In the past three years, *New York Times* bestselling author **Sherrilyn Kenyon** has claimed the number one spot seven times. This extraordinary bestseller continues to top every genre she writes. With more than 25 million copies of her books in print in over one hundred countries, her current series include: The Dark-Hunters, The League, Chronicles of Nick, and Belador. Since 2004, she has placed more than sixty novels on the *New York Times* list in all formats including manga. The pre-eminent voice in paranormal fiction, with more than twenty years of publishing credits in all genres, Kenyon not only helped to pioneer, but define the current paranormal trend that has captivated the world.

Visit Sherrilyn Kenyon online:

www.darkhunter.com
www.sherrilynkenyon.co.uk
www.facebook.com/AuthorSherrilynKenyon
www.twitter.com/KenyonSherrilyn

Praise for Sherrilyn Kenyon:

'A publishing phenomenon . . . [Sherrilyn Kenyon] is the reigning queen of the wildly successful paranormal scene'
Publishers Weekly

'Kenyon's writing is brisk, ironic and relentlessly imaginative. These are not your mother's vampire novels'
Boston Globe

'Whether writing as Sherrilyn Kenyon or Kinley MacGregor, this author delivers great romantic fantasy!'
New York Times bestselling author Elizabeth Lowell

Time Untime

Sherrilyn Kenyon

piatkus

PIATKUS

First published in the US in 2012 by St Martin's Press, New York
First published in Great Britain in 2012 by Piatkus
This paperback edition published in 2013 by Piatkus

A CIP catalogue record for this book
is available from the British Library.

ISBN 978-0-7499-5772-8

Typeset by Phoenix Photosetting, Chatham, Kent
Printed and bound by CPI Group (UK) Ltd, Croydon CR0 4YY

Papers used by Piatkus are from well-managed forests
and other responsible sources.

MIX
Paper from
responsible sources
FSC® C104740

Piatkus
An imprint of
Little, Brown Book Group
100 Victoria Embankment
London EC4Y 0DY

An Hachette UK Company
www.hachette.co.uk

www.piatkus.co.uk

For my husband, for too many reasons to count.

For my boys, who make me laugh and fill my life with joy.

For my friends, who keep me sane.

And for my readers.

Thank you all for being a part of my life and for filling my heart with love.

Time Untime

PROLOGUE

In the distant, unrecorded past

It wasn't fun being the gatekeeper to hell. The only thing worse was being evil's bitch, and Makah'Alay Omawaya had been that, too.

Willingly.

A tic beat in his sculpted jaw as the harsh winds whipped his long black hair, flogging him while he stood on top of a high precipice, his muscled body and sheathed weapons silhouetted by the Hunter's Moon. Soul-sick and weary, he surveyed the red canyon that was awash with moonlight and dancing shadows that reminded him of his past.

How could one man ruin so many lives?

No, not ruin.

Destroy.

He no longer had a right to live. Not after all the blood he'd greedily spilled with his knife and arrows. Not after all the atrocities he'd committed. Yet here he stood. Alone.

Ashamed.

Undead.

A twice-designated guardian to a world he'd done his damnedest to annihilate. Yeah, it didn't make sense to him either. The spirits were ever a mystery. He couldn't even begin to fathom their reasoning in allowing him to return here.

But then the one lesson he'd learned through all of this was the truth in the old saying—*man has responsibility, not power*. After all these years, he finally understood what that meant.

I will not fail them.

Or himself.

I am resolute. . . .

He lived his current life by conscious decision, not random chance. The spirits hadn't chosen him for this task. He'd volunteered. With no more excuses to blind and impede him, he would make changes for the better.

This time, he would be motivated to excellence and not manipulated by evil. He would be useful and not used. Excel rather than compete. From this moment forward, he would trust his own inner wisdom and ignore the counsel and opinions of others. His worthless self-pity finally spent, he would endeavor to learn self-esteem.

To live the life of honor he should have had all along.

His gaze skimmed the deep cavern below where he'd once battled a powerful immortal for a year and a day. He still didn't know how or where he'd found the strength for the fight. But then his adrenaline and years of a humiliating past that still stuck in the craw of his throat had kept him from feeling any pain. It had kept him from feeling any fatigue or injury. That unleashing of decades of caged fury had succored him better than mother's milk.

If only he had that solace now. But with the fight done and the blood on his hands, he felt tired and sick. Disgusted. He wanted to blame someone else. Anyone else. Yet in the end, he couldn't run from the one simple truth.

He, alone, had done this to himself. He'd made the decision and allowed his thoughts to be controlled by another.

Now it was time to make amends.

You're not free, Makah'Alay. You will never be free of my service. And now I have you for all eternity.

"No, you don't," he shot back in his mind loud enough for it to carry from this realm into the West Land where the Grizzly Spirit was imprisoned.

Hopefully for all time.

The Grizzly Spirit had owned Makah'Alay Omawaya.

"Makah'Alay Omawaya is dead." Killed by his own brother's trickery. And that, too, had been justified.

Now he was reborn as Ren Waya—the treacherous wolf—and his soul was in the hands of an immortal from a faraway land.

Art-uh-miss. She had spun the magic that had brought him back into this realm. And he'd sworn himself to protect this world from her brother's creatures, who preyed on the souls of mankind. The symmetry and irony of that wasn't lost on him.

But then his people had always believed in cycles and circles—

Be kind to all, for you will meet each other again. It was why his clan didn't believe in ever saying good-bye. People were ever the same, but circumstances did change.

And Artemis owning his soul after all he'd done seemed right. Not to mention, it allowed him to watch over his own brother to make sure that Coyote didn't scar the land even more than Ren had when he'd been its overseer.

Even so, he couldn't deny that while the Grizzly Spirit was trapped in the West Land, that bastard still possessed a part of him that was forever corrupted.

A part he hoped was sealed as tight as the gate that held the Grizzly Spirit.

Yet deep inside with the powers Ren had cursed since the hour of his birth, he saw what was to come. Those gates would be weakened. And while he was strong, a man, even an undead one, only had so much strength within. Grandfather Time was ever marching forward and as he spiraled across the lands, he forever changed them.

His strong hands molded and shaped this earth.

Like Ren, he scarred it.

One day, Grandfather Time would come for him and demand an accounting for all he'd done.

For all he *hadn't* done.

May the good spirits of the earth help them all when that day came. Change was never without dread and sacrifice. And while he knew his strengths, he also knew his weaknesses.

So did the Grizzly Spirit and his handmaiden Windseer. They had already claimed him once as their own.

When next they battled, Ren would fight with everything he had. But he knew it wouldn't be enough.

They would have him again, and then ...

4

Ren winced at his visions of the future and what awaited this hapless world that had no idea about the things men like him kept at bay.

It didn't matter and it changed nothing. He would fight for good even harder than he'd fought for evil. If he won, all would be well. And if he lost . . .

Death wasn't without its benefits.

Chapter 1

December 10, 2012
Las Vegas, Nevada
3:00 a.m.

"The feathers are forming in the heavens and the Cold Moon is almost upon us. Soon Father Snake will open his eyes, and with them, the seven gates."

Ren tilted his head down as he heard Choo Co La Tah's deep proper British accent disturbing the solemn darkness where he sat, listening to the silence around him. Those feathers were the crown on the head of the Snake constellation that ruled their ancient calendar. When the feathers were in full plumage and the winter solstice aligned, the gates between this world and others would open. And into this world would spill all the evil that had been driven out by not only his people, but those from the other six continents as well.

Eleven days.

12/21/12. 11:11 A.M. At that precise instant the heart of the universe would cross through the tree of life. The head, heart, and body would be aligned for the first time in centuries.

How perfect was that? If anyone had ever doubted the balance and cycles of the universe, that should be proof enough to convince them that while everything might seem random, it wasn't. No one, except the Great Creator, could have timed this so perfectly.

Eleven days to the Reset.

Ren could hear the clock ticking. Every heartbeat brought them closer to the inevitable. Closer to all hell busting loose.

Be a good time to call in sick to work.

If only. But such luxuries belonged to humans, not to immortals such as he. For creatures like him, there was never a sick day or even a lazy one. Win, lose, or draw, they would fight to the bitterest end and take as many of their enemies with them as they could.

United we stand.

United we die.

And for an immortal, death was much scarier than it was for a human. When you died without a soul, it was utter agony for all eternity.

Hell had nothing on the existence that would become his should he fall.

Ren inclined his head respectfully to Choo Co La Tah. "I've been watching the signs." During which he'd had a vision that still haunted him. Even with his eyes wide open, he saw her clearly. Felt her presence as if she were here, right now.

8

But he had no idea who *she* was. A mere slip of a woman with the courage of the cliff ogre, she'd come to him through the darkness. Dressed in yellow buckskin, she'd twisted up her dark brown hair and laced it with white feathers. Like the goddess who'd taken his soul, she'd knelt by his side while he lay wounded on the ground. Her sweet voice had soothed him as she sang in a language he hadn't heard a woman speak in over two thousand years.

Death had held him tight until she'd laid her tiny hand to his bloody cheek. Leaning forward, she'd continued to sing, her breath falling against his skin. Her kind touch and soothing voice had driven away his pain until he felt nothing except the heat of her flesh against his. Her gaze had held his as she brushed a kiss to his lips. One so light, it felt like the wings of a hummingbird.

"I'm here for you," she'd whispered an instant before she stabbed him straight through his heart. As the pain seared him, she'd laughed, then left him there to die alone.

He'd barely finished that vision before Choo Co La Tah had appeared in his backyard. For the last half hour, he'd been in solemn observance of the sky above, watching for something to belie what he knew was coming for them.

No one can stop a train. The best they could do was bleed on the cattle scoop and tracks.

Ren stood up slowly in the middle of his backyard, then turned to face the ancient immortal. Centuries ago, they had been in the same clan together. Choo Co La Tah had once been his brother's most trusted friend and advisor.

But things changed. And so did people. Too often you

woke up to find that the person you were the closest to was the one you knew the least about. And as Ren had learned firsthand, the friend saturated with evil was the one thing to fear the most. While enemies could wound your body, an evil friend wounded the heart and mind—two things that could prove fatal.

"There's no sign of the Keeper." Choo Co La Tah glanced up at the Pleiades above them to where the first gate lay. The same stars Ren had been focused on. And the ones that held a special place in his heart. "What if she's dead already?"

"A good friend once told me not to dread the future. One way or another, it would come. The trick was to meet it with open arms so that when it ran me over, it wouldn't break anything."

Choo smiled. "I was much younger and far more flexible in those days."

Ren laughed at the ancient who physically appeared to be a well-muscled man in his early thirties. Dressed in a tan buckskin coat and jeans, Choo wore his long black hair braided down his back—the same style as Ren's. And each of his eight fingers bore a silver ring that protected a sacred stone. Like him, Choo had once been the best of their clan's warriors. They had gone to war together and they had fought against each other. Ironically, Ren had been the only one to ever defeat Choo Co La Tah.

Something he'd cheated to do.

Luckily, Choo didn't hold a grudge.

Much.

Ren crossed his arms over his chest as he noticed how cool the night air had become. While he'd been meditating, he hadn't paid attention to the dropping temperature. Now, the cold desert wind made itself known. "Besides, it's not her death we should fear as much as the possibility that her stone is now in the hands of something it shouldn't be."

Choo Co La Tah nodded in agreement. "And that is what I fear most. The ghighau should have contacted me by now. Since she hasn't . . ." His frustration was tangible. "I don't even know who she is in this life."

Neither did Ren. In order to protect her from all the predators who would kill her if they could, the Spirits had never allowed the Guardians to know her identity until it was a necessity. Where the Guardians were immortal, the Keeper wasn't. A human child, she passed her sacred stone from mother to daughter, along with the story of their most sacred duty. Whenever the time came for the Reset, the Keeper always sent a dream to Choo Co La Tah to let him know who she was.

With two of the four Guardians slain, Choo and Ren's brother Coyote, were the only ones left who could assist her in resetting their calendar and keeping the gates closed.

One Guardian who would protect her.

His brother who would kill her.

Ren, who had been a Guardian until his brother had stolen his position, now lay between the two. While he intended to stand and fight with Choo Co La Tah to the best of his abilities, he wasn't sure what he would do against his brother. A part of him still hated Coyote with a vengeance that left him bitter. But beneath that was a guilt so profound that he wasn't even angry that

Coyote had tortured him last year when he had taken Ren captive.

How could he be when he'd done far more harm to Coyote?

Betrayals were never easy. When they came from a stranger, they were hateful. When they came from a friend, they were hurtful, and when they came from family . . .

They were vitriolic.

He clapped Choo Co La Tah on the back. "Look on the bright side. At least no one's uncapped the Anikutani."

"Yet, my dear boy. But remember, we still have eleven days to go. One 'oh shit' moment can undo all of our best efforts to protect this world, and there's nothing more dangerous in this existence than a moron on a mission."

Ren snorted at his optimism. "Sure there is, Choo."

"And that would be?"

"One with an Internet connection and a six-pack of Red Bull." But all joking aside, Choo Co La Tah was right. If anyone were to uncap the stone seal that kept Ren's brethren imprisoned during the Time Untime . . .

He really was going to call in sick to work.

And find a hole to hide in.

At the mere thought of their return, his stomach tightened and chills ran up his arms as if his unconscious was trying to warn him that it was already too late to contemplate running. It felt as if the seal had been broken.

Stop. It's the wind.

That he had no doubt about. But the question was, did that wind come from the desert?

Or from the Anikutani being released?

Chapter 2

December 10, 2012
Tuscaloosa, Alabama
4:00 a.m.

Kateri Avani jerked in her sleep as her dreams tormented her. No longer a woman full grown, she was again a little girl sitting in her grandmother's house, playing with the dolls her grandmother had made for her and her cousin Sunshine Runningwolf from the corn that grew in the garden out back. Barely twelve, Kateri brushed her small hand over the black corn-silk hair of the male doll. She didn't know why, but she always made a small bow for him to hold on to.

Her grandmother sat beside her, at the old-fashioned red kitchen table, shelling peas as she spoke to Kateri in that ever-gentle tone that never failed to make her feel safe in a world that had been anything but. "You know,

Ter, it's a common saying among people that the love of money is the root of all evil. But nothing could be more wrong." She dropped the strings and ends of the pea stalk into the compost bucket at her feet. "Before the invention of money, or even monetary systems, there was plenty of evil to go around."

Not sure why her grandmother was telling her this, Kateri quirked a brow at the serious tone.

Her grandmother's snow-white hair was braided and twisted around her head in an intricate coil Kateri had tried over and over to master. Unlike her grandmother's, her hair always ended up in a mess that would leave her braids to fall loose as soon as she moved swiftly.

After pushing her glasses back with her knuckle, her grandmother paused her lecture to pull more unshelled stalks from the handmade straw basket on the table and put them into the silver pan she held in her lap. Pointing at Kateri with one of the long pea stalks, she pierced her with those golden eyes that held all the fire of a strong, spirited medicine woman. "Heed my warning, child. Neither money nor greed destroy humanity, and they definitely don't ruin the life of a single individual. Rather, it's something much more sinister. Those are merely the symptoms of the true disease that can rot you from the inside out."

Kateri's eyes widened. "What rots people, Grammy?"

"Envy," she said in a chilling tone. "It is the deadliest of all things, child. It was what motivated the first crime known to mankind, when brother struck down brother and left him dead for no reason other than the fact that he thought his brother was more favored. On the surface, it's such a beautiful word. But like all true evil, that beauty is deceptive and it lures the unwary in for capture and ruin. Just like the devil's whirlpool, before you realize it, you're drowning in it and can't escape it no matter how hard you try."

Her heart thumped hard in her chest. Those words scared her. She never, ever wanted to feel it. The problem was, she didn't know what "it" was. "What does 'envy' mean?"

Her grandmother snapped the peas apart, her movements more frenetic than before. "From the Latin *invidi,* which means to cause resentment or to calculate ill will toward another, envy is that inability to feel happiness at someone else's good fortune or to wish them well even though they deserve it. It's when you begrudge someone their moment in the sun or just the fact that they have a life that you think is better or easier than yours. But heed my words, child, we all have more than our share of pains and sorrow. Embarrassments and things that haunt us. From that, no one is ever immune, no matter how good or perfect a life you think they live. Shame and hurt spare no one."

"I would never do such a thing, Grammy," Kateri assured her. "I know better."

Her grandmother smiled kindly. "I know, baby. But the warning bears repeating. It's so easy to fall into envy's grasp, and to let that hatred and bitterness destroy your own happiness." She handed Kateri several raw peas to eat while she continued shelling them. "When I was a girl about your age, my grandmother told me a story that her grandfather had told her. Even though I was young when I heard it, it has stayed with me throughout my entire life."

Kateri crunched the peas while she listened. She always loved her grandmother's tales.

"One day, a young boy went up to his grandfather, who was an old Cherokee chief. 'Edudi?' the boy asked. 'Why are you so sad?'

"The old chief bit his lip and rubbed his belly as if his stomach pained him unmercifully. 'There is a terrible fight inside me, Uhgeeleesee,' the chief said sternly. 'One that will not let me sleep or give me any peace.'"

She touched a pea stalk to Kateri's nose as she mimicked the boy's wide-eyed wonder. "'A fight, Grandfather? I don't understand. What kind of fight is inside you?'"

Kateri stole another handful of peas from her grandmother's pan.

"The old chief knelt in front of the boy to explain. 'Deep inside my heart, I have two wolves. Each strong enough to devour the other, they are locked in constant war. One is evil through and through. He is revenge, sorrow, regret, rage, greed, arrogance, stupidity, superiority, envy, guilt, lies, ego, false pride, inferiority, self-doubt, suspicion, and resentment. The other wolf is everything kind. He is made of peace, blissful tranquility, wisdom, love and joy, hope and humility, compassion, benevolence, generosity, truth, faith, and empathy. They circle each other inside my heart and they fight one another at all times. Day and night. There is no letup. Not even while I slumber.'

"The boy's eyes widened as he sucked his breath in sharply. 'How horrible for you.' His grandfather shook his head at those words and tapped the boy's chest right where his own heart was located. 'It's not just horrible for me. This same fight is also going on inside you and every single person who walks this earth with us.'"

Kateri touched her own heart as she wondered if those wolves were inside her, too.

"Those words terrified the little boy," her grandmother continued. "'So tell me, Grandfather, which of the wolves will win this fight?' The old chief smiled at his grandson and he cupped his young cheek before he answered with one simple truth. 'Always the one we feed.'"

Her grandmother's voice echoed through Kateri's dream as she tried her best to wake herself. *Be careful what you feed, child. For that beast will follow you home and live with you until you either make a bed for it to stay, or find the temerity to drive it out.*

But her grandmother wasn't through with her warnings. She took Kateri's hand and pulled her forward through time. Into a place that was eerie and foreign, and at the same time, it was familiar. Like she'd been here before and forgotten it.

Or banished it.

Though the sweeping winds were hot, they made her blood run cold with dread—as if there was something innately evil here. Something that wanted her dead. All around them, stalagmites and stalactites formed misshapen beasts that added to her discomfort. The red earthen walls reminded her of a Martian landscape. More than that, those walls held sketches of past battles between warriors and a feathered snake that rose up above them, breathing fire from its nostrils as it tried to defeat them.

"This is where the end begins."

Before she could ask her grandmother what she meant, Kateri saw a shadow move across the floor. It grabbed her from behind and jerked her back against a rock-hard chest. She felt swallowed by the size of the man who held her with an ease that terrified her. Dressed in a white linen shirt, black vest, and jeans, he had long ebony hair that fell to the middle of his back. Dark eyes flashed in a face so perfectly sculpted that he didn't appear real.

Familiar with this stranger, she relaxed.

Until he spoke.

"For all time," he whispered in her ear an instant before he plunged a knife deep into her heart, then threw her to the ground to die. Her last sight was of him turning into a crow so that he could fly away from her.

Shaking and scared, Kateri woke up in a cold sweat to the sound of her alarm clock blaring. At 4:30 in the morning, her bedroom was still pitch dark, but even so she sensed a presence near her bed. More than that, she smelled the faint scent of peppermint and Jurgen's lotion.

Her grandmother's scent. There had only been one other time when she'd awakened to this sensation and smell—the night her grandmother had died while she'd been in college. Goosebumps ran over her body as tears filled her eyes.

"Eleesee?" she breathed, using the Cherokee word for grandmother.

Lightning flashed, highlighting the shadows in her room. Kateri gasped as the one in the corner appeared to be the solid form of a woman.

Only it wasn't her grandmother. Instead, it was twisted and horrific. Ugly.

18

Worse, the shadow lunged at her.

Reacting on pure instinct, Kateri threw her arm up and whispered the ancient words of protection her grandmother had drilled into her so that she could fight her nightmares whenever they came for her. As she'd been taught, she pushed against the invader with her thoughts, willing it from this existence into the realm that had spawned it. The creature screamed as it reached her bed and its face came within inches of hers. Its hollow eyes flickered like flames before it recoiled as if it had hit a force field. With a shrill caw, it exploded into a fiery creature that twisted and flew through the window in the shape of a crow.

No. Not a crow.

A raven.

Chills ran down her spine as her memories shot her into a place and time she didn't want to go. *It's a raven mocker.* Withered beings who only revealed themselves to those about to die.

To the souls they intended to devour.

Kateri shook her head harshly. No, she didn't believe in such things. No one or nothing could take a soul from a person. Those were stories her grandmother had told her to amuse or scare her with as a child. Ancient legends.

I'm a scientist. I know there's no such thing as shapeshifting beasts who steal the souls of the dying.

It was impossible.

But her grandmother had believed in them, as well as many of the Cherokee who'd lived on the reservation her grandmother had serviced. So much so that her grandmother had been summoned any time someone

19

was dying. Day and night, until they passed, her grand-mother had kept vigil to protect the dying from the raven mockers.

I have battled many of them in my day, child. And like me, you will one day have the ability to see them, too. To fight them for the souls they come to steal. It is your honor to follow after me. And when my time comes, I want you to hold my hand as I cross to the next adventure and protect my soul for me until it's free of this old body and safely through the gates of heaven. Then I shall live among the stars and stare down at you every night as I watch over you.

It was a dream that had never come true. Instead of dying peacefully in her sleep as she'd envisioned, her grandmother had been murdered by a home invader while Kateri was thousands of miles away.

Don't think about it. Any time she did, rage—dark and foul—set her on fire and it took everything she had not to go rabid vigilante. Her grandmother had been the kindest, gentlest creature ever born and some psycho had kicked her door in and . . .

Stop! She had to get to work so that . . .

Her thoughts scattered as her gaze went to her dresser. There on top, next to the small picture of her and her cousin Sunshine sitting on her grandmother's lap, were the corn dolls she'd been dreaming about. Dolls she hadn't seen in years. Not since the summer when she'd turned sixteen and her grandmother had led her through the ritual to symbolize her walk from childhood into that of an adult.

Those dolls had been burned to ashes on that day and then their remains scattered in the garden to feed the new

20

crop of corn—the symbol of life and the cycle of birth, renewal, death, and rebirth. . . .

But their presence on her dresser wasn't what truly scared her.

While she'd slept, someone had come into her room and written on her mirror with a bar of soap—something else her grandmother had done whenever Kateri had stayed with her. Little notes such as "I love you," "Good luck with your test," "Have a good day at school," "Don't forget your sweater," or some such trifling.

But this note wasn't sweet.

Take my nayu into the Valley of Fire, where the pure earth must tame the crow. Listen to the buffalo and protect the butterfly. Together, you are stronger than any foe. And remember, Waleli, when the coyote comes and the snake attacks, either you eat the bear or the bear eats you.

In the middle of the day, that would be irritating to read. This early in the morning, it was downright cruel.

I'm in no mood for this crap.

"Who's here?" she shouted.

Only the sound of her own heartbeat answered her. She'd call the police, but to what purpose? *Hey, officer, I woke up and found this really cryptic message on my mirror, written by someone who was high or drunk or . . . No, officer, I'm not on anything. And no, they're not here now and I have no idea why they'd do something like this, but could you find out who they are and ask them not to leave me notes anymore? Who do I suspect? No idea. Only my late grandmother left me notes like this.*

Yeah, that wouldn't go over well, and with her luck, they'd haul her in for filing a false report.

Or worse, call a psych unit on her.

But what really disturbed her about the note was that it called her *Waleli* . . . Hummingbird. It was her real first name that her grandmother had given to her on her birth. One that hadn't been entered on the paperwork her mother had filed for her birth certificate. No one alive knew of it.

No one.

So either her grandmother had visited her or . . .

You don't believe in ghosts.

True, but what other explanation could there possibly be? Why would a complete stranger break into her house, steal nothing, do her no harm, and write that? The reasoning defied logic.

How would they know about her grandmother's nayu that had shown up in mail addressed to her the day after her grandmother had died, or the name her grandmother only used when they were alone?

Kateri shook her head.

Maybe that was what the raven mocker had been doing.

Yeah, okay, the idea of a raven mocker writing in soap on her mirror sounded even more ludicrous and far-fetched than the ghost theory, but what was left?

Once you eliminate the impossible, whatever remains, no matter how improbable, must be the truth. She rolled her eyes as her mind reminded her of the Sir Arthur Conan Doyle quote.

"I don't believe in this crap, Grammy!" she shouted up at the ceiling. She never had. Paranormal, raven mockers, tsinooks, spirits, and such . . . hokey poppycock.

She was a scientist. She only believed in what she could see, taste, touch, smell, and hear.

Quantify.

The rest was fodder for novelists and Hollywood. It just didn't exist outside of dreams.

It didn't.

All of a sudden, something squeaked. Kateri snapped her head toward the sound that had come from her dresser.

There on her mirror, more words appeared as she watched them.

But I believe in you, *Waleli. Do not fail me.*

Above all, do not fail yourself.

Chapter 3

Noon

Jotting down the time and date for her notes on the soil sample she was testing, Kateri felt as if she was moving forward while stuck in reverse. Her limbs heavy, every movement was lethargic and difficult. Like the entire world was out of synch and she was caught between two competing forces. And no matter how hard she tried to focus on her work, she couldn't stop her mind from replaying her crazy dreams.

What did I eat last night?

Banana ice cream.

That's it. From now on, it's off the menu.

After hours of internal argument that left her doubting her very sanity and condemning her own flagrant stupidity for even thinking otherwise, she'd finally managed to convince herself that everything she'd imagined until she'd gone into the bathroom to brush her teeth had been a dream brought on by too much stress, ice cream, and . . .

Something in retrograde. She'd have to check with her cousin later. Sunny always kept up with that weirdness. If anyone could tell her what planet or astrological sign was playing havoc with her life, Sunny was she.

Still, Kateri couldn't get the image of that dark-haired warrior out of her mind. Of course, it would help if the man would keep a shirt on whenever he came into her unconscious mind. What kind of person didn't have enough decency to keep himself clothed while barging into her dreams?

A little modesty went a long way.

Yeah, but clothes on a body so fine was its own form of obscenity.

Shh, mind, have some decency yourself.

But it was hard when all she saw was the pain in his dark eyes as he held her in arms that were warm and welcoming. As his breath tickled her skin. Even now, she could feel his heart pounding against her shoulder and feel the slight trembling in his arms. Almost every time she dreamed of him, he'd press his cheek to hers while he seemed to savor being near her. In those moments, she was always so serene. So happy.

Until he killed her.

It's just a stupid dream.

She really did believe that now. When she'd gone back into her bedroom to dress, the mirror had been free of writing and there had been no sign of the dolls, the raven mocker, or anything else out of the ordinary.

Thus proving her imagination was as active as ever.

And friends wonder why I never experimented with drugs. With her family history, she didn't dare. She had enough insanity without them. Last thing she needed was more.

Ever since her grandmother's death, she'd seen "visions" she couldn't explain. Caverns in the desert and ancient hieroglyphics that were painted on stone walls. Animals that would charge her. But the one thing that had always been constant in all of them was the dark-haired man who either fought by her side or who . . .

Stabbed her dead.

Suddenly, her lab door opened to show her grad assistant, Enrique Martinez, coming in with a giant package in his hands. At twenty-three, he was gorgeous and well aware of the fact. Something he took full advantage of with female coeds whenever they needed "tutoring." His list of ever-revolving girlfriends was so long that Kateri had quit trying to keep up with it weeks ago.

"*Hola,* Dr. Avani." He set the huge box down on the table next to her.

Sitting back on her stool, she smiled at him. She'd told him repeatedly to call her Teri or Kateri. But for some reason, he could never bring himself to be so formal. "Hi, hon. How did your date go last night?"

He made an unhappy sound with his tongue. "Not as well as I'd hoped. She threw me back into the river. Oh well. I'm not too trashed over it. She wasn't exactly what I was looking for either."

"How so?"

He flashed a dimpled smile. "She complained about her food so much to the waiter that I was afraid to eat mine. You never know when an irate cook is going to spice

27

your meat with something *extra* special. Last thing I need for a woman is a harpie, know what I mean?"

Laughing, she reached for her package to open it. Dang, it was heavy. Had someone mailed her a stack of bricks? She now had a new appreciation for Enrique's strength.

"You laugh at misery, Doc, but Montezuma's Revenge is nothing to play around with."

She gave him a peeved glare. "You're never going to let me live down Gus Guatemala's, are you?"

"You're not the one who lived in the bathroom for three days, Doc. Thanks for *that* birthday present, by the way."

She snorted. "Yeah, well, at least you'll always remember it. Never let it be said that I don't know how to make a lasting impression."

This time he joined her laughter as he pulled a butterfly knife out of his back pocket, twirled it open, then sliced through the tape on her box.

Arching a brow, she was rather impressed with his knife skills, and didn't want to contemplate why he, a geology grad student, had them. "Aren't those illegal?"

His expression would make an angel weep at his innocence. "Are they?"

She loved how he always answered questions he didn't like with another question. Deflection had its place in the world and he was a master manipulator. Shaking her head, she opened the box to expose a ton of Styrofoam peanuts and something wrapped and taped as if on a dare.

Great. Just what she wanted. A broken nail and tape burns.

Enrique slid his knife into his pocket before he lifted up her notebook from the desk. "Nice drawing, Doc. Is this your boyfriend or something?" There was a strange glint in his eyes. If she didn't know better, she'd swear it was a light of recognition.

Heat radiated from her cheeks as she realized what Enrique had in his hand. *Why didn't I close it?*

'Cause she'd been a little preoccupied with convincing herself the subject of her drawing was a delusion brought on by one rom-com too many.

"No. I sketch sometimes to clear my head." It'd been her attempt to drive the mysterious warrior out of her thoughts so that she could focus on her research and tests.

Hadn't worked. But it'd been a valiant effort on her part that had blown up in her face. Instead of clearing her thoughts, every line of his chiseled face and rock-hard body was now permanently branded into her mind.

For some reason, she'd drawn him from the side profile, looking to the left with the light falling across his face and highlighting his features and bare torso in a pose so sexy, she was sure it was outlawed in most states. She'd left his long hair down and his throat was bare of the silver, bone, and turquoise necklace he wore in her dreams. In his hands, he held a massive war club. It reminded her of a canoe paddle, except the paddle's edge was spiked with thin jagged pieces of glass. A forgotten weapon modern man only knew about from prehistoric glyphs, the club had a flat side that allowed Mayans to knock their victims unconscious while the obsidian glass could cut through flesh and bone faster than a scalpel or bone saw. She didn't know why she saw him with a Mayan weapon, but it was one he'd used several times in her dreams.

Even without it, though, he looked lethal and powerful. Mesmerizing, and absolutely lickable.

Things she didn't want Enrique to know she thought about. Ever. She slid the pad out of his hand and closed the cover.

With a devilish grin that said he knew more than he should, Enrique took it in stride. "By the way, did you hear about Dr. Drake?"

"Which Dr. Drake?" There were four of them on campus, and two of them in the geology department where she and Enrique lived most of the time.

"The one you went on your dig with last summer down in Mexico. It's in your e-mail. I forwarded you the notice earlier. He dropped dead on a plane a few days ago."

She gasped in shock at his lack of tact. *Dang, boy, didn't your mother teach better? You don't just firebomb someone with tragic news. . . .*

A little warning would have been nice.

The Drake he referred to was Fernando Drake from the sociology and anthropology department at Millsaps College in Mississippi. She'd been friends with him since they'd met in Reed Hall as sophomores at the University of Georgia—Fernando had been kind enough to kill the bug in her dorm room that had been terrorizing her for days.

Something he'd done with flair as he heard her screaming for a shoe to kill the beast. Flame-red Doc Martens boot in hand, he'd rushed through her open door, and killed it on the floor by her roommate's bed. Even more heroic, he'd taken its remains and given it a burial at sea in the boys' bathroom.

No one could ever accuse Fernando of being anything less than the best of gentlemen.

And since they were barely thirty, Fernando was way too young to just fall over from anything. She'd never even known him to have a cold or a headache. "What?"

"Yeah. Freaky thing, too. They said there wasn't a mark on his body anywhere, but that when they did the autopsy, his heart was missing. How weird is that, huh? It's like something out of *Fringe,* you know?"

The room spun as old tales whispered through her head. She literally felt as if she were free-falling. Reaching out, she touched the table to center herself before she fell off her stool. "You're joking."

"Why would I joke about something so grisly? I'm not that big a jerk." He frowned. "You okay, Doc? You look a little sick."

She was a lot sick as her mind went to a place she definitely didn't want it to go. Raven mockers were said to eat the heart out of their victims and to leave no external trace whatsoever. The only way to see their work was to open the victim's chest and find the heart gone.

Unable to breathe through her constricted throat, she opened her e-mail so that she could read the article about Fernando's death herself. But it did nothing to calm her. If anything, it made it all the worse.

Enrique was right. Fernando had been flying home when the flight attendant had tried to wake him so that he could put his seat upright for landing. She'd discovered him dead and had assumed it a heart attack. Yet during that flight someone, or something, had removed his heart with surgical precision while not leaving a single mark on the body anywhere.

Not something one came across every day. Not unless one was completely insane or a medicine woman or man guarding the hearts and souls of the dying.

Yeah, right.

I don't believe in raven mockers. At least that was what her head kept saying. Too bad the rest of her consciousness wasn't listening.

Over and over, she heard her grandmother's stories and saw the twisted figure from her dreams that had flown out her window.

Stop it! This was the twenty-first century, not the first. She was sitting in a state-of-the-art lab facility at the University of Alabama—not some wattle-and-daub hut in a North Georgia field.

She forced herself to look around the room. She wasn't surrounded by cave paintings and questionable herbs that doubled as hallucinogens. She was here with the gas and ion chromatographs, an inductively coupled plasma mass spectrometer, electron microprobe, isotope ratio mass spectrometer, her electron microscope . . .

Her world consisted of things such as Betsy guns, single- and three-component geophones, StrataVisor seismic acquisition systems, and CHIRP sub-bottom profilers. She was a scientist, not a medicine woman doling out concoctions made from things she grew in her garden.

She refused to believe in any of this. There was a logical explanation for what had killed Fernando. There had to be. "What do you think happened to him?" she asked Enrique.

Like her, he was a scientist who didn't buy into mumbo-jumbo.

"*El chupacabra*."

Well, so much for that theory. She rolled her eyes at him. "Really? A goat sucker? Last I checked, they only drank blood, and that from animals. I've never heard of one taking a human heart."

"Yeah, but you don't know, right?" His accent changed from regular American to a thicker Spanish that only came out whenever he was excited or angry. "*Abuela*, she used to tell me stories of *el peuchen* where she grew up."

And here she'd foolishly thought she was up to date on the scary legends. Leave it to Enrique to find one she'd never heard of before. "*El peuchen?*"

"*Si*. It's a gigantic flying snake, right? Or sometimes it can change its shape to other things, but it's mostly a feathered snake that hunts at night. And it's a cousin or something to *el chupacabra. Abuela* used to tell me how it would come out and suck their blood or eat their hearts. In the morning, they'd find the hapless victims in fields or near streams. Her mother was the village *machi* and, to protect the village, she would drum it out whenever it started feeding. So I'm thinking *el peuchen* must have hitched a ride on the plane and got him."

"Then why did you say *chupacabra?*"

"'Cause no one outside of Chile or Argentina has ever heard of *el peuchen*. It's not exactly big up here, you know? Besides, I've never heard of one of them coming this far north. *Chupacabra*, on the other hand . . ."

As much as she hated to admit it, he had a point. Still . . . "You don't really believe that, do you?"

"I know you want me to say no, Doc. I do. But . . . *Abuela* knew things. She saw things. Things no one could explain, no matter how much science you want to put on it. She said they were visions given to her by the Holy Mother back in the day. When I was a boy, she told me I could see them, too. But I didn't want to see them and so I didn't. Just because we study science, it doesn't mean there aren't things that defy us. For everything we know, there is much more we don't. Things no one can find out with an empirical test." He jerked his chin at her computer screen. "And that is something we definitely don't know."

He was right about that.

Not wanting to admit it, she went back to unwrapping what felt like a giant round rock.

Enrique helped her until they uncovered . . .

A giant round rock.

His scowl deepened along with hers as she pulled the plastic back to reveal a hand-chiseled wheel the likes of which she hadn't seen since they left the dig months ago.

"What is that?" he asked.

She ran her fingers over the intricate carvings as she studied the giant red stone that had to be thousands of years old, judging by its worn condition. "It appears to be a Mayan calendar, but the glyphs aren't exactly Mayan." More than that, there was writing on it, too. Not glyphs, but something that appeared to be an ancient Greek script.

Okay . . . someone had to be screwing with her. They had to be. One of her friends must have made this up as a joke.

Because she'd never seen anything like this. No one

had anything ancient Greek with Native American. There was no way for it to exist.

But what if it was real?

It can't be. Those two cultures had never intermingled. Ever.

Frowning, she dug through the peanuts until she located a note near the bottom. Prepared to have it say "April Fool's," she quickly skimmed it.

> *Teri,*
>
> *We found this seal in the center of our site under an ornate headstone unlike anything I've ever encountered. I have never seen glyphs like this. The other script looks Greek to me—yeah, I know, go ahead and laugh— which shouldn't be possible. I've sent a photo of the writing to Dr. Soteria Parthenopaeus in New Orleans to see if she can read it and I've asked her if she has any idea how anything European could be on a Preclassic stone in the Yucatán. My initial test results say the stone is 14,000 years old. Not a typo. Believe me, I know it's impossible, but I've checked and rechecked a thousand times. It can't be right, so I'm sending this to the best geologist I know for corroboration. Or for you to tell me it's time to update my equipment and better ventilate the shafts we've been working in. I've included several soil samples for you, too. Please call me as soon as you get this.*
>
> *Fernando*

Chills spread over her arms as she stared at his name on the paper and a million memories assaulted her. Even now, she could see him sitting outside the pyramid last summer as the sun set behind him. Grimy and sweaty with his hair matted and sticking up all over his head, he'd been happy and excited even though they'd been excavating for ten hours straight in the worst sort of heat. Flashing her that boyish grin of his, he'd popped open a lukewarm beer and handed it to her. *"Después del trabajo—cerveza!"*

Tears welled in her eyes. That had been the worst-tasting beer she'd ever drank, but his company had made it seem perfect. Fernando had always been a good friend to her and she would miss him terribly.

Why did he have to die? He was too young. He'd had too many plans.

She clenched her teeth, forcing her tears down as she focused on what Fernando would want her to do. Work always came first. It was why he didn't have a wife or even a girlfriend.

Focus, Teri. . . . By the date and time on the package, he'd sent it to her the same day he'd boarded the plane to come home. No doubt it'd been too heavy for him to pack or carry, what with all the airline restrictions nowadays.

Not to mention, the stone was huge.

In more ways than one. If this really was fourteen thousand years old, and if that was Greek writing on it, it would entirely rewrite the historical record and change everything they thought they knew about the ancient world. Both here in the Americas and in Europe.

Fourteen thousand years predated any known script-writing system. Come to think of it, it might even predate ancient Greece. . . .

She frowned at the thought. When was Greece founded? She had no idea. That wasn't her area of expertise. She'd never been all that fond of traditional history. That had been Fernando's scope of knowledge, and while she'd picked up a great deal of information on her digs with him, most of it was Mesoamerican and not European.

But even with her limitations, she knew this was epic to the extreme. One of the greatest scientific discoveries of all time . . .

There is no such thing as a coincidence. The universe and spirits are always sending us omens and signs. You must learn to see and read them. Only then will you be able to control your destiny.

Her grandmother's words haunted her.

But what was this a sign of?

"Do you believe the world's going to end in two weeks?" Enrique asked, dragging her thoughts back to where she was.

"What?"

He jerked his chin toward the calendar in her hands. "You know, the Mayan thing? Isn't the world supposed to end any day now?"

At least that added a small twinge of humor to her sadness. She'd listened to Fernando rant and rave against that all summer long. It'd been his sore spot the way she couldn't stand how some people left their shopping buggies in the middle of the aisle so that no one could get past them. Rudeness always set her off.

"No, sweetie. There's absolutely nothing in the Mayan culture or writings to suggest the world will end this year. Like the Cherokee and other natives, they have a cyclical calendar system, and the fourth cycle ends on the 21st, but they never once wrote anything about it being apocalyptic."

Fernando would be so proud to know that she'd actually been listening to his tirades. That thought caused pain to lacerate her heart as she finished Fernando's diatribe in honor of him. "That was a distortion made back in the days when we could only read about thirty percent of the Mayan glyphs . . . if that much. Then back in the nineties when everyone was terrified of Y2K, some scholars repeated the old misconception and cashed in on it. So don't start giving away your personal effects. You'll be needing them on the 22nd and whatever you do, don't forget to buy something for your mother and *abuela* for Christmas. They'd be very upset at you."

He let out a sound of supreme aggravation. "So the date's not important to the Mayans at all?"

"Yes and no. They'd think of it the same way we throw parties on December 31st and why we partied like it was 1999. It's the end of an era for them, and the beginning of a new one. But other than tossing down a few drinks, or taking a few heads as the Mayans were prone to do, it's no cause for alarm."

"Unless you're one of the heads they have their eyes on."

She laughed. "Exactly."

Enrique sighed like he was disappointed that time would carry on. "Well, damn. I better pay my light bill when I get home. I was hoping I could let it slide."

Before she could comment, a new voice interrupted them. "I wouldn't rush home if I were you. The world may yet come to a bad ending."

Kateri sucked her breath in sharply at the thickly accented male voice that intruded on their conversation. Neither Spanish nor Indian, his accent was more a soft blending of the two. One that made the deep rich timbre sound exotic.

Frowning, she looked past her assistant to find what had to be one of the sexiest men she'd ever seen in the flesh. He'd paused just inside the doorway so that he could watch them. Though she doubted he was much over average height, if that, he had an aura so powerful that it seemed to fill the entire room. It was the raw intensity of someone used to being worshiped and feared . . . most likely at the same time.

Dressed entirely in black, he wore his thick ebony hair pulled back into a ponytail. He pinned her with a stare so unsettling, it made her hands shake. There was something about him. Magnetic and scary, it set fire to the very air around them.

It literally sizzled.

His skin the same color as a perfect piece of caramel, he moved with the feral lope of an accomplished predator. Even though his gaze never wavered from hers, she had the distinct impression that he could see everything around him.

For that matter, she wouldn't be surprised if he could see behind his back, too.

"Why would you say that, Mister . . ." She dragged the word out, hoping he'd fill in the missing detail.

Luckily, he took the hint as he closed the gap between them. "Verastegui, Kukulcan Verastegui. But most people refer to me as Cabeza."

The way he said his full name, she could almost taste something sweet and luscious . . . like warm cocoa.

Except one thing destroyed the image. The fact that she knew what his nickname stood for. "They call you . . . Head? Why?"

One corner of his mouth quirked up into a smile that was both amused and threatening. "Pray that you never find out."

Her gaze dropped to the gold ring on his left pinkie. It bore a Mayan symbol, but she wasn't close enough to identify it, and though he was hotter than hell, she didn't want to get even a micro-inch nearer to him. His lethal persona said he might take her arm off if she tried.

"Is there something I can do for you, Mr. Veracity?"

"Vair-ross-STUH-gee," he corrected, rolling his R so that it sounded like a purr.

Enrique put himself between them, forcing Cabeza to stop short of reaching her.

Go, Enrique. Twenty-two-point bonus on your next test. God love that boy for being overprotective.

The scary glint in those soulless black eyes said Mr. Head didn't like or appreciate the interference. Cabeza spoke to Enrique in Spanish, but his accent was so thick that Kateri couldn't catch the individual words. However, there was no missing the way Enrique curled his lips before he shot back with a fiery retort.

Somehow, she didn't think they were discussing the weather or getting directions to something off-campus. They rather reminded her of a *telenovela*.

Cabeza laughed in a low, throaty tone as he tossed a smug expression at her. "You should call off your

40

Chihuahua, *chica*. I'm really not in the mood to clean blood from my clothes."

Enrique started for him, then all of a sudden, froze as if someone had flipped an off switch. He stood stock still with one arm raised and his features contorted by anger.

Yeah, okay . . . that wasn't right.

Gasping, Kateri took a step back, only to collide with the lab table that cut off her retreat. Crap!

"Relax, *bonita*. If I wanted you dead or harmed, you'd already be so."

Right . . . He didn't know her at all if he thought that.

Her hands shaking with controlled fear, she reached into the pocket of her lab coat so that she could clutch her tactical pen—something her uncle Danny had insisted she always carry in case someone attacked her. If Cabeza didn't freeze her too, she had one heck of a surprise for him. She might be short and comparatively tiny, but thanks to her uncle Danny and cousins, she was all muscle and trained to fight dirty with the best of them. "What do you want?"

"You own a certain item that I require."

"And that would be?"

"A stone."

That was like asking the ocean for a single molecule of water. "Look around the room. I'm a geologist." She gestured to the shelves on her left that were lined with boxes of rocks— kind of what he was if he thought she was going to give him anything while he threatened her.

And that display was nothing compared to the ones she had at home. "Been collecting stones since I started walking. I need a little bit more than one noun. Could I buy an adjective there, Pat?"

41

His gaze turned dark. Deadly. "How about you just cooperate and give me what I need?"

Kateri pulled her pen from her pocket. "Let me think . . . um . . . no." She ran for the door.

Unfortunately, he ran faster and cut her off halfway to her destination. She slashed at him with her pen, but he caught her wrist in a move that was so fast she didn't see it until he had her pinned. Damn, he was a lot stronger than Mr. Hulk appeared. And that said it all.

"Give me your time stone," he growled in her ear.

"My wha—Who?" Her gaze went to the calendar Fernando had sent. Was that what he was talking about?

Okay, *that* he could have. Whatever it was, it definitely wasn't worth her life.

"You mean that?" She pointed toward it. "Take the stupid thing. It's all yours."

He glanced toward it, then did a double take. He released her so fast, she stumbled backward.

She ran for the door, but when she tried to open it, it wouldn't budge. Where was a grenade when you needed one?

Better yet, a key.

His features reverent, Cabeza ran his hand over the ancient carvings. He caressed the calendar like a lover he thought was lost to him. "How did you get this?"

"UPS."

He curled his lip and raked her with a sneer. "Where was this found? Tell me!"

Not the appropriate tone, buster. She'd never been one to be ordered around by anyone, anytime. Anywhere. Ignoring his command, she tried the knob again. *C'mon door . . . open, open, open!*

42

Why wasn't the damn thing opening?

'Cause this day just didn't suck enough already.

That thought had barely finished, before the whole door blew apart in her hands. Shielding her face with her arm, she fell away in an effort to protect herself. Cabeza launched himself at her. Dodging his grasp, she ran for the opening, only to collide with a solid wall.

No, not a wall— A giant mass of a man who had to be seven feet tall stood in the center of the doorframe. One who snarled something at Cabeza in a language she'd never heard spoken before.

Kateri barely got out of the line of fire before the two of them went after each other with everything they had. They let fly blows that should have killed any normal human being. But neither of them did more than growl and attack as they continued to block her exit.

It was like being trapped by Godzilla and Mothra.

With no thought other than survival, she ran toward the closet in back. If nothing else, she could try to hide there.

As she broke even with the last table, where she'd left her purse, she grabbed her phone out of it. Intending to call security, she cursed as it started ringing in her hands.

Dammit! It better not be a telemarketer.

She flipped it open, and started to tell whoever it was that she was a little busy when she heard her cousin's voice.

"Teri? Is everything okay?"

"Sunny! I need help in my lab. Now! Call campus security for me. I'm being attacked." She'd barely finished the last word before her phone went dead.

"We can't be having that, can we?" Cabeza asked as he kicked the mountain away from him.

He started toward her.

Her eyes widened as the other man ran at him and slammed him against the wall. That had to hurt, but since he was doing her a favor, she was actually rooting for the mountain to win.

I have to get out of here. Especially before they turn that hatred on me. One hit like that, and she'd never recover. Kateri ran toward the front again. *Please have heard me, Sunny. Please call help.* She loved her cousin dearly, but the woman could be extremely absentminded and oblivious at times.

She glanced at Enrique, who was still frozen mid-gesture. He needed help, too.

What do I do?

Kateri was almost to the closet door when someone grabbed her arm and pulled her to a rude stop.

Furious, she turned on the newcomer, intending to attack. But as she raised her arm for the blow and focused on her latest annoyance, she sucked her breath in sharply. Recognition hit her like a sucker punch.

"Talon?" It was Sunny's husband. All six foot four, rippling muscles tattooed with Celtic tribal marks, of him. "What are you doing here?"

Had he been in town? Was that why Sunny had called?

He didn't answer her question as he pulled her back and put himself in the line of fire to protect her. His blond wavy hair was cut short except for two long, thin braids that fell from his temple. Just as Cabeza would have hit him, a fourth man caught Cabeza and lifted him off his feet. He slammed Cabeza to the ground before he kicked the mountain away from them.

"Get her out of here, Celt," he growled at Talon over his shoulder.

Without hesitation, Talon tossed her over his muscular shoulder as if she weighed nothing at all and ran with her out of the room. Not the most comfortable of sensations. But she was too grateful to be out of that room to protest.

Talon didn't set her down until he reached her office at the end of the next hallway.

"Enrique's still in the lab," she told him.

"Cabeza will get him."

She sputtered at his lackadaisical tone. "That's the problem. I don't want him to."

"Why not?"

Why not? Really? "I like him. He's a good assistant, and those are really hard to find."

Talon scowled at her. "Then why don't you want him saved?"

"I *do* want him saved. Not fed to Cabeza."

Talon's frown deepened. "We are both speaking English, right?"

"Yeah."

"Then why do I feel like we're not?"

Before she could answer, the tall, scary man who'd slammed Cabeza to the floor appeared by his side. Literally—by his side.

How had he run in so fast that she hadn't seen it?

Not that it mattered right this instant, because . . . *Holy firecracker . . . How had she failed to notice him?*

Yet during the fight, she'd barely registered the man.

Now the sheer ferocity of his presence jarred her. Just over six feet, he was built like a tank, and those black clothes added an even more sinister look to him. Not that he needed it. His black hair was slightly longer than Talon's and he wore it with his bangs covering a pair of obsidian eyes that froze her the instant they met her gaze and held it in a tight fist.

Her knees went weak from terror. How had he appeared in here without using the door? It was still closed from Talon and while the man might be fast, she would have surely seen it open and close. Not to mention, hear the bell on it.

Unlike her, Talon didn't seem to think it unusual that he had materialized in her office. "Did you get the kid?" he asked the man.

"Barely. I stashed him in the public toilet. He should be safe there until he regains use of his body." The man jerked his chin toward the windows. "Help a brother out, Celt. I could have gone up in flames just now, you bastard. Think ahead. Ask for my help. Blow me up. Shit. What kind of friend are you?"

"Screw you," Talon snarled before he moved to the blinds and closed them. "Mess with me, boy, and I'll bring the daylight inside where you stand."

The man gestured at Talon with something she assumed must be obscene.

Talon flashed a taunting grin. "Not on your best day, Cabeza. But feel free to keep fantasizing about me. Most *women* do."

The man scoffed and grabbed his "package" and shook it. "Yeah, I got your woman for you, Celt. Right here."

Kateri held her hands up before they started a fight to equal the one she'd just left. "Wait, wait, wait ..." She pointed to the man. "He's named Cabeza, too?"

The man quirked a brow at her. "Too? I'm pretty sure I'm it. Haven't ever come across another."

Her own head was starting to throb. "The other man in the lab. The one you attacked. He said his name was Cabeza."

"His mama named him Head?" Talon snorted derisively. "Damn, that's cold. And here I thought this Cabeza had it bad."

"It was a nickname. His real name was Kukulcan Verastegui."

The Cabeza in front of her broke off into a fierce round of what sounded like Mayan cursing. She had no idea what he was saying, but it was raw and explosive as he gestured furiously to punctuate his tirade.

She turned her frown to Talon. "What's he saying?"

Talon shrugged. "I'm from Britain, not Mexico. No idea."

"That *pendejo* is *not* me." Cabeza broke off into a mixture of Mayan and Spanish and then returned to English, but this time his accent was much thicker and he rolled his Rs viciously. "His name, for the record, is Chacu. *Ese cabrón hijo de la gran puta*, pretending to be me. I should have cut his throat for my Act of Vengeance!"

"The real question is, did you cut his throat today?"

Hands on hips, Cabeza glared at Talon for asking such a thing. "No. He got away, along with the ... what's the word? Uh ... Pigeon crap?"

"Chicken shit?" Talon offered.

47

"*Si!* . . . that was with him. They vanished before I could kill them."

"Why were they fighting?" Kateri asked. "And why were they after me?"

Cabeza arched a brow at her. "Don't you know?"

"Why would I ask if I knew?" She turned her attention to Talon. "And how did you get here so fast? Where were you?" Talon and Sunshine lived in New Orleans . . . not here in Tuscaloosa, Alabama. Last time she'd made that drive, it'd taken her four hours, and she didn't drive slowly.

"You'll want to sit down for this." Talon turned the chair in front of her desk around for her.

A sick feeling settled deep in her stomach. "Think I'll stand. Now, what's up?"

The men exchanged a solemn look as if they were silently willing the other to speak first.

"Did Chacu say anything to you, other than pretending to be me?"

"He said he wanted my stone."

A tic started in Cabeza's jaw. "And the other . . . creature with him? What did he say?"

"Nothing. He showed up and Cab—" She broke the word off as his eyes snapped ebony fire at her. "Chacu attacked him."

"Any idea why he's handing out your name?" Talon asked.

"No idea. His hatred of me is legendary. But he's not exactly engraved in my heart either. My want-them-dead list, however, is another matter."

Kateri cleared her throat to get their attention. "And you're *both* avoiding *my* questions."

Talon let out a sarcastic laugh. "That's because you're going to freak and neither one of us wants to deal with it."

Well, at least Talon was honest.

"I'm not going to freak," she assured him.

It was now Cabeza's turn to mock her. "That's what they all say, *chica*. And then they all freak."

Talon laughed again—for real this time—as he met Cabeza's gaze. "You remember that time when . . ." He glanced at her. "Never mind."

She ignored that segue entirely. "Look, whatever it is, I can handle it. I'm not a child, and Talon, you know I don't ever overreact to anything."

Cabeza crossed his arms over his chest. "Is this true?"

"So far. But I've never dumped anything like this on her before. There's always that first time for everything."

That offended her. "So far? Thanks for the vote of confidence, Talon."

He held his hands up in surrender. "At least it's something."

"You better tell her, Celt . . . before another comes. We need to get her to shelter while we can."

Kateri definitely didn't like the sound of that. "Shelter from what?"

Talon let out a long sigh. "All right. Fine. You asked for it. Let's see you not freak when we tell you that you're the mother of Armageddon."

Chapter 4

Kateri stood completely still as those words sank in. She wasn't sure what reaction to have to his news. But it was a good thing that she'd told them she didn't overreact, otherwise, in spite of her bravado, she'd be running for the door.

Probably screaming the whole way.

Maybe . . . if her shaking legs could manage it.

Instead, she took a deep breath and met her cousin-in-law with the calmest stare she could muster. "Have you been into Uncle Danny's peyote?"

Talon opened his mouth to respond, then closed it.

Cabeza laughed.

Talon cut a menacing glare toward him before he softened his features. "I know this is hard for you to hear and I know you're not going to believe me. But . . ." He hesitated as he visibly searched for words.

Cabeza gave him no reprieve. "We need to get out of here. Chacu will return for her and he'll bring reinforcements."

"Who is Chacu?" Kateri snapped, wanting real answers from both of them. "Why was he here?"

Most important, why the hell was he after *her*?

Cabeza put his hands on his hips. "Do you know what the Snake Kingdom was?"

Something to be avoided at all costs, no doubt. But she kept that sarcasm inside. "Not a clue."

"Of course not . . ." He growled low in his throat as if he found her lack of knowledge offensive, then he mumbled in Spanish under his breath. After a second, he took a breath and spoke. "Really short version, Chacu's name means 'to pillage' or 'to ravage.' The other *puta* with him, and yes, I'm using the feminine on purpose, is called Veneno—as in 'venom' or 'bane.'" He narrowed his gaze on her. "Is the picture starting to paint in your mind yet?"

With a clarity that horrified her. After all, their parents hadn't named them "Fluffy" or "Bunny." Obviously Chacu and friend were hard-asses. "And this time stone thing that Chacu wanted from me?"

"In short, it's called the Kinichi. With it, he can rule the world and even time itself. Your grandmother was one of the sacred keepers of the Kinichi. Your mother should have followed her into that role, but since she died before your grandmother, that role went to you."

Fabulous. She was overwhelmed with gratitude, and yes, that was sarcasm, too. "Why me?"

"The stone passes from daughter to daughter to ensure the bloodline."

Mama's baby. Daddy's maybe. That had been the philosophy her grandmother had used when Kateri had asked her why the Cherokee were matriarchal while most societies weren't. Everyone knew who their mother was without a doubt. But paternity, especially in the past, could be dicey and relied solely on the mother's character and morals . . . provided she wasn't raped.

But that still didn't leave her as the sole heiress. "I'm not the only female in my family." She gestured to Talon, who was married to her cousin.

"Sunshine is half white," Talon said simply. "The stone has to go to a full-blood, Teri. . . . You."

Great. Could she win the lottery?

No. With her luck, she'd win the multi-mega-millions and still end up owing someone a check for it.

A sweepstakes once in a while?

Again, double heck no.

Mother of the Apocalypse . . .

Well, of course, honey. Come on up and claim your prize.

Life was so unfair. And just once, Kateri would like to see the bad-luck fairy prey on someone else. Preferably not someone she liked, but still . . .

Was the bitch bored today? Or could she really not find another victim?

"We also have a bigger problem," Cabeza said to Talon.

By all means, let's pile it on.

Talon stepped back. "Dare I ask?"

Cabeza snorted. "I wouldn't. But unfortunately, you need to know that someone unearthed the Seal of the Anikutani."

Talon gave him a dark scowl. "You say that like I should know what you're talking about."

Cabeza mumbled under his breath. "It's a ... *kala kratu* ...A ..." He paused, struggling to find the right word. "How you say in English? Guard stone? Spell stone? Not the right word, but you know what I mean. It was placed over the tomb where the last seven Anikutani warriors were imprisoned. Now that it's uncovered, anyone can summon them back to this world. Whoever does such, they owe a favor to, and they will do what he commands them to. Then they will breach the gates and fight with the evil they unleash. You see the problem now, Celt? Chacu knows the seal is missing and he knows what that seal is."

Kateri cursed at that knowledge. No wonder Chacu had been so interested in the calendar when he'd seen it on her table. Why did she feel like she was suddenly in a horror movie?

Cabeza grabbed her arm and pulled her in to Talon. "Take her and go. We have to get her to her stone and then to safety so that she can seal the gates again."

"What about you?" Talon asked.

Someone should bottle Cabeza's evil laughter for a haunted house. It would definitely put the fear of death into any living being. "I live to fight, *m'ijo*. If they're dumb enough to come back, I have some questions I want answered and I'm sure I can pound it out of them.... *Adios.*"

Talon inclined his head to him. *"A beber y a tragar, que el mundo se va a acabar."*

Cabeza was less than amused. "You're a cold bastard, Celt. *Hombre prevenido, vale por dos."* With that said, he walked backward, out of the room.

Kateri arched a brow at Talon. "I understood your 'Eat,

54

drink, and be merry 'cause we're dying tomorrow.' But what did he say back to you?"

"One man forewarned is worth two. Now let's get you—"

Before he could finish that sentence, something dark pooled around her. Eyes wide, she reached for Talon, who lunged toward her.

He didn't make it.

Just as her fingertips brushed his, she was sucked into some kind of spiraling vortex. Nausea rose up as she sank downward. *I am not Dorothy.* But if someone dropped a house on her, she was going to be even more put out than the Wicked Witch had been.

Fear me. . . .

At least that was her thought until she slammed hard into utter darkness. There was no light whatsoever. The blackness was so thick it made her eyes hurt as she strained to see something. Anything. Pushing herself up from the earthen ground where she'd landed, she tried to get her bearings.

A low whine sounded in the distance.

Her mind struggled to name it. Dog? Child? She couldn't tell for sure. She started to call out, then stopped herself. Just in case something meant her harm, the last thing she wanted to do was let it know where she was.

I've seen that horror movie a few times. That stupid puta *always buys it first.*

At least I don't have on high heels or a short skirt. Screaming or not, that character always died.

She reached out with her arms, trying to find a wall or furniture or—

55

"Ow! Son of a . . ." She pressed her lips together as she reached down to rub her shin. Surely, there had to be another purpose to that body part other than finding furniture in the dark.

Only she hadn't hit furniture, she realized as she explored the hard surface with her hand. It felt more like rock.

What I wouldn't give for the flashlight in my purse.

Something brushed against her leg.

Gasping, she twirled, trying to find out what it was. *Please don't be a rat. Please don't be a rat. . . .*

That was her worst phobia.

"Where's the stone?"

She jumped at the sudden raspy voice. "Who are you?"

"Where's the stone?" That was another voice from the other side of the darkness.

When she didn't answer right away, light flared. Horror froze her into place. Never in her life had she seen anything like this.

The entire cave—and she now knew it was a cave she was in—was filled with . . .

Chupacabra?

El peuchen?

Where was Enrique when she needed him? Better yet, his great great-grandmother's drum to drive them out.

The small area she stood in was packed with creatures possessed of sharply pointed teeth. Their bodies were painted from head to toe in designs that reminded her of a totem pole caricature. Paint that gave them the illusion of frowning in displeasure.

Even more terrifying, they appeared to be splattered with dried blood.

Her bravado gone, she knew she could never win a fight against this many. Their sheer number would beat her down and kill her.

One of them hit her from behind. "Stone!" he snarled. "Give it. Now!"

"I-I-I don't know what you're talking about."

Wrong answer. They beat spears against painted round shields as they screamed their displeasure at her.

I'm so dead. Her limbs shaking, she ran to her right, where there appeared to be a shaft.

The monsters cut her off.

With a move Peyton Manning would envy, she stopped, dodged, and reversed direction, heading toward another tunnel.

This time, by some miracle, she made it. But that didn't say much. She slowed down as it became dark again and she could no longer see anything.

And again with the whining and hissing.

Now that was just mean ... toying with her like this when they knew she couldn't see them. They better be glad they outnumbered her. Otherwise—

I have lost my mind. It was the only explanation for her strange panicked calm. How could somebody be both petrified and in full control of themselves?

Be grateful. She could be screaming....

Then again, maybe she was. Maybe this calm was a fabrication of her inability to cope.

The cave began to thump around her like some deep, heavy heartbeat. Everything echoed and pounded.

Everything.

Kateri turned to run. She'd barely taken two steps before something slammed into her so hard, it stung.

No, not stung. It'd wounded her. Suddenly light-headed, she touched her ribs where it hurt the most. Sticky blood coated her fingers as the sounds grew louder.

Closer.

They were everywhere now.

She moved as fast as she could, but it was no use. No matter what she tried, she couldn't escape the creatures after her—whatever they were. They continued to toy with her as they whispered over and over, "Give us the stone."

"Shut up!" she snarled. "I don't have it!"

Something slapped her across the face.

She kicked out at it and was happy to hear it groan in response. *Good. I hope you feel it for a while.*

But that didn't change the fact that she was in serious trouble. Clutching her injury, she limped through the darkness, hoping to find some kind of exit.

I'm going to die.

She knew it. There was no alternative.

Her hand trembling, she applied more pressure to her wound. It wasn't that deep, but it throbbed unmercifully and made it all the harder to breathe. Worse, it was making her extremely dizzy, and if she didn't get it tended, she could bleed out.

Through the darkness, she heard more shrill cries. Different ones this time.

Cries she knew all too well from her dreams.

Raven mockers.

Even more terrified, she fell back further into the shadows, praying they wouldn't find her.

As she felt her way down the wall, she cringed at what was happening. She just didn't want to believe her grandmother's stories were real. They couldn't be.

Because if they were . . .

I am not that person. I'm not. I don't believe in magic or spells.

But what other explanation could there be? She wasn't stupid and her denials were bordering on that at this point. No matter how much you believed something—how much something had been proven—part of being a scientist was learning how to accept new findings that completely changed the way people viewed things.

So accept it. Your grandmother was right.

All of it was real.

Yet it was hard because she didn't want to have the responsibilities her grandmother had held. Everyone had depended on her for every little thing. She'd been responsible for people's lives and their immortal souls. . . .

As if her thoughts reached across the worlds, she felt her grandmother's presence in the room with her. Smelled the Jurgen's and peppermint. "Kateri? Help me. I need you, child. My soul will die if you don't come."

She took a step forward instinctively, then caught herself. It wasn't her grandmother calling out to her. Her grandmother had been dead for years and she would be using the name only the two of them knew. *They're trying to trick me.*

"Help me, child!"

Hoping to put more distance between herself and the

things after her, Kateri pressed her back against the cold stone wall and took another step away from the opening.

Someone tsked in her ear. "Where are you going, tidbit? You're not trying to leave us so soon, are you?"

Her vision dimmed as a bony hand sank like a claw into her shoulder, piercing it with pain. Unlike the other things in the cave, she knew this one. It was a raven mocker.

Suddenly, a deep masculine voice thundered, speaking a language she didn't know.

But the raven mocker knew it. She could tell by its sharp, angry intake of breath. Releasing her, it lunged at the voice and shrieked so loudly that it made her ears ring.

The moment it struck the man, light bathed the small shaft with an orange glow. A glow that came from the man's skin . . .

Kateri wanted to run while they fought, but she couldn't. She felt as frozen as Enrique had been in her lab. Her entire body tense, she watched closely, praying the newcomer was friend and not foe.

She was so over her foe quota for the day, and it was barely noon. . . .

As she watched, her gaze went from the twisted, hideous raven mocker to the man it fought. Swathed head to toe in black, he was even larger than the raven mocker. Because of the eerie glow he was giving off, she couldn't make out his features clearly, but his long black hair was loose, falling to the middle of his back as he turned and dodged, then attacked the raven mocker with movements so graceful they reminded her of a dancer's.

The raven mocker slashed at his throat.

In an elegant, quick move, the man jerked back.

Instead of the raven mocker cutting his throat, it caught his bone-and-turquoise necklace, and snatched it free. It flew through the darkness to land on the ground at her feet.

Kateri picked it up, then froze as her gaze focused on the silver circle that held the imprint of a thunderbird.

From the east, the Thunderbird will fly into the direction of the death lands. Beware the Thunderbird, child. For in his path, all will perish. None can stand against him.

Not even you.

Her grandmother's words had barely whispered through her head before the warrior caught the raven mocker a blow that caused it to explode into bright, flickering flames.

The man turned toward her.

In that instant, her heart stopped beating as she clearly saw his entire body. His eyes were as black as his hair and clothes. Every line on his handsome face sculpted to perfection, he held the expression of a merciless fighter who was more used to taking lives than saving them.

And as he focused that cold, dark gaze on her, she felt the hand of death brush her cheek.

For all time . . .

This was the man who always killed her in her dreams.

Chapter 5

Ren froze as his gaze locked with the woman's. When Cabeza had called and told him the Ixkib, or ghighau as she was known in his language, had been found and then lost, he'd envisioned her as an elder woman. It was what she'd always been in the past.

But never had he foreseen *this*. . . .

Or anticipated *her*. . . .

Her presence slammed into him like an unexpected fist in his gut. *This* was the woman in yellow who'd killed him in his visions. Time and again. The one whose gentle touch always paralyzed him for her lethal blow.

One she'd never failed to deliver to him with a smile on her lips. *"I'm here for you."* That voice haunted him as his head reeled from a reality he didn't want to face.

By her hand, I will die. And he couldn't deny it. His precogs were never wrong.

Never.

And in the flesh, she was even more beautiful. More compelling, she had her long, dark brown hair pulled back into a ponytail. Strands that had come loose during her capture and escape curled around her face in an attractive mess that begged him to sink his hand into it and see if it was as soft as it appeared. And even though she was well muscled for a woman, she was tiny. The top of her head barely reached the middle of his chest.

Just like in my dreams.

Still, even knowing that she would eventually kill him, he couldn't bring himself to harm her. Not while her sweet scent filled his head. There was something about her that appeared soft and delicate. Fragile.

Or so he thought until she narrowed those dark eyes and lunged at him with an object in her hand.

Reacting on pure instinct, he fell back, allowing her to unbalance herself when she didn't make contact with his body. He clamped down on her wrist with enough pressure to control her attack, but not enough to harm her. And as he held her immobile, he realized she was hurt and bleeding.

Badly.

He would have admired her bravery and spirit even if she wasn't wounded. The fact that she fought when others would be on the ground, crying, said a lot about her character and resolve.

"I'm not going to let you kill me," she snarled in his face.

He opened his mouth to respond, but before he could draw a single breath, her eyes rolled back in her head and she passed out.

Ren barely caught her before she collapsed. Swinging

her up in his arms, he debated what to do. He'd ventured here in his crow form. It'd been so long since he'd last tried to teleport someone from one realm to another that he wasn't sure if his powers would work or not. And then there was the small matter that it was a lot harder to teleport dead weight than someone whose conscious energy he could use for a power source. Not to mention, his brother had drained a good portion of Ren's strength to summon the Na'ha Ala to pull the woman from the human realm into this one.

I hate you, Coyote.

But it wasn't productive to focus on something so negative. Especially not while another Na'ha was entering their small haven . . . and it wasn't alone.

A large group of hairy, smelly friends had decided to join it.

Like it or not, Ren didn't have a choice.

Either he tried . . .

Or they died.

Hoping for the best, he summoned every bit of power he could and forced himself to take a very rare leap of faith. His head buzzed as he felt the surge.

Light flashed and he felt his body shift, but not how he wanted it to.

Shit . . .

He didn't go far. In fact, he went *toward* them instead of away.

Only I have this kind of luck. Thank the Spirits that the woman was unconscious and couldn't see his incompetence. It was bad enough *he* was awake to witness it. All he needed was for her to laugh at him.

You're worthless, Makah'Alay. I weep for the day you were brought into this world to be a hindrance to us all. . . .

He flinched as he heard his father's acerbic voice across the centuries. *Would you die already, you bastard? I had enough of you while you lived.*

But sometimes dead just wasn't dead enough.

Pushing those thoughts away and forcing himself to concentrate on only the positive, Ren tightened his grip on the woman.

With a savage hiss, the Na'ha came at him, fangs bared, claws gleaming in the dim light.

Ren twisted at the waist so that the creature would hit his spine and not the woman. Then, he tried to at least teleport them back to where they'd been a moment ago. The Na'ha's hot breath scorched his neck as it clamped a clawed hand onto his biceps.

That pain boosted his powers as he cried out and rage took hold of him.

This time, with that boost, it worked.

One second they were in the cave, the next he was in his living room. . . .

With the Na'ha's hand still attached to his arm.

Curling his lip at the grisly sight, he moved to lay the woman on his couch so that he could tear it free and throw it into his fireplace where he'd left a fire burning. While his journey had seemed to last only a few minutes, time here passed differently than it did there.

Here, it was already night and his small house was silent and empty. Except for the sound of the fire popping and destroying the physical remains of something he'd hoped would never be able to breach the gate to this world. Things he'd hoped to never face again.

Thanks, Coyote.

Bastard. Rat. Asshole.

Son of a belly-licking rodent's backside.

Ren cringed at the smell of burning demon flesh, which triggered memories he'd spent eternity trying to forget. But some wounds went far deeper than the bones. Some went all the way to the soul, and they stung even after he'd sold that same soul for peace.

Or, more to the point, war.

Trying not to think about it, he returned to the woman and lifted her shirt so that he could see her injury. Yet all he really saw at first was her smooth, tanned skin. Skin that looked as soft as the hair he really wanted to bury his face into so that he could inhale her delicate scent.

God, it'd been so long since he'd last slept with a woman. Felt her breath and hands on his skin as he lost himself to absolute pleasure.

For many reasons, he'd done his best to stay away from women as much as possible. It wasn't that he didn't trust them.

He didn't trust himself.

After enslaving himself to the last woman he'd been with and allowing her to completely and utterly control him against all sanity, he had no desire to surrender his will or body again to any female. Not even long enough to scratch a base urge.

It wasn't worth it.

And that succeeded in reminding him why he didn't need to think of this one as an attractive woman in the

67

least. She was just another stranger who would be out of his life in a matter of days.

No more. No less.

In the back of his mind, he saw an image of her stabbing him. But that, too, he pushed aside. He knew to watch out for it. So long as he kept his guard up, there was no chance of her harming him. He was too lethal a warrior for that. He wasn't the same man who'd allowed Windseer to take control of his hatred.

I am the Thunderbird. The fiercest of all legends. The deadliest of predators.

The only thing that had ever defeated Thunderbird was the Thunderbird when he'd allowed himself to be tricked by Raven.

And that will not happen to me.

Never again.

His thoughts finally where they should be, he narrowed his gaze on the deep gash that ran along her rib cage. It looked painful and terrible. Having received more than his fair share of wounds, he knew how much such a thing stung. It amazed him that she'd lasted as long as she had before passing out.

Heaven knew, Coyote had never been so strong.

Tasting the bitterness on his tongue brought up by that particular memory, he pulled his T-shirt off, over his head, and used it to apply pressure with one hand while he called Talon with the other to let his friend know that he'd found their target.

Talon didn't answer.

Frowning, Ren tried Choo Co La Tah next. When Choo didn't pick up . . . that made him nervous. *Don't panic.*

They're not back in this realm yet. That's all it is. Hard to get cell phone service when you're beyond the reach of cell towers.

It could be true. They'd each gone to different realms where the woman could have been taken. Since his friends didn't know he had her, they would keep searching for a while.

Which meant he was stuck with her until their return. Alone.

It's not the same as before. He wasn't the same.

And she definitely was not Windseer.

Yeah, but look what that got you. A quick kick in the teeth and crotch, *and* a gelding would have been far superior to Windseer's treachery and abandonment.

It was why he didn't want to be alone with this woman.

I can resist anything except temptation. But at least he knew that about himself and he accepted it. He now understood what to guard against. It was why he was a recluse to the worst extent of that word. Why he, unlike the majority of other Dark-Hunters, didn't have a human servant to look after his affairs.

The fewer people around him, the better. For centuries only Choo Co La Tah had been trusted as his friend. And a hundred years ago, after Buffalo had been reincarnated and then slain, Ren had taken his one true friend under his wing to protect him.

He didn't need anyone else in his life.

But as he tended her side and the warmth of her skin caressed his, he remembered a time when he'd wanted so much more than this barren existence. A time when he'd craved being a part of the world. Having friends and family to share his fire with.

Why? He had no idea. The world had never welcomed him. His family damn sure hadn't.

Prove to me that you're at least worth the grain it takes to feed you. Protect your brother. At all cost. Even if it means your own life. That had been his only use to any of them.

Bleed for others.

And it was still his sole reason for living. *The more things change, the more they stay the same.*

Grinding his teeth, Ren pushed all those thoughts back to the place of darkness where they belonged.

If only they would stay there.

Angry at himself for a weakness that shouldn't exist, he finished cleaning and binding her wound, then got up to put away his bloody shirt and get a fresh one.

As he stepped away, lightning flashed brightly and was followed by a clash of thunder so loud, it jarred his entire home.

At midnight, the Reset would officially begin. A ten-day festival of counting down to the opening of the gates. The first day of fun would be violent storming. Followed by tornadoes, floods, and hail so severe only a fool would venture into it. And with the dawning of every day, Windseer would be one step closer to release.

Once she was out, then she would set free the Grizzly Spirit.

And then, they would come for him.

Ren ground his teeth as he remembered the day Windseer had taken him before her master. At first, Grizzly had appeared old and withered. It'd only been when their gazes met that Ren understood the power of the immortal bastard. What it would take to restore the ancient being to health.

"Release me and I will make all your dreams a reality."

The Grizzly had required a blood sacrifice from a child of the Stars. His heart filled with utter hatred and contempt for the world that had kicked him in the teeth one time too many, Ren had gladly performed the ceremony and restored the Grizzly Spirit to the human realm. And just as gladly, he'd welcomed Grizzly to use his body as Grizzly's own.

In blood and sweat, Ren had been reborn a new man. But not a better one. Strange how he hadn't really found his humanity until after he'd sold his soul to Artemis. Only then had he learned what mattered most in life.

Only after he'd lost absolutely everything.

I'm coming for you, Makah'Alay. I can't wait for our reunion. The Grizzly's voice was getting louder and stronger.

And the only thing that could stop one of the oldest, deadliest creatures to ever walk the earth was a tiny slip of a woman who slept on his couch. If it wasn't so pathetic, he'd laugh.

From the doorway, he glanced back at her. Her features pale and relaxed, she breathed so lightly that she didn't even appear to be alive. How could someone so small stand against a creature who made Ren appear dainty and frail?

Grizzly would eat her alive.

It didn't matter how strong she was. If the Guardian didn't return to battle Grizzly, there would be no hope for any of them. Even if she reset the calendar, it would change nothing.

71

Evil would not be denied. Having once served it, he knew that for a fact.

With a heavy sigh, Ren went to clean up.

Dressed all in white with an eagle's feather tied in her dark hair, Kateri followed a path through a dense forest. The scent of pine hung thick in the air, stinging her throat. She didn't know why, but she'd never cared for that smell.

"Because your father told you to fear it when you were a baby. Though you don't remember him, you remember his words of warning."

She paused at the sound of her grandmother's voice. "Grammy?"

Her grandmother stepped out of the woods in front of her. "It's so easy to lose your way, child." She gestured to the trees around them. "When you're in the middle of something and you're surrounded by so much that overwhelms you, it's easy to focus on the wrong thing."

"I don't understand."

Instead of answering, her grandmother rushed forward as a wolf ran at Kateri.

Gasping, Kateri fell back.

Without hesitation, her grandmother drove the wolf off until it was just the two of them again.

Her grandmother faced her with a stern glower. "Now do you see?"

Yes, she did. "But this is just a dream."

"Dreams are the mind's way of dealing with reality, Waleli. It's why they're so important, and why we need to remember them." Her grandmother started away from her.

"Grammy?"

Follow me. The voice was in her head and didn't come from her grandmother's lips.

Kateri rushed forward until her grandmother stopped at the edge of a field. There she saw a strange stone building in the middle of a thriving, ancient town. Though different, it reminded her of a Mayan pyramid. It was cut at a sharper angle with a more rounded top, and had things that appeared to be windows in it. Never had she seen the like. Fernando would be impressed to see this.

The people moving around it looked to be Native Americans, but their clothes were unlike anything she'd ever seen before. They were more stylized, and dyed bright colors with exquisite beadwork. Many of the people wore feathers either for jewelry or hair accessories. And while the women had no makeup whatsoever, the men who appeared to be warriors had their faces heavily painted.

She didn't know what her grandmother was trying to tell her about this town until the warrior who'd saved her stepped out from the building. Another man, a few inches shorter, trailed behind him. The man at her warrior's back had his face painted white with brown buffalos on his cheeks, meanwhile his was painted black. Two red stripes cut sharp angles from his eyes to his jawline. Another red mark went across his brow with white dots placed above it.

They came down to stand in a small courtyard at the base of the stairs as if they were waiting for someone else to join them.

Others filed in from all directions until they formed a small army of men. Most of them were heavily armed with blowguns, atlatls, or spears. A few with those vicious war clubs.

But not her warrior. His sole weapons were a simple bow and a short knife that was tucked into his boot.

"They'll be here soon," the shorter man said.

Her warrior nodded. Dressed in a very thin black buckskin jacket and pants, he wore no shirt beneath it. And well he shouldn't, given how chiseled and rigidly defined his muscles were. The front of his long black hair was pulled back to the crown of his head, where it was held by a thick leather cord, the ends of which were attached to a black and white feather.

He wore the bow crossed over his back, and a small quiver of arrows at his waist. Even though he was surrounded by fierce warriors, he stood out. Not just because he was the tallest, but because of the way he watched those around him. As if he expected an attack at any moment.

And who could blame him? Contempt bled out of the expressions of the others whenever they glanced in his direction. Why did they hate him so? Was he so evil that they couldn't stand to look at him?

Turning, he spoke to the man beside him with short, rapid hand gestures that made no sense to her whatsoever.

The man arched a brow. "Why would you think that?"

Her warrior shrugged.

Suddenly, silence fell over the gathered warriors as the doors opened. Moving with slow, deliberate strides, four older men who were dressed in the cloaks of priests descended from the building. Each of them had a different feathered headdress and mask. One appeared to be a deer, complete with antlers. Another was a white buffalo, followed by a black bear, and lastly a gray wolf. They also carried ornate feathered fans.

The oldest began speaking in a language she couldn't understand. But after a second, the words became clear.

"It has been decided and agreed upon. For his bravery against the mighty boar and for saving his brother's life, Coyote will lead us after the death of our chief, his father. Word has been sent to the Deer clan that we will welcome their strongest daughter to be his wife. So let it be done and may we grow even more prosperous under the leadership of Coyote and his bride, Butterfly!"

Kateri heard those words, but it was the expression on her warrior's face that held her real attention. He looked as if someone had just kicked him in the stomach.

The man with him started forward, but her warrior grabbed his arm and shook his head sternly.

"They should know the truth," his friend said in a fierce whisper.

"They don't c-c-c-care." His stutter stunned her. She'd have never expected that from a man so predacious.

"It's not right! *You* saved Coyote. How can he take credit when you're the one who was almost killed defending *him* and *his* stupidity? But for you, he'd be dead now."

A tic worked in her warrior's jaw as he began to sign to his friend.

His friend returned his comments with one last gesture she assumed must be obscene given the angry reaction of her warrior. Turning sharply on his heel so that he could stalk off, his friend left him.

"They should be told the truth," his friend growled under his breath.

Ignoring him, her warrior removed the bow from his back. His expression blank, he walked forward to lay it at the feet of the head priest before he bowed low.

The priest smiled in approval. "An offering to our future chief from his elder brother. Thank you, Makah'Alay. Your brother will be touched by your gift. Let you stand as an honorable example to all."

"Honorable my ass," one of the men said off to the side. "But for his brother, he'd be dead."

"Nah, he'd have been cast out years ago." They all laughed while her warrior stood there with nothing showing on his face at all. It was as if it was so common an occurrence that he didn't even hear them anymore.

"We respect you, priest, but please don't hold up a defect as an example of anything except why malformed children should be left in the woods to die."

The man came forward and snatched the bow from the ground before he shoved it into Makah'Alay's hands. "Our future chief doesn't need *your* castoff. No one wants the twisted bow of a deformed, retarded idiot."

The fire returned to Makah'Alay's eyes as he clutched the bow so tightly his knuckles blanched. Even Kateri feared for the other man. It was obvious Makah'Alay wanted to plant his offering in a very uncomfortable place.

Self-preservation must have finally kicked in. Without another word, the man quickly retreated from her warrior.

With his head tilted down and his expression darker and deadlier than before, Makah'Alay watched the others with an unspoken threat that he was plotting their deaths. Even though he was terrifying to behold, there was something intrinsically hot and sexy about that pose.

He was like a predator in the wild that was one breath from attacking.

Any wrong move or word . . .

And someone would be missing a throat.

Finally, her warrior pulled the bow around his body to lie diagonally across his back. He held the string with both hands, then he walked away. Only when his back was to them and none could see his face did he let the hurt show. His eyes betrayed the depth to which they'd wounded him. But even worse was the shame and self-loathing that he didn't deserve to feel. The tragic despair.

And that brought tears to her own eyes.

How could people be so mean to each other? She'd never understood what it was about some people that they couldn't allow anyone else to have a moment of dignity. That they had to rob others of any semblance of pride or happiness.

It was so wrong.

"Teri?"

She turned at the familiar voice, but she couldn't place it.

"Teri? Can you hear me?"

It came from a distance. But she didn't want to go toward it. She wanted to follow the warrior and make him feel better. To tell him that the others were wrong for what they'd done. . . .

"Teri!"

She jerked awake so suddenly that she had to grab the couch to keep from hitting the floor. It took a second before her gaze cleared enough to see her cousin Rain Runningwolf standing over her.

Frowning, she tried to get her bearings. "What are you doing here?"

Where *was* here?

"Sunshine didn't want you to be alone. She threatened the boys if I didn't haul ass over to you ASAP. Since I'm rather fond of my boys"—he flashed a devilish grin—"here I be, cuz."

Tall, dark, and irritating, Rain would be gorgeous if A) he wasn't her cousin and B) he acted like a man and not a five-year-old kid.

She scowled at his short, military hairdo. He used to pride himself on his long raven locks. "When did you cut your hair?"

"A year ago when I decided I didn't want to work with my family for the rest of my life. You really never check your Facebook page, do you?"

Without pausing he continued with his ADD, "Love them, but distance doth make the heart beat stronger. It also does wonders for my social life, since women tend to look down on men who work for their dads and live over their father's club."

She pressed her hand to her temple as she tried to follow his train of thought. "I don't understand. You still live over your father's club."

"Yes, but now they don't *know* it's my father's club. I went from being a mooch to interesting with one little job change."

Deep, masculine laughter drew her attention to the man behind Rain.

Her heart stopped as she saw the one who'd rescued her. The one she'd wanted to comfort in her dreams. Only he didn't look so vulnerable now.

78

Rather he looked like the fierce warrior who'd been one step from carving the heart out of the man who'd insulted him.

Not sure of his intent where they were concerned, she tried to get up, but Rain stopped her. "Easy. Ren said you were cut pretty badly."

"Ren?"

He indicated her warrior watching them. "Intense dude over there, staring a hole through me. I know you haven't missed his presence. Only Sunshine could be that oblivious."

So his name was Ren and not Makah'Alay. . . . Much easier to pronounce.

But she still wasn't ready to let her guard down. Especially not with someone so lethal. "He's a friend?"

Rain glanced over at him. "God, I hope so. While I'm tough, I'm pretty sure he could kick my ass. Don't really want to test it. Know what I mean?"

Yes, she did. "Where am I?"

"Ren's place."

She winced as pain lanced her side and reminded her of how nasty a wound she'd taken. "Shouldn't I be at a hospital or something? Why am I here? And *where* is here?"

"Vegas, and this place is protected to keep you safe. Hospitals aren't."

Her head hurt so badly she could barely follow his rapid-fire weirdness, which left her feeling like she was in the middle of a puzzle with missing pieces.

How had she gotten to Vegas from Alabama?

No, she couldn't be here. Rain was being stupid or playing a prank of some kind.

"I'm not in Nevada, Rain. I can't be."

"'Fraid so, hon."

No, no, no. Her head reeled over what he was telling her. It just couldn't be. It wasn't possible. She couldn't get halfway across the country without knowing it.

Could she?

All of a sudden, thunder clapped so loud, it jarred the entire house.

Squeaking in alarm, she shot to her feet, then winced at the pain in her side. "What in the world was that?"

"Bad thunderstorms and flash floods are moving in."

A weird sensation went through her at Rain's words. It was the kind of chill her grandmother would say came from someone walking on her grave.

She caught the look on Ren's face. "You felt it too, didn't you?"

But he didn't respond. Rather, he turned and left the room.

Rain shrugged at her. "He doesn't talk much. I haven't really gotten much more than a single word out of him. Talon said having a conversation with him is like pulling teeth. And here I thought Storm didn't talk much. I think I've found the only person alive who speaks less than my bro. Who knew, right?"

Was it because of the stutter . . . ?

No. That was a dream. Not reality. Just because she saw it in her head, it didn't mean Ren had a stutter.

It didn't.

Or could it?

Curiosity settled on her back and rode her with spurs. "I'll be back in a sec." She headed after Ren, wanting some answers.

"Bathroom's the first door on the left," Rain called after her.

She barely registered that as she headed down the small hallway, looking for Ren.

She found him in a bedroom that had been converted to a gym in the back of his small, ranch-styled house. Probably no more than 1,800 square feet, the house was sparsely furnished and had few decorations. Some old pottery, rugs, but nothing on the walls except for a TV in the living room where she'd awakened and a smaller one here in the gym.

Strange.

Sitting on a weight bench, Ren was texting someone. He glanced up at her approach and cocked a puzzled brow.

The beauty of his face captivated her. If not for that overwhelming masculinity, he'd be considered pretty. And even though he was sitting down, he commanded attention. Respect.

Fear.

A lot of fear.

"I-uh . . . I wanted to talk to you." Although now that she was alone in a room with him, that didn't seem like such a good idea after all.

Rising to his feet, he turned his phone over and slid it into his pocket, but didn't say a word.

Kateri swallowed hard. *Why did you have to get up*? He was absolutely huge in comparison to her. The power of his presence made her want to step back, but she refused to be intimidated by anyone. Even someone who could probably palm a basketball without fully extending his hand.

Gah, he was massive.

She cleared her throat. "I'm just trying to understand everything, okay? You were the one who rescued me, right?"

He nodded.

"Where was I? I mean, where did they take me from my office? How did I get there and how did you get me *here*? Did we fly or something?" Surely they wouldn't have allowed a man on an airplane with an unconscious woman and no ID? But nothing else made sense. "We couldn't have driven this far? Right?"

Ren debated what to tell her. On the one hand, she needed to know if she was to fulfill her duties, but on the other . . .

Without the Guardian's return, her part of the ritual wouldn't really matter. The Ixkib's duties were to reset the calendar. The First Guardian was the only one who could choose new Guardians and reseal the gates.

If he wasn't here . . .

"Are you not going to speak to me?" she asked.

Ren hesitated. He wanted to, but he didn't trust himself not to do something embarrassing . . . like stutter. God, how he hated that affliction. While it very rarely occurred now, it had been horrendous in his youth. So much so that he'd been relentlessly ridiculed—which had only aggravated the severity of it.

Finally, he'd stopped speaking at all.

For over three years, he'd remained mute rather than listen to the laughter and insults of others as they'd cruelly mimicked his stutter. But for his friend, Buffalo, he'd have never spoken again to anyone.

Unlike the rest of their clan, Buffalo hadn't minded it, nor had Buffalo thought him stupid because of it.

Together, they'd invented their own sign language so that Ren could speak without using his voice.

Yet it wasn't just his stutter that kept him silent now. He didn't know what to say to her. He'd always been awkward with women. Buffalo used to joke that Ren could lead an army of men into battle and never hesitate. That he could face down an entire den of bears with his bare hands and not flinch.

Put a woman in front of him and he trembled like an errant child facing an angry parent.

If any clan wants to bring us down, all they have to do is send a woman after you and you'll run screaming for the woods.

That was because as bad as he hated to be mocked and insulted by men, it was even harder to take from a woman he found desirable. Nothing stung worse than to muster the courage to talk to a woman and then have her shoot him down before he could get more than a badly stuttered word out.

And if they laughed at him . . .

There were some humiliations no one needed.

As much as he despised it, he was extremely attracted to this woman. All he could think about was tasting her lips. Of making love to her until they were both spent and dizzy.

To have one moment in her arms . . .

But he wasn't brave enough to risk it. He'd been mocked enough in his life. Now, he only wanted to exist in solitude.

Suddenly, his phone rang.

Ren would have ignored it had it not been Talon's ringtone. He still needed to tell them that the Ixkib was safe.

Pulling his phone out, he turned his back to the woman and answered it. *"Osiyo?"*

Kateri froze at how deep and resonant his voice was as he said "hello" in Tsalagi. It sounded nothing like it did in her dreams. It was much, much more masculine and baritone—like rumbling thunder.

And while his back wasn't as terrifying as that penetrating grimace he wore whenever he faced her, it was every bit as well formed as his front. The kind of back that begged a woman to run her hand down it so that she could feel those hard muscles flex.

Her throat went dry as a wave of desire seared her. *Stop it, Ter . . .*

That was much easier said than done. There was something about him that was absolutely magnetic.

"She's here." Then Ren was silent again as he listened.

Well, at least I'm not the only one he ignores. She was surprised he wasn't tapping out his answers on the phone—one tap meant yes. Two for no.

After a few seconds, he spoke again. "Later." He hung up and closed the phone, then turned back around.

"So, you *can* speak," she teased.

His face completely somber, he nodded as he slid the phone into his pocket.

"Can I ask who was on the phone, since it was obviously about me?"

"Talon."

At least she finally got a word from him that was

84

actually directed *at* her. "You know . . . wow, these two-syllable answers . . . impressive. Can I ratchet it up to three? Oh heck, let's go for broke and get a whole sentence out. What do you think?"

Ren wanted to be angry at her, but for some reason he found her charming. She wasn't attacking him . . . she was playfully teasing him about the very things Jess, Choo, and Talon got on to him for.

Because of the way he'd been treated as a human, he never liked conversing with people. It was easier to pretend they didn't exist. After all, he'd been invisible to most of them while he'd lived. Hell, even in death people rarely acknowledged him. It was why he kept to the shadows, out of their sight.

"C'mon, big guy," she said, rising up on her tiptoes so that she could lay her hand against his jaw.

The moment her flesh touched his, his entire body went white-hot. Every hormone he possessed fired into overdrive. For a moment, he couldn't breathe as that heat seared him and he tried to imagine what she'd taste like.

With a smile that caused his stomach to flutter, she moved his jaw up and down. "You can do it. Look how easy. . . ." Then she deepened her voice to mimic his. "Wow, Teri. I never knew speaking would be so easy. Thanks for telling me. I might even want to try and do this on my own one day."

In spite of himself, he smiled at her antics. No one had ever been so playful around him. Most kept a wide distance out of fear.

Pulling her hand away, he stared down at her. "Ha ha."

She scowled. "You really can't go over two syllables,

can you? What? Did you lose a bet with a sorcerer or something? If you let out three does your head explode or do you get some form of ED?"

Erectile dysfunction? She did not just go there. . . .

'Cause from where he was standing, there was no chance of that. He was harder right now than he'd been in a long time. And all he could think about was pressing her hand against the part of him that was begging for a taste of her.

C'mon, Ren . . . just one small kiss. . . .

Determined to keep her at a distance, he dropped his gaze to her arm.

His breath caught as his gaze focused on something that couldn't be right.

No. Not possible. It couldn't be. It was an illusion of the light. His mind playing some kind of sick joke . . .

It had to be.

His heart pounding, he reached out to take her right wrist. Turning it over, he saw the faint mark at the crook of her elbow that was in the shape of a spider.

It's a coincidence. . . .

But what if it wasn't?

"Where did you get this?" he asked, brushing his hand over the mark.

She looked down and her frown deepened. "I was born with it. And I'm impressed. See, you can speak a whole sentence and not spontaneously combust into flames. Amazing, isn't it?"

Honestly, he didn't register a single word of what she was saying. He couldn't. All he could focus on was a mark only one other person had ever borne.

One that no one else should have.

"What does your father say about this?" he asked her.

She shrugged. "Nothing. He walked out on us when I was a baby and I haven't seen him since."

His head reeling, he took a step back as everything started coming together.

She wasn't just the Ixkib. She was also the daughter of the First Guardian. . . .

Chapter 6

"What aren't you telling me?" Kateri asked with a very subtle drop in octave that told him she suspected she should be afraid. But other than that, she hid her panic well.

Damn. Ren should have recognized who she was the moment they met. Strange how the mind colored things and hid them from conscious thought. How something could be right under your nose and you missed it entirely . . .

Now that he knew the truth of her, it was obvious, and he had no idea how he could have been so stupid as to have been blind to it.

While her features and height were nothing like the First Guardian's, she had his same eerie gold-tinged eyes that held a probing, deep intensity that seemed to strip away all lies, bravado, and pretenses so that their owner could see straight into the naked soul.

The first time he'd met the Guardian, that penetrating stare had reduced him back to the cowering dog that had lived only to gain his father's approval. The pathetic shadow of a human who'd allowed his own brother to walk all over him while he protected the bastard with his blood and bone. The dog that had accepted the kicks of everyone who came into contact with him, thinking he deserved nothing better than their contempt.

For most of his life, Ren had honestly believed that rather than be angry or bitter, he should be grateful that anyone was willing to offer him a home at all. Dignity was something reserved for his betters.

As much as he'd convinced himself that he hated his father and Coyote over how they'd treated him, the truth was he'd hated himself more. He had been the one to swallow their abuse and say nothing. The one who had allowed them to treat him as if he was lesser.

All the while, he'd had the strength and skills to silence them. But rather than risk his "home" and what little security he knew, he'd taken their verbal assault and made himself believe that he couldn't exist on his own.

That he really was weaker.

And the moment the First Guardian had looked into his eyes and stripped away the vengeance-seeking monster Windseer had awakened so that he was again a vulnerable human, Ren had unleashed that hatred all over the ancient for daring to see the truth. But in the end, the First Guardian had been right. It wasn't the First Guardian Ren had ferociously battled for that entire year so much as himself.

He, and no other, had always been his worst enemy.

Anyone else would have condemned Ren for his past atrocities and demanded his life. Instead, the First Guardian had embraced him like a brother. *You allowed someone you loved to blind you with her lies. You trusted in her to look after a fragile heart that had never beat with acceptance before. While you committed evil at her command, the evil wasn't inside you. You took no pleasure or comfort from your actions. No pride.*

I see your heart, Makah'Alay. You are shamed and horrified by what you've done. You know how wrong it was and you don't hide from that fact. You flog yourself far worse than I ever could.

But what you have to remember is that there are only two men in life who are perfect. The one not yet born and the one who has died. We all make mistakes. It's part of growing. The trick isn't to be perfect. It's to find a place of solace in the mind so that it doesn't cane you for trusting the wrong person or following after the wrong dream. All of us fall victim to harmful guile at some point.

Even I.

But hatred and rage solve nothing. Like a mighty fire, they quickly consume whatever is fed them. Yet it can't last. Soon enough, they devour all around them and burn out, leaving nothing but a hollowed shell no longer capable of feeling anything at all.

You, Makah'Alay, are the mighty Thunderbird. Born of human sorrow, you are the bringer of storms that swept through the land, destroying everything in its path.

Now spent, it is humble and giving. A protector who will sacrifice his life to save another.

How could I ever fault or punish that?

The cycle of the universe is birth, growth, death. And death, while unwelcome, is always necessary. Without death, there is no birth and no growth.

Most men die many times in their lives. The man we become invariably slaughters the child we once were. His knowledge of the world murders the babe's innocence. With the step you have just taken, the wise Makah'Alay has now laid the warrior Makah'Alay to rest. While you still know how to fight, you have now learned when to fight. . . .

And most important, what to fight for.

Others and not himself. The First Guardian hadn't said the last four words, but that had been the lesson Ren had learned. Until the First Guardian had spared him, he'd always fought for his own glory, even while he claimed he was fighting for Coyote and his father. He hadn't really been protecting his brother. He'd been hoping that his father would take notice of his skills. That his father would, just once, embrace him and be proud to call him son.

But no one could change the mind of someone else. That was for them to do. And if they weren't willing, then there was no magic in existence to make them see what they didn't want to see.

His father had never held any use for him.

It wasn't my opinions that changed. It was my perceptions. That had always been Buffalo's quip whenever someone accused him of capriciousness.

Now, centuries later, Ren stared into the same pair of eyes that had once motivated him to murder. . . .

"How much do you know about your father?" he asked her.

"Nothing really. My mother didn't speak about him.

My grandmother told me the memories were too painful for her to bear and that I shouldn't mention him around her. So I never did."

"Your mother still won't speak of him?"

"My mother died when I was a girl."

So that was it, then. The First Guardian must have known that the Ixkib's line would die out and so he'd intervened to protect that from happening during one of their most crucial times. Knowing her mother would perish, he'd given her a child so that there would be a new Ixkib to carry on.

Which still begged the question of where the First Guardian was now. It wasn't like him to be missing while his daughter was in danger.

Maybe she's not really his daughter.

But he knew better. Between the mark all Guardians had and her eyes . . .

He had no doubt about her. While her powers lay dormant, they were still present to anyone who looked past the surface. In all his life, he'd only been defeated one time.

By her father. And even then, it hadn't been through her father's superior battle skills. Rather, the First Guardian had won the fight mentally. He'd verbally stripped Ren bare and left him exposed until his will to fight was gone.

It was the dirtiest trick anyone had ever used on him. And given his past, that said a lot.

She arched one probing brow. "What are you hiding from me?"

"What do you mean?"

"I've always had the ability to know whenever someone was keeping a secret. You have a deep one. I can feel it."

Oh yeah, she was definitely the daughter. No one else had ever been able to read his moods—not the way the First Guardian had.

And he really wasn't into sharing. "You don't need to know anything about me."

Her other brow joined the first in a look that said he'd offended her. "You don't have a lot of people skills, do you?"

If she only knew the truth. . . .

"Don't want them."

Kateri frowned as the image of Ren being mocked went through her head. That would explain his hostility toward people. And who could blame him?

But this couldn't be the same man. She knew better. Those images had come from her dreams. Some weird holdover maybe from her dig last summer. Her grandmother had firmly believed that objects could carry the essence of previous owners. That the human spirit was so powerful, it could leave impressions on virtually anything. Kateri had handled a lot of different Mayan fragments. Any one of them could have "infected" her and caused her subconscious to create fictional scenarios.

While it wasn't the most satisfactory of answers, it was certainly a lot better than believing he was some reincarnated warrior or immortal vampire or something else bizarre and farfetched.

Which led her back to the oddest question of all. "How did you get me out of that hole?"

"Carried you."

Nice sarcasm there, buddy. Never had she held a stronger desire to kick anyone. Not even the little boy who'd stolen her purse in kindergarten to aggravate her. But this man . . . he was purposefully being vague and difficult.

Unlike the little boy in her class, this one ought to know better. . . .

"You're really going to play this game with me?"

His gaze dropped to her lips. For the merest nanosecond, she saw the spark of desire in his eyes. But no sooner did it flame than he extinguished it. "You asked and I answered. No games."

"What? You don't play those either?"

He wore the most emotionless expression she'd ever seen in her life. Man, *he* should have played the Terminator. He'd have been better than even Schwarzenegger. "No. I do not."

"You should. There's a lot to be learned from games. As Socrates said, a person can discover more about another in one hour of play than in two years of conversation."

He seemed to consider that until his phone rang an instant later.

Ren pulled it out of his pocket and checked the ID, expecting it to be one of his few friends. His heart stopped.

Not a friend, after all.

It was Coyote.

Don't answer it. Nothing good could come of talking to his brother. Nothing.

But his curiosity was too great. He wasn't even sure how his brother had his number, never mind why the

95

bastard would be calling him. Before he could stop himself, he flipped it open. *"Osiyo."*

"Greetings indeed, big brother. It has come to my attention that you have yet again stolen the very thing I need. I want it back."

Ren tsked at him. "Poor Anukuwaya. You never could hold on to a woman, could you?"

As Ren had intended, Coyote sputtered in indignation. Then he broke off into a round of cursing him.

In spite of the gravity, Ren was amused by his brother's colorful choices. "That is your father, too, Anukuwaya. More so, actually, since he was never interested in claiming me."

Coyote snarled in his ear. "I want her. *Now.*"

Yeah, and people in hell want ice water. "Will not happen."

"Not even for Choo Co La Tah's life?"

Ren froze at the unexpected question. No . . . surely Choo wouldn't have been captured. "You lie."

He heard something that sounded like a fist striking flesh. It was followed by a deep grunt. "Say hi, dog."

A deep English-accented voice spoke over the phone. "There is nothing more frightening, Renegade, than ignorance in action." Choo was one of the few who knew what Ren was short for. His way of letting Ren know Coyote really had him.

Not that he had to doubt. An instant later, a photo text message buzzed, showing him Choo tied down to a chair and beaten brutally.

"His future is up to you, Makah'Alay."

Ren gripped the phone as fury tore through him. The

man he'd learned to become wanted to save his old friend. But the warrior in him knew better.

When the coyote was hungry, it fed. There was no appeasing the beast until it'd eaten its fill. No matter what he did, it wouldn't change Coyote's actions or Choo's fate.

"Does Choo Co La Tah live or die?" his brother taunted.

Ren ground his teeth before he spoke the only answer he could give. "That decision is yours alone to make. The Ixkib stays with me."

Coyote laughed before he mocked him. "You were ever st-st-st-stupid."

The line went dead.

Ren could have definitely done without that last bit. His gut knotting over what he was sure he'd just condemned his friend to, he closed his phone and met the woman's gaze. His only comfort came in knowing that his other friend, Sundown, was safely hidden from Coyote along with Sundown's wife, Abigail. Ren and Choo Co La Tah had sent them off months ago so that Coyote wouldn't find them. Not because Sundown and Abby were cowards, but because Abigail was pregnant. None of them were willing to risk the baby to Coyote or any other danger.

Until their child was born, Ren would not go near them or ask for their help.

"What happened?" the Ixkib asked.

Right as he started to answer, something slammed into the roof of the house so hard, it sounded like it might have come through the tiles.

Ren rushed to the door to find Rain running up the hallway.

"Man, there's something wicked outside. Like a tornado or . . . I don't know. I didn't go to meteorology school."

Ren grabbed him by the shirt and hauled him into the room. "Guard her."

Kateri scowled as Ren left them alone. "What was that action?"

"I don't know. The man scares me."

She scoffed at Rain's words. "That's not saying much, cuz. As I recall, spiders render you catatonic and even ladybugs make you scream like a girl."

Rain stiffened indignantly. "Not my fault. I promise you. If you ever saw my dad dressed like a Killer Ladybug with my uncle, Seamus, for Mardi Gras, you'd be terrified of them, too. Just saying. Ain't nothing more scarring to a young mind than two straight men in drag, singing 'It's Raining Men' to me, and then telling me I was named after that song. And if that wasn't damaging enough, my mom agreed with them. It wasn't until I was old enough to realize my birth predated the song that I finally calmed down."

An image of Uncle Daniel, who was a scary man in his own right, in a dress and bad makeup went through her mind and made her laugh. Yeah, she could easily picture him torturing his son that way, and so would her aunt Starla. They were hilarious people. "I've never met your uncle Seamus."

"Be glad. Seamus is like a head injury. Funny as hell so long as it's happening to someone else. . . . Imagine Dad, taller, meaner, thicker, and wielding an Irish brogue."

Yeah, that was something that would probably motivate her to gouge out her eyes. "Okay, no more jokes about ladybugs making you their bitch."

"Thank you."

The lights flickered.

Kateri froze for a minute as she heard things breaking. She looked back at Rain. "What did you see, exactly?"

"Honestly? I think it was a vortex. It looked like something out of *Doctor Who*."

Glass shattered from the direction of the living room. Even though she'd seen enough horror movies to know better, Kateri went to investigate.

Rain crept along behind her. "I don't think we should leave the room."

She ignored him as she moved cautiously down the hallway, closer to the sounds of fighting. As she came even to the living room, her head spun. Once again, she saw Ren in a different time and place. In her mind, he was fighting in a deep valley with his peculiar war club. His chest bare, every vein stood out while he fought against an older man.

Blood covered both of them. It soaked Ren's hair and stained the white feathers that were attached by leather cords.

"You don't really hate me, Makah'Alay. You know this." The older man's voice was thick with fatigue. "And if you don't change direction, you're going to wind up where you're headed."

"I am sick of your pithy sayings, old man. Do us both a favor and die already."

The old man ducked his swing and kicked him back.

"They say that your love has blinded you and that your greed is insatiable. But you're not greedy. Not for material things. I know that and so do you."

"Shut up!" Ren bellowed.

"The truth bites hardest through the deepest treachery. You are nothing but a tool being used, Makah'Alay. As you were with your father and your brother. Are you telling me that that is all you ever aspire to?"

She saw the agony in Ren's dark eyes as those words stung him.

"If Windseer loved you, she would be here now. But she isn't, is she? No. She opened the door for the Grizzly Spirit and then he freed her. Like everyone else, she has abandoned you to die alone."

"So what?" Ren challenged as he swung his club at the man's head. "I entered this world alone, and alone I shall leave it."

He dodged the blow. "And the time in between? You are content to have nothing throughout your life? No one? Ever?" Those words were punctuated by blasts of fire that Ren tried to deflect with his club. They caused him to stagger back and drove him to the ground.

Pain echoed in the older man's eyes as he moved to stand over Ren. "Who will weep for you when you're gone? Tell me, boy. What do you live for?"

Ren blasted him in turn. "Revenge!"

The old man paused so that Ren could regain his feet. "You are right to be hurt, Makah'Alay. But your actions have turned a little right into a great wrong. And your vengeance has spilled over to the innocent who have never caused you harm. Would you have the seed you have

100

planted take root in the heart of another boy? What crops do you sow with such vim? Do you really want them to grow uncultivated? For those boys, those orphans, to have the same venom in their veins as you?"

"What do I care? This world has never shown me kindness. They have never once welcomed me."

The old man dropped his club. "But you do care. Don't you? I see it in your eyes. Even now. Even after all you've been through. You still want what all men do. Comfort—"

Ren bellowed so loud, he drowned out whatever else the old man said. "I want nothing! Nothing!" He renewed his fight with such vigor and rage that his blows came too fast to be seen by a human eye. Only the thunderous sounds of them could be heard.

Just like what was going on in the living room.

In that heartbeat, Kateri pulled out of the past or her dream or whatever it was she saw and found herself back in Ren's house in Las Vegas. Thunder and lightning echoed as Rain pulled her back into the hallway.

In the living room in front of them, Ren was surrounded by dark spirits that attacked as one and then split apart to fight separately. Even so, he held his ground with an admirable skill.

The wolf is never tamed through violence. But rather with a kind, gentle, and above all, patient hand. The most ferocious of beasts see enemies everywhere. They have to in order to live. All they know is how to be attacked and how to fight. They expect treachery from all. Her grandmother's voice whispered through her head.

One of the beasts caught Ren a blow that sent him to

his knees. He rolled with it, but didn't make it completely free. Another one caught him and kicked him hard.

They were about to defeat him.

Refusing to watch him go down while he fought to protect her, Kateri ran forward. . . .

Then realized she had no weapon to fight them with.

Oh snap . . .

Ren glanced up as another shadow approached him. He drew back to strike the beast, only to see the woman there.

For a full heartbeat, her unexpected presence paralyzed him. He couldn't move as he waited for her to attack him, too.

Instead, she went after those he was fighting. . . .

It was so unexpected that it took several seconds before his brain could reconcile the incongruity of someone fighting *for* him.

Until it dawned on him that she wasn't a match for them.

His only thought to save her, he ran at her and wrapped himself around her body, then teleported them out of his house and into the only other haven he knew.

Kateri couldn't breathe through the tight hold Ren had on her. Completely surrounded by a wall of muscle, she had her face pressed against his chest. His heart pounded under her cheek while the warm, masculine scent of his skin soothed her. There was an underlying spicy smell. Something that made her mouth water.

After a few seconds, he loosened his arms and took a half step back so that he could look down at her.

The concern in those dark eyes caught her off guard.

It was such a hot, sexy look. One that set her on fire. Especially when he cupped her face in his hands and leaned down so that their heads were level.

"Are you all right?"

She nodded. "You?"

"I'll live."

To her chagrin, he released her and stepped away. The sudden absence of his warmth sent a chill over her. And as she glanced around the room, she sucked her breath in sharply.

It was a *nice* hotel suite. The kind of penthouse suite that a billionaire playboy would rent.

What the . . .

"I am having one wicked dream," she breathed, wondering what was going on with her unconscious mind.

Ren shook his head. "It's not a dream."

She snorted. "Then how did we get here?"

"I have the ability to teleport."

Sure he did. She laughed nervously. "Yeah. Beam me up, Scotty, right? Did you guys slip me something? Is Rain in on this?"

"You don't really believe that."

Kateri ran her hand along the dark blue curtain beside her. A curtain that didn't vaporize and turn all of this into some psychotic dream. "No, but I want to." She wanted to believe anything other than what this appeared to be.

I'm insane. I have to be—that at least makes sense.

Otherwise . . .

She flinched at a reality she wanted no part of. Personally, she liked having an address in the state of Denial. "This is real, isn't it?"

"As real as it gets."

Covering her face with her hands, she tried everything she could to come up with some other plausible explanation.

There wasn't one. *When you have eliminated the impossible, whatever remains, however improbable, must be the truth. . . . Damn you, Sir Arthur Conan Doyle. Damn you!*

And in that moment, everything overwhelmed her. The death of Fernando, her recent spree of brushes with death, her crazy, weird dreams . . . Everything.

Oh God, it's true.

All of it.

No, he can't be the same man in the past. He couldn't be. He couldn't . . .

Ren recognized the shock she was falling into. Knowing he had to ground her, he closed the distance between them and cupped her face again in his palms. The softness of her skin caressed his and made him yearn for things he knew he could never have. Things he knew he shouldn't even want.

"What's your name?" She'd called herself "Teri" earlier, but it didn't seem to fit what he knew of her.

Kateri blinked at his unexpected question. "Huh? What?"

"I don't know your name, little one. What do they call you?"

That made her laugh. "Of course you don't. Why should you? You've only saved my life twice now. Pulled me out of . . ." Her brain went from her situation to another one that scared her even move. "Is Rain okay?"

"They won't hurt him. They're after you."

Of course they were. . . .

"What are *they*?"

Ren hesitated. Being told that basically everything wanted a piece of you wasn't conducive to calming someone down. While he didn't have a lot of people skills, he knew that one bit of knowledge was best kept to himself. "Enemies."

She screwed her face up at him. "Really?" she asked, her voice dripping in sarcasm. "Enemies? That's the best you can do?"

"You still haven't told me your name," he reminded her.

"Kateri Avani, though most people call me Teri."

Ren repeated it in his head. It was a beautiful name, like the woman who bore it. "I'm Ren."

"I know."

"But I didn't tell it to you."

She frowned at him. "Does that make a difference?"

"Where I come from, it does."

Kateri bit back another retort as she stared into eyes so black, she couldn't even make out his pupils.

From the deepest part of her brain, she remembered something her grandmother had once told her about the way her people viewed names. Why "Waleli" was only known to the two of them and no one else. "It's a sign of trust."

He nodded. "When someone knows your name, you give them a small piece of yourself. It's the first step toward friendship."

And in that moment, she had another insight into why he so seldom spoke. That, too, was giving her a part of himself. If he really was the man in the past, then he was trusting her not to mock him should he stutter. "So we're past that whole two-syllable thing, then?"

One corner of his mouth quirked up into the most devastating smile she'd ever seen on a man. "We are . . ." and then as if realizing he was about to give her only two syllables as an answer, he tacked on, "Kateri."

Dang . . . the way he said that with his accent . . . It sent shivers over her. She'd never particularly liked her name. While it was uncommon, it came with the annoying drawback that no one ever could spell or pronounce it.

But her name rolled off his tongue like a caress.

Against her will, she felt a part of her melt toward him. He really was sweet when he wasn't being a total ass.

And that made her wonder if his lips would taste as good as they looked. . . .

Teri! She never had thoughts like that. She was too focused on her career to bother with something so trivial. But for once, she couldn't seem to quell her desire.

She really, really wanted to bury her face into the crook of his neck and inhale his warm, masculine scent.

Licking her lips, she leaned in to him. She was almost home free when they heard a sound at the door. At first, she thought it was a mistake.

Until the lock turned.

A moment later, the door was blasted open, spraying debris all over them. Ren shielded her body with his. Violent winds tore through the room. They were so strong that it stole her breath and whipped her hair around her body. If not for Ren holding her, she'd have

106

been sucked out of the room. How he continued to stand strong against the ferocity of a hurricane, she had no idea.

And as the winds picked up speed, she met Ren's gaze. Her heart stopped.

His black eyes had turned blood-red.

Chapter 7

Ren braced himself as he felt the steel claws of Kyatel rip across his body. As the wind-demon had intended, it stung his flesh like a thousand scorpions. Tears of vicious pain welled in his eyes while he struggled to remain on his feet. If he went down, the demon would have the woman and the fight would end here and now. She would die and all the gates would open.

I will not be defeated. . . .

Never again.

Angry for getting them into this situation and for failing to teleport her to his intended haven, he forced himself to stand strong in spite of the physical agony as he mentally reached deep inside and summoned every piece of power he could. This was so not where he wanted to be. Why . . . why had his powers screwed them over like this? For once, couldn't something work the way it was supposed to? His fury rising, he bared his fangs and threw his arm outward. As hard as he could, he drove a fireball straight into the demon's chest.

Screaming, Kyatel fell back, through the doorway. The winds stopped howling long enough for Ren to grab Kateri's hand and pull her forward. They needed to get deeper into the first realm if they were to survive. He would try to teleport them again, but after this misstep, he didn't dare. His powers were waning and with two of them . . .

Better to be locked here than to fall into the second realm.

As he tried to lead her, she shook her head in denial and literally dragged her feet, slowing them down. "What are you?"

"The only one in this realm on your side. Come with me or they *will* kill you."

He saw the hesitation in her eyes an instant before she nodded. His only thought to put as much distance between him and his former ally as he could, he ran toward a door and threw it open.

Kateri slowed again as she saw the burning room they needed to cross. Giving him a look that said she thought he was insane, she refused to go into it.

Ren fought down his irritation. Unlike him, she wasn't used to demon tricks and traps. "It's an illusion."

This time her gaze called him a liar.

"Trust me."

"Why should I?"

He deserved her doubt. After his past, he wasn't entitled to anything except contempt and disdain. Still, it stung on numerous levels. "You want to live?"

Her gaze scorched him with a trust he'd never seen in any woman's eyes before. "Yes, I do. So please, don't be lying to me. I don't have much to live for, but I definitely don't want to die tonight." Those words were whispered as she stepped forward and retook his hand.

Hoping, praying he was right about it being an illusion, Ren pulled her into the flames. For the merest instant, he thought he'd misjudged the situation. But as they crossed the burning room and he recognized the stench of this hell, he knew what had happened.

Coyote had breached this first gate and sucked them into it. Somehow his brother had opened the doorway to Hi'hinya and released Kyatel. Or worse, Coyote had broken Choo Co La Tah and Choo had done it for him.

Either way, the gate for Hi'hinya was open and it was bad for all of them.

Not wanting to consider what it would take to force Choo's hand to do this, Ren used his telekinesis to slam the door shut and seal it behind them before Kyatel came through. They wouldn't have long and he wasn't exactly the fiend of the month around here. No doubt there were wanted posters for him everywhere. Ones that held a huge bounty. If a demon could capture him and take him to the Grizzly, they would be rewarded beyond measure. There was nothing in the universe the Grizzly Spirit wanted more than to have Ren back in his custody.

For that reason, Ren was as much a threat to her as the demons were.

Maybe he ought to let her go it alone.

But he knew better. She wouldn't last long in this first realm of the dead. She had no idea how to fight or avoid

111

them. And at least the demons here weren't that strong as a rule. Many were nothing more than shadow walkers—demons that straddled the two worlds. The biggest problem with them was that they had no loyalty whatsoever. Ambiguous and capricious in the purest sense of those words, they were as likely to kill someone as to help them.

If they were really lucky, the shadow walkers wouldn't care about their presence at all.

Of course, luck was always one fickle bitch.

And tonight she seemed to have it in for them.

Suddenly, the wall to his left exploded, showering them with sheetrock. However, that wasn't the bad part. The bad came in the form of a herd of demons who were hell-bent to claim his heart, and her life as a bonus.

Ren let go of the woman so that he could face them.

Kateri fell away with a gasp as Ren manifested the club she'd seen him use a thousand times in her dreams. And he made use of it like a champion. With the flat end, he swatted them back before slicing them open with the obsidian glass.

The twisted demons screamed as they went down. Many retreated, but others persisted, climbing over the bodies of the fallen so that they could pursue him.

Kateri glanced around, seeking some way to help. Unfortunately, she wasn't sure what exactly they were fighting and she didn't have a super weapon to combat them with. Going up against them with her bare hands didn't seem like the smartest thing to do. Rather, she decided not to be a distraction to the one who knew how to fight them. Better to guard the wall and make sure Ren didn't accidentally hit her with that club than to run forward and get them both hurt.

It was actually quite impressive to watch Ren wield his club. He treated it like an extension of his arm. He held a fluid grace to his movements that said he'd spent his life training for battle.

And as he fought, more images filled her head.

"Why do you fight me, Makah'Alay? I am not your true enemy. He lives much closer to home. We could be allies, you and I. Fight with me for those who can't fight for themselves. Let go your anger and, for once, embrace something good." She didn't know who the old man was who fought against Ren, but something about him seemed so familiar. . . .

Ren didn't respond as the two of them went at each other like primordial gods fighting for supremacy.

"Is this really what you want?" the old man tried again. "Is it *all* you want?"

Ren glared at him. "What I want is for you to die already, old man! And shut up while you do it!"

"That's not you talking. It's Grizzly. He fears the truth because he knows that will send him back to where he belongs. Let your hatred go and purge him from your body. Whether you believe it or not, you're better than this, Makah'Alay. You do deserve to be happy and valued."

"Fuck you!" Ren had renewed his fight with greater vigor.

Both of them were sweaty and grimy from their battle. They looked like they'd been fighting for months. . . .

For . . .

"A year and a day," she breathed.

Ren turned to scowl at her. "What did you say?"

"Duck!" she shouted as one of the demons went for his back.

Turning, he barely caught it with the club. The twisted demon thing let out a piercing shriek before it burst apart. The flames flared brighter until they were blinding. Kateri held her hand up in front of her face to shield her eyes.

Ren turned and grabbed her, then tried to teleport. It didn't work. Dammit. He had to get her out of here. But he couldn't take them both out with his powers so depleted.

It's a good day to die. If he was gone, no one would care.

But unlike him, she mattered.

He cupped her face in his hand, then locked gazes with her. "Think of your grandmother. Call her to you and ask her to guide you home."

Kateri scowled at his order. "I don't understand."

He put something solid in her hand and held her fist closed over it so that she couldn't see what it was. "Just do it. Now close your eyes and think of her."

Kateri did. One second, she could feel the room warming up—feel the flames starting to lick her skin to burn it—and in the next . . .

She was beside Talon in his living room in his New Orleans home.

What the . . . ?

Completely confused, she turned in a small circle, surveying her cousin's house. Decorated in bright pinks and purples, it was completely out of synch with the overtly masculine man Sunshine had married. But he indulged her in everything. Even to the point that all of their towels were pink.

Sunshine sat on the couch to her right with her infant son, Declan, sleeping on her lap.

At Kateri's sudden appearance, Talon shot to his feet. He took a step toward her.

Relieved, Kateri started for him, then remembered Ren had given her something. Glancing down, she opened her hand to find a small, white, opalescent, tumbled feldspar that was in the shape of a teardrop.

A moonstone. Her grandmother had carried a similar one in her *degalodi nvwoti* or medicine pouch that she kept either in her pocket or tied around her neck. Every morning when her grandmother awoke, she'd pull out her crystals and stones that she kept in her night stand and choose the ones her Spirit Guide told her she would need for the day. Whispering a prayer, she'd place them in her *degalodi nvwoti* and draw the strings closed so that she could bravely face whatever challenges the day would send for her. Every morning it was a new set, but the one stone that never changed was her sacred moonstone.

"Why do you always keep a moonstone with you, Eleesee?" she'd asked one day after her grandmother had taken it out of her *degalodi nvwoti* and held it as if in prayer.

Her grandmother had pulled Kateri into her lap and placed the moonstone in her palm for her to examine it. Even now, she remembered how beautiful the milky translucent stone had appeared as the bright sunlight made it flash blue. *"It's a stone of destiny that will help you see your future clearly so that you can better attain it. For that reason, it's a strong wishstone—whisper your dreams to it and it will echo them to the heavens for the Great Spirit to hear. It can also heal and protect those who are in need. And it is a stone of new beginnings and good fortune. You should always carry one whenever you travel, Waleli. They are a most precious gift from Grandmother Moon, who guides us through the cycles of our lives and who watches over us while Grandfather Sun slumbers. In our darkest hours when our enemies are hidden from our sight and wish to do us absolute harm, it is she who will guide us to safety. She who will make us see truths we don't want to face."*

Tears choked her as she held Ren's moonstone, and understood the significance of what he'd done for her. In their culture, gifts were never expected from others, not even on birthdays or at weddings or festivals. In fact, it was usually the one being celebrated who gave to the attendees, as a way of letting them know how much they were valued and how much the person being honored appreciated other people taking valuable time out of their lives to come be with them for the event.

The importance was never on receiving something. The importance was on the act of giving to another, especially when it came unexpectedly and from the heart. The monetary value of a gift was even less important. The most valued gifts of all were those that held personal or spiritual significance to the giver.

And Ren had sent her away with his protection and destiny stone—with one of his most sacred possessions that he'd thought enough of to have it with him—knowing that he stayed behind to fight for her without it to watch over him.

No one had ever given her anything more valuable.

"Teri?" Worry creased Sunshine's beautiful brow. "Are you all right?"

Kateri couldn't answer for the lump in her throat as she clutched at Ren's most precious gift. A single tear for him slid down her cheek.

In that moment, she felt something grab her from behind.

Talon lunged for her.

It was too late. Whatever had grabbed her, sucked her out of the house and back into darkness.

"Grammy!" Kateri called, attempting to do what Ren had instructed her. She tried her best to stay focused on her grandmother. But it was useless. Her grandmother couldn't help her stop whatever this was.

So instead, her thoughts turned to a tall, gorgeous man who always murdered her in her dreams.

Ren's head swam from the pain he was in. It was so foul that it kept him from shifting forms to escape. He'd used up his reserves to send the woman to Talon. Worse, his Dark-Hunter powers were making him sleepy—something they always did whenever a Dark-Hunter was wounded. Asleep, the Greek dream gods could help them heal. But if he went down in this fight . . .

They'd kill him for the very blood he hated.

He felt so sick. And still the demons kept coming.

Just lie down and let them have you. Really, there was no reason for him to fight anymore. He'd more than made amends for his human atrocities. And he'd survived long enough to see his bargain with Artemis fulfilled.

It was time for his next adventure.

If you die without a soul, you will be in utter misery for eternity.

He laughed at the thought. How would that be a change from normal? Hell, he wouldn't even notice the difference.

Kyatel shimmered in front of him. His demon's eyes were a bright fluorescent purple. "You owe me your blood."

Ren sneered. "I owe you nothing."

The demon bared his fangs before he went for Ren's throat. Ren caught him and swung him around. But instead of flying away from him, Kyatel embraced him like a brother. The demon sank five claws deep into Ren's previously injured shoulder.

Ren cried out in agony of the additional wound.

"Remember your debt," Kyatel breathed in his ear.

Ren's sight dimmed as that one word took him back to the distant past. Back to the time when he had ruled here as Grizzly's overlord.

When he had owned everything . . .

It had been the only time in his entire life he had felt no pain. No shame. He had walked this realm with the knowledge that he was king. No one could touch him.

You are mine again. Grizzly laughed, the sound echoing through his head.

No! Ren struggled to hold on to his last shred of humanity. But it was impossible. No matter how much he denied it, he knew the truth in his heart.

He wanted to belong to something. Anything. Just once. No one else had ever wanted him. Evil had been the only thing that ever welcomed him to its bosom. . . .

But this wasn't belonging and he knew it. All of it had been a lie. The demons hadn't welcomed his presence any more than his family or the world in general. And the only reason Grizzly had pretended to want him was so that he could use Ren's body to get at his enemies.

As for Windseer . . .

She'd abandoned him as soon as she had her freedom. Ren had been just as lonely here as their overlord as he'd been in the human realm.

Nothing changed. He was a worthless throwaway then. He was worthless now.

Closing his eyes, he waited for the demon to end him.

"Let. Him. Go."

At first, Ren couldn't place that angry tone. And even once he'd identified it, he couldn't believe his eyes as he saw Kateri standing behind Kyatel.

And she was pissed at the demon holding him. As incredulous as it was, she appeared ready to tear the demon apart. He wasn't sure who was more shocked by her reappearance. Him or the demon.

That being said, Kyatel recovered first.

Then laughed.

Ren took advantage of the distraction to stab the demon. Too bad, it couldn't kill him. But the blow to Kyatel's carotid would weaken him. Kyatel would have to stop the bleeding and replenish the missing blood, or he'd be too weak to fight. Something no one could afford to be in this realm.

Kyatel's eyes glowed a deep vibrant orange that obliterated their normal purple hue. "This isn't over."

Ren gave him a taunting grin. "It is for now."

As the demon vanished, Ren turned to grab Kateri's arm. "What are you doing here? I sent you away."

"I don't know. I was at Talon's and then I vanished ... and came back."

Ren cursed. Kyatel was stronger than he'd been before. Much stronger. But for her timing, he'd have probably been killed. And now, thanks to the wound in his shoulder, he was even weaker than he'd been before.

Which meant she was in extreme danger. If something attacked her, he was in no condition to put up much of a fight. And if it came for him, he wouldn't be able to keep it from getting her.

Shit ...

"You shouldn't have come back here."

Kateri didn't respond to that. Her attention was diverted by the amount of blood on his clothing. His arms had cuts all over them. And his left shoulder looked as if someone had tried to shred it. "You're hurt."

"I'll live." He leaned his head over to glance past her shoulder, where more creatures were piling in on them. "We need to leave."

"And go where?"

Ren hefted his club up, over his uninjured shoulder. "Preferably some place *they're* not."

"I couldn't agree more." She followed him out of the room, down a long hallway where there were more demonlike creatures, but they didn't attack. Rather, they stayed to the shadows, watching with an eerie intentness that made her extremely uncomfortable. "Where are we?"

He twisted his club around on his shoulder before he

answered. "Someplace neither of us needs to be ... The first level of the West Lands."

Kateri scowled at the term. "Why does that sound familiar to me?"

"It's where our ancestors locked away the worst evils of the world to keep them from preying on humanity."

Oh yeah ...

Her eyes widened as she remembered her grandmother's stories about the Guardian who'd been chosen to keep mankind safe. Benevolent and kind, he'd sought to protect the first humans by banishing all threats. Unfortunately, mankind had been tricked and, like Pandora in Greek mythology, had cracked open the door to release just enough evil to keep them from having a life free of pain and suffering.

It's just a legend.

That thought died as another demon turned around and viciously hissed at them. Huge, green, and smelly, it was as real as she was.

This wasn't playtime and that definitely wasn't make-believe. As much as she wanted to deny it, she couldn't. These things were real.

Baring his own fangs, Ren angled his club at the beast, letting it know what would happen should it attack. It shrank away in fear. He put her in front of him while he rushed her through the building, and away from the rest of the creatures.

Too grateful to argue or even question Ren's peculiar dental problem right now, she rounded a corner, then pulled up short as she saw three divergent hallways. With no idea where they were going, she allowed Ren to choose the correct direction.

He headed left with huge predacious strides.

Kateri practically ran in order to keep up with him. One of his strides equalled two and a half of hers. "How did we get here, anyway?"

Ren winced at a question he didn't want to answer. He couldn't stand looking stupid or being mocked. But apparently, his sole purpose in life was to serve as the poster child of imperfection and incompetence.

Thanks, fate. Appreciate the consideration.

So rather than hide it like a coward, he told her the truth. "I was trying to take us to Sin's and somehow I landed us here. I know it was a stupid mistake, okay? I'm doing my best to fix it as quickly as possible."

"Hey." She pulled him to a stop. "It's all right. You were trying to help me. I'm not about to complain when you saved my life, especially since you bled to do it. What kind of person do you think I am? And by the way, thank you. For everything." She rose up on her tiptoes to place a quick, chaste kiss on his cheek.

Ren couldn't speak as those words echoed in his head and his skin burned from her soft lips. Lips that left him swollen and aching for a much more thorough physical exchange.

Honestly, he was baffled by her. No one had ever given him the benefit of the doubt before. In the past, whenever he screwed up, he was held accountable, and usually rather rudely. "I should have known better."

She snorted. "I don't think knowing has much to do with it. Besides, we were a little preoccupied with our near-death experiences. Give yourself a break. Out of everything that has happened in the last few hours, this isn't so bad." She gestured to his club. "At least we're armed and ready to battle. Well . . . you are, anyway. Thank goodness."

Her generosity of spirit charmed him. He'd often heard it said that people had good hearts, but he'd so seldom seen them that hers caught him off guard. The majority of people he'd dealt with had been self-serving and cold. Unforgiving.

And that had been his family.

Ren slowed down as they left the building. The moment they were through the door, the glamour spell was broken and instead of appearing as the Ishtar Casino he'd thought it to be, it took on its true form—an old gray stone structure that looked weathered and aged, in a town full of similar buildings. They were burned-out hulls against a dark landscape of utter misery. There was nothing inviting or beautiful about this place.

Worse than that, he hated to be back here where he was forced to face the memories he'd wanted to keep buried. The First Guardian was right. He flogged himself more than any torturer ever could.

And that thought reminded him of the first time he'd met Acheron—the immortal who led the Dark-Hunters. Though Acheron appeared physically young—he'd barely been twenty-one when he was killed—he was one of the oldest and wisest men Ren had ever known.

His features perfect and chiseled, Acheron held the swirling, silver eyes of a true ancient. "Life is messy, Ren. It's not easy and it's definitely not for the timid. Everyone has a past. Things that stab them right between the eyes. Old grudges. Old shame. Regrets that steal your sleep and leave you awake until you fear for your own sanity. Betrayals that make your soul scream so loud you wonder why no one else hears it. In the end, we are all alone in that private hell. But life isn't about learning to forgive those who have hurt you or forgetting your past. It's about learning to forgive yourself for being human and making mistakes. Yes, people disappoint us all the time. But the harshest lessons come when we disappoint ourselves. When we put our trust and our hearts into the hands of the wrong person and they do us wrong. And while we may hate them for what they did, the one we hate most is ourself for allowing them into our private circle. How could I have been so stupid? How could I let them deceive me? We all go through that. It's humanity's Brotherhood of Misery."

Ren had locked gazes with the Atlantean youth. "Tell me, Acheron. How do we find peace again when we have wronged ourselves and others?"

"If we're lucky, we find the one person who will hold our trust and keep it sacred and safe against all attackers. That one soul who will restore our belief that people are decent and kind, and that life, while messy, is still the most wondrous gift anyone can know. But until that day comes, we have to try and remember that home isn't a specific place or person. It's a feeling we carry inside ourselves. That touch of the divine that lights a fire inside us that burns out the past and consumes the pain until nothing is left but a warmth that allows us to love others more than ourselves. A warmth that only grows when we do right even while others seek to do us wrong. Peace is knowing that one life, no matter how trivial it seems, touches thousands of others, and learning to respect that about all people. While you may not mean much to the world, to those who really know and love you, you are their entire world. And it is the knowledge that no one can hurt you unless you allow them to. The only power they have isn't something they've taken or demanded. It's what we give them by choice. And while it is imperative that we value the lives of others, it is equally important to value our own."

Even though he'd wanted to believe Acheron's words, Ren scoffed. "You make it sound so easy, Atlantean."

Acheron had let out a short, bitter laugh. "The truth is always simple, but the path to it is overgrown with thorns and lined with traps. Our fears and our emotions cloud even the brightest day and the clearest truth. Talk is cheap, but actions are bloody. You can't plant the garden until you've overturned the soil. And nothing new can grow until the old dies. Lay your past to rest, Ren, so that your future can grow unimpeded by those ghosts. We can't change what we've done, but we can always change what we're going to do."

Those last words had branded themselves into Ren's heart and he had carried them through the centuries.

And tonight, he was going to protect the woman by his side with everything he had.

Kateri's features went pale as she surveyed her dismal surroundings. Never had she seen a more frightening place. A huge sallow moon hung over a town that reminded her of a Tim Burton landscape. Mournful cries for mercy and tortured screams echoed all around, many punctuated by the sound of insane laughter as if someone or something took pleasure from their pain.

A chill of foreboding ran up her spine. "Is this hell?"

"As close to it as I want to get." Ren stopped, then gently tugged her into a shadowed alley.

When she started to speak, he placed his finger over her lips. Only then did she hear the sound of something slithering by the area they'd been in only a heartbeat before. Bug-eyed, she held her breath until it vanished and all was relatively quiet again.

"I have to get you out of here," he whispered in her ear.

She couldn't agree more. "And you, too."

He glanced to his wounded shoulder. "I've been tagged. I won't be able to leave now. Wherever I go, they'll follow and drag me back."

Her heart ached at the sad resignation in his voice. It was as if he accepted the fact he was going to die here, and *that* she had no intention of allowing to happen. If she was nothing else in her life, she was loyal to a fault. "It's not right to leave you here alone to face them."

"I'll live."

"You keep saying that. But—"

"I'm immortal, Kateri," he said, cutting her off. "You're not. Your duty is to save the world and my only duty now is to save *you*. I have to get you back to the human realm so that you can fulfill your sacred role. It's that simple."

She shook her head at the ludicrousness of those statements. And nothing was ever simple. Rubik's Cube had taught her that when she was four years old and had arrogantly boasted that it couldn't be *that* hard.

Yeah, *that* had learned her.

"You know, Ren, twelve hours ago, I'd have called

126

you nuts for talking about sacred roles and all of this." She gestured at the bleak, twisted buildings surrounding them. "Luckily, I'm a little more open-minded now. Not sure if that's a good thing or not, but ... At least I'm not wasting time with denial anymore. I accept the fact that the weirdness in my life has just shot up the epic scale of redonkulous."

After all, what more could happen?

Death and dismemberment notwithstanding.

Yeah, okay, maybe she shouldn't test the bad-luck fairy since the bitch was already gunning for her. But dang ...

Didn't they deserve a break tonight? And not one on their bones.

All of a sudden, one corner of his mouth quirked up as if he was amused by her comments. "We have to get off the street and find a safe place to hide until I recharge my powers enough to get you out of here."

"Okay. But I still don't understand why it has to be me to do whatever it is I'm supposed to do. How did this chore fall to my bloodline anyway? What did we do to be so cursed?"

"It's not a curse. Your ancestor stood strong before the gods when no one else would."

There was an answer she hadn't expected. "What do you mean?"

Ren grimaced as if his wound pained him, then rolled his injured shoulder. He led her back to the dark street. Keeping to the shadows, they headed in the direction that, given the moon's position, she assumed would be east. "Before recorded time, there was a god who came to this realm and—"

"What god?" she asked, cutting him off. While her people believed in an overall divine being, and other paranormal entities, they didn't think of the Great Spirit as a god in the traditional sense of the term. It was extremely hard to explain their beliefs to others who came at it with preconceived notions.

And the way he used the word "gods"...

It didn't make sense to her.

"Ahau Kin was, for lack of a better term, the Mayan god of their underworld and of time," Ren explained. "It's why he's usually shown at the center of their calendars."

She scowled as she remembered seeing the image all over the Yucatan last summer. "The guy who looks like a jaguar or has a jaguar face?"

He nodded.

Fernando would be so pleased that she recalled that. But her happiness died instantly as she remembered her friend's death, and grief went through her all over again.

Clearing her throat, she waited for Ren to continue.

He didn't. Rather he seemed to be lost in either thought or memories.

After a few minutes, she prompted him. "You were saying?"

Ren ground his teeth as his thoughts went back to his youth—to a time and place he hated with every part of his being.

Even now, he could see himself running through the bright summer forest of his island home, chasing after the buck he'd been hunting. The beast had been elusive and it'd led him to a clearing where a woman bathed alone in a pond that was at the base of a whispering waterfall.

Never had he seen a more beautiful maiden. Her long black hair had fanned around features that were perfection incarnate. Her dark, tawny skin had been so flawless that his mouth had watered for a taste. And even though he was invading her privacy, he'd been unable to tear his gaze away from her.

Completely naked, she was floating on her back, her eyes serenely closed while her breasts jutted out from the water. Her hands had moved through the water in a mesmerizing dance that was in synch with the pleasant, gentle tune she was humming.

His prey forgotten, he'd moved closer, taking care to be as silent as possible.

All of a sudden, as if she'd sensed his presence, she opened her eyes and pinned him with a harsh glare. Narrowing her gaze, she rose out of the water to show him her entire naked body as she walked toward the land where he stood, gawking.

Ashamed and embarrassed that he'd spied on her, he'd felt his face heat up. Turning away, he tightened his grip on his bow and started to run.

"Wait!"

Her unexpected command had literally frozen him in place. Before he could think better of it, he stopped moving. With his back to her, he'd heard her leave the pond and make her way over to him.

A few seconds later, her hand had brushed across his shoulders, smoothing his braid. And when she'd moved it to trace the line of his jaw, his entire body turned molten. She sucked her breath in sharply as she fingered his biceps. "Aren't you a handsome one? You know, if you're going

129

to spy on a woman during her bath, the least you could do is kiss her first."

Stunned, Ren hadn't known how to respond to that. He wasn't used to women coming on to him. All the women in his town knew who and what he was, and they either avoided him or mocked him for it.

None of them had ever tried to seduce him.

Licking her lips, she'd fisted her hand in his hair and pulled his head down for her kiss.

His senses had reeled from it, and when her tongue brushed against his . . .

He'd been blinded by pleasure.

Windseer had pulled back to give him a salacious grin. Then, taking his hand into hers, she'd led it to her breast so that her hardened nipple teased his palm. "You act as if you've never seen a naked woman before."

The softness of her skin had amazed him. Her body was so different from his. Supple. Sweet.

Succulent.

And he'd been long past the age most men lost their virginity . . . another truth that shamed him and left him open to attacks from others whose vicious cruelty rammed home why no woman would have him. Ever. Until that moment, he'd never been kissed.

She'd nipped at his chin with her teeth. "Are you not going to speak to me?"

He hadn't dared. The last thing he'd wanted was for his stutter to betray him and leave him open to more ridicule. She'd think him stupid and push him away like everyone else.

So he'd kissed her again while he fingered her puckered

nipple. Within a few minutes, he'd lost both his virginity and his will to her. After that afternoon, he'd been a fucking idiot where Windseer was concerned.

She asked. He gave.

He'd have done anything to keep her.

Even kill his own father ...

Ren winced at a memory he wished with the whole of his being he could take back and change. But there was no way to undo any of it. Windseer had claimed him with her body and he had been her most willing slave.

How could anyone screw up their life so badly? One wrong move. One foul decision ...

An eternity of regret.

And all because she and Grizzly had needed a blood sacrifice. Not from a worthless piece of shit like him, but from a whole-blood ...

His father.

Damn you both.

But that wasn't really what hurt him most. They weren't the ones he hated.

Damn me for it all.

The saddest part? He *had* damned himself.

Sighing, he lowered his club, taking care not to let the razor-sharp glass touch his leg as he turned his thoughts to the present and what Kateri needed to understand about all of this. "Ahau Kin was the father of the Anikutani."

Kateri frowned up at him. "You mean the legendary Cherokee fire priests who were put down for their arrogance and licentiousness? How could he be their father? He was a Mayan god, right?"

He nodded. "The Maya were our ancestors. We come

131

from common ground and people, but we split off from them centuries ago. While the Maya built their cities, the Anikutani, as the direct descendants and chosen people of Ahau Kin, fortified their posts. They were essentially gate-keepers charged with holding the darkest evil back from the world—to keep it locked in their father's underworld realm so that it couldn't harm humans. There are a total of eleven gates that can be opened to access it. Four main ones in what is currently the U.S. and the other seven that are spread over the rest of the world. It was their most sacred duty, and for generations, the Anikutani bred the greatest warriors the world has ever known to combat that evil should it ever escape. No one could defeat them. . . . Until the day the monster with white eyes came for them."

Kateri slowed her pace as she walked beside him, and dread consumed her now that she realized these legends weren't just farcical stories made up to scare and entertain children. And this one in particular she knew well . . . it was something her grandmother had even written down for her. "From over the great Eastern water, the monster that was possessed of terrifying power and great evil came and laid waste to everything in its path. The attack was so vicious that Mother Earth bled and her heart-beat grew so faint that not even the little people could hear it anymore. Though it was fought off, legend says it will return one day to finish what it started. To end the world." All ancient Mesoamerican cultures described a Caucasian god who had destroyed them, or one who would return to kill them. Scholars had been debating the origins of those myths for decades.

He inclined his head to her. "That monster's name was Apollymi. A goddess from Atlantis."

But that didn't make any sense to her. "Why would an Atlantean goddess destroy our people?"

"Vengeance over a wrong done to her."

"What did we do?"

"Nothing, other than having a gate on an island that was near Atlantis. In her mind, our inaction was the greatest sin of all. But her anger wasn't really for us, we just got caught in the cross fire. Her fury was for the Greek god Apollo. Most of all, it was against her own family."

Her frown deepened. "Why?"

"She had a son who had been ordered killed by her husband. To protect her baby, she hid him in the human realm to be raised as a prince. Instead, he was abused and then brutally murdered by Apollo. In retaliation, she put down her entire family and then sank her Atlantis into the ocean. Still not appeased, she vowed to see the whole earth destroyed. And so she went on a rampage that brought her here. Not because we'd harmed her, but because none of us had been there to help her child."

Kateri gaped at the irrationality of that. Honestly, she expected better from a goddess. "But if they didn't know—"

"It didn't matter to her, Kateri. Trust me. Her rage and loss, I completely understand, and I don't hold that against her in the least. There is no worse feeling than to have your entire world shattered when there's nothing you can do to stop it. To be in complete and utter agony and misery, and to look around at a world that truly doesn't give a shit about you . . . It hits you on a level I am grateful to

133

the gods that you can't understand or imagine. Because no one should *ever* know that place in hell. You are lost to the pain, and inside you're screaming at the top of your lungs for help, and no one hears you. No one cares. They go on with their putrid lives, oblivious to your agony. And when that moment comes that you realize just how alone you really are—how little you matter to anyone else, you lose all higher cognitive functioning. You devolve into a rabid animal. All that matters then is that you make them understand your pain. That you shake them out of their blind complacency so that they share the hell that is yours. In that moment, you want to feel *their* blood on your hands. To taste it on your lips. To bathe in it until you're drunk and pruny. There is this place of insanity that lives deep inside everyone. Most people might tap at it, once, maybe even twice in their lifetime, but they never breach it." His eyes burned her with his sincerity. . . .

And madness.

Something that absolutely terrified her. She wasn't even sure what kind of creature he was. Demon, god, or other. Yet here he was, livid, and she hadn't done anything to provoke him.

"Others are like animals who have been abused one time too many," he continued. "They have suffered and been hurt to a level that doesn't understand anything except cruelty. The rage takes hold and it drives out everything else that makes them human. All they want is to make the world pay for what it's done to them. I cannot imagine the pain and brutal betrayal Apollymi felt as she held her son's lifeless body in her arms and saw what had been done to him. Truthfully, I can't even begin to comprehend a love of that magnitude. But I do understand the need for retribution that drove her across the ocean and made her attack us."

His gaze turned darker, but the anger was gone now.

Kateri's heart ached in sympathy at the torment she saw in his obsidian eyes. In that one moment, his heart was bared to her. This wasn't a fierce immortal warrior standing by her side.

He was a man whose heart had been shattered.

She wanted to hold him and make it better, but she knew it wasn't that simple. Only in early childhood could everything be cured by a kiss and a hug. *That* was the saddest part about growing up. The biggest loss.

Some scars went too deep to ever be fully concealed. While you might succeed in hiding them from time to time, they always came out and reopened a wound that never fully healed.

And his were massive.

Ren moved his club to his other hand before he spoke again. "In a matter of minutes after reaching their shores, Apollymi destroyed the Keetoowah homeland and sank their island to the bottom of the ocean. But because of their superior skills and technology, many of them escaped to the mainland, where they sought shelter." He had a bitter catch in his voice.

"What happened?" she asked, knowing it had to be bad.

"Within a few weeks of setting up their new town, they were attacked by seventy tribes who blamed them for the destruction Apollymi had wrought. At least that was what they claimed. The truth was, they were jealous.

They felt that the Keetoowah were more favored by the heavens, and since the Keetoowah were weakened by Apollymi's attack on them, the others saw it as a rare opportunity to go after them and kill them off before they had a chance to replenish their numbers."

That was beyond cowardly. But as her grandmother had so often said, envy was the root of the greatest evil in the world. Since the dawn of mankind, it had been used to fuel the worst acts of cruelty.

And while she'd heard a different version of the story, she wondered if one part had been true. "My grand-mother told me that the Keetoowah won because of the Spirit Warriors who aided them in the fight."

A wry grin twisted his lips. "They weren't Spirit Warriors."

"What were they?"

Ren paused as they reached the end of town. He scanned the dark forest in front of them, wondering if it would be safer or more dangerous than to try and hide among the city dwellers.

The number of demons who lived here was staggering, both in the city and the outlying areas. But at least in the forest he'd feel more at home.

As a child, he'd spent hours upon hours hiding in the woods, pretending that he would never have to go home again.

But this wasn't the time to think about that.

Hefting the club, he used it to beat a trail through the thick foliage so that they could find shelter and give his body a chance to heal and his powers a chance to charge. "On the island that Apollymi had destroyed, the Keetoowah's main city was directly below the Pleiades constellation. Because of that, the seven goddesses who called it home were able to look down and watch them go about their daily lives."

He paused to glance back at her to ensure himself that she was safe and still following him. "One of the Pleiades, Sterope, fell in love with the chief's son. . . . She must have hit her head or something to give herself brain damage to love that bastard, but what the hell do I know?" he mumbled bitterly. Then louder, he continued, "For years, she watched over him, dreaming of a time when they might be together. And when the tribes attacked his people, she saw it as a prime chance to win his heart."

"I don't understand. Why didn't she help him with Apollymi?"

"She couldn't. The Greeks were the ones who'd pissed Apollymi off, and they were her prime target. Had Sterope reared her head during that fight, Apollymi would have taken it and stuck it on a pike. So Sterope didn't make her presence known to the chief's son until he was under fire from the seventy tribes. Unlike with Apollymi's attack, there were no gods rallying to stop the brutality. She knew if she didn't do something, they would all die."

Kateri was impressed with his depth of knowledge. He told the stories as if he'd witnessed them. "Were you there when all of this happened?"

He shook his head. "It was before I was born."

"How do you know so much about it, then?"

"I grew up with people who'd lived through it. When the elders would get together, they'd talk about it and warn the rest of us to be wary of those who might still want to do us harm because of it all."

Kateri took a second to digest everything he was telling her. And that made her curious over something. "How old are you?"

He laughed bitterly. "By the calendar you know ... over eleven thousand years."

She stumbled at that unexpected disclosure. Whoa ... that was old ... Even by her geology standard. "I have to say, you look great for an old geezer. What's your secret? You bathed in Ponce de Leon's Fountain of Youth as a kid?"

He gave her a droll stare. "Sold my soul."

Okay, between the red eyes and the fangs ...

What am I doing here?

"You're a demon, aren't you?"

"Not by blood."

A chill went down her spine. "What does *that* mean?"

"You don't have to be born demonic. There are plenty of people I've met who are worse than any demon ever born."

Those words calmed her a bit. He was right. She'd met a few of those herself.

He stopped and turned to face her. To her complete shock, he laid his hand against her cheek. "Don't be afraid of me, Kateri. While I lived at one time for no other purpose than to make the entire world tremble in my presence, I've long since put that battle to bed. I sold my soul, not for personal gain, but to make right a wrong I committed against the people I should have protected with every part of me."

"And did you make it right?"

He released a weary sigh. "It took a long while, but yes.

138

I did. Eventually." He dropped his hand from her face. As he started away from her, she stopped him. He met her gaze with one arched brow.

There in the moonlight, with the play of shadows over his handsome face, he took her breath. Not because of the way he looked, but because of the vulnerability she saw in the heart of a man who seemed invincible.

"Why did you give me your moonstone?"

"To protect you on your journey." He said that like it was nothing, but she knew better.

She glanced down to his wounded shoulder. "You're the one who's fighting. Wouldn't you need it more than me?"

He shrugged. "Grandmother Moon never thought much of me. I was hoping she'd like you better."

Still, it meant a lot to her that he'd done it. And she'd offer it back, but if his people were like hers, that would be the ultimate insult. When a gift was made, it was from the heart. To return it was a rejection.

And this man had been rejected enough.

"Thank you, Ren."

He inclined his head to her, then returned to cutting a path for them through the woods.

"Ren? Can I ask you something?"

He paused to look back at her. "Have you not been doing that since we met?"

"Yeah, but this is personal."

"More personal than asking about my gift or age? Or if I was a demon? I shudder with dread over the possibilities."

She smiled at his sarcasm. "Fine. Does the name *Makah'Alay* mean anything to you?"

He hissed as his grip on his club slipped and he narrowly missed hitting himself with it. "Where did you hear that name?"

Kateri hesitated. Talk about personal. Admitting she'd seen him in her dreams for years was kind of creepy. Could that be considered a form of stalking? She hadn't done it intentionally. Still ...

Oh c'mon, Teri. Every friggin' thing about this is creepy. He was creepy.

Might he have the power to walk in her dreams? He was old ... and he was as paranormal as anything could be. It was possible that he'd been the one to make her dream those things.

Hoping for the best, she opted for the truth. "I've seen visions of you, but in them you're always called Makah'Alay."

Ren couldn't breathe as he heard that. Why would she dream of him? Dreams had great power. They were the key to all creation.

To all life.

If he saw visions of her and she saw them of him, then that meant they were tied together.

Intimately.

Was she the tool the Grizzly would use in this time and place to destroy him? It was the only thing that made sense. It would explain how she knew his name and why he'd been warned about her.

Whatever he did, he couldn't let his guard down where she was concerned. She was his assassin.

"And in these visions ... what does Makah'Alay do?"

She didn't flinch or hesitate with her response. "Usually, he kills me."

"Have no fear, *ta'hu'la*. I would never kill you. It's forbidden."

"Forbidden by whom?"

"The one who owns me. I came back to this life to protect humans, not harm them. So long as you're with me, I will give my life for yours. As for Makah'Alay, he died a long time ago."

That seemed to placate her. "So what does *ta'hu'la* mean?"

"Little one."

Kateri felt heat rush over her face at his endearment. She wasn't the kind of woman who normally brought that out in a man. And definitely not in one who looked like Ren. Heck, her own lab assistant, who wasn't that much younger than her, couldn't even call her by her nickname. Wanting to cover her embarrassment, she returned to their former conversation. "I interrupted your story. You were telling me about the Pleiades. I take it Merope rallied her troops?"

"Sterope," he corrected. "Merope is actually her sister, who married Sisyphus."

"And people wondered why I had a C average in the one Classical Studies class I took in college. Who can keep all these names straight?"

"There are many who would argue that the Greek is easier to pronounce and remember than our names."

"Yeah, well, those are people who weren't raised with our writing system ... which is different than yours, isn't it?"

"It is. Ours was more like the Maya. Glyph based."

Kateri's mind reeled at that. "Wait ... the stone that was

sent to me." The one that was fourteen thousand years old. "It had strange writing on it with something that appeared to be Greek."

"Not Greek. And not Mayan. Keetoowah. But you're getting ahead of the story."

"Sorry. Back to the Greek confusion. I take it our ... Ope woman rallied her troops to help the Keetoowah fight off their attackers."

He wiped the sweat off his forehead with his arm. "Not until after she made a bargain with the chief's son."

Ooo, this was getting good. "Which was?"

"She would save his people if he would agree to spend a week with her once the battle was won."

"Horny little booger, wasn't she?"

Ren cast her a glare so malevolent that she actually took a step back from it. "She loved him."

Okay, she'd struck a nerve there. She'd ask him more about Sterope, but decided it might not be the wisest course of action. Better to get the scary immortal man off his sensitive topic, especially while he held a war club that still had the blood of demons on it.

Kateri cleared her throat. "So she made her bargain and he agreed to it?"

Ren returned to his hacking, which made her feel a whole lot better.

Yeah, kill the bushes. They didn't care about living.

She did.

"After the agreement was made," he said, "she convinced her sisters to help her save his people. Because they were family and they loved her, they agreed. The seven goddesses came down together and chose the seven

142

strongest warrior-priests among the Keetoowah to fight with them. They were the ones who drove the seventy tribes back and then divided them up so that they couldn't attack the Keetoowah ever again. When the fighting was finished, Sterope claimed her fee, not knowing that the chief's son was already married to a woman he loved dearly."

Kateri gaped. "Are you serious?"

"Very much so."

"That dog. How could he do that?"

Ren shrugged. "In his mind, he was making a sacrifice for his people. One week of servitude seemed like a small price to pay for everyone's life."

Okay, so when put in those terms, it made sense. Still . . . *What a two-timing bastard.*

"For the record, I'd absolutely *kill* my husband if he did that to me."

"Believe me, his wife wasn't happy about it. Especially since her husband impregnated Sterope during that same week."

Ouch! Kateri cringed with dread. Something told her this wouldn't have a happy ending. "I imagine it wasn't exactly the highlight of Sterope's life, either."

"Actually, they say she was thrilled to be pregnant with his baby. But because the father was a mortal man and she was a goddess, the other gods shunned her for it. Zeus, driven by jealousy since she was the mother of two of *his* children, ordered the mutant baby killed. The last thing he wanted was to suffer the humiliation of having the mother of his children prefer the touch of a mortal man over his."

Kateri cringed for the poor woman and the baby. "That is so harsh. So did she kill it?"

"No." Ren led her deeper into the forest. "Instead, Sterope went to the goddess Artemis."

"Why?"

"At one time, she'd been Artemis's most trusted handmaiden and had kept the goddess's secrets. To repay her, Artemis saved the baby and lied to Zeus. They both swore it was stillborn. Zeus wasn't happy, but he didn't hurt Artemis over it. Off the hook, Artemis then took the infant to his father, who was furious over it. The last thing he wanted was to have a permanent reminder of his infidelity around the wife he loved—a wife who was, at that precise moment, in labor with her own child. Not to mention, he didn't want a half-breed mutant son that wasn't good enough to be kept by its own mother."

Kateri flinched in sympathy. Poor baby boy, but it made sense. If the Keetoowahs were matriarchal like her people and the mother didn't keep the child, it would be viewed as seriously defective and lacking. Unworthy.

To this day, all babies born to her tribe were presented to the grandmother, if she was still living, to be inspected and named. If the grandmother wasn't alive, then it fell to the mother.

For that child to be rejected . . .

"I'm surprised they didn't kill it."

Ren snorted. "I'm told he tried and couldn't."

Well, that made her feel better. "He loved the baby too much to hurt it?"

"Hardly." Ren returned to hacking a path for them. His strokes were more brutal and sharp. "The first time he left it to die, an old woman found the babe and brought it back to town not knowing it had been intentionally abandoned. When Artemis learned about it, she struck down his beloved wife in retaliation."

Kateri winced at that. How awful for all of them. But even worse . . . "'First time' implies he tried again."

Ren nodded. "The second time, a crow-demon found and nursed the baby. When he was a year old, she returned him to his father and warned him that if he didn't raise it to manhood, she would return to kill his cherished son for his neglect, and then make him live with the pain of knowing he killed both his beloved wife and treasured child."

In a sick way, that was almost touching. "Why did the demon care?"

He sighed heavily. "Honestly? She couldn't have cared less. But she didn't have a choice."

"Why not? And where was the baby's mother during all of this? Why didn't Sterope bitch-slap him for his cruelty?"

Ren fell silent as bitterness swelled inside him. "For her sin against Zeus, Sterope had been banished back to the stars. To make sure that she never shamed him again with her human lover, Zeus turned her into a comet that would only pass over the earth every seventy-five years— his way of guaranteeing that she would never see her son. That the boy would most likely die prior to her return. But before she was punished, Sterope had made Artemis promise her that the goddess would ensure no one killed her son before he had a chance to become a man. Artemis promised, however she was too afraid of Zeus to see to the baby herself. So she sent a demon in to protect the boy and make sure that his father didn't kill him."

"Poor kid. So did the demon stay with him after that?"

"No. She kept him only until he was weaned and didn't need a mother's milk anymore. Then, after threatening the father, who had no more love for the boy than she did, she left the child and walked away. The boy cried himself sick for the only mother he'd ever known, but the demon never returned and he never saw her again."

Kateri shook her head at the horror. "How could even a demon leave a little baby with a father who hated him?"

Ren shrugged with a nonchalance that defied her comprehension. "After a while, the boy didn't mind his father's hatred. The feeling was quite mutual. In fact, most days, he hated his father more."

"Oh, but it had to be horrible for the little guy. Growing up like that . . . can you imagine?" Tears welled in her eyes as she felt so bad for the innocent baby who had no part in any of it. Her emotions overwhelmed her. Anger, pity, grief.

Most of all was a tsunami of indignation on the boy's behalf. She wanted to hurt all of them for treating him that way.

How could people be so selfish and cruel?

Ren turned to stare at her with a puzzled scowl. "Why do you cry?"

She wiped at her eyes, then waved her hand over her face in an attempt to stop any more tears from falling. "I'm sorry. I can't help it. I'm being a girl. I know. I just can't stand the thought of a little boy going through something so terrible. Alone. It's just not right. Please tell me that he grew up to be a ruler or happy or something really good."

When he didn't speak, a bad feeling went through her.

"His father didn't kill him, did he?"

"No. He lived."

She waited for him to say something more.

When he didn't, she reached out to touch his arm. "C'mon, Ren. Finish the story. You can't leave me hanging like this. What happened to the baby? Did he grow old? Did he father a boatload of kids and shower them with all the things he didn't have? Please, tell me after all of that evil misery he found someone who loved him and treated him right." She knew she was babbling, but she couldn't help it. Something inside her was desperate to know the baby's fate. "Well? Did he?"

His gaze searched hers with a probing stare she couldn't fathom. When he spoke, his tone was low and incredulous. "No. While he was in the fullest bloom of his manhood, his brother tricked a spirit into killing him. Then the boy sold his soul to come back and make right a wrong against the only real friend he ever knew."

It took a full minute for her to grasp the meaning of his words. For her mind to put all the pieces together into the only conclusion she could make.

"*You're* the baby."

Chapter 8

A thousand tangled emotions ripped through Kateri as she stared up at Ren with an understanding that burned her raw. He had been the baby that no one wanted. The baby banned from seeing the only person who'd ever wanted him.

His mother.

She knew from her own experience how much it hurt not to have a mother. How many times in her life she'd ached over the loss. Every time she'd seen a mother with her child, regardless of age, and they embraced, or just laughed together . . .

When she'd moved in or out of her college dorms and she'd seen her classmates with their families, their moms with tears in their eyes as they said good-bye and wished them luck with their classes. Graduations, birthdays, proms . . .

All family occasions.

And those damn sappy family commercials . . .

It always cut her to the bone because it rammed home with brutal clarity what she was missing. What she lacked most in her life. When there was a true mother-child relationship, there was no stronger bond. No greater love or sacrifice. That was what Ren had meant when he spoke of Apollymi destroying everything over the death of her son and why he couldn't comprehend that kind of love. *That* was how much a child meant to a real mother.

Their child *was* their world.

And when you didn't have that bond, there was no greater misery. It left a hole in your heart and a never-ending longing that was indescribable because you knew it was out there for others. You saw it constantly. Everywhere. And you wondered why you were exempt from having someone love you like that.

Why were they so lucky and you so cursed?

In her case, she'd at least known her mother for a brief time. She had memories of her mother holding her in her arms and rocking her whenever she felt bad, of her mother wiping away her tears and singing lullabies while her mother placed warm cloths of Vick's VapoRub on her chest whenever she was sick. Of kisses and hugs that came for no reason whatsoever, and with no strings attached. Of placing her own hand inside her mother's and feeling safe and secure in a world that was seldom kind to the innocent.

Most of all, she'd felt loved beyond measure every time her mother had looked at her.

It was also why she hated Mother's Day with a passion that burned like the fire of a thousand suns. Everywhere she looked, for weeks on end, was a vicious reminder that she no longer had a mother to buy a present for. No one to call. A woman to say "thanks for being there, Mom" to. While it was a great thought for those blessed with a mother who loved them and who was still with them, it was a brutal assault on those who'd lost theirs. She could only imagine how much worse it would be for someone like Ren who had no concept of what a real mother could be. Of what it felt like to know there was someone on this earth who would kill or die for you without reservation or hesitation.

And she knew exactly how lucky she was. She'd had two mothers who had loved her and cared for her. Two women who made her feel like she was everything to them.

Her mom and her grammy. Even though they were gone, their love lived inside her and gave her strength and character to this day. And she still wasn't alone. Not really. She had her aunt Starla, who would call and check on her. Make her laugh no matter how bad her day had been. Starla might only be related by marriage, but she'd always treated Kateri like another daughter.

Ren had never had anyone.

Ever.

She sniffed back the tears that threatened to become an all-out crying jag for the real tragedy of his life. "I'm *so* sorry."

And still he appeared puzzled as he watched her. It was as if compassion and sympathy from someone else were so alien an experience that he couldn't fathom anyone caring about him. "Why?"

"Why?" she repeated incredulously. "Because no child should grow up like you did. No one should ever be abandoned by the people who shouldn't have to be threatened to do right by their own blood. For the fact that you've never met your mother and that stupid demon-bitch abandoned you to a total asshole. I'm sorry for all of that. Most of all, I'm sorry that you think I'm nuts for caring about you. And for your being shocked and baffled that someone else could actually care about and be indignant over what was done to you as a child." She reached up to touch him, but he moved away.

Who could blame him? He didn't know how to bond with anyone. His own brother had killed him.

She winced at a reality so harsh, she wondered how he could be sane. Then again, maybe he wasn't. There were times when she doubted her own sanity. Times when the world kicked her so hard it left a permanent scar on her heart.

A heart that now wanted nothing more than to soothe him. "Has anyone ever just held you?"

He scowled. "What do you mean?"

And even that, he couldn't comprehend. Of course no one had ever held him close.

Held him like he mattered.

"I'm sorry, Ren. It's none of my business, I know. I'm just trying to imagine how hard it had to be on you growing up like you did." She winced as another wave of tears made her eyes water. "Did your father ever learn to love you?"

His features were as empty and blank as his tone. "No.

He blamed me for the death of his wife. And he blamed my mother for the destruction of his homeland."

Something she was sure he took out on Ren.

"Why did he blame her for that?"

"He refused to believe that Apollymi came on her own to attack us. In his mind, my mother concocted all of it so she could have him."

How vain could one man be? "What? He thought your mother murdered Apollymi's son and destroyed two continents just to sleep with him?"

"I never said my father was a bright man. Thank the gods I inherited my intelligence from my mother and not him."

With those words, another vision went through her head. She saw Makah'Alay as a boy around the age of ten. He stood in the doorway of a room, staring at a bed that was surrounded by people who had their backs to him. She recognized the priests and medicine men. It was obvious they were there to cure someone, and it couldn't be his father since he stood at the head of the bed, looking down.

The oldest priest turned to face Ren's father. "I'm sorry, Chief Coatl. There's nothing left to do except prepare sacrifices in hopes the spirits will take mercy and leave Anukuwaya in this world."

Coatl's gaze darkened as he turned to see the son he hated standing there, hale and whole. His rage and hatred were tangible. Cursing, he headed for Ren.

Ren's eyes widened as he realized his father had become aware of his presence. He bolted for the hallway, but it was too late.

His father was on him before he could scurry away. He snatched the boy by his arm and shoved Ren against the stone wall. "What did you do to him?"

"N-n-n-nothing, F-f-f-father."

He backhanded Ren so hard that Ren fell to the ground. "Don't you dare lie to me! I know you're jealous of my son. That you covet his perfection." He grabbed Ren by the hair and wrenched him to his feet. Ren's lips and nose were bleeding as he clutched at his father's hand, trying to get him to let go.

"You better pray, boy, that nothing happens to my son. If Anukuwaya dies, I will gut you myself as an offering for his safe passage to the next realm. Do you understand? Now, whatever it is you have done to him, you better undo, or I will have your life as payment for it."

The vision vanished, leaving Kateri to stare into the eyes of the adult version of that little boy's face. A face that still had bleeding lips from the battle he'd fought *for her*.

Overwhelmed by it all, she reacted without thought and pulled him into her arms.

Ren froze at the foreign sensation of being held by someone as she buried her face against his neck and tightened her grip around his waist. Her tears dampened his skin, raising chills all over him. He was so stunned that he didn't know how to react to her fierce hug.

And in that one moment, something inside him shattered. It unleashed a long-buried dream that he knew better than to have. One where he lived a normal life with someone who would miss him if he was gone. Someone who would fuss at him if he was late and hadn't called . . .

Closing his eyes, he inhaled her scent—a mixture of valerian and primrose. And all he could think about was being inside her. Of spending hours with her wrapped around his naked body.

Was this what it felt like to be loved? Not that he thought for one instant that she loved him. How could she? She didn't know him at all, because if she did, she'd be terrified and running for the nearest hole to hide in.

But love or not, this was the first time anyone had ever held him like this. Like she cared about him.

She'd been right. In all his life, he could count every hug he'd ever received. They were so rare and brief that he'd actually committed them to memory.

No one had ever held him to comfort him. Ever. His head reeled from emotions he couldn't even begin to name, and from the warmth her hug gave him. And here, for one single heartbeat, he allowed himself to feel that maybe, just maybe, he might be worthy of being loved by someone.

Don't be stupid.

The last time he'd entertained that fantasy had been with Windseer.

To this day, he could hear her mocking laughter after he'd made the mistake of confessing his love for her. "You didn't really expect me to say I love you, too, did you? While you are physically appealing and okay in bed, you're weak. Pathetic. You let everyone walk all over you and then wipe their feet on you when they're done. You cower into the shadows and shirk away every time your father draws near. Instead of being a man and standing up for yourself, you allow your brother to take credit for your skills and your kills. You're just a mewling little boy. You won't even accept the Grizzly Spirit's offer because you're too afraid to do so. How could any woman love something as pitiable as you?"

"I'm not p-p-p-p-p-p . . ." He'd been so upset by her attack that he hadn't been able to get anything else out. He'd stood there sputtering like he was as mentally defective as everyone thought him to be.

"Try 'nugatory' or 'inferior,'" she'd sneered at him. "Maybe you won't stumble over those."

At that point, his fury had been such that he'd feared he was about to strike her. So he'd turned sharply on his heel and headed for the door.

"Wait, Makah'Alay! Don't forget to take your meager p-p-p-pride with you!"

That had been the taunt that sent him over the edge. The one that gutted the hardest.

Intent on proving her and everyone else wrong, on proving to himself that he wasn't the piece of shit everyone thought him to be, he'd left her and gone straight to the Grizzly Spirit to make his bargain.

That had been the last time he'd seen her, and those her last words to him. Once he realized she'd only been using him to free Grizzly, he'd vowed to himself that no matter what, he'd never again love any woman. That he would never, ever open himself up to that kind of pain and humiliation.

It just wasn't worth it.

And he wasn't so weak that he needed validation from another. He lived his life for himself and he preferred it that way. He didn't need anyone else in his world.

"We need to get you something for your pain and wounds."

Kateri's voice dragged him back to the present and to the fact that she was still holding on to him.

For a second, he thought she was talking about his memories, until he again felt the physical pain of his fight. Releasing her, he took a step back, brushing his hand over the worst of the wounds in his side. "There's nothing to be done for them."

"What do you mean?"

"I told you, Kateri. I'm immortal. They'll heal on their own."

"Don't they hurt?"

Of course they did. While he'd beat the crap out of the demon, the demon wasn't inexperienced. Little bastard had kicked the shit out of him.

But she was being kind, so he kept his sarcasm to himself and nodded.

"Then we can—"

"Nothing will take the pain away, Kateri. Dark-Hunter powers don't work that way."

She frowned in confusion. "Dark-who? What?"

He rubbed his clean hand over his face as he remembered that she wouldn't have a clue about his brethren, even though Talon had once been a member of their elite brotherhood.

Although technically, Ren wasn't really one and never had been. He pre-dated the first official Dark-Hunters by a couple thousand years. And because of that, he was the only one considered a Dark-Hunter that Acheron, their leader, hadn't trained. In fact, Acheron hadn't even known

Ren existed until Cabeza had crossed over four thousand years ago, and the Atlantean had gone to train him for his Dark-Hunter duties in the Yucatan.

Acheron had been as shocked by Ren's existence as Ren had been by his.

Unlike the other Dark-Hunters, Artemis had resurrected Ren only because of her promise to his mother that she wouldn't let him die as a child—she'd sworn a sacred vow on the River Styx that she would watch over him.

To breach that oath would have cost her her own life.

Since Artemis was immortal and rather self-absorbed, she didn't have the best grasp on what differentiated a human child from an adult. So she'd returned him to life out of fear that if she didn't, she'd die, too.

And because of the dark powers she had to use to restore his life, it had "gifted" him with fangs and an inability to walk in daylight. Artemis told the other Dark-Hunters she'd created that those were a result of what they were pledged to hunt.

But once he'd been brought back, Ren had slowly learned the truth of his own birth and of the secrets of his mother's Greek pantheon.

The power to bring the dead back to life was one Artemis had stolen from Apollymi's son. As such, Artemis couldn't control it entirely. But it didn't matter to him. He'd been too grateful to come back and try to rectify his own stupidity that he wasn't about to complain about hers.

Right now, he didn't want to go into any of that with Kateri. Nor did he want anyone else to know how different he was from the others. The Dark-Hunters accepted him as one of their own, and since none of them knew his true age, they didn't question his Dark-Hunter designation.

They assumed he was a lot younger than he was and he didn't bother to correct them. Only Acheron knew the truth about him and only he knew the truth about who and what Acheron really was. A fact he kept from Acheron. Having lived his own crappy life, he wasn't about to dredge up Acheron's past that made Ren's look like a walk through Disney World. Since both of them wanted their pasts forgotten, Ren was more than happy to oblige their Atlantean leader.

So he gave Kateri the simplest explanation. "Dark-Hunters are immortal warriors who protect humanity from the preternatural beings who prey on them."

Kateri frowned. This was one of the moments when a sane, rational person would throw down the bull *caca* flag on the field. But . . .

Sanity had waved bye-bye to her several hours ago. At this point, she was ready to go with space aliens, flying fat Elvi, and anything else someone wanted her to believe in.

Even Santa and the Tooth Fairy.

Heck, why not throw the Easter Bunny in for good measure.

And assuming that the Dark-Hunters were as real as all the other . . . things she'd met since she got up this morning, she had a few questions. "So how does someone get to be a Dark-Hunter? Are you born to do it?"

"No. They're usually someone who dies during a brutal betrayal of some kind. One so violent and harsh that their soul screams loud enough to carry to Artemis's temple on

Olympus. When she hears it, she goes to make them a bargain. For a single Act of Vengeance against the person who hurt them, they give her their soul and spend the rest of eternity hunting down Daimons for her."

"Daimon as in demon?"

He laughed bitterly. "Another very long, complicated story. Suffice it to say, they're soul-sucking vampires who serve the Atlantean goddess Apollymi. Since they collect souls and souls cannot live inside a body not their own, a Dark-Hunter is charged with killing the Daimon before the soul dies so that it can return to where it needs to be."

A shiver went down her spine at the thought of losing her soul. "You sold your soul to Artemis?"

"Trust me, it wasn't much of one, and it was no great loss. I really haven't missed it at all." There was a note of bitterness in his voice as he spoke.

But that got her to thinking. . . . "Then they're not worth anything?"

"Not as long as you're alive. But if you die without one, it makes your concept of hell look like a picnic."

Oh, okay, that didn't sound so pleasant. . . . "But if you're immortal, you can't die, right?"

"Easily. There are certain things no one survives."

This she had to hear. "Such as?"

"Beheading. Total dismemberment. Heart removal. Basically anything that utterly destroys a body, such as fire, and of course my personal fave—letting sunlight touch you. We tend to spontaneously combust into flames whenever that happens."

"Why?"

"You want the lie or the truth?"

Kateri wondered what made him ask such a question. Who would want a lie if they could have the truth? But her curiosity did get the better of her. "Oh, what the heck, let's live a little and hear both, shall we?"

One corner of his mouth twitched as if he started to smile, then caught himself. "Artemis tells everyone that it's because of her brother, Apollo, god of the sun. It's his curse that keeps the Dark-Hunters from daylight. But it stems from Apollymi. Since the Daimons can't go out in sunlight, she made it so that the Dark-Hunters who pursue them can't attack them unfairly. If the Daimons can't walk daylight, the Dark-Hunters can't walk daylight."

Made sense, but it stunk for the ones caught in the middle. "It sounds like Apollymi and the Greeks are still at war."

He inclined his head to her. "They are. The gods are worse than the Hatfields and McCoys when it comes to grudge matches. They don't know the meaning of the words 'Halt. Enough.'"

"And I still don't see how any of this ties in to me."

Ren paused at the opening of a cave. He pulled the knife from his boot. "Can you handle a knife?"

"I'm a better archer, but I think I understand the basic concept of stabbing someone."

His eyebrow shot up at that. "You can shoot a bow?"

Could she shoot a bow? Really? His astonished tone and expression seriously offended her. "Honey, I was on the 2008 Olympic archery team in Beijing. I didn't take home the gold, but I was ranked number four in the world. Compound, crossbow, or traditional . . . whatever propels an arrow. If I can nock it, I can shoot it accurately. Never go to rubber-band war with me. You *will* be sorry."

This time he did smile, and it was devastating enough to make her forget all about feeling offended. Damn, he was gorgeous when he did that....

It lit his face and made him appear boyish and sweet.

Then a panicked look darkened his eyes as if he realized what he was doing and it instantly embarrassed him. Clearing his throat, he returned the knife to his boot. A bright light flashed an instant before a recurve bow appeared in his hands with a quiver of arrows, armguard, and shooting glove.

He handed them over to her. "Would you prefer a compound bow?"

"No way. Recurve's my baby. Not as forgiving, true, but I don't need forgiveness. I'm Sagittarius, Sagittarius rising. My grandmother always swore I was born with a bow in my hands."

That seemed to please him. "All right then. I'll be right back." He paused to look at her. "On demons, aim for their eyes. Anything else will just piss them off."

She flashed him a grin as she strapped her glove on. "Good to know. Thanks for the heads up."

Ren hesitated as he watched her put the armguard on and then nock an arrow and test her line of sight. She shot the same way he did—one over, two under. Her flawless form was a thing of beauty. While he'd seen plenty of women archers over the centuries, he'd never seen one who was truly united with her bow the way Kateri was.

Like the Guardian . . .

Yeah, that bastard had shot so fast and so furiously that his arrows had blotted out the sky. While the Guardian wasn't the most accurate, he was one of the fastest on the draw that Ren had ever faced. The first time they'd fought, Ren had taken three arrows in his right thigh. But for Buffalo drawing his fire away from Ren, Ren wouldn't have survived it.

Never underestimate an enemy.

Pushing those memories away, he went to explore the cave. His current wounds were taking their toll and he wasn't sure how much longer he'd be able to function. Every heartbeat was threatening to send him to the ground.

Luckily, the cave was empty and appeared to be relatively clean. Thank goodness something was starting to go in his favor.

He headed back to the opening to find Kateri sitting on a rock as she scanned the woods around her like a true hunter. The sallow moonlight highlighted her silhouette, showing him the perfect angles of her face. She'd pulled her hair back into a tight bun that exposed her neck and reminded him of how good she'd smelled when she held him.

His throat went dry as his hormones roared to life in spite of the pain he was in. What was it about her that made him crave her so? That made him ache to be near her when he knew he shouldn't?

Proximity. Yeah, he'd blame it on that. That was safe and easy. Anything more bordered on terrifying.

He was just horny. He'd be like this with *any* woman.

And yet he knew better. He'd been around enough

women over the centuries to know they didn't do this to him. Ever.

Not even Windseer had made him ache to hear his name on her lips. . . .

"Kateri?"

She jerked her head in his direction.

"C'mon, I found us a place to hole up for a bit."

She slid off her makeshift seat in a way that reminded him of an exuberant child, and made her way over to him. A slight smile hovered at the edges of her lips—one that made her eyes sparkle. An urge to kiss her grabbed him by the throat and it was all he could do not to give in to it.

"You wouldn't happen to be able to think us up a cheeseburger, would you?"

Her question amused him. "Hungry?"

"Very. Who knew running for your life would give you such an appetite? I think I could actually eat a bear right now."

He really didn't want to be charmed by her, but it was impossible to resist. She spoke to him like she'd known him for years. Like they were old friends.

In the midst of all this crap that had hit them in the last few hours, she'd been brave and reasonable. Calm. Things he could definitely appreciate and respect.

She arched her brows at him. "Where are you taking me?"

That was a loaded question. He'd like to take her right here and right now.

Harness those thoughts. Now!

Yeah, that was only going to get him into trouble.

"Um ... b-b-back here."

Fuck! The sound of that damn stutter iced every hormone in his body. Why did he have to do that with her? Why?

Hating himself and with his fury riding him hard, he started away.

But she caught his jaw in her hand and gently turned his face until their gazes met. The warmth of her hand scalded his flesh, but it was the sincere concern in her gaze that set him on fire.

"Ren ... Did you know that Winston Churchill, the greatest orator of all time and one of the greatest leaders in the world, had a speech impediment? All of us botch our words from time to time. And honestly, I'd much rather stammer than put my foot in my mouth, and I've done more than my fair share of that. You have no reason to be embarrassed or ashamed for a biological misfire you can't help. It's not an indictment on your intelligence, but it is on the humanity and decency of anyone cruel enough to mock you for it. Besides, I think it's adorable."

Those words, combined with her touch and the look on her beautiful face, shattered every piece of resistance he had where she was concerned. In all his life, no one had ever made him feel like she did right now.

Normal. Whole.

Human.

There was no disdain or mockery. No judgment. She stared up at him the same way the Butterfly had looked at his friend Buffalo.

Like he meant something to her.

Before he could stop himself, he dipped his head down to taste her lips.

Kateri couldn't breathe as Ren kissed her with a passion the likes of which she'd never experienced. He sank his hands in her hair and explored every inch of her mouth with a hunger that set her on fire. It was as if she was the air he needed to live. Her head reeled from it and it made her so weak, she surrendered her weight to him.

When he finally pulled back, he still didn't release her. Rather, he buried his face against the crook of her neck and held her there as if savoring her very essence.

"You're not going to bite me with your fangs, are you?"

Ren blinked as those words registered past the daze that had claimed him. "No," he breathed. "I'm sorry. I don't know what came over me."

She gave him a smile that played havoc with every part of his body. "Don't apologize. That was one heck of a kiss. But if you're through, you might want to put me back on my feet."

He felt heat scalding his face again as he realized that during their kiss he had picked her up entirely. Her feet were several inches above the ground.

But in spite of his embarrassment, he slid her down the front of his body, savoring her curves against his chest. Too bad they were both clothed. It would have been infinitely more enjoyable had they both been naked.

Kateri watched the play of emotions cross his face. He would most likely die if he knew how transparent he was to her right then. How vulnerable. This wasn't the face of the warrior who had fearlessly fought demons.

This was the face of a man more used to rejection

than acceptance. One who was still waiting for her to say something nasty to him.

"Just so you know, Ren, I think you're wonderful."

Ren scowled at her. "For what?"

He truly didn't know. . . .

It amazed her that anyone could be so handsome and strong, kind and giving, and not have a clue about how superlative they really were.

"For protecting me. For your gift, and for that amazing kiss. And if you want to conjure me up a burger, I'll consider you the greatest human of all time."

To her complete shock, he laughed. "You want fries with that?"

"Sure. And a big old thick chocolate shake." Yeah, that very thought made her stomach rumble.

He took her hand and led her deep into the cave.

She slowed as the darkness completely enveloped them. "I can't see anything."

A green light flared instantly. Ren handed her a small glowstick he must have conjured like he'd done her bow. "That unfortunately is about the last thing I can do right now. Sorry." He sank down on the floor as if he was too weak to take one more step.

Concern tore through her at his actions. "Are you all right?"

Ren nodded. "I have to sleep for a while." He went down on all fours, then basically collapsed on the ground.

Even more worried than before, she rushed to him and knelt by his side. He was still breathing, but he was frightfully pale. Sitting back on her haunches, she glanced over the small area, taking a mental inventory of everything around them.

She did a double take at a white bag on a nearby rock.

No . . . it couldn't be.

Could it?

With a curious frown, she went to it and sure enough, it was a cheeseburger, fries, and a large chocolate shake. Laughing in happiness, she pulled a fry out and ate it. She glanced back at Ren, amazed by his kindness. "You are so not what I thought you were."

At least not entirely. He was still scary and huge, and very skilled. But he wasn't the ogre he'd appeared to be at first.

He was surprisingly gentle, and, though he'd probably hate to hear her say it, sweet.

How could his father and brother treat him the way they had? What kind of beasts could hurt someone like Ren?

I wish I knew more about you.

While she'd gathered a great deal of information, there was still a lot more she lacked.

Like had he ever married? Did he have children?

When did his brother kill him and why?

Most of all, what was the wrong that he'd come back to right?

For that matter, she still didn't know how her destiny was tied to his past. Why was she here with him? Why he couldn't take her home himself?

So many questions. No real answers.

Sighing, she ate her food, wishing she had a crystal ball. Not that she could use one if it'd been here. But . . .

"You would be amazed at what you can do."

Kateri went completely still at the deep, thunderous voice. Her heart hammering, she turned slowly to see a tall, imposing older man. One who had red eyes and a scar down the length of his face . . .

And he stood between her and her bow.

Chapter 9

Kateri reached for the knife in Ren's boot.

"Easy," the older man said, holding his hands out to show her that he was unarmed—not that that meant much, given what she'd seen over the last day. Some of the most lethal things after her hadn't been armed.

Oh, for the days when people fought with weapons she could actually see. . . .

But the man didn't appear to be threatening her.

Please don't let looks be deceiving. She was really tired of being attacked and all she wanted was five minutes to regroup.

To be honest though he appeared rather pleasant. Friendly, even. Clean-shaven and tall, he wore his long gray hair loose about his shoulders. The front of his hair was pulled back from his face and secured at the crown of his head with a set of three feathers. Two white and one black. Something about him seemed old, even though physically, he looked around forty. "Do you not know who I am?"

She started to shake her head no until something in her mind flashed to her childhood. To images of this man watching over her from the shadows—only his hair had been dark and he'd been younger ... closer to her age. All throughout her life, she'd caught tiny glimpses of him from time to time. Usually whenever she was upset or extremely happy.

She'd even glimpsed him at her graduations ... and at her birthday parties in the park.

He'd always been a shadow figure in the background— more illusive than real. She even had an indistinct, fuzzy image of him in one of her old photographs. "My grand-mother called you my guardian angel."

His gaze turned warm and gentle. "Oh, sweetie, I am definitely that. But I'm also your father."

Yeah, right. Did she look like Luke Skywalker? Uh-uh. No. This was too much. Out of all the other weird things that had happened to her since she woke up, this ... this was the straw that broke it. She refused to believe him. Her father had run off and abandoned her when she'd been a baby. Something her mother had never gotten over.

This was *not* her father.

Shaking her head in denial, she scampered over Ren's body, to put him between them. Not that he offered much protection while he was unconscious. Still, she felt better with him providing some form of a barrier between her and Captain Weirdo Liar.

The man claiming to be her father took one step for-ward, then froze as he saw her reaching for Ren's knife.

"Kateri, please. I'm not strong enough to fight you and stay here. You have to listen to me. I don't have long and there's much I have to tell you."

She kept her hand on the knife's hilt, but left it in its sheath. "What do you mean?"

"I'm no longer corporeal. I haven't been since I physically vanished from your life—something I did not do voluntarily. I swear. I loved you and your mother. More than anything. If I'd had any choice in the matter, I would never, ever have left you. And I've come to you every time I could. As long as I could." He gestured to Ren. "It's why I sent Makah'Alay to you. Even though we were once enemies, he is the only one I trust now to keep you safe. He's the only one capable of saving you."

"I don't understand."

"I know, baby. It's all confusing." He sighed wearily. "Things did not turn out the way I wanted them to. But then life so seldom cooperates with our plans for it." He took another step toward her. With the greenish light now at his back, she realized he was translucent.

"You're a ghost?"

"In a manner of speaking." Tears filled his eyes as he swallowed hard while staring at her as if he couldn't believe she was here in the cave. "You're so beautiful ... just like your mother. I should never have interfered, but I couldn't help it. The moment I saw your mother, I fell in love with her. No one could resist her smile, least of all me. I knew what I did was wrong and I couldn't stop myself. And you were the sweetest bonus that I never expected."

Her own eyes watered as tears choked her. Was there any truth to what he said? Could there be?

He jerked his chin toward Ren. "Makah'Alay thinks that he needs me to reset the calendar, but I'm not the necessary one. *You* are. For the first time since the Great Dawn, the Guardian and the Ixkib are united in one person. While they are dormant for now, you have all my powers, as well as all of your mother's and grandmother's, and when the time comes and you need them, they will be there for you. No one has ever been so strong. But you're the one who has to believe that those powers are yours to command. Let no one tell you otherwise. And you, alone, will have the power to designate the new Guardians for the gates. Choose better than I did. I allowed myself to be blinded by hope. You're more pragmatic than I ever was. And you do me prouder than any child has ever done their parent."

His gaze returned to Ren. "While I trust Makah'Alay for now, be cautious, little one. His heart was turned once. It makes it easier for it to be turned again, and having met your mother and being unable to resist her even though I knew I should have, I completely understand him now. And that knowledge scares me. There is still much inside him that is angry and dark. So long as it lives in his heart, he will never be free. And he will never be truly safe. Artemis isn't the only one who owns a piece of him."

Her heart pounded at his words. If she couldn't trust Ren, who could she trust?

And there was still the biggest puzzle of all. "What about the stone everyone wants? Where is it?"

He smiled at her. "You will discover it when the time is right. Your grandmother took care of that for you. Your enemies can't find it. Only *you* can."

The walls around them began to flicker. Images flashed across them so fast, it was hard to focus on any one. She saw Ren fighting her father. Blood soaked them both as they tried to tear each other apart. It was a brutal, gladiatorial fight.

Her father laughed. "He is the only one who ever defeated me in battle."

She scowled at that. "I thought you won."

He shook his head. "No. By all rights, he had won the fight and defeated me, but I tricked him at the end. Like everyone else in his life, I lied to him and used his insecurity against him so that he faltered and defeated himself. That is his only weakness, and it's the one you can use should you need to kill him."

That thought horrified her. "Kill him?"

Her father gestured to the wall on his left.

The scenes flared bright. And then, larger than all the others, was an image of Ren staring straight at her. The wind blew his long black hair around his shoulders and handsome face. He was dressed in a light brown buckskin suit that was decorated with elaborate red and black embroidery. The fur of a jaguar hung over his shoulders and was secured to his suit by two ornate brooches. Like her father, he had three feathers in his hair, only his fell from his left temple. Two black and one white. He wore a red stone in the shape of a teardrop from a leather cord around his neck. It was reminiscent of a drop of blood.

In his right hand was an ornately carved black bow and in his right was a pure white arrow. But it was his eyes that pierced her. One was as blue as a perfect summer sky and the other was as red as blood. They seared her with his anger and hatred.

Kill the jaguar. That voice was demonic and cruel as it directed Ren.

He nocked the arrow and aimed it straight for her heart.

Her father started to fade. "If the Grizzly takes him over again, you will have to kill him, Kateri. You are the only one who can. Kill him. Stab his heart and he will be no more. If you don't, he will destroy the world of man, and he *will* kill you. Remember that I love you, daughter. Always."

Then her father was gone completely.

Ren's image stayed on the wall with that one red eye glaring at her. "You will not weaken me!" he snarled, then he let loose his arrow.

Kateri ducked instinctively. But it was just an illusion. No part of it was real.

None.

Except for the man who slept beside her. Her hand trembling, she brushed the hair back from his battered face. So he really was the Makah'Alay she'd seen in her visions and dreams. How weird to know him so well and yet not know him at all. To have someone from her dreams here in the flesh . . .

Makah'Alay.

That was also the name of a demon her grandmother had told her about when she was a little girl. *He is evil to the core of his soul. Those who see him, die by his hand. Always. He takes pity on none and can control the raven mockers. Fear him, Waleli. Pray you never meet him. And if you do, run with everything you have.*

Could he be the same creature her grandmother had warned her about?

Swallowing hard, she ran her hand over his sculpted jaw where only a few whiskers were there to tease her skin. Asleep like this, he looked more boyish than threatening. More human. But awake, he could be terrifying and overwhelming.

And with that thought came another image of him with both eyes so red, they glowed. He stood with his legs apart and body tensed as if about to battle an unseen enemy.

"What did you do to make them all fear you so?" *Why* had he done it?

Kateri sighed as she tried to sort through information that came at her so fast, she felt like she was in the middle of cramming for finals. If she learned one more thing, her brain was going to shut down in revolt and leave her a drooling vegetable on the floor.

Needing a minute to clear her head, she stretched out by Ren's side. But it wasn't comfortable. The hard, earthen floor was cold and gritty. In fact, it said it all about how much he needed sleep that he could be out so soundly on something so miserable.

Ugh, this is not going to work. She tried everything she could think of, twisted into every position. She put her arm under her head, then took it out.

Useless.

Until she slid her gaze to Ren's lush body. Yeah, *that* was the only thing in this dismal place that looked appealing. Desirable . . .

Inviting.

Don't do it. He's bleeding.

True, but there were areas of his body that weren't blood-soaked. Areas that were ...

Comfy-looking. Before she could stop herself, she rolled him over, onto his back, then scooted closer so that she could use him for a pillow.

Oh yeah, much *better*.

And in the next second, she took a deep breath, then was out cold.

Ren came awake slowly. His body was still aching. Damn it. He felt like someone had beat the hell out of him, which they had. Literally. Or more appropriately, he'd beat the hell out of the demon.

I should have beat the bastard harder. . . .

Wincing from the pain of his ribs and back, he opened his eyes, then froze at the last thing he expected to see.

Kateri was snuggled up against him with her head on his shoulder. Her left hand rested in the center of his chest while her breath tickled the flesh of his neck.

His body hardened so fast and furiously that he sucked his breath in sharply. Against his best efforts, an image of her naked and writhing, and in his arms, went through him. He could just imagine her running her hands over his back while he made love to her.

That did nothing to help his discomfort.

Or his mood.

He tried to think of something unpleasant. His father. His brother. Grizzly ...

Smelly socks.

Nothing worked. Not while he could feel her on top

of him like a familiar lover who was completely at ease with his company. Biting his lip, he pressed his hand against his swollen groin, trying to force his will on the treacherous beast that couldn't listen to him. Or if it did, then it was definitely mocking and ignoring his wishes right now.

I should have gelded myself after Windseer left.

True. It wasn't like he'd ever needed it. It'd only gotten him into trouble and it reminded him of just how alone he really was in this world.

How different he was from other men.

All of a sudden, Kateri stretched like a languid cat, arching her back and pressing her body closer to his. Something that also gave him a perfect view down the neckline of her shirt, straight to her purple lace bra and a set of tawny breasts that made his mouth water for a taste.

He clenched his hand into a fist to keep from obliging himself with a grope he was sure would get him bitch-slapped. And justifiably so.

With a contented sigh, she slid her hand over his chest, brushing against his nipple.

Ren moaned deep in his throat as tortured pleasure erupted through his entire being. Oh yeah, he was dying now. This . . . this *was* hell.

At the sound of his hiss, Kateri opened her eyes instantly and met his gaze with a startled gasp. "Oh, hey." She relaxed into a sweet, welcoming smile. "Morning, Sunshine. Ready to take on the day?"

Gah, she was a morning person. . . . *Kill me.* How could anyone wake up in such a pleasant mood? He'd never understood that disposition.

Not that it mattered. Right now, he couldn't respond had he wanted to. Not while his body was so aroused.

"Are you feeling better?" she asked in that chipper voice that hadn't been annoying yesterday when it hadn't been so early.

And the answer was simple. Hell, no. But that wasn't what she was referring to and he knew it.

There's no need in being an asshole to her. Not her fault you're horny.

Yeah, well, bullshit on that. He wouldn't be in this condition without her. *She* was definitely the reason for his raging hard-on. However, it wasn't her fault she felt really good in his arms or that she was unbelievably sexy with her hair tousled around her face, her cheeks flushed from sleep.

So he gave her a grudging, "Yes."

She flashed him an adorable grin that made his cock jerk in response.

Down, boy. No need in making us both miserable. You're not going anywhere so you might as well deflate and save us our dignity.

She stretched again. "By the way, did you know you talk in your sleep?"

He arched a brow at that. Since he'd never spent the night with another person, he'd had no idea of it. *Please tell me I didn't stutter there, too.* That was all he needed.

"So who's Windseer?"

Oh wait . . . it just got worse. But at least that question finally succeeded in icing his hormones. It slapped him down faster than an arctic bath. How horrifying to talk about that bitch in his sleep to the Ixkib.

I'd rather stutter. . . .

"She's no one."

Kateri gave him a doubting stare. "It didn't sound like no one. You called out to her like you wanted her badly. Is she an old girlfriend?"

Great. What the hell was wrong with his subconscious? Why would any part of him want Windseer for anything except to slaughter the bitch where she stood?

Your unconscious is even dumber than you are. And that was an accomplishment, given his average daily stupidity.

Grinding his teeth in anger at himself, Ren curled his lip. "She's nothing to me. I don't want to think about her."

Kateri sucked her breath in at the hatred in his tone. Obviously, Windseer had hurt him.

Badly.

She detested the fact that she'd inadvertently kicked him by mentioning the woman's name. "Sorry. Duly noted and now permanently removed from my vocabulary." As was anything that had "wind" attached to it and that included her own middle name, Wynd. No need in making him this upset ever again. She'd had her inherent share of bad relationships she didn't want to revisit. So she fully understood his need not to go to the past. It was an ugly place sometimes.

And people could be total jerks when they wanted to.

She started to move away, but he caught her in an iron grasp that startled her even more than his tone had. To her shock, he kept her by his side.

His gaze searched hers as if he sought something he'd lost. "Why are you on top of me?"

181

Heat scalded her cheeks as she realized just how intimate they were in this position. "You were comfy. The floor wasn't. . . . And I was cold so I figured you were too." She bit her lip as that heat lit her entire body up and she realized that her excuse wasn't really viable. "I was trying to conserve body heat for both of us."

Yeah, it sounded phony to her too.

His breathing ragged, he brushed his hands through her tangled hair. The desire in his eyes set her own heart to pounding. Gracious, he was hot and unsettling. Or rather her body's reaction to him was unsettling. She never responded to a man like this.

But there was something about him that was irresistible. Something that called out to her against all sanity and rationale. Right now, all she wanted to do was nip that chin and explore every inch of his hard body.

"What have you done to me?" he breathed.

She frowned at his agonized tone. "Nothing."

He shook his head. "I've never had trouble as an immortal remaining celibate. But all I can think about is being inside you."

She should be offended by that. Instead, those words made her heart race even faster. It was nice to know she wasn't the only one having issues with their close proximity. It would really stink if she was.

And those words made her twice as curious. "You've been celibate? How long?"

"Eleven thousand years."

Kateri choked on his answer. *Holy* . . .

Was he serious?

She'd expected him to say a few months . . . tops. Given

the way he looked and the way he moved, she wouldn't have been surprised had he said a few hours.

But centuries? Really? Thousands upon thousands of years?

No . . .

Who could do that? How could *he* do that in *that* body? As gorgeous as he was, women had to be throwing themselves all over him. All the time. What did he do? Beat them off with a whip?

Her look turned chiding. "Well, honey, that's probably your problem. Been a little long between uh . . . well . . . you know—and I know you do. I admire your fortitude. I do. A lot. Not many people could do what you've done, and it explains a lot about why you're not a happier person."

He snorted at her attempted humor. "Don't be impressed. The last time I slept with a woman, I damn near destroyed the world because of it. When you do something *that* record-breakingly stupid, it tends to stay with you awhile."

Yeah, but thousands and thousands of years?

That, right there, told her exactly who and what Windseer was to him. She must have been the one who had led him astray and burned him to a level so foul that he had never gotten over it. "Out of curiosity, why would you have tried to destroy the world?"

"Ever attempted to hunt down a parking space at Christmas? Buy a shirt in a store the day after Thanksgiving? Those two things alone will make you doubt the human-ity of humans, and question if survival of the species is in anyone's best interest. What are we fighting for, anyway? Better department store sales?"

He did have a point.

Still . . .

Ren hesitated before he continued with his sarcasm. A part of him wanted to lie to her, and keep the topic light. Not because he didn't trust her, but because he didn't want to face the truth himself. The why was what burned the worst in his memory and heart. What cut him the deepest.

If there had ever been a Dumbass of the Day Award, he'd be in the Hall of Fame for it.

But before he could catch his tongue, it betrayed him. "Honestly? I did it to prove to her that I was a man and not a spineless piece of shit."

"Did it work?"

He shrugged. "I never saw her again, so I guess in her eyes it was futile. But I got my point across to all the others who thought I was weak. Nothing like a good ass-kicking to put fear into others." But that wasn't the same as respect. He'd gone from being a pathetic milksop to a homicidal psycho, and learned that the only things that changed were the names they called him and the tone and volume level they used when they did so.

Neither position was desirable or enviable. Both left you isolated, lost, alone, and insecure. No one to trust.

No one who gave a shit about you. The only real difference was that when they thought you weak they didn't try to kill you when your back was turned.

Sighing, he released her, then rolled over and rose to his feet. She got up and dusted herself off.

When he started to walk away from her, she put her hand on his arm to stop him.

"For the record? You're not a pathetic wretch, Ren, and you don't have to end the world to prove it."

He snorted at her naiveté, but a part of him he didn't want to acknowledge took flight over her kindness—even if it was feigned. "I have the blood of three competing pantheons, two of which are born warring, flowing through my veins. Since the hour of my birth, I've been at war with myself. You want to know why I stutter?"

"Why?"

"I was suckled for a year by a demon. Her milk infected me with her venom and it was her language I learned first. It's so radically different from anything human that I was five before I could even begin to comprehend our speech patterns. By that time, they all thought I was slow and stupid because of it. Then when I finally learned how to make their sounds, I stuttered with them because I have to translate from demonspeak to human. It's taken me a million lifetimes to speak without hesitation. And still whenever I think or dream it's never as a human." His gaze burned her. "Because of what Artemis sent to care for me, I became a conduit of evil. *That* is my true nature."

She shook her head. "I don't believe you. If you were truly evil, you wouldn't fight that nature. You'd go with it and let it swallow you whole. Yet you don't. You came for me when you didn't even know me, and rescued me. You have fought for strangers for centuries. How is any of that evil?"

"I killed my own father while he begged me for mercy."

Kateri hesitated at his confession. But as soon as she felt compassion, she remembered her visions of his father's cold brutality. "The same father who left you to die in

185

the woods alone when you were a defenseless infant? The one a demon had to threaten in order for him to care for you?" One who had abused and belittled him? "Pardon me if I don't shed a tear for that bastard. I mean c'mon, Ren, really? You've kept yourself celibate for eleven. Thousand. Years. Eleven," she repeated.

He scoffed at her tone. "You don't have to keep saying it. Believe me, no one is more aware of how long that is than I am."

"Yeah, well, excuse me for being impressed. That kind of self-control is off the grid. Seriously, off-grid. Especially to a woman who can't pass by a donut without having a bite of it. Sad, but true."

He snorted at her disbelieving tone. "It wasn't as difficult as you think. Trust me. It's kind of hard to have sex when no woman wants to be seen in public with you, never mind share your bed."

Yeah, right. What woman in her right mind would turn down all *that* yummy goodness? He was far more tempting than even a chocolate-drenched donut.

"Obviously you've been living in a closet. Alone." The instant those words were out of her mouth, she saw Ren in his past. . . .

He was with his friend who spoke to him in sign language.

His friend kept glancing over to a group of women who were shopping at a nearby vegetable stand. Two of them were insanely beautiful—the kind of perfectly formed women every woman wanted to be, but only a tiny handful were lucky enough to attain. The third was cute, but she paled in comparison to the two goddesses flanking her.

"Go on, Makah'Alay," his friend urged him. "It's a perfect opportunity to speak to her."

Ren shook his head.

His friend rolled his eyes. "You are the fiercest fighter we have . . . fearless in battle. Eldest son of our chief. Are you honestly telling me that you're so scared of a woman that you won't even go talk to her? Really? You're going to let a mere woman cow you?"

Rage darkened his gaze at his friend's insult.

Clenching his teeth and glaring at him, Ren turned and headed over to the women.

Kateri held her breath, expecting him to go to one of the two perfect girls.

He didn't. Instead he skirted around them to the third girl, who didn't have enough to pay for her purchase.

Tears swam in her eyes. "It's all I have. Please. I can't return without it. My mother told me that I had to have it or else."

"We don't lend credit here. You'll have to go beg from someone else. There's a price to be paid for every drop of sweat." The vendor reached to take the bundle of maize back from her.

Ren stopped him. "I'll cover it."

The man curled his lip. "How do I know *you* have it?"

Ren pulled out a piece of gold and handed it over.

After inspecting the gold, the vendor returned the maize to the girl.

"Thank you," she said to the vendor, not Ren. In fact, she wouldn't even look at him to acknowledge his presence.

Placing it in her wicker basket, she moved to join the other two, who were waiting for her.

"Itzel?" Ren called as he tried to catch up.

She hesitated before she turned to pin him with an irritated grimace. "What?"

"I-I-I was w-wondering . . ." He hesitated as if searching for the right words. The quivering in his jaw worsened as her look turned from irritation to disdain.

"Wondering what?" she snapped.

He bit his lip before he tried again. "W-would you m-m-mind if I c-c-c-"

"If you're asking to see me, yes I mind." She glanced toward her friends. "Do you think I want to be laughed at and mocked? That I'm desperate enough to be courted by *you*?" She sneered that word, twisting her face up into an ugly mask of cruelty. "Forget it. Go find yourself a woman as stupid as you. Oh wait, there's no one here that dumb. Not even the whores will take you when you pay them for it. Maybe you can find a horny goat or something in one of the other towns."

Ren stood ramrod stiff as she stalked off and left him to hear the vendor's laughter. As soon as she reached her friends, they all three looked at him and burst out laughing. He lifted his head, but as Kateri watched, the pain in his eyes brought tears to her own.

His friend started toward the girls, but Ren stopped him. "Don't m-m-make it worse."

Shaking his head, his friend headed off in the opposite direction, leaving Ren to glance back at the girls with a wistfulness that shredded her heart.

Kateri winced over what they'd done to him. No wonder he was celibate. Those bitches had trained him well to avoid women. Drawing a ragged breath, she sniffed back her tears. What could she say to ease that kind of mean-ness? What could ever undo such cruelty?

Unable to stand it, she pulled him into her arms and held him close.

Ren was completely stunned by her actions. Worse, his body roared to life as she pressed her warm curves against him. He stood there completely stiff, in more ways than one, unsure of what to do. "Why are you hugging me, Kateri?"

"Someone needs to."

That only confounded him more. "I don't understand."

Kateri pulled his lips to hers so that she could give him a scorching kiss the likes of which he'd never expected. The intensity of it, the sensation of her tongue danc-ing with his, made him light-headed and breathless. He growled low in his throat as he wrapped his arms around her and reveled in the taste of her lips.

He didn't think anything could be better. Not until she slid her hand down his chest and stomach, blazing a trail that left him trembling. Then, to his complete shock, she cupped him in her hand.

Completely stunned as she stroked and fingered him through his jeans, he broke off their kiss. "What are you doing?"

"I'm about to rock your world."

Chapter 10

Kateri had never been so forward with any man in her life. She had no idea where the courage came from, but she wanted to soothe him in a way she'd never wanted to soothe anyone. No one should be so alone. So abandoned. So humiliated. Especially not a man who had spent eternity protecting others.

A man who had bled to keep her safe. No one had ever given so much to her, and he barely knew her. No wonder he'd gone after the world so ferociously. All it had ever done was kick him in the teeth. She couldn't get over the cruelty she'd witnessed.

For once in his life, he needed to feel appreciated and cared for by someone he'd reached out to.

She nipped at his chin as she unbuttoned his jeans and slid her hand inside to touch him.

Gasping, he caught her hand in his and pulled it back. His breathing ragged, he shook his head. "Don't."

She frowned at his actions. "What's wrong?"

The raw agony in his dark eyes made her ache for him. "I c-c-can't."

His rejection stung her hard. She'd more than felt the proof that he *could*. He was already hard and wet. What he meant was that he didn't want *her*.

Clenching her fist, she nodded in understanding. "I'm sorry. I didn't mean to offend you."

Ren scowled at the catch in her voice, at the embarrassed humiliation in her eyes. It was a feeling he knew all too well, and he hated himself for making her feel it now. But the last thing he wanted was to be her pity fuck. That was the only thing worse than being rejected and ridiculed.

Even knowing that he meant nothing to her, it would weaken him where she was concerned and turn him into a mindless toy for her to jerk around. It was what he hated most about himself. If anyone ever managed to show him an ounce of kindness, he was pathetically loyal to them over it.

I am a wretch. . . .

Still, he didn't want her to feel bad. It'd been a kind offer. More than anyone else had ever given him. But he didn't mean anything to her and he knew it. She felt sorry for him and that was all. She didn't really want to sleep with him and he wasn't desperate enough to take advantage of her kind heart.

"It's not you, Kateri. It's not. The last time I slept with a woman, I almost ended the world. I've been twice adopted by evil and I know better than to tempt that part of me. I can't trust myself where you're concerned. If I let my guard down for even an instant, the darkness takes hold of me and I'm lost to it completely."

"I'm not asking for your soul, Ren. I'm only offering you comfort."

He laughed bitterly at his own frail stupidity. "And that is my weakness. Do not be nice to me."

Kateri stood there, staring at him in the dim light. He was serious about that. He honestly wanted her to hate him. And for what?

Fear of intimacy?

No, it wasn't that. She could feel it inside her. He was terrified of becoming her lapdog. Because in his mind, he was so desperate for any kindness at all, that once given, he would do anything to get more of it. Like a junkie wanting a fix.

Her heart broke for him. "Comfort is not a weakness."

"Yes, it is. In the wrong hands it's the cruelest weapon of all. And I don't want your kindness or your comfort. I don't need it."

But she knew better. He wanted to be held as much as she wanted to hold him. How sad that he couldn't trust her for the most basic human needs of all.

To be accepted and valued.

"Is there really no one you trust?"

"Only Buffalo."

An image of the handsome man in her visions flashed through her mind. "The friend you had as a boy who stood up for you? The one you used to sign with?"

His face went pale. "How do you know about that?"

She held her hands up to assure him that she wasn't intentionally prying into his past. "I've seen a lot of your life through visions. I never asked for them. I swear. They just come and go, in snippet pieces that I don't understand most of the time. But they've told me a lot about you. I even know that Ren is short for Renegade because you consider yourself a traitor to your family and people."

He stood in front of her, looking bereft of everything except self-loathing. "I don't consider myself a traitor. I *am* one. I have twice over betrayed everyone who trusted me. And I do mean *everyone*."

She didn't believe that for even a heartbeat. "Your father never trusted you."

"My brother did."

Kateri drew her brows together as she tried to picture what he described. Oddly enough, she'd never seen a single vision with his brother in it, other than the one when his brother had been ill as a child, and even then, his brother had been nothing more than a shapeless lump underneath bedcovers. She'd only seen allusions to his brother, but never his face or form.

But the one thing she had seen and that she could feel was that he did love his brother. Dearly. "I can't believe you'd betray him without cause."

His features hardened. "You don't know me, Kateri. What I'm capable of. I swore a sacred oath to protect my brother and for over a year I brutally tortured him."

A shiver went down her spine at what he said and from the look of hatred on his face. "Why?"

Shame filled his eyes as he stepped away from her.

As she suspected, he hadn't done it for pleasure. He'd been motivated to it by something or someone. "Tell me, Makah'Alay."

He turned back toward her faster than she could blink. Rage contorted his features as he curled his lip. "Don't call me that!" he snarled between clenched teeth. "Ever!"

His anger caught her off guard. She'd never seen any inclination in her visions that his real name bothered him. "Why?"

"It's not my name either." He returned to stand directly in front of her so that he dwarfed her with his height. His ravaged emotions were tangible as he glared down at her.

Yeah, okay, he was really fierce and scary. But she refused to cower. She would stand toe to toe with him no matter what, because that was what *she'd* been taught.

The Cherokee don't run. Sometimes they might want to. Sometimes they ought to. But the Cherokee don't ever run. Whatever the danger, you stood strong against it and faced it with everything inside you. That was her grandmother's greatest legacy and it was hardwired into her DNA.

"Do you know what Makah'Alay means?" His eyes flashed bright red in the darkness. But it came and went so fast that she wasn't sure if it happened or she imagined it.

She shook her head.

"It's the Keetoowah word for crow-demon. Since my mother didn't name me and I was returned to my father by a demon wet nurse, it was what they called me."

No one had given him a name?

"What of your grandmother?"

He scoffed bitterly. "I know nothing of my maternal grandmother. Not even her identity. As for my father's mother . . . She refused to even look at me or acknowledge me. It was why my father took me to the woods and left me there to die. After refusing to give me a name, she told him I would bring nothing but shame and sorrow to his clan. That I was defective and unworthy of being the son of a chief. And she was right. I brought nothing but misery and embarrassment to all of them."

It wasn't that cut-and-dry. She'd never seen him say or do anything in her visions that would embarrass someone else. While he would at times strike out at someone and fight, he wasn't the one who initiated the conflict. At least not that she'd witnessed.

Which made her wonder one thing. . . . "Why did you torture your brother?"

The look on his face would melt an iceberg. But instead of answering her question, he pulled her against him and held her there in an iron grip.

Before she could ask him what he was doing, she stood in the past with him.

They were in a huge gilded dining hall, filled with people celebrating the arrival of a beautiful woman and her entourage. Dressed in a bright yellow gown that was decorated with bright embroidery, the woman came into the room surrounded by painted warriors from her clan. She wore an ornate headdress of feathers and gold that stood up around her head like a halo. Her parents followed behind her, standing proud as they presented her to the chief and his sons. Something that was very different from the customs of Kateri's tribe where the husband went to live with the wife's clan when they married.

Ren stood next to a man who looked so much like him that they could easily be mistaken for twins. The only way to tell them apart was by their posture. Ren kept his eyes cast down, his head lowered, and shoulders slumped. His brother stood straight with an arrogance that couldn't be missed. It was as if he knew he owned the world and he expected everyone to bow down before him.

Even Ren.

Their father stepped forward to welcome the woman and her parents to their home.

"Butterfly, it is an honor to have you here. You are as beautiful as they have claimed. More so, in fact."

Her dark eyes glittered like gems in her perfect face. She smiled up at him and it was dazzling. "You are far too kind, Chief Coatl." Then, seductively biting her lip in eager anticipation, she looked past him to where Ren and his brother stood. "But no one told me you had twin sons. They are both handsome and strong. I'm sure they bring great honor to you and your clan."

Ren looked up in stunned surprise at that kind comment to meet her gaze. The moment he did, his jaw went slack and hunger filled his eyes. He straightened his spine to show that he was actually taller than his brother. And with his shoulders squared, it became obvious that he also had a larger, more defined physique. The sight of him actually having a degree of pride brought a smile to Kateri's lips. How kind of Butterfly to say something so sweet and make him feel better about himself.

A tic worked in his father's jaw as he stiffened indignantly. "They're not twins, Butterfly, and they're nothing alike. Believe me. No one matches my heir in any capacity. He is truly the finest warrior ever born."

Ren winced as if he'd been physically slapped.

197

With his back to Ren, his father continued speaking to Butterfly. "I fear *I* am the only thing they have in common. . . . They couldn't be more opposite—in all things." His father took her hand, then led her toward his brother, but not before he rudely shouldered Ren out of the way.

Deflating immediately back into his former stance, Ren glanced about as he realized how many people had witnessed his father's verbal and physical swipe at him. Butterfly's father scowled at Ren, but said nothing as Ren's father introduced Butterfly to his brother.

"It is with the greatest honor that I present you to my son—the future chief of our people, Anukuwaya."

Pride of the Wolf Clan. Kateri sucked her breath in as she finally caught the dual meaning of his brother's name. It not only meant the pride of his clan, it was an ancient name for Coyote—the great trickster.

Coyote stepped forward to take the hand of his future bride. "Butterfly . . . you are truly the most beautiful woman ever born. You honor our home by being here and I swear I will spend the rest of my life making sure you never regret your decision to accept me as your husband. Welcome."

Her smile was dazzling. "It's my pleasure and honor to be here, Anukuwaya. I promise that I shall always strive to bring nothing but happiness to you and your clan." She turned expectantly toward Ren. When no one moved to introduce them, she exchanged a nervous, puzzled frown with her mother, who shrugged in awkward confusion as to why he was being publicly dissed.

Ren's friend stepped forward to address her curiosity.

"His name is Makah'Alay, and he is the elder brother of your future husband."

"Buffalo!" his father snapped. "Mind your place!"

Ever loyal, Buffalo shrugged innocently. "I was only being hospitable, my most honored chief. She was curious about your eldest son"—Kateri cringed as Buffalo recklessly rammed that dig home—"and so I obliged her. No offense was meant to anyone." He offered Butterfly a smile and something unspoken sparked between them. A mutual admiration that left Kateri wondering about the two of them and their relationship.

Coatl passed a cold smile to Buffalo before he spoke to Butterfly and her parents. "You'll have to forgive my warrior. Since Makah'Alay was born mentally retarded, Buffalo champions him constantly and is his voice since he doesn't have one of his own."

Several of the others present laughed and whispered among themselves while Ren swallowed hard. He tightened his grip on his bow until his knuckles turned stark white.

"I'm surprised you kept him," Butterfly's father said. "It was my understanding that your people killed such infants at birth. I am glad to know that your clan has more mercy and decency than I was led to believe. You are indeed a most noble and admirable chief to take pity on a son so afflicted."

Coatl cast a smug glance at Ren. "I try to be patient with him, though he doesn't make it easy. I believe he was sent to remind me that no matter how much we might attain in our lives, we are all still frail humans in the end." He clapped Coyote on the back. "Just a few weeks back, I almost lost Coyote when he rushed to defend Makah'Alay from a vicious wild animal. There aren't many men who'd risk their life to save someone so afflicted."

Her expression one of worship, Butterfly smiled up at Coyote. "You are indeed a most wonderfully brave man. I am thrilled to be marrying such a hero."

Coyote smiled at her, then glanced to Ren. Something that appeared to be an unspoken apology passed between them.

What had really happened?

But Ren didn't give her time to explore that. He pulled her out of his past and stepped away from her as if he was afraid of being too close to her for too long. "I didn't care about being chief. Since my mother wasn't Keetoowah, I never expected it to come to me. It couldn't. Yet by all rights, Butterfly should have been mine. As the eldest, I should have married first. But my father refused, saying I wasn't man enough to provide for a wife. That I wasn't smart enough to have one. So I let my jealousy over their engagement infect me to the point that I took things out on my brother I had no right to. Coyote was a good and decent man until I turned him into the monster he is today."

Somehow, she doubted that. "Why did he give you that look when your father spoke of his saving your life?"

He clenched his teeth hard enough to make the bones in his jaw protrude. "We were hunting."

"Just the two of you?"

He nodded. "We ended up in a fight. Coyote wanted to head to the south where I knew boar made dens.

200

Since we didn't have the right equipment with us to hunt them, I wanted to head east for other game. He wouldn't listen and stormed off without me. Angry, I went east, but I kept having a bad feeling about Coyote so I doubled back. All of a sudden, I heard him yelling for me. By the time I reached him, a wild boar had him treed. I killed the boar, but almost lost my life doing it. By the time I came to, I was in my bed at home and everyone was celebrating Coyote for saving my life."

That irritated her. "Did he not tell your father the truth?"

"He tried, but my father thought he was being humble and didn't believe it."

Kateri narrowed her gaze on the ground as she saw a different play of events in her mind.

Coyote ran toward their town to get help for Ren. Luckily not too far from where he'd left Ren, he came upon two men who were also out hunting. She knew one to be Buffalo. The other she'd seen a few times in other dreams, but he never spoke.

"Choo Co La Tah, Buffalo . . . I need your help."

"Did you kill your brother?" Buffalo accused as he saw the blood on Coyote's clothes.

"No!" Coyote snapped. "We were hunting when Makah'Alay was attacked by a boar. I managed to kill it, but he's badly wounded. I need help carrying him—"

Buffalo grabbed him by the arm and started running with him before he could finish his sentence. "Show us!"

Coyote took them to where Ren lay beside the boar that was riddled with arrows. The animal had torn him apart.

"Makah'Alay?" Buffalo breathed, reaching to see if he was still alive.

Ren moaned low, but it was enough.

Buffalo picked him up and carried him. "You killed the boar?" he asked Coyote.

"Yes."

"Then why do you have a quiver full of arrows and Makah'Alay has none?"

Coyote curled his lip and gestured to the injury on his own leg. "I was injured, too!"

Buffalo rolled his eyes. "From what? Climbing up a tree like a scared little bitch? You think we're so stupid we don't know the difference between the gash from a boar's tusk and skinning your knee on tree bark?"

Coyote turned to the other man with them, who had retrieved Ren's blood-soaked bow and quiver. "Choo, you believe me, don't you?"

Choo Co La Tah sent a pointed stare at Buffalo. "A wise man does not question his future chief."

Buffalo snorted. "Between wisdom and loyalty, Choo, I pick loyalty and truth. One day, brother, you're going to have to choose too. I hope when that day comes that you're even wiser than you are today."

Coyote snarled at them both. "You may not believe me, but my father will."

"I'm sure he will," Buffalo muttered.

Kateri shook her head. Yeah, for all of Ren's denials, Coyote wasn't the one who had stood by him in her visions.

Only one man had never wavered with his loyalty.

"Your friend, Buffalo . . . why was he always so quick to defend you?"

"He was a fool."

She laughed at his deadpan tone. "I doubt that. Tell me, Ren. What did you do to make him see the truth?"

Crossing his arms over his chest, Ren let out a long breath before he spoke. "When I was fourteen, a bad epidemic ravaged in our town. It was one of the worst you can imagine. The priests couldn't keep up with the number of deaths, and many of them were too sick to help anyone else, so bodies were piled in the street. People were starving and everyone was scared of catching it. Since I was one of the few who wasn't ill, I'd go hunt and leave fresh meat for those who couldn't feed themselves. One night, as I was leaving some for Buffalo's family, he caught me before I could get away."

Kateri was baffled by his charity, especially given how young he was and how badly they'd treated him. "Why did you help them?"

He shrugged. "I felt guilty. I never had a cold of any kind. Not even a sniffle. I don't know if it's because my mother was a goddess or my nursemaid a demon, but I was always healthy. For weeks, my father and the priests had been sacrificing to no avail, and they blamed me for bringing the sickness to the town. I didn't want the innocent punished because of me so I tried to help as best I could by leaving foodstuffs for the homes that were stricken the worst." He laughed bitterly. "Everyone thought it was Coyote who helped them. They regaled him for his charity for years afterward."

"You never told them the truth?"

Snorting, he shook his head. "No one would have believed me so I kept silent. The last thing I wanted was for my father to beat me for lying about it. When Buffalo finally recovered from the fever, he came to thank me. I told him to forget what he'd seen. Not to tell anyone what I'd done. He swore to me that he was forever in my debt, and that so long as he lived, he would be the most loyal friend ever known."

Now that sounded like the man she'd seen. "And he never told another soul?"

Ren sighed in disgust. "Stupid fool. He never listened to me about anything. He only saw the best in everyone. And he was a firm believer in the old adage that the truth was always the best course of action to take. So, he tried to tell the town who really left the food while they were ill."

"And?" she prompted when he failed to continue the story.

"His father beat him for lying."

She gaped at that. She'd ask if he was serious, but she could tell by the angry look in his eyes that he wasn't making it up. "Why didn't Coyote tell them you were the one who did it? He had to know he hadn't done anything."

"He said if they knew it had been left by me, they wouldn't have eaten it. They would have assumed it tainted. And I knew he was right. They would have, and rather than eat what I left, they'd have starved themselves to death."

Indignant rage for him darkened her sight. She really wanted to beat someone over it. "Your brother was *not* a good man, Ren. Had he been, he would have told your father the truth."

Still, he defended his brother's actions. "You can't tell the truth to someone who doesn't want to hear it, Kateri. Every time Coyote tried, my father thought he was being kind to me, and humble, so all it did was elevate Coyote in his eyes while it lowered me. Coyote always apologized and felt badly for it, but there was nothing he could do. I never held any of it against him until Butterfly. She became the symbol for every slight I'd been given by every person, and it was her presence in our home that made me realize I would never have a life like other men. That no one would ever welcome me as a husband. That I was only a charity case to be pitied at best, ridiculed at worst. Her presence rammed home just how much of nothing I really was in the eyes of everyone."

"You weren't nothing."

"Don't patronize me, Kateri," he growled. "You weren't there. You may have had visions about things that happened, but you didn't really see it. You definitely didn't live it. There's no worse feeling than being trapped in a situation from which you can't escape. In retrospect, I should have found the courage to walk away from all of them, but I was too afraid. I kept thinking that if this was how the people who were supposed to love me treated me, how much worse would a stranger be? Not to mention that those not related to me were every bit as cruel, if not more so. So even if I'd left, it would have been the same wherever I went. I'd be alone and outcast." His gaze cold, he dropped his voice an octave. "And I've since had eleven thousand years of moving from place to place to know just how right I was. Nothing ever changes except hairstyles and clothing."

She wanted to deny it, but she knew in her heart that he was right. People could be unbelievably cruel, and in spite of what he thought, she wasn't naive. She'd had her own share of insensitive comments over the years.

Still, there was much he wasn't telling her. "So what did you do when they married?"

He shrugged. "They didn't marry. She fell in love with Buffalo the moment he spoke up for me on the day of her arrival."

"Oh . . ." She cringed internally over something she hoped hadn't been blamed on him. "I take it that didn't go over well."

"No. It did not." Ren brushed his hand through his hair. "I destroyed all their lives. But for me, Coyote would have married her and they would have had a good life together."

She didn't believe it. "Had you not saved him, your father wouldn't have arranged the marriage. Butterfly would have married someone else anyway." She moved to lay her hand on his cheek. "They were responsible for their own lives, Ren. And all but Buffalo were cruel to you. You were in pain and none of them cared."

He started away from her, but she caught him again.

"You can trust me, Ren. You can. I would never take advantage of your heart."

Ren wanted to believe that, but as he'd said, nothing ever changed. He never changed. "I was born broken, Kateri. I'm not like other men. I can't have what they have."

"You're wrong. But I won't push you." She rose up on her tiptoes to place a chaste kiss on his cheek. Then, she whispered in his ear. "And for the record, I think you're the sexiest man I've ever seen."

Those words meant everything to him. Everything. *This is just more torture for you.*

It was true. Her presence. Her kindness. How cruel to have her here, knowing there was nothing he could do to keep her.

And he was tired of being kicked.

"We have to leave. We've been lucky that nothing has found us."

She nodded. "What do you need me to do?"

Stay with me. He wasn't sure where that thought came from or why it was there. It'd popped into his head before he could stop it.

"Just stay focused. I think I've healed enough that I should be able to get us out."

Kateri inclined her head to him. "All right. Fingers crossed."

Cabeza barely made it to Talon's before the sky unleashed a furious blood-red downpour. Thunder clapped so hard it shook the house, while lightning flashed again and again.

"You all right?" Talon asked as Cabeza took body inventory to make sure he hadn't been singed by anything. Or that Chacu hadn't ripped something off while he wasn't paying attention.

"*Si.* Yeah." Cabeza turned to find Talon's wife Sunshine on the black leather couch next to Acheron Parthenopaeus, who was holding her infant son. He did a double take on Ash's short black hair as a sick feeling went through him. *"Madre de Dios* . . . it is a sign of the Apocalypse. What happened to your hair? Did someone scalp you?"

Never in all these centuries had he seen Acheron with

short hair. No matter the fashion or time period, it'd always been down to the middle of his back.

Always.

"Relax," Ash said with a hint of laughter in his voice. "Tory and I donated our hair to Locks of Love on Bastian's first birthday to show our appreciation for having a healthy baby. It'll grow back."

Grow back?

Maybe, but this . . . this had evil written all over it.

"Hey," Sunshine said to Cabeza with a wide grin. "You should have seen it six months ago. It started out as a crew cut."

Bug-eyed, Cabeza was momentarily speechless as he tried to imagine the intrepid Dark-Hunter leader with a crew cut. "Out of all the shit I've seen in the last two days, that is the only thing that truly frightens me. I think we just sped up the final countdown."

Rolling his eyes at him, Acheron handed the baby back to its mother, then stood. His long, black leather coat settled down around his dark red Doc Martens. Though Acheron was the oldest of the Dark-Hunters by years, he physically was their youngest. He'd only been twenty-one when he'd died. And honestly, he looked more like a teenager until you saw his eyes. Only they betrayed his ancient age. . . .

And his wisdom.

Rain came out from the rear of the house. He still had a black eye from where Cabeza had rescued him in Las Vegas. "Any word on Teri?" he asked Cabeza.

"It's worse than we thought. They are in Xibalba."

Acheron cursed. "No wonder I couldn't find them

with my powers." He glanced over to Rain to explain. "I can't see into another pantheon's hell realm without going to it physically."

Talon let out a nervous laugh. "I try to avoid descending into hell realms as much as possible."

Ash scratched at the back of his neck as if that comment made him uncomfortable for some reason. "Out of curiosity, do you know what level they're in?"

"As far as I can tell, the first."

Ash let out a relieved breath. "You think Ren knows better than to descend past the fourth level?"

Cabeza thought it over. Ash was right, if Ren and the Ixkib descended below the water level, there was no coming back. They would be in Xibalba forever. "Since it's Mayan, I wouldn't count on it. He might not even know where he is."

"Well," Talon said, "we can look on the bright side."

This, Cabeza had to hear. "And that would be?"

"No one can reach the time stone, right?"

Cabeza inclined his head to him. "True. But there is a problem."

"And that would be?" Talon explained.

"If she doesn't make it to the temple by week's end, the Daimons won't be our worst fear, *amigo*. Imagine every known piece of evil from all pantheons unleashed simultaneously on this earth. Every demon and predator that has been put down by priests and shamans for centuries . . ."

Ash went completely still at those words.

"Is something wrong?" Talon asked.

Ash didn't respond. Rather, he vanished from the room

where they had gathered, and took himself to his own realm. Katateros. It was the Atlantean heaven realm where their gods had once ruled their island kingdom and made war against the Greek pantheon.

It was here that Ash's mother, Apollymi, had destroyed her family over what they'd done to Acheron when she'd been forced to hide him in the human realm.

Using his god powers, he threw open the ornate doors at the main hall and walked across the foyer where the symbol of their power lay. The moment he did, his jeans and T-shirt turned into the ancient robes of his people and his own symbol of a sun pierced by three lightning bolts appeared on the back of it.

"Alexion!" he called as he entered the throne room.

His friend and servant appeared instantly. Barely three inches shorter than Acheron, Alexion had once been an ancient Greek soldier and was one of the first Dark-Hunters Artemis had created.

He was also the first Dark-Hunter who'd died without his soul. To save him from suffering over Acheron's mistake, Acheron had pulled him into Katateros, where Alexion existed in a noncorporeal form. While not ideal, it wasn't nearly as bad as the alternative.

His blond hair tousled, Alexion was still buttoning his shirt. "What's wrong, akri? You never bellow like that. Simi eat someone she shouldn't?"

Ash ran his hand over the dragon tattoo on his forearm that was Simi in her dormant state. She was his Charonte demon and his personal bodyguard.

But more than that, she was his daughter, and he would do anything to protect her from harm.

"No, she's fine. It was you I was worried about. Has anything happened?"

"In terms of what?"

Ash didn't want to scare him, but at the same time he couldn't take a chance on not warning his steward what might happen in the coming days.

"The gods might awaken."

Alexion froze for a full minute. Then he blinked. "You mean the creepy statuary in the basement is going to start moving around?"

"If they don't reset the calendar, yeah." That's exactly what's going to happen. And when they do, they're going to be pissed.

"Well, that sucks." Alexion sighed. "They're not friendly to us, are they?"

Ash shook his head. "They have one hell of a grudge against me and my mother. You, they *might* spare."

Alexion laughed nervously. "I'm Greek and they hate us so I'm going to take that as a major nugatory. They spent a lot of time trying to kill us. So how do we stop this?"

"We have to retrieve the son of Sterope from the Mayan hell realm, along with Sunshine's cousin."

Feigning laugher, Alexion slapped at his thigh. "You're hilarious, boss. You ought to do stand-up. Stop, stop, you're killing me."

Ash pressed his fingers to his forehead. Though he couldn't get headaches, right now, he swore he had a migraine. "Times like this, I wish you were corporeal so I could give you a head slap."

Alexion sobered. "In all seriousness, can you go there?"

211

"Yes and no. I *can*, but I don't know what my presence in that realm might unleash. The Mayan gods have been dormant like ours. But I don't know if that means they're asleep or on lockdown like my mother. If they're on lockdown ..."

"A foreign god in their domain is an ugly thing."

"Exactly."

"So who would know the answer?"

Ash considered it. "The Chthonian in charge of them is dead. Thank you, Savitar, for that PMS."

"Ah ... So what Chthonian is in charge of South America, and are they friendly?"

"Ecanus, and he's not on our side. He's very much like Savitar and has withdrawn from the world to let things run their course. Since most of their gods aren't active, neither is he. So long as the other Chthonians stay out of his territory, he doesn't come down out of his mountain home."

"Ah ... So who do we know who can go fetch our boy?"

"I can go."

They turned to see Urian standing in the doorway. Tall, and lethal, he had long white-blond hair that he wore in a ponytail.

Ash sucked his breath in sharply. "You're the son of a god, too."

"Half-god, and I'm dead and soulless. I have no allegiance to any pantheon." Urian screwed his face up. "Except yours, of course, but no one gives a shit about the Atlanteans, no offense."

No offense ... why did people always use those two

212

words whenever they knew they were being offensive, as if it excused their behavior?

Alexion laughed before he spoke to Acheron. "And here I thought I went out of my way to annoy you." He laughed again. "Dang, Urian, you make it look so effortless."

Urian flipped him off.

Ash ignored the two men, who argued like brothers most of the time. "You really want to go do this?" he asked Urian. "Last time I checked, you were all about killing humanity, not protecting them."

Urian shrugged. "My father readjusted my attitude. And you're going to need someone who can draw on major source powers to get them out of there. Someone who's used to going in and out of hell realms."

Urian was definitely the expert in that. His father was the leader of the vampiric Daimons the Dark-Hunters had been created to fight against. For centuries, Urian had been his right hand, until Stryker had killed Urian's wife because Urian had lied to his father to protect her.

And if that wasn't cold-blooded enough, then Stryker had left Urian for dead. If not for Ash, Urian wouldn't be here now.

But more than that, Urian was the grandson of Apollo—the Greek god of the sun and plagues. It might not be a bad thought to send him in, since there was no telling what kind of pestilence might be all over Ren. If anyone could curb it, Urian would be he.

"All right, but you'll need someone to help track them down."

"I'll call Sasha. Worst-case scenario, like me, he has no

one to mourn him should he die valiantly from this rampant stupidity."

Ash narrowed his gaze on one of the very few people he trusted and one of only a handful he considered family. "That's not true and you know it."

"I'm not talking about friendship, Acheron. We die, all of you would get over it. It's not the same as losing your spouse or a child. As I said, we have no one to mourn us."

Ash winced for the pain he knew Urian lived with every day. The man had watched, one by one, as all of his siblings and his mother had died or been killed. He'd lost two adopted children and countless friends. But more than that, Urian had lost his most cherished Phoebe.

His heart aching for the man, Ash spun his wedding ring around on his finger with his thumb. While he'd known how much Phoebe's loss had crippled Urian, he now, because of his wife Tory, had a new perspective on it that horrified him. The mere thought of losing his wife tore a hole so deep inside him that he was amazed Urian could function at all.

And he couldn't even think about losing his son without wanting to kill everyone around him. For the first time in his eleven thousand years of life, he fully understood his mother's rage where he was concerned. If anything ever happened to his family, he would make his mother's anger look like a gentle summer breeze.

Every day Urian got up and managed to make it through without going ape-shit on the world was a victory for him. Ash had never known anyone stronger, and he respected the man immensely.

"I want you two to be careful and take Cabeza with

you. You'll need someone who knows the pantheon and who can speak and read their language."

Urian scoffed. "I read and speak Greek, Acheron. Tell me what on earth is harder than that?"

"Olmec and Mayan. You ever tried either?"

"That would be . . . no. Never had a reason to. Besides, I thought they were space aliens."

Alexion snorted. "He's been watching a lot of History Channel lately."

Urian curled his lip. "Have to do something to drown out you and your wife. Wish you two would soundproof your room. Although I have yet to figure out how two noncorporeal beings could . . . never mind. I do not want to go there."

"And on that note, I'm heading back to the realm of humanity to help combat what's already being unleashed against them."

"Are you sending Tory and Bas here for protection?" Alexion asked.

Ash shook his head. "I sent them to my mother when all of this started. Should we fail, I figure that's the safest place. At least I know how far she'll go to protect them."

"True enough. All right, I'll go watch the statues and let you know if one of them twitches."

"Please do so."

Urian inclined his head to Acheron. "And I'm off to rendezvous with Sasha and Cabeza."

Ash didn't move as the two of them vanished to attend to their duties. He ran his hand over his Simi tattoo and considered sending her to his mother as well. But he knew better. Simi would never leave him alone to battle what was coming for them, and that bothered him most. No matter how hard he tried, he could never let himself forget that he was the sole reason Simi had no mother— that Simi had been an orphan before he adopted her. Her mother had died trying to keep Apollo from gutting him. The poor Charonte had failed, but at least she'd tried.

Every time he looked at Simi, he saw her mother's face and guilt stabbed him hard. It was why he couldn't deprive her of anything, except for the killing of other creatures. That was the only thing he forbade her to do. Unless they threatened her first, and then it was open season on them and Simi could grab BBQ sauce and have at them. No holds barred.

Closing his eyes, he tried to see the future, which for him shouldn't be a problem. But because it involved so many people he cared about, he saw nothing at all.

The one thing he could feel was the heartbeat of the world that thrummed like a solid hum under his feet. It vibrated through him as the constellations aligned and the gateways were weakened.

Evil was coming and it wasn't going to take prisoners.

Let the war begin. . . .

Chapter 11

Ren cursed under his breath. Never in his life had he felt more worthless—which basically said it all about their situation and his inability to get them out of this realm. "I'm sorry, Kateri."

"Hey ..." She pulled him to a stop as they walked through an endless forest. "You don't need to keep apologizing for something you can't help. We'll make it out. We will."

"How can you have such faith?"

"Oh c'mon, you defeated death and came back to life. You have to have faith, too. I know you do."

The edges of his lips twitched at her words. Amazed by her ability to find amusement and to make light of an extremely bad situation, he stared into beautiful eyes that seared him.

Step away from her. Now!

For once, he didn't listen. Before he could stop himself, he kissed her. The scent of her skin and the taste of her mouth sent his body into overdrive. Everything around them was going wrong. Everything. His primary powers weren't working. They had demons after them. The First Guardian was missing. Choo was captured. . . .

And she felt like heaven in the midst of hell. It didn't make sense. He should be hating himself for his incompetence, but when he looked at her, he didn't see disdain or contempt. He saw friendship. Kindness. Encouragement.

Worst of all, the same desire he had for her.

Instead of making him feel like he was lacking for getting them into this, she smiled and retorted with jokes that lightened his spirit. She didn't call him stupid or worthless. Or accuse him of condemning her to this.

She made him feel like the man he'd always wanted to be. Like maybe, just maybe, he had some degree of value and sense. That he was worth being lost with.

Pulling back, he buried his face in the crook of her neck so that he could smell the faint remnants of her perfume. Valerian had always been one of his favorite scents, and on her . . .

His mouth watered.

Kateri held Ren close as she felt his heart pounding against her breasts. It'd been so long since she was close to a man. Not eleven thousand years by any means, but quite a few months. The one thing she and Fernando had shared was their philosophy that work came first, no matter what. That there were many discoveries yet to be made and papers to be written. Lectures to be given and kids to be encouraged. She'd never found a man who could respect that. One who would share her with her work schedule.

You're a geologist. What the hell do you have to work on at night and on weekends?

Research papers and class prep waited for no one, and writing took up a great deal of her time. For reasons she didn't understand, she seemed to get caught in strange time warps. She'd sit down and start working on a paper, then the next thing she knew, it would be five hours later and her phone would be buzzing or ringing with either a text or call about why she wasn't at home or wherever it was she was supposed to be. It was like the world stopped moving whenever she worked, and she would sit still for hours on end without getting up or sometimes even blinking.

But the simplest truth was that none of the men she'd dated had been worth her keeping up with the time to make sure she wasn't late meeting them. While they'd been fun to hang out with for a little while, they invariably started bitching about her schedule and weird beliefs and habits to the point she hit the door running to escape them. They were never her priority.

Ren was different.

His beliefs made hers seem normal. If she were to talk about raven mockers, instead of laughing or rolling his eyes, he most likely would be on a first-name basis with a few of them. And the moonstone he'd given her said that he understood her fascination with rocks and minerals. That he felt the power they held and knew what it meant to reach for one in the middle of a crisis. He got it.

Most of all, she found him fascinating. The things he

219

knew . . . the things he could do. She hadn't thought about work once while they'd been together.

Well, okay, granted they were running for their lives, but still . . .

He held her attention completely. For him, she would gladly put her research aside. To make him smile a real smile, she would be late to class. How sick was that?

She barely knew him and yet . . . she'd been with him for years. "Did you ever see visions of me?"

He pulled back to stare down at her. Cupping her jaw in his large hand, he teased her chin with his thumb. At first, she didn't think he'd answer. But after a brief pause, he gave a subtle nod.

"What did you see?"

Ren's first thought went to the images of her killing him. Now at least he understood why he never fought her for his life. But those weren't the only dreams of her he'd had. "I've seen you in a yellow dress with hummingbirds on it and a matching yellow sweater. You were a young teenager and had yellow ribbons in your hair. You were happy about something and you threw your arms around an older man."

A winsome smile curled her lips, reminding him of how she'd looked in his mind. "My sixteenth birthday. My grandmother made that dress for me. I hated it, but I didn't want to hurt her feelings so I wore it."

"And the man?"

"My stepfather. He adopted me right before my mother died. It's why my last name is Avani. He was from New Delhi and used to joke all the time about which of us was more Indian."

"What happened to him?"

"He died of cancer while I was in college."

"I'm so sorry."

She swallowed against the grief that choked her. She'd loved him so ... Every day, she missed him terribly. "Thank you. He was a good man. He married my mom when I was four and you'd have never known he wasn't my biological father."

"You were at a dance with him when you were older. You wore a short blue skirt and white blouse."

She nodded. "It was a father–daughter charity dance that was sponsored by his office."

He frowned at her. "Why did you burst out crying during one of the dances? Did he hurt your feelings?"

"Oh God no. He'd just been diagnosed with cancer and they started playing the Bob Carlisle song, 'Butterfly Kisses.'"

"I don't know it."

"It's a song about a woman and her father and—" She broke off into a sob.

"Sh," he said, pulling her back into his arms. "I'm so sorry, Kateri. I didn't mean to make you cry."

"No, it's okay." She sniffed back her tears. "I wish you'd known a father like him, Ren. He was so good to me. There's not a day that goes by that I don't feel his loss as much as I do my mother's and my grandmother's. I was so lucky to have him. And he loved my mother more than you can imagine. To the day he died, he had their wedding photo on his desk, and his one request for his funeral was that I place a photo of her on his heart and lay his hands over it. I remember asking him once, years after her death, why he never dated anyone. He told me that he'd found his one perfect soul mate and that there was no reason in trying to find another. No woman would ever mean as much to him as my mother had and that he didn't have room in his heart or life for anyone else. Keeping up with me was a full-time job and it was the only job he really wanted."

Ren had no way of relating to the love she described. But it sounded incredible. "I'm glad he was good to you."

Kateri burst into deep, wrenching sobs.

What did I do? Ren pulled back and cupped her face in both of his hands. Never had he felt so lost. He hadn't meant to hurt her with his comment. Stupidly, he'd thought to make her feel better. He'd spent so little time around women that he had no idea how to help her. Did all women do this?

Was it normal? Or had he broken her with his ignorance?

And still she sobbed as if something inside her had snapped. What could he say? After what just happened, he was terrified to even try.

"Don't look at me," she wailed.

He released her and started to turn away.

She grabbed him and threw herself into his arms. He stood there, stunned. Okay. She wanted him to hold her, yet not look at her. Weird, but okay.

Dammit, Sundown, where are you when I need advice? Surely, his married friend would have a clue.

Maybe . . .

Ren searched his mind for something he could do to soothe her. The only thing he could remember was seeing

222

mothers with crying children. They would hold and rock them.

Scooping her up in his arms, he carried her to a small clearing and sat down to hold her in his lap. He brushed the hair back from her face while she sobbed against his chest and clung to him. Wow, all this over what he thought was an innocuous comment meant to cheer her up. *You will never understand people.*

That was definitely true. They'd never made sense to him in any way.

So he held her against him and rocked her gently, hoping they didn't get attacked until she had time to finish.

Kateri hated that she'd fallen apart like this. It was what she hated most about grieving. Most days, she was fine. But every now and again, a sight or smell would ambush her, or she'd hear a song, see something that evoked a buried memory, and it would hit her all over again just how much she missed them. How much she wanted them back and how much she hated that she'd never see them again. It wasn't fair. Other people got to keep their parents most of their lives. But not her. Until last night, she'd never even met her biological father.

And as bad as that was, she couldn't imagine the pain of not having them at all. It made her wonder what was worse. Not knowing what you were missing or knowing exactly how it felt to be loved and cared for and then having it ripped brutally away from you.

She covered her eyes with her hand and groaned at what a basket case she must look like to poor Ren. "I am so sorry, sweetie. It's just been a horrendous last few days.

I'm tired. I'm scared, and I lost a really good friend right before all of this happened."

Ren didn't respond. He just kept rocking her.

Frowning, she wiped at her eyes and looked up at him. "Are you all right?"

He nodded, then brushed away more of her tears.

"Then why aren't you speaking to me?"

Panic flashed across his features. He glanced away as if trying to think of a response.

"Ren? Talk to me."

His lips twitched before he finally spoke in a low tone. "I don't want to say the wrong thing again and make you cry more."

The pure innocent sweetness of that wrenched another sob from her.

"Ah, see now what I did. I'm sorry, Kateri. I won't say anything else. I promise."

She laid her head down on his shoulder and wrapped her arms around his neck. "It's so not you, baby. You did nothing, absolutely nothing wrong." She squeezed him tight, wishing she could make him understand. "All you've been is wonderful. . . ."

Ren knew she was speaking, but he couldn't make out the words. Not after she'd called him baby and sweetie. No one had ever used an endearment for him before. Until now, the closest anyone had come was to call him friend or brother.

But baby . . .

He'd never been anyone's baby.

"Are you listening to me?"

You should probably say yes. That would be the smartest

224

thing to do. But for some stupid reason the truth came out before he could stop it. "Um . . . no."

"Why are you tuning me out?" she snapped as fury lit up her eyes.

Ren moved his jaw, trying to explain, but no words would leave his lips as he stammered over the word *I*. *Why do I always do this shit when I least want to look like an idiot?*

He expected her to be angry. Instead, she kissed him senseless. Every part of him went into overdrive as his cock hardened.

She pulled back. "What were you trying to say?"

Heat scalded his face. "I didn't hear anything after you called me baby."

Kateri laid her hand over his cheek at the anguish she saw on his face. Her heart lurched. Given what she'd seen of his life, she was willing to bet it was the first time anyone had ever used an endearment for him. While most people grew up being called "sugar" and "darling" by others, he never had, and he'd secluded himself to the point that he most likely hadn't even been called that by a waitress, let alone someone who actually cared about him.

"I know that place deep down inside where it feels like no one cares. No one sees you. No one knows you. But I see you, Ren, and I do care. I know exactly how it feels to be alone in this world." She laughed bitterly as she remembered something Fernando had said to her about one of the most influential innovators in the field of archaeology and anthropology. "Margaret Mead once said that one of the oldest human needs is having someone to wonder when you are coming home at night."

She smiled at him. "There's nothing lonelier than an empty house when you're going to bed. I've lost everyone I've ever loved and I'm scared as hell at the thought of letting you or anyone else into my heart to hurt me like that again. Because every time I lose one of them, a part of me goes to the grave with them and I'm not sure how much of me is left anymore. But I'm willing to take that leap again . . . *for you*."

Ren swallowed as he understood what had motivated her to burst into tears. No one had ever said anything kinder to him. Her words touched a place inside him he hadn't known existed. A part of him that had never been touched before.

"I could never hurt you, sweetie," she breathed.

In that single moment, he was completely lost to her. *I'm such an effing idiot.* He hadn't even gotten laid first, this time, and he had no business letting her get close to him, yet somehow she was already there. He had no idea how it'd happened, but he'd basically been a goner the first moment she smiled at him.

"Are you going to say anything?"

Ren didn't trust his voice. So instead, he kissed her slowly and tenderly, savoring every stroke of her tongue against his. Breathless, he laid her back against the ground and covered her with his body. Stars blinded him as an unbelievable pleasure tore through him.

Kateri smiled as Ren left her lips to trail hot kisses down her neck. Had she not understood why he didn't speak, she'd be offended. But that wasn't his way. He was a man of very few words. He spoke through his actions, not with his voice. In a way, she preferred it. There was no way to misinterpret his tenderness.

226

He slowly unbuttoned her shirt, then ran his hand over her breasts. Arching her back, she moaned at how good he felt. The hunger in his eyes was searing as he struggled with her bra.

She smiled at his confusion. "It snaps in the front."

He still had no clue.

"I guess they didn't have these back in the day, eh?"

"No. It's like a puzzle box."

Laughing, she took his hands and showed him how to undo it.

Ren sucked his breath in sharply at the sight of her bare breasts. He'd assumed some of their size was from padding, but that was definitely not true, and while he didn't have a lot of experience in this department, he knew she was well endowed. "You're so beautiful."

She took his hand into hers and led it to her mouth so that she could kiss, then nip his knuckle. A shiver went over him. She returned his hand to her breast before pulling his head down to hers to nibble his lips. If he could, he'd die right now in this perfect moment of sensory overload.

Kateri felt the muscles in his jaw tighten as he clenched his teeth. Damn, he was the sexiest man she'd ever been near. The raw strength and power. The adorable vulnerable innocence that shouldn't exist inside someone like him. It combined into the most irresistible package imaginable.

Wanting to please him, she pulled his shirt off, over his head, then rolled him onto his back. She paused as she saw the scars and injuries that riddled his body. But the scar that wrung her heart was in the center of his chest. Jagged and raw, it was bigger than her fist.

Her hand shaking, she placed it over his heart to finger that scar. The moment she did, a brutal vision came to her with a clarity so clear, it stunned her. . . . Ren and Coyote were in a grand dining hall where they were fighting over the corpse of a man who'd been beaten so badly that she couldn't tell who it was.

His entire body coated in blood, Coyote sneered at Ren, who gaped in horror at what his brother had done. "This is all *your* fault," Coyote sneered. "You and your petty jealousy. Why couldn't you have been happy for me? Just once in your miserable life. Why? Had you left us alone, none of this would have happened. There would have been no Grizzly Spirit. No need for Guardians and he"—Coyote gestured to the floor with a knife—"would never have come here to claim her."

Ren didn't respond. His gaze was fastened to the red on Coyote's hands. It went from there to the floor where . . .

Buffalo lay dead in a pool of blood. She only knew the man's identity because Ren knew.

He winced as unmitigated grief tore through him. "How could you do this? He was a Guardian." *And my best friend in the world.* The one and only person who'd stood by him without question.

Even when evil had claimed possession of his body and he'd served it willingly, Buffalo had stayed with him. Protecting him.

Now he lay slain by Ren's own brother.

My cruelty drove him mad. . . .

His brother had been pure and decent until Ren had tortured him. *It's all my fault. All of it.*

228

Coyote spit on Buffalo's body. "He was a bastard and he stole her heart from me."

Ren shook his head slowly as guilt and sorrow ripped him apart. "Hearts can never be stolen. They can only be given."

Coyote sneered at him. "You're wrong! That's your jealousy speaking."

But it wasn't. Ren had learned to banish that. He no longer felt anything except guilt and remorse.

Now it was too late. He'd destroyed everything that was good in his life.

Everything.

Sick to his stomach, he went to Buffalo and knelt beside him to whisper a small prayer over his body.

A shrill scream echoed through the room.

Looking up, Ren saw Butterfly as she ran to her Buffalo. She sobbed hysterically, throwing herself down on top of him. She paid no attention whatsoever as his blood soaked into her clothes and left her covered in it.

Her features twisted by rage and accusatory grief, she glared at Coyote. "Why? Why? Why would you hurt me so?"

Coyote curled his lip. "You tore my heart out."

"And you killed mine." She laid herself over Buffalo and wept with shrill screams that raised the hair on Kateri's arms.

Ren stood up and left her there to grieve while he confronted his brother.

That was his mistake. He didn't think about what would happen if Butterfly was allowed to cry her misery out to the gods and spirits. To wail and shriek for her lost Buffalo.

But it was too late now. The doors of the room blew open. A howling wind came screaming through, dancing around their white-buckskin-covered bodies. Those winds joined together to form two trumpeters who blew their horns to announce the most feared creature of all.

The Avenging Spirit. Something that could only be summoned by the cries of a wronged woman who wanted vengeance against the ones who'd hurt her.

Nebulous in form, he was bathed all in white. His hair, the translucent skin that covered his skeletal features. His feathers and buckskin. The only break from the color was the dark blue beadwork along his neckline.

"Why was I called forth?" he demanded.

Butterfly looked up. Her beautiful face contorted by grief, she appeared old and haggard now. Her hair blew around her body as she leveled a furious stare at them.

She pointed her finger at Ren's brother. "The Coyote killed my heart. So I want his as payment for what he unjustly took."

The Avenging Spirit bowed to her. Then he turned toward the men. His face changed from that of an old gaunt man with stringy hair to the face of ultimate evil. He opened his mouth and it dropped to the floor, contorting and elongating his features. The sight left Kateri horrified. Forget Hollywood, this was scarier than anything ever conceived by Wes Craven. . . .

Out of his mouth flew a giant eagle with a lone ghostly warrior on its back. The warrior lifted his spear.

Ren stepped back, away from Coyote, and braced himself to fight.

With a discordant cry of vengeance that shook the

very fabric of Mother Earth's gown, the warrior let fly his spear at Coyote's heart.

One moment Ren was standing out of the way. In the next, he was across the room where Coyote had been a heartbeat earlier, and Coyote was in his place. Before he could gather his wits and move, the spear flew through the center of his chest, piercing his heart. The force of it lifted him off his feet and pinned him to the wall.

Pain exploded through his body as he gasped for breath. The taste of blood filled his mouth. His eyesight dimmed. He was dying. After all the battles, all the fights . . .

He would die by treacherous trickery.

By his brother's viciousness.

The warrior turned his eagle around and flew back into the Avenging Spirit's mouth. As quickly as they'd come, they were gone.

His breathing labored, Ren stared at his brother. "I would have given you my life had you asked for it."

"You taught me to take what I wanted." Coyote crossed the room and snatched the bone necklace from Ren's throat that held his Guardian seal—a turquoise thunderbird. He untied the pouch from Ren's belt where he kept his strongest magic and stones. "And I want your Guardianship."

Blood trickled from the corner of Ren's lips. In all his life, the Guardianship had been the only thing good that Ren had been chosen for. The only thing that had ever given him an ounce of pride, and made him feel worth something more than disdain and contempt. "You weren't chosen."

"And neither were you. Not really. The Guardian gave

it to you out of pity." Coyote raked a sneer over him, and clenched Ren's necklace tightly in his fist. "You were never worthy of this." He seized the spear and drove it in even deeper, then laughed in triumph as Ren choked on his own blood.

With one last agony-filled gasp, Ren fell silent.

The pride on Coyote's face was sickening as he turned his attention to Butterfly. "I'm a Guardian now. You can love me again."

She curled her lip in repugnance. "I could never love you after what you've done. You're a monster."

He snatched her up by her arm. "You are mine and I will *never* share you. Make yourself ready for our wedding."

"Never."

He slapped her across the face. "You do not argue with me, woman. You obey." He let go of her so fast that she fell back across Buffalo's body, where she wept until she had no more tears.

She was still there when the maidens came and dressed her for Coyote.

At sundown, he returned for her. But before they could begin the ceremony that would join them together, the First Guardian . . . Kateri's father . . . appeared in the middle of the room. His dark eyes radiated fury as he glared his hatred at them both.

"I am here to claim the life of the one responsible for killing two Guardians."

Coyote gasped in terror. His mind whirled as he tried to think of some trick that could save his life. And while his brother's magic was powerful and had allowed Ren to battle the Guardian for a year and a day, it wasn't *his* magic. And it wouldn't be enough for him to save his own life.

Her father crossed the room in a determined stride that promised retribution. From his belt, he drew the sacred Dagger of Justice, and without hesitating, plunged it straight into the heart of the one who'd caused such turmoil and misery.

Butterfly staggered back as blood saturated her dress and ran across her braids. Instead of showing pain, she sighed in relief. Blood ran from her lips as she turned to Coyote. "I will be with my love now. Forever in his arms." She sank to the floor, where she died with the most blissful of smiles on her face.

His features contorted by his confusion, Coyote shook his head. "I don't understand."

Her father shrugged. "You were the tool who killed Buffalo. But Butterfly was the cause. Had she not been born, you wouldn't have taken the Guardian's life. She is the one responsible for his death, and for that of Makah'Alay."

"No, no, no, no. This isn't right. This wasn't how it was supposed to end." Raking his hands through his hair, Coyote went to his true love and cradled her in his arms one last time. She was so tiny and light. Her blood stained his wedding clothes and he wept at the loss of her.

And it was his loss.

She wouldn't be waiting for him on the other side. The pain of that knowledge tore him apart. She would greet that bastard Buffalo. A man who had caused him infinite grief and tried to alienate him from his father and from their people.

No . . . it wasn't right that bastard would have her. Not

after Coyote had endured torture and pain to come back to her and take her as his wife.

Damn you all!

Throwing his head back, he screamed in outrage. It wouldn't end like this. He'd been a good man. Obedient. All his life. And one by one, all of them had killed that.

First Makah'Alay, then Buffalo, and finally Butterfly.

They'd ruined his life and changed him forever. There was no way he would let them live a happy eternity together. Not after he'd assumed an immortal Guardianship that would leave him alone for eternity.

He reached into Ren's pouch and summoned the strongest demon elements there. "I curse you, Buffalo," he growled between clenched teeth. "You will live a thousand lives and never be happy in any of them. You will walk this earth, betrayed by all who look upon you. There will be no one place you call home. Not in any human lifetime. And you will never have my Butterfly." He blew his magic from his palm into the air so that it could be carried to the spirits who would make it so.

Then he looked down at the serene beauty of the Butterfly. So gentle. So sweet. The thought of cursing her stung him deep.

But she had scorned him. Betrayed him.

"Because of what you did to me, you will never marry the one you love. He will always die on his way to unite with you and you will spend your lifetimes mourning him over and over again. No peace in any of them. Not until you accept me in my true right. And if you do marry another, he will never trust you. You will never be happy in any marriage. Not so long as you have human blood within you." He reached into his pouch and drew the last of his brother's magic, then sent it into the wind.

"Do you know what you've done?"

Coyote looked up at Choo Co La Tah's approach. "I settled the score."

Choo Co La Tah laughed. "Such magic always comes back on the one who wields it. Whatever you cast for, you bring to shore."

"How so?"

He gestured out the window, toward the sky and the trees. "You know the law. Do no harm, and yet you have done much harm here today."

"They hurt me first."

Choo Co La Tah sighed. "And you have sown the seeds of your ultimate demise. When you curse two people together, you bind them. With that combined strength, they will have the ability to break their curse and kill *you*."

Coyote scoffed at him. "You don't know what you're talking about."

"Arrogance. The number one cause of death among both peasant and king. Beware its sharp blade. More times than not, it injures the one who wields it most of all."

Coyote dismissed Choo Co La Tah's words. He had no interest in them. He would never suffer more. He'd already paid his dues. It was time for him to get his just rewards.

And he would ensure that they did, too. For all time.

Kateri pulled back as she experienced Coyote's hatred firsthand. It was a malevolent beast all its own. She left it there in the past, and looked up at Ren while he held her.

"Am I doing something wrong?" Ren asked with a

furrowed brow. "I haven't hurt you, have I?" The concern in his tone warmed her.

How could anyone not treasure someone so sweet?

"No, honey. You definitely haven't done anything wrong. I just felt a jolt of hatred from your brother for you. It was so foul, it momentarily stunned me."

He started to speak, but she placed a finger on his lips to stop him. "Don't say it's your fault. You have suffered far more than he ever did. Yet you are still human. You never left that part of you behind."

"I wasn't always so."

"You were possessed. That's different."

Ren wasn't so sure about that. Yes, he'd allowed the Grizzly Spirit to take possession of his body, but he'd been aware even then what he was doing. And the Grizzly hadn't been inside him at the point he'd killed his father.

That, he'd done on his own.

He glanced down at the scar near his left hip where his father had almost gutted him. It had been a brutal fight. For all of his age, his father had still been an accomplished warrior. Ren was lucky he'd survived the fight.

It was also his self-awareness that had finally allowed him to break from the Grizzly and free himself. But that was a lot easier said than done. It'd taken weeks to get his life back.

And a mere heartbeat to lose that life again.

Kateri laid herself over him. He sucked his breath in sharply at the sensation of her naked breasts on his chest as she began to lave his jawline. All thoughts scattered. His body erupted as his head swam from sensations he'd all but forgotten.

Straddling him, she pressed the center of her body against his groin, making him even harder. *Please don't let me embarrass myself.* Afraid he wouldn't last long for her, he rolled her over so that he could peel her shoes and jeans from her.

His heart stopped beating as he saw her lying there, completely naked and inviting. She opened her legs for him and bent her knees, giving him a prime view of the part of her body he craved most. Her smile was warm as she reached for him.

He wanted to tell her how much that meant to him, but his mind couldn't formulate a single word past the thrumming heat in his blood.

Kateri arched a brow at Ren's hesitation. She saw the deep-seated need in his eyes. Still, he made no move to touch her. Rather, he licked her entire body with his hungry gaze.

Finally, he approached her like a feral predator on all fours. Crouching low, he slid his cheek against her calf in a tender caress that sent chills all over her. His gaze held hers captive as he reached to gently finger the part of her that was begging for his touch. He ran his thumb slowly down her cleft in a move that only made her want him more.

A slight smile curled his lips as he used his thumb to open her up for him, then he replaced his hand with his mouth.

Kateri cried out as pleasure singed her. Reaching down, she sank her hand into his thick hair while his tongue teased her mercilessly. For a man who hadn't had sex in eleven thousand years, he was doing a mighty fine job of it.

Ren closed his eyes as he savored the taste of her and let her cries wash over him. He took a lot of pride in the fact that she was enjoying his touch as much as he enjoyed pleasing her. The last thing he wanted was to be compared to her other lovers and be found lacking in any way.

He wanted her to be more than sated. Her hands played in his hair, stroking his scalp while she murmured endearments. And then, in one heartbeat, she tensed up and screamed out as she spasmed.

Amazed at how quickly she'd come for him, he waited until she was completely through before he undid his pants. When he went to remove them, she stopped him.

At first, he thought she'd changed her mind, until she rolled him over and pulled them free of his body.

Kateri took a moment to appreciate the sight of his tawny, naked body. Never in her life, other than on the cover of a bodybuilder's magazine, had she seen a man more ripped. Dang, he was fine. He could eat crackers, soup, anything he wanted ... what the hell, he could come to bed covered in sand and she wouldn't care.

She purred at him, causing him to arch a brow at the sound. Laughing, she slowly crawled up his body, stopping only long enough to lave and tease him.

Ren cried out at the sensation of her sliding her mouth over his cock. Windseer had never done that for him. His breathing labored, he knew he was forever lost to Kateri. For this kindness alone, there was nothing he wouldn't do for her. Nothing.

It's just sex.

Yeah, but she didn't have to have it with him. And the

care she took, it was almost enough that he could pretend she had real feelings where he was concerned. What he wouldn't give, just once, to make love to a woman who would cry over his body the way Butterfly had cried for Buffalo.

The way Abigail would cry for Sundown.

I sound like an old woman.

But as soon as he had that thought, he heard Kateri in his head—*one of the oldest human needs is having someone to wonder when you are coming home at night.* As much as he hated admitting it, she was right. While jealousy was the root of all evil, love was the source of all good. Jealousy brought out the worst in everyone. Love created the best. It was for jealousy that he had destroyed his own brother. But it was love of his best friend that brought him back and made him a defender again.

What about Coyote? He loved Butterfly. And there was nothing beautiful in that relationship.

That wasn't true and he knew it. Coyote hadn't loved her. He'd lusted for her and he'd wanted to possess her. If he had really cared about Butterfly, he would have rather seen her happy with Buffalo than miserable with him. It was why his mother had released his father. She'd loved him enough to want to be with him only briefly. But she'd known that he would never be happy with her. Not while his heart belonged to another.

It was why Choo Co La Tah had married the love of his life to his best friend. Because they'd grown up together, Choo had never told her of his feelings. They were from the same clan and a marriage would have been forbidden. While Choo had dreamed of it, he'd let

239

that dream go when she'd met another and fallen in love with him.

That selfless sacrifice was why the First Guardian had chosen Choo Co La Tah to be one of the Gate Guardians. Choo was able to put aside his interests for the benefit of others. While the Guardians had competed for the honor of their posts, those competitors had been chosen from warriors who had proven that they knew how to love. Warriors who understood that others came first.

Ren was the only exception. Forbidden by the First Guardian to compete for his stewardship, Ren had been chosen because of the hold Grizzly had on him.

If anyone understands why evil must be kept locked away, it is the one who danced with it for over a year. The one who has tasted its sweetness and then been burned by its bitter taste.

But Ren had never known the flavor of love. Not until he looked into a pair of gold-tinged eyes that reminded him of the man he'd once wanted to be.

He shook all over as she slowly licked her way up his body. She lifted herself up to look down at him with the most amazing smile he'd ever seen. Biting her lip, she slid herself onto him. Growling low in his throat, he shuddered at the sensation of his body inside hers. It took every bit of his self-control not to come instantly.

She took his hand into hers and rode him slow and easy while she smiled down at him. Ren lifted his hips, driving himself in even deeper. Until this moment, he'd never understood what it felt like to be welcomed somewhere. To be wanted. But as he looked into her eyes, he finally felt the warmth of home. Of belonging to someone other than himself.

Kateri watched the play of emotions on Ren's face. She wrinkled her nose teasingly at him. "Sorry I broke your record."

He scowled at her. "My record?"

"Longest stretch of celibacy ever. Guinness would be most impressed. And I seriously doubt you'll ever find a contender for your title."

He rewarded her with a warm, rich laugh. One that ended in a moan as he released himself inside her. He drove himself even deeper while he shuddered.

Once he was finished, she started to move to his side, but he held her on top of him. For once his emotions were completely hidden as he cupped her face in his hands, then kissed her.

Pulling back, he nuzzled his cheek against hers so that he could whisper in her ear. "I won't let anything happen to you."

"I know, sweetie. And I won't let it get you either."

Ren smiled at the endearment. For the first time in his extremely long existence, he felt truly intimate with someone. And it wasn't just because he'd seen visions of her life, nor was it from the sex. It came from the fact that he actually believed her promise.

He believed in her.

Yeah, the world was definitely going to end. He'd had sex and he trusted the woman he'd had it with. If that wasn't the sign of impending doom, he didn't know what was.

She kissed him on the tip of his nose before she slid off his body and dressed.

Pulling on his own clothes, Ren knew they should

hurry, but he didn't want this to end. He'd had so few perfect moments in his life. He could count them on one hand. And none of them came close to this.

"Dadgumit!"

He arched a brow at her irritated tone. "What's wrong?"

"I broke a stupid nail." She held it up to show him. "I know it's ludicrous, right? But I still hate to lose one."

Then the smile faded from her face as she stared at him as if he was a stranger.

Dread hit his stomach hard. This couldn't be good. "What?"

"Why are your eyes blue?"

Ren went to conjure something so that he could see for himself, but the moment he tried, he made a frightening discovery.

He had no powers whatsoever. That, combined with blue eyes, could only mean one thing. . . .

Dear gods, I'm mortal.

242

Chapter 12

Kateri couldn't breathe as she stared into a pair of eyes that were so vibrant a blue they practically glowed, especially in contrast to his dark tawny skin and black hair. "What's going on?"

"I-I-I-I . . ." He slammed his eyes shut and ground his teeth. After a few seconds, he tried again. "I-I-I've lost all m-my p-p-powers."

"Okay, so we can't conjure anything."

He shook his head. "I'm m-m-mortal ag-gain." He tried to say more, but he couldn't get it out, which only frustrated him more. Damn it! Without those powers, he was a stammering, effing moron.

She reached up and gently pulled his head down until she had her forehead pressed against his. Smiling, she brushed her hands against his cheeks. "Breathe, sweetie. Take your time. The only part about your speech that bothers me is how much it upsets you. Give yourself a break and stop calling yourself names in your head."

He frowned.

"Yes," she continued, "I know you're doing it. Now stop."

He took a deep breath before he made another attempt. "I can die now."

"Okay, I liked it better when you were stuttering and couldn't get that out. Are you serious?"

He nodded.

Releasing him, Kateri took a step back. "What do you need me to do?"

He shrugged, then hesitated as if he dreaded speaking. But when he did so, his voice was calm and perfect. "I've never lost them completely before. I have no idea."

As Kateri opened her mouth to speak, she heard a rustling in the trees behind him.

Ren turned at the same time a fireball came flying toward her. It was so close that she felt the burn of it an instant before Ren threw her to the ground and covered her with his body. He flung his hand out to return the fire, then cursed as he remembered he didn't have his powers.

Beautiful timing there.

Fine. He still had his bow, and even as a human, he could do a tremendous amount of damage with it. While more fireballs bombarded them, he started to move in front of Kateri to cover her, but before he could, she let fly her own shot.

It went straight between the demon's eyes. Three more arrows went past him in rapid succession, taking out more demons.

Damn, she was impressive.

He moved in for cover fire. "Deeper into the woods."

She shot two more arrows, then complied.

Hiding behind a forked tree, she covered him as he ran to join her.

Gah, what he wouldn't give to be able to conjure armor for them. While it wouldn't save them completely, it would at least give them a little more protection than bare skin.

And at the rate they were firing, they'd be out of arrows soon.

He met Kateri's nervous gaze. "Keep moving forward."

She did and he stayed one step behind her. All of a sudden, one of the black trees reached to grab Kateri.

Reacting on instinct, Ren let out his demon crow's call. The tree shirked away from her.

A slow smile curled his lips. He might be mortal, but he still had the demon in him. While he wasn't happy with Ravenna, at least she'd given him a few handy things no one could steal.

With that thought, he yanked his quiver over his head and handed it to Kateri.

Kateri froze as she tried to understand what Ren was doing by shoving his arrows at her. Before she could ask, he changed from man into a huge crow. Stunned, she watched as he took flight and went to engage the other demons.

"Keep running." His voice was inside her head.

"What are you doing?"

"I'm preventing them from harming you. Go, Kateri. They can't harm me like this."

She wasn't sure if she believed him or not. "You said you were mortal."

"I am, but even as a mortal, I had a few things that weren't normal. Now, please, go deeper and avoid getting close to the trees."

Though she'd never been a follower as a rule, she obeyed him. After all, he was used to these things. She wasn't. Best course of action was to withdraw until you had a chance to study your enemy. Thank you, Sun Tzu.

She scurried through the brush, dodging the trees that came at her. She'd just hit a clearing when something bright flashed in front of her. Temporarily blinded by it, she held her hand up to shield her eyes.

One minute she was facing nothing. In the next, three men were there.

Reacting on pure instinct, she let loose an arrow, then gasped in horror as she realized she'd just shot Cabeza.

Yet as the arrow reached him, he literally grabbed it out of the air and gave her a peeved glare.

"You know, that wouldn't have killed me, but it would have hurt and pissed my ass off."

"Sorry," she offered.

"Damn, Base," the blond with short hair said from beside him. "Don't ever take her hunting. She's one of those 'I heard a noise, let's shoot at it without finding out what it is first' people. It's what I hate most about trying to roam free in the modern world. Last thing I want is to have buckshot enter my hindquarters while I'm trying to take a leak because no one can spare a second to ascertain who's around them in the woods before they shoot it. America doesn't need gun control. What they need is idiot control."

Cabeza and the man with a blond ponytail laughed.

"I don't have a gun," Kateri reminded him as she realized that she and the blond with short hair were the only two non-fanged beings in this group.

He snorted. "Bullet or arrow . . . really, would it make a difference to you if you had to have someone dig it out of your ass?"

The man had a point, but she wasn't about to concede it.

"You better lay off her, Sasha," the other blond said. "Or she's liable to shoot you on purpose."

As if in response to his words, an echoing gun blast sounded behind her.

Gasping, she jerked around, praying it wasn't Ren who'd been hit.

More gunshots sounded in rapid succession.

Kateri started for them, but Cabeza pulled her to a stop. "Don't. It's just pest control driving out the rodents."

"How do you mean?"

Another blast. This one a *lot* closer.

In spite of what Cabeza said, she nocked another arrow and prepared to send it between the eyes of whoever was shooting that gun.

The brush in front of her rustled.

She aimed for it.

Out of nowhere, Ren, still in crow form, flew at her bow, knocking her sight off.

"What are you doing?" she asked him.

"Friendly fire. Don't kill him." Those words had barely registered when the source of the noise entered their clearing. For a full minute, she couldn't move as she stared into the face of the last man she'd ever expected to meet.

Buffalo.

Tall, dark, and swathed in black from head to toe, he was identical to her visions except for his short hair, Stetson hat, snakeskin shit-kickers, and long black duster.

Flipping his Henry rifle over his shoulder, he inclined his head to the men with her. "Thank you, boys, for the assist. Mighty kind of y'all to scratch yourselves while we were fighting for your lives." And that thick Mississippi drawl had to be the most shocking thing of all.

Sasha held his hands up in surrender. "Hey, I was protecting the woman. She's the priority. Right?"

"I thought Cabeza was going with you to fight. I didn't know he'd pull back to the woman's position."

Cabeza glared at the guy in the ponytail. "Are you calling me a coward, Urian?"

Urian made a rude noise. "Do I look like Acheron? No, I don't. And for the record, I don't do vague. If I want to call you a coward, I will bock at you in no uncertain terms. Chicken shit."

Ren landed on the ground between her and Buffalo before he turned back into a fully clothed man.

While Ren shook his change off, Buffalo tipped his hat to her. "Nice meeting you, ma'am. Or rather, Doctor. I know a lot of you college intellectuals get a bit riled when you don't get called that."

She lowered her bow. "Call me Kateri."

Ren cast a strange glance at her that she didn't quite understand before he gestured to Buffalo. "Kateri, meet Sundown."

"Sundown?" she asked in her head.

Ren answered in kind by returning her thoughts. *"He*

was reincarnated several times. His last incarnation was as a man named William Jessup Brady. Jess for short to most people. He, too, is Cherokee, and his mother named him Manee Ya Doy Ay." Which meant "sundown" in Cherokee. *The quiet time between night and day when there's perfect balance between light and dark.* Though that name certainly didn't fit with the exceptionally loud shotgun rounds he seemed to enjoy letting loose.

But who was she to judge?

Ren went on to the others. "You know Cabeza from your earlier attack. The blond with long hair and fangs is Urian, and the other is Sasha."

"Hi," she said, offering them a smile.

Moving to stand beside her, Ren folded his arms over his chest. "Just so you know, the reason Sasha lacks fangs as a human is that he's a lycanthrope."

Fascinating, and that knowledge made her realize something. The sun was shining. . . .

She glanced up at the sun meaningfully. "Shouldn't you, Urian and Cabeza be bursting into flames or something?"

Cabeza looked up at the sky. "That's not the real sun."

Which brought up one interesting question. "Okay . . . so where are we?"

He slid his gaze to Ren. "Xibalba." Could he have made that sound any more sanitizer?

Ren cursed as she gasped, then looked around the area with new sight. This was the Mayan hell?

Great. Leave it to her to get sucked into some prehistoric underworld. How many people could say that?

Sundown laughed at their reactions. "See now," he said to Kateri. "I had to have all that explained to me. I'm impressed you know the answer without asking. But then, that's why you got them letters after your name."

Ren ran his thumb down the side of his mouth. "They haven't *really* bothered us. Should I be concerned by that?"

"Well, there are nine levels here," Cabeza said. "This is level one. Mostly made up of phantoms and ghosts, and lower-class demons, it's not so bad. But there are twelve Lords of Xibalba. They're the ones we don't want to run into. Especially not Ixtab."

"Ixtab?" Sundown asked.

"A suicide goddess," Urian answered.

Cabeza looked impressed. "You know our pantheon?"

Urian glanced around their small group with a wry grin. "As the oldest one here . . . yeah. I've been to a lot of places over the centuries, hunting food. Mayans were always one of my favorite menu choices."

"Why?" Sasha asked with a puzzled frown.

"They had a suicide goddess, Scooby. You showed up as a demon, claiming you came from Xibalba, and they were eager to give up blood and their souls to you. Mayans viewed life as nothing more than a gateway to death. They had a whole different point of view about it all that we milked. Plus the blond hair really helps when they have a whole prophecy about a white foreign snake demon. Whether they called us Waxaklahun Ubah Kan or Kukulkan, they were eager to give us their throats. Damn shame their cities collapsed."

"Probably 'cause you overfed," Sundown mumbled. "Where the hell were the Dark-Hunters?"

Urian winked at him. "Very few and very far between

250

in Mesoamerica, which was another reason we loved it here."

Sasha shook his head. "Nice dissertation on Daimon mind-set. I can't believe we share common genes. Damn, Uri, you guys were cold and you give my people a bad name."

Urian's glare could melt ice. "Cold is having your own grandfather condemn you to die horribly on your twenty-seventh birthday over something you had no knowledge of or participation in. Hell, I was a baby living in Greece when the Atlantean queen bitch had Apollo's mistress slaughtered."

"Bitter much?" Cabeza asked.

The malevolent glare went to him next. "How'd you get to be a Dark-Hunter again?"

Cabeza laughed evilly. "I not only own the bitter card, I play it every chance I get. It serves me better than my people thinking you were my direct ancestor."

Kateri wasn't sure she caught that correctly. "You're related to the Mayan gods?"

"It's why I'm named Kukulkan. Unfortunately, though, the genes were watered down so much by the time they got to me, all the powers that came with the bloodline had been lost." He turned an irritated grimace toward Urian. "Probably 'cause someone sucked it all out of us. Oh for the days when I could stake you."

"All right, children," Ren said, interrupting them. "I have neither the energy nor inclination to play referee." He indicated himself and Cabeza. "You and I—"

"Why are your eyes blue?" Sundown asked. "Man, they're freaky-looking what with your coloring and all."

Kateri went ramrod stiff. "They are not! They're beautiful."

Sundown laughed. "Beautiful like a woman, huh?"

She took a step forward, but Ren caught her. His features softened as he brushed a strand of hair out of her face. "It's all right, Kateri. He means no offense by that and I don't take any. If I did, I'd have shot him."

Those words caught everyone's attention and made her the center of a curious scrutiny she didn't relish.

Ren cut a gimlet stare to Sundown. "Obviously, Captain Observant, my powers are down. I'm hoping they come back soon."

Urian let out a low whistle. "You found your Achilles' Heel. I hope you took notes so as not to do it again. That's the kind of information I used to kill to obtain."

Ren ignored his comment. "As I was saying, since Dark-Hunters drain each other's powers, I'm thinking mine might not come back so long as Cabeza is near me."

"Yeah, well, too bad. I have to stay around you to navigate you out of here. Otherwise, you might as well build a cabin and settle down for the duration."

Sasha let out an evil laugh.

They turned to stare at him.

"Oh, like I'm the only one who figures if all the evil gets out, we only have to camp here for eight more days. Your threat's not as badass as it would have been a hundred years ago."

Cabeza growled at him. "If I give you a dog biscuit, would you go lick your balls and leave us alone?"

Sasha took a step toward Cabeza, but Sundown caught

him with one arm. "Easy, pup. You don't want to get blood on your clothes."

"I can make new ones."

"Yeah, but I'd rather not have to bury one of you here. So let's pretend we have some degree of social skills and a little bit of home training, and get the nice lady back so she can stop this and I don't have to worry about my babies that I left alone to come do this with y'all."

Cabeza held his hands up in surrender and inclined his head to Sundown's wisdom. "We need to head north, away from the pathway to the second level. I should be able to find an exit there."

Kateri frowned at the weird dip in his tone. There was something Cabeza wasn't telling them and that worried her.

"Why can't we just teleport out?" Urian asked.

Cabeza grinned, showing off his fangs. "Go for it."

Urian did, then cursed. "Okay, explain this shit."

"It's a hell realm. They don't want you to leave and there's no god here on our side who's going to give us a free pass. We'll have to earn our way home."

Urian growled low in his throat. "No good deed goes unpunished."

As they started forward, Ren pulled Sundown back. She stopped, waiting to see what was going on.

Ren offered his friend a smile. "Thank you for this, Jess. But I'd have rather you stayed with Abigail. I'm sure she needs you more than I do."

Sundown clapped him on the back. "The baby came yesterday while you were in the middle of all hell busting loose, otherwise I'd have been there, too. Now, I have them both tucked in with Zarek so they're safe. This morning, Abby and I decided that you needed me more than she did. So my goal is to get you back to meet your goddaughter."

Ren congratulated him. "I'll bet she's beautiful."

The pride on Sundown's face made Kateri smile. "Like her mother. Perfect, precious, and liable to make me crazy for the rest of my life." He clicked his tongue and winked at Ren. "Thank God I got a shotgun and no compunction against riddling a suitor's backside full of buckshot should he ever disrespect my girl."

"So what did you name her?" Ren asked.

"Well, Abby and I had a long and, at times, not so friendly discussion. She wanted to name her Hannah after her sister, but I didn't like that so much. Naming a daughter after a Daimon, even one who's family, just don't sit right with me. Besides, never been all that fond of that name. Andy suggested we name her Andrewa after him. So I tossed his ass out the door so we could have a serious discussion. I wanted to call her Rena after you, but Abby said they'd call her Renal Gland at school and she'd have to kill me over it. So after some debate where certain areas of my body were seriously threatened and my manhood questioned repeatedly by the love of my life, we decided to name her Mikayla Laura for you and Abby's mama."

Kateri pressed her lips together to keep from laughing out loud at Sundown's hilarious explanation. Though she barely knew him in this life, she really, really liked him. And while she now saw the subtle differences between the cowboy Jess Brady and the Keetoowah warrior Buffalo, she also saw the core of his soul that carried through all of his lifetimes.

No wonder Ren had been willing to sell his soul to help his friend beat Coyote's curse. Sundown was definitely a treasure. She also noticed that Ren never stammered even the least bit while talking to him. He was completely relaxed and at ease—as if he knew Sundown would never judge him harshly. That more than anything made her love the cowboy.

Ren moved to walk by her side while Sundown quickened his pace to tell Cabeza something.

"I have a weird question."

"Yes," Ren answered before she asked it. "His wife Abigail is Butterfly."

She was glad that Butterfly had finally claimed her Buffalo. "Are you okay with them naming the baby Mikayla?" Given his earlier reaction to the name Makah'Alay, she wasn't so sure he'd be keen on it.

"I am deeply honored." But there was a sadness in his eyes. Not jealousy. It was something else. Something she didn't understand.

"What's wrong?"

Ren started not to answer. Sharing his feelings had never been easy for him. But for some reason, he found it natural to confide in Kateri. Like it was something he was born to do. "I've done so much harm to Butterfly that I wish Sundown wasn't here. The risk is too great. I wouldn't be able to live if I caused Buffalo to leave her again. I keep thinking that maybe this is Coyote's curse on steroids. That now that they're together and happy, the curse will steal him from her."

She took his hand into hers and gave a light squeeze. "Life is never a sure bet. If I know nothing else, it's that one thing. But . . . I have faith that we're all going to get out of here and Sundown is going to live a long, happy life with Abigail while Mikayla and her sisters make him wish he'd neutered himself when they bring home dates and spouses."

He stopped dead in his tracks. Not just because she'd taken his hand and held it as if she was proud to be seen with him, but because of what she said and the tone of her voice when she spoke. It was the tone of a medicine woman speaking prophecy. "Can you see the future?"

Kateri hesitated. She'd never once told anyone the truth. It was something she hated and had tried many times to get rid of. Yet it always came back. "Yes. But what I see doesn't always happen. Sometimes, my visions get derailed by other things that I don't see. Things that cause it to change."

Ren laughed. "So what you're saying is if he doesn't die horribly, he'll have a good life."

If not for the teasing note in his voice, she'd be offended. "Exactly," she teased back.

Ren glanced down at their joined hands. "Thank you."

She frowned at the catch in his voice. "For what?"

"Treating me like I'm human."

Those sincere words wrung her heart. "You are human, Ren. Me, on the other hand, I'm a complete freak of nature."

Smiling, he lifted her hand and kissed the back of her knuckles. The moment his lips touched her flesh, she gasped as images flooded through her. They came so fast and furious that they left her dizzy.

She heard people screaming, crying out for help. Everywhere she looked, she saw chaos and smoke.

Her grandmother stood on an isolated hill, her eyes filled with tears. The setting sun silhouetted her frail body as she turned to face Kateri.

"Beware the wolf, Waleli. He will never be tamed. All he knows is death and killing. His heart is black and filled with a bitter hatred that can't be undone. Do not be led astray by your heart that is pure. A heart that sees only the good in others. There are some who lie and deceive. Shadow walkers who live off the humanity of others. They can never be trusted. They live only to betray, to twist our words into ugly lies to be used against us. And he will betray you, my child. Don't let your kind heart blind you."

Her grandmother's words circled around her head until she thought of something she hadn't considered before. Ren's *name is Ren Waya.* . . .

Renegade Wolf.

Terror consumed her as she pulled her trembling hand from his grasp. He was the wolf her grandmother spoke of. The one her father had warned her about.

Evil owned him once.

It was going to own him again.

Ren scowled at her. "What's wrong?"

Panicking, she glanced about at their small group. She saw Cabeza lying beheaded on the ground. Sundown had his throat cut. Sasha was torn into pieces. And Urian . . .

He lay on a sacrificial altar where someone had removed his heart.

Ren was nowhere to be seen.

Someone was chanting in her vision. She scanned the

room until she saw a priest in golden robes who wore a huge feathered mask, obscuring his identity. Red demonic eyes glowed from behind it as he went through his ritual sacrifice. But she knew who it was. She had no doubt.

The priest was Ren and he was summoning Grizzly back to the world.

Chapter 13

"Kateri? What is it?"

She heard Ren speaking, but she couldn't respond. It was as if she was torn between two worlds and grounded in neither while her head swam with out-of-context events and images she didn't understand.

Finally, one came into focus. Dressed in formal Victorian attire, Urian fed off the blood of a woman. There was so much pleasure on his face that it sickened her.

Then the image shifted to show him in modern times, dressed in black pants and a black button-down shirt. Fire was all around him as he worked to save the life of a beautiful blond woman. She was terrified as he held his hand out to her.

"Trust me, Phoebe. I won't let you die. I swear it."

From there she saw him and Phoebe alone in an apartment where he held her so tenderly it brought tears to her eyes. Leaning back against his chest, Phoebe fed from his wrist while he stroked her hair and nuzzled her neck.

"I'm not taking too much, am I?" Phoebe asked.

"Don't worry about me. Take what you need."

Kateri could feel the love between them. It was so strong, it was tangible.

Then she left them to find Sasha in ancient Egypt embroiled in a furious battle where he fought with a clan of wolves against an ancient Greek army. Kateri sucked her breath in sharply at how young he appeared. While he fought, it was obvious he lacked the experience of the others.

And as one of the Greek soldiers came at his back with a spear, a wolf launched itself to take the fatal blow instead.

"No!" Sasha screamed, reaching for the wolf. But it was too late. The wolf had died instantly.

He was still holding the wolf when one of the soldiers came forward to seize him by his hair and pull him into a cage. "I hope they roast you over an open pyre," the soldier snarled at him.

Then those images faded while more flashed like a panicked strobe light. The motion made her sick to her stomach until everything settled again.

This time, it was Cabeza in ancient Tikal. Dressed as a Mayan warrior with his face painted into a fierce mask, he was under attack by a group of seven men led by a prince from Calakmul.

"We will feed on your blood," one of the men shouted in Cabeza's face.

Cabeza laughed. "Crawl back to Calakmul, Chacu. So long as I live, my father will own this land *and* yours."

Kateri's heart pounded as she realized that this was the same Chacu who'd attacked her in her lab. No wonder Cabeza had lost his mind. Their enmity was centuries old.

And still the images shifted again, making her feel like Alice falling down the rabbit hole. But the next time she was able to focus, she gasped.

Coyote stood with Buffalo in the same hall where she'd seen Buffalo's body after Coyote had killed him—wearing the same clothes he'd died in. It was strange to see this version of the cowboy. While their features were the same, Buffalo had long black hair and wasn't nearly as well muscled as Sundown Brady. Nor did he have the same cockiness or sense of humor.

Buffalo glanced around the room in confusion. "Where's Makah'Alay? I received a message that he needed to see me. He's not hurt, is he?"

A tic worked in Coyote's jaw. "No, he's not hurt. He's healthier than ever."

"Then why—"

"I was the one who sent the servant after you," Coyote said, interrupting him.

His scowl increased. "I don't understand."

"I'm your future chief, Buffalo. Not my brother. You'd do well to remember that."

"Is that a threat?"

Coyote scoffed. "Why would I threaten the man who stood by and allowed my torture? I ask you?"

"I didn't know what he was doing to you."

"You didn't bother to find out, did you?"

Shame filled Buffalo's eyes. "I never dreamed he'd do something like that. It wasn't really him, you know.

261

Getting Grizzly out of him almost cost the First Guardian his life."

"How commendable of you to keep defending him. How sweet."

Buffalo went ramrod stiff at the insult. "What are you implying?"

"Nothing. I merely find it odd that you have always been so quick to defend a mentally defective retard when no one else will. Tell me honestly, don't you get tired of kissing his ass all the time?"

Buffalo took a step toward him, then stopped. "You're not going to goad me into a fight. So you might as well stop this now. I protect him because I owe him a debt that cannot be repaid. My sister and mother were on the brink of starvation until he began bringing us meat. I wouldn't have them now but for Makah'Alay, and for that charity, he will always have my loyalty."

"How nice for my brother. It's a shame your loyalty goes no further."

"How do you mean?"

Coyote moved to stand just before him. He raked a condemning sneer down the length of Buffalo's body. "You know exactly what I mean. I saw you earlier today."

Buffalo's face blanched at the last five words.

"Oh yeah . . . I see the guilt in your eyes. You have stolen the affections of my promised bride."

"I stole nothing."

Coyote snorted. "Bullshit! That was why you didn't help me when Makah'Alay tortured me. You were hoping I'd die so that you could have her *and* a clear conscience."

"That's not true."

"Isn't it?"

Buffalo shook his head. "I never meant to love her. I didn't. Any more than she meant to love me. But when you went missing, Butterfly refused to leave until she knew you were safe. She worried herself sick over you. For hours on end, she'd walk the halls, weeping and begging the spirits to bring you safely home."

He curled his lip at Buffalo. "Yes." His voice dripped with sarcasm. "I saw her concern this afternoon when she threw herself against you with a passion she's never shown me."

"It's not like that, Coyote. Neither of us meant to hurt you. She cried herself sick every single day. I only came here in your absence to reassure her that you were still alive and that you'd be back home soon. We were very circumspect and respectful of you. Always."

Coyote backhanded him. "Liar!"

He wiped the blood from his mouth with the back of his hand, then swiped at it with his tongue. "It's not a lie. It's just that the more time we spent together, the more we realized that we couldn't live without each other. I began to live only for the seconds when I'd be able to see her face again."

"What do you think got me through a year of torture?" Coyote ground through clenched teeth. "Huh? It was knowing that she'd be waiting here when I returned. *She* was the only thing I hung on to. And you took her from me. Damn you! Damn you!"

"You've every right to be angry, but ..." Buffalo's voice broke off into a sharp gasp. He staggered back to see the blood spreading over his tunic. Pressing his hands to the wound, he gaped at Coyote, who plunged the knife in again and again in a furious rage that descended so rapidly, Buffalo had no chance to defend himself.

Yet somehow, he managed to remain standing as he confronted his killer. "I never touched her. She *never* betrayed you. We never even kissed."

"I saw you hold her!"

Buffalo staggered, then caught himself. "A hug. Nothing more. We were saying good-bye so that she could marry you on the morrow. We'd already relegated ourselves to living apart. We both intended to honor her vows to you." He sank down to his knees. "Your heart is so evil, Coyote, that you have never been able to be happy. Even though you were always the favored son, you couldn't allow Makah'Alay to have even a tiny bit of your father's affection or any note of praise from anyone."

"Shut up!" Coyote shouted as he kicked Buffalo in the ribs. "Die already, you worthless bastard!"

But Buffalo had been right. She saw the images now of them as boys. Anytime someone attempted to praise Ren, Coyote would insert himself so that their compliment would go to him instead.

She saw them together as young teens. Ren was stringing his bow while Coyote bragged about a banquet being served to honor him.

"Can you believe it, Makah'Alay? After tonight, I will be considered a man!"

"B-b-but you, you, you d-didn't kill it."

"It doesn't matter, does it? Father's always said that because of your mental defects you'll be a perpetual child and that we'll always have to care for you. Now I will have all the respect of a real man." Coyote rushed over to Ren so that he could lean against his back and whisper in his ear. "It'll be our secret. You kill the game and I'll bring it in."

By his face, it was obvious Ren didn't like the idea at all.

Coyote scoffed at him. "Stop pouting like a baby. No one would ever give you credit anyway. They all think you're incompetent. So what does it matter?"

She could hear Ren's thoughts. *It matters to me. Just once, I'd like for someone to tell me I did a good job, too.*

"Kateri!"

The images scattered until she was staring into the face of the man that boy had grown into. "Why did you stop stuttering when the Grizzly possessed you?"

He frowned at her. "What?"

"Your stutter went away when he possessed you. Was that part of the bargain?"

Ren glanced to the others to make sure none of them overheard her question. Luckily, they were far enough away that her voice wouldn't carry to them.

"Yes. He returned it when I cast him out, but by then I'd learned to mitigate it most of the time."

And he never stuttered around Buffalo.

She winced as pain lacerated her skull. "My head hurts. Badly."

Ren brushed a tender hand over her forehead. The concern on his face touched her deeply. "You were crying out like you were in a nightmare. What happened?"

She pressed the heel of her hand to her eye socket, trying to relieve the pain of it.

"Here."

Before she realized what he intended, he swung her up in his arms to carry her.

"What are you doing?"

"I know your head hurts, but I would think it obvious."

She groaned at his density. "Let me try this again. *Why* are you carrying me?"

"You don't feel well."

"People don't normally carry other people for that reason."

He winked at her. "I'm not most people."

That was certainly true. "Can I ask you something?"

"If I said no would it stop you?"

She smiled. "Of course not." She laid her head down on his shoulder and savored the comfort of his arms around her. "How did you learn so much about hunting?" It seemed incongruous that anyone in his clan would have taught him given their contempt.

"Artemis is . . . for lack of a better term, my godmother. Since she's goddess of the hunt, I always assumed it was a gift from her."

"Mmm."

Ren had to tighten his arms around her to keep her from falling as she went completely limp. "Kateri?" He shook her slightly. Her head lolled back.

She was out cold.

Fear shredded him. "Sundown!"

They all slowed down to look at him.

Jess came running over immediately. "What happened?"

"I don't know. She just passed out."

And in the next heartbeat, she stopped breathing entirely.

Chapter 14

Raking his hands through his hair, Ren stood back with tears in his eyes while Jess tried to resuscitate Kateri, who lay on the ground at his feet. But she didn't respond at all.

She was dead. . . .

How?

The answer didn't really matter to him. Not even a little. The reality was that she was gone, and the pain of it slammed into him so hard that it left him weak in the knees. He couldn't breathe or focus. Nothing in all eternity had hurt him *this* much. Nothing. He felt like the world around him was crumbling to pieces. Like the very ground he stood on had swallowed him whole.

She'd just entered his life, turned it on its head, made him feel again, and now she was gone. Why? Why would the gods have done this to him?

He'd been all right alone. He'd gotten by without

having any real ties to anyone. Maybe not deliriously happy, but not really miserable either. Muted emotions had worked for him.

At least they beat the hell out of this utter agony that made him want to shout his anguish to the gods and kill whichever one had taken her life.

Panting, he glared up at the muted underworld sky.

I want her back! Damn you! I want her back!

How badly?

His heart stopped its rapid beating at the foreign voice in his head. But it wasn't foreign. It was familiar, though he couldn't place it. Before he could remember, a flickering shade appeared to his right.

Windseer.

More beautiful than any mortal woman, she stood there as a wraith with an unamused expression that made her cheekbones even sharper, her olive skin more luminescent. It was as if she was listening to someone else in her head.

And he knew exactly who would be pulling her stings.

Grizzly.

Get thee behind me, bitch, he growled at her.

She shrugged nonchalantly. *Fine. Let her die. She means nothing to me.* She started fading.

Kateri might mean nothing to them, but she meant everything to him.

"I'm really sorry, Ren," Sundown said, rising to his feet. He pulled his hat off respectfully as he shifted his weight to one leg. "There's nothing more we can do. She just won't respond."

"*Hijo de puta,*" Cabeza snarled. "Who's going to reset

268

the calendar now? Huh? We just got screwed, *mi hermanos*. Might as well stay here and set up camp. Once those gates open, everything here will head to the surface. This will be a ghost town."

Urian rolled his eyes. "That's a really indecent pun, Khan."

Jess sighed. "This ain't good. Not good at all."

Sasha nodded in agreement. "Blows chunks, my friends. Blows serious chunks. Thank the gods I'm not human. Can't wait for the gates to fall." His tone dripped sarcasm. He passed an irritated smirk to Sundown. "And we thought it was bad when we were attacked with the plagues. Woo-hoo, Field Day II here we come. Who wants popcorn?"

Their words did nothing to ease the ache in Ren's chest and throat. While they were worried about the world as a whole, he honestly was only worried about one person.

The woman who lay dead.

Sundown looked over at Cabeza. "Is there a place here where we can bury her body?"

Those words slammed into him with a force so strong it made him take a step back. Ren returned his attention to Windseer. *Wait!*

Windseer solidified with an arched brow while the others started looking for a place to put Kateri.

Ren panicked even more. *What do you want in exchange for her life?*

The smile on her face was cold and calculating. She slid her gaze down to Kateri. *The Grizzly wants his freedom and he doesn't want to fight for it or share it. We bring the bitch back, she resets the calendar. Then you free him, alone. No other entities are invited to our party.*

269

It wouldn't be that simple. He knew better. For one thing, he'd have to kill his brother in order to release the Grizzly. But at this point, sacrificing Coyote, who was hell-bent on destroying the world himself, didn't seem as bad as it once had. *Is that all?*

She laughed evilly. *Of course not. You return to him as his servant.*

Ren shook his head. *I won't fight for Grizzly. Never again. Makah'Alay, Makah'Alay . . .*

Ren could have definitely done without her patronizing tone. Her expression was pitiless. *You misunderstand me. He doesn't want you to fight for him. He no longer has faith in your loyalty. You will be his eternal slave to do with as he pleases.* Total *subjugation.*

His stomach cramped with dread at the very thought. *I can't do that. Artemis owns me.*

Windseer tsked at him. *Then let her come for you if she wants you so badly. . . . But you know the truth, just as we do. She doesn't care about you, any more than anyone else does. She won't waste three seconds trying to find you, because she won't even know you're gone. Face it, Makah'Alay, you're worthless. You have no value to anyone. Not even us.*

Those words slapped him hard. Mostly because they were true and he knew it. The only person who seemed to value him was now dead at his feet.

Or was there more to this?

If I have no value, then why does Grizzly want to own me?

To torture you, idiot. Why else? You betrayed him and he wants your blood for that. No one makes him look like a fool. The only so-called value you have to him is that you can get close enough to Coyote to sacrifice him and release Grizzly

270

faster than anyone else. But if you have no wish to have your beloved toy returned to the land of the living, fine. I'll find someone else who will have the balls to do what he has to for the ones he loves.

Ren ground his teeth. She was wasting her time insulting him. He couldn't care less what she called him. Those barbs had lost their sting a long time ago.

The only one who could hurt him now was Kateri, and with her gone, his heart was broken.

I can save her life.

He looked down at the only person who'd ever made him feel welcomed. The only one who'd made him smile while hell rained down on him, and his gut wrenched with grief. He couldn't say no to their offer and they knew it.

How can I be willing to sell my freedom for a woman I just met?

The same way Buffalo had been willing to risk Ren's anger and retaliation by visiting Butterfly during Ren's brief reign. When Ren first discovered what Buffalo was doing, he had been furious. Not because he wanted Butterfly for himself, but because he felt betrayed that Buffalo had feared him so. That his friend had thought so little of him that Buffalo had honestly believed Ren would turn on him and kill him for loving her.

That was what had taught him how ludicrous and unreasoning fear was. Had Ren wanted Butterfly, he'd have taken her once he held Coyote as his prisoner.

Instead, Ren had left her alone. Even though she was beautiful beyond belief and he would have been proud to call her his own, he had envied his brother's happiness that had been bought with Ren's blood and dignity, not his bride. Even then, Ren would never have taken Coyote prisoner had his brother not poisoned him and then tried to cut his throat.

And he wouldn't have tortured Coyote had his brother kept his mouth shut and not insulted him day after day. Ren had gone insane from it all. Between being possessed and the pain of Coyote and his father mocking him, he'd lost it completely. All he'd wanted was for it to cease. For someone, just one person, to look at him like he was human and had feelings. Hell, even when he'd gone to kill his father, the man had laughed at him.

"You're not man enough, dog." And then his father had spat in his face.

When Ren had attacked, his father might have been able to survive had he taken Ren seriously. But he'd mocked him right up to the point Ren had stabbed him.

In all his life, Ren had never felt treasured, not even by Buffalo. Theirs had been a relationship born out of a debt Buffalo thought he owed him and because he felt sorry for Ren. While they had grown close, Buffalo hadn't befriended him because he liked him or because they had anything in common.

Only Kateri had done that. She owed him nothing. Nor did she pity him. She actually liked him as a person and teased him playfully. He could see it every time she looked at him. Every time she touched him.

His eyes watering, he met Windseer's gaze. *Save her. Whatever it takes.*

Windseer smiled cruelly. *We told you you would come back to us one day.*

Damn them for being right.

An instant later, Kateri took a deep, ragged breath and opened her eyes.

His heart pounding in gratitude, Ren sank to his knees and pulled her into his arms to hold her as his tears finally fell.

Windseer moved to stand between Cabeza and Jess, neither of whom could see her. *Remember your word, Makah'Alay. If you fail us, we won't kill her. Grizzly will take her as his own, and you know what he does to his property. She will be well used.*

Ren ignored her as he inhaled the scent of Kateri's skin and felt her warmth against him.

"Anyone else feeling *really* awkward here?" Sasha asked. "Guys, get a room."

Ren let out a puff of laughter before he pulled back to cup her face in his hands so that he could assure himself she was fine.

She touched the tears on his face. "Did I miss something?"

Sasha snorted. "Nah, nothing too important. Just your death."

"What?" she asked with a stern frown.

Ren nodded. "You died in my arms."

"How?"

"I don't know." But he had a good suspicion it was something Grizzly had caused. Just as he was certain Grizzly was the reason they hadn't been attacked. The bastard had most likely allowed them that time knowing what Ren would do. Knowing what she'd come to mean to him.

First Grizzly had sent Windseer to screw him over and

now he'd done it with a woman who had no idea she'd been used as a tool against him.

But that wasn't her fault. He was the moron who couldn't keep his heart and his body separate. He couldn't just screw a woman and walk away. He'd felt too used by the world too many times to give that feeling to someone else.

And now his enemy knew exactly how to cripple him. Grizzly knew his greatest weakness. Kateri.

I am so fucked. . . .

Kateri choked as Ren tightened his hold on her. "Sweetie, I can't breathe. You're killing me."

He loosened his arms, but still kept her pressed up against him as if he was trying to merge their bodies together.

Jess cleared his throat. "Maybe Sasha's right and we ought to leave them alone for a bit."

"Yeah, sure, what the hell?" Urian said snidely. "Not like the fate of the world hangs in the balance or anything important. You two take your time. There's a clump of bushes over there that should give you some privacy."

Ren let go and got up with a look on his face that actually scared her. He leveled a killing glare at Urian. "If anyone should understand me right now, it's you." Bracing his legs into a warrior's stance, he held his hand out to her as Urian looked away bashfully.

Kateri took Ren's hand and allowed him to pull her to her feet. She brushed the tears away from his face, amazed that he would allow anyone to witness them. Especially after all the visions she'd had where he went to great pains to make sure no one saw him weak or hurt. She placed a kiss on his cool cheek. "Are you okay?" she whispered in his ear.

The burning sincerity in his gaze pierced her. "I am now." He turned toward the others. "What are you waiting for? Don't we have humanity to save? The Apocalypse waits for no one."

Sasha stroked his chin as they started forward once more. "You know, I have to wonder about that. Does it really wait for no one or do you think it would wait for the four riders? Maybe we ought to have someone kidnap them."

Urian scoffed. "That idea didn't work out so well for Sisyphus. Last I heard, Hades was still making him suffer."

"Good point, and I learned well not to meddle in the affairs of gods, or pick one over another. You get seriously trashed." Sasha started whistling "Heigh-Ho."

Until Urian grabbed him by the throat. "In case you have forgotten, we are in a hell realm that is inhabited by demons and some of those gods you don't want to piss off. I suggest we draw as little attention to ourselves as possible."

Sasha knocked his hand away from his throat and made a face at him. "You don't have to be an asshole."

"You don't have to be an idiot."

"Enough," Ren said sharply. "Let's save our venom to fight the ones who want to kill us, and not attack each other."

While they walked onward, Kateri fell quiet, observing the men. They fascinated her. Such a mixture of personalities. Yet they came together as warriors to protect people they'd never met. The kind of people who hadn't been kind to them in the past. Each of them had been bitterly betrayed by someone they trusted.

Sundown shot dead by his best friend on the steps of the church where he'd gone to marry the woman he loved. Urian by his father and grandfather. Cabeza by the only woman he'd have died to protect. Sasha by his own brother. And Ren . . .

Her heart aching for him, she took his hand in hers. Because he wasn't used to anyone being so familiar, it startled him.

"Are you going to jump every time I touch you?" she teased.

Ren savored the sound of her light tone. He'd never get used to her being so at ease with him.

"I wonder if he's ticklish," Sasha said, wagging his brows at her. "Not like I'm going to find out, as I'm rather fond of my non-gutted state. But you'll have to test it out and let me know."

She gave him a playful smile. "Are you?"

Ren shrugged. "How would I know?"

Kateri winced at those emotionless words. There for a single heartbeat, she'd forgotten that such things hadn't been part of his childhood. No one had ever played with him. He'd been all but grown before Buffalo had befriended him, and while he'd had a brother his own age, Coyote had played with friends and left him alone to watch them while they frolicked.

Her mind drifted to a bright summer day in his past where it was so hot, everyone complained about it.

"Hey, Makah'Alay, we're going swimming. Want to come?"

Around the age of twelve or thirteen, Ren had looked up from his chores to see Coyote with a group of boys his age, including Choo Co La Tah. "I-I-I-I have to f-f-f-finish."

"Oh c'mon, we won't be gone that long. You can finish when we get back. It's the middle of the day. Everyone's taking it easy due to the heat."

Even though he sensed something about it wasn't right, he nodded. Since they'd never invited him before, he was afraid to turn them down lest they never ask him again.

Ren set his tools aside and wiped at the sweat on his brow before he joined them. The whole way to the bathing lake, they joked and laughed with each other and ignored him.

Once they reached the small clearing where the lake rippled, they stripped down to loincloths, then jumped into the water.

Ren hesitated. Would they mock his body? He'd never removed his clothes in front of anyone before.

"C'mon, Makah'Alay," Coyote called. "You're missing out."

Bracing himself for the worst, Ren stripped to his own loincloth, then waded in. To his relief, they ignored him while they splashed and played.

Ren ducked under the water and let the coolness ease the summer heat. For several minutes, he floated peacefully on his back with his eyes closed.

Until someone grabbed him.

Before he could recover, Choo Co La Tah had yanked his loincloth off and they ran for the shore, laughing.

Ren went after them. As soon as he was on dry land, Coyote caught him about the waist and lifted him off his feet, then threw him back into the water. He came up, coughing and sputtering for air, to find them all gone. Along with all his clothes.

He tried to call them back, but nothing would come out. His jaw spasmed and the words hung in his throat.

Humiliated and angry, he swam back to the shore and got out. He should be able to make it back to town without being seen. There were several alternate paths that weren't traveled much.

Once home, he could ...

That thought died as he came face-to-face with a group of teenage women who had come to bathe. At the sight of his nudity, they shrieked and laughed at him.

His face red, Ren cupped himself and ran to the woods to save what little dignity he could. But inside, he was mortified.

By the time he made it home, his father was waiting for him. The girls had come straight back to tell everyone they had caught him masturbating in the public pool.

"Where are your clothes?"

"Th-th-th-th-"

His father backhanded him so hard, it knocked him to the floor. "Answer me!"

Ren tried, but he was so upset he couldn't say anything in his own defense. No words would come out at all.

His father yanked him up by his arm.

Ren stumbled, his eyes filled with tears of pain. He tried to get his freedom, but his father wouldn't let go. They were headed to the whipping post. Ren fought harder.

Still his father hauled him naked through the house. As they passed Coyote, who watched them with wide eyes, Ren reached for him.

"P-p-p-" He was trying to say please so that his brother would tell their father what happened and spare him his beating.

Coyote ignored him and followed them to the back courtyard. His father tied him to the post, where Ren was given twenty lashes for defiling the pool.

"You are *never* to go there again," his father snarled in his face, "you understand?"

Tears soaked his cheeks as his lips quivered from trying to speak.

His father buried his hand in his blood-soaked hair and wrenched it. "Do you understand me, you retarded bastard?"

Sobbing in silence, Ren nodded.

His father untied him. "Now go clothe yourself and finish your chores. If there's one thing left undone by sunset, we'll be back here for twenty more." His father stalked away and left him on the ground.

Ren tried to push himself up, but he hurt too much to stand. His limbs trembled from the pain even worse than his lips did.

He lay there for several minutes until Coyote brought him a blanket and covered him with it.

"I'm sorry, Makah'Alay. We were just having fun. I didn't know the girls would say that. We thought they'd laugh about it and tease you. We never dreamed they'd tell others you were doing something lewd."

Still, his back burned from the lashes. "W—w-why didn't you s-s-say-"

"I didn't want to get in trouble. Besides, you know how Father is. He'd have found some reason to beat you for it. There was no need in both of us being punished."

His brother was right. Either way, he'd have been beaten.

Coyote helped him to his feet. Placing Ren's arm over his shoulder to help him, he started toward Ren's room.

Halfway there, their father met them in the hallway with a smile for Coyote.

"My precious son, you're ever kind to those least worthy. While I appreciate your charity, you shouldn't have done it." He curled his lip at Ren. "You can't pamper wrong-doers after they've been punished. Otherwise, they never learn any lessons. Now let him go and take the blanket. He thought it was funny to be naked . . . let him walk to his room that way."

Ren waited for his brother to say something in his defence.

Instead, Coyote nodded. "Sorry, Father. I won't do it again." He took Ren's blanket.

Ren struggled to stand alone. His eyes filled with tears, he watched as his father ruffled Coyote's hair and kissed his head.

"Come, my precious son, I have a present for you."

Kateri couldn't breathe as the raw pain of that memory hit her hard. How sad that compassion was so rare for Ren that he hung on to his brother's selfishness and defended it as good. How could Coyote have been so mean to him?

A raw, bitter fury took hold of her. Before she even realized what she was doing, she quickened her steps and shoved Sundown.

Shocked, he turned to stare at her as if she'd lost her mind. "What was that for?"

"You bastard! Why did you wait to become his friend? You know, you could have been nice to him before you were obligated to!"

"What are you talking about?" Sundown scowled. "Is she *loco*?"

Ren turned her around to face him. "Kateri, he doesn't remember being Buffalo. I mean, he has bits and pieces of it, but he doesn't recall much. While they have similarities and they look the same, Sundown is an entirely different man."

Clenching her eyes shut, she nodded. "I'm sorry, Ren." She looked up at the cowboy. "Jess. I just get so mad at all of them . . ." She turned back toward Ren. "They had no right to treat you that way."

"Did you have another vision?"

She nodded. "Now I understand my grandmother. We'd be walking down the street and she'd flinch for no reason. Whenever I asked her about it, she'd say, 'It's the past, baby. For some people it's so vicious that it creates a loop of bad memories that runs constantly inside their hearts. A loop so bad that sometimes it reaches out to those of us capable of seeing it to let us know to take extra care of the ones who were hurt. It tells us to let them know that just because the world is eaten up with mean, it doesn't mean we all are. That even though the past hurt them, it doesn't have to destroy their future. Give as many smiles away as you can. They're free and they make the world a much prettier place. You may not have the best clothes or the latest *in* shoes, but everyone has a unique designer smile that is worth millions, especially to those who need its warmth.'" She clenched her hands in her hair. "Ugh! I think Jess is right. I am crazy."

Ren ran his hand down the line of her jaw, causing chills to rise on her arms. "You're not crazy. You're coming into your powers and you don't have control of them yet. Trust me. We all think we're going crazy when it happens. You should have been there the first time I turned into a crow. I flew straight into a tree and then had to figure out something to explain away the huge bruise I had in the center of my forehead for two weeks."

She shook her head at him. "You're terrible."

"He's right," Sasha said from behind him. "When I was learning to teleport, I accidentally flashed some unknown wedding party. You talk about humiliating. And of course the powers that got me there decided to abandon me a blink later. So there I stood in all my glory, cupping my junk and wondering, 'Why me, gods . . . why me?'"

They all laughed.

"I hear you," Urian said. "I accidentally turned my brother into a goat for a week. I was so scared of what my dad might do that I didn't tell him. It wasn't until my mother figured it out when she found him in my bed that he was restored to his real body. I'm really glad he had a sense of humor about it and didn't kill me. But he did guilt the shit out of me over it for the rest of his life."

Kateri felt for his brother. "Was he okay?"

"Yeah, but he did have this strange craving to chew on leather after that. At least it kept his fangs sharp."

Cabeza drew up short and motioned for them to be silent. Without a sound, Jess pulled his gun off his shoulder while she and Ren each nocked an arrow.

Off to the left something was running.

And it was headed straight for them.

Chapter 15

"Use me for cover."

Kateri gaped as Ren moved to stand between her and whatever was approaching them. "Ren—"

"I'm immortal and I just got you resuscitated. You're a lot more important than I am. Now do what I say ... please."

Those words had her riled up until the please at the end. That one word coupled with the break of fear for her in his voice took every bit of the sting out of his sharp order. And it rammed home what he was really saying.

He who never cried, had cried over her.

"A'ight, baby," she said with a smile. "But just so you know, you get hurt, I'm opening up a can of 'Bama whup-ass on them so big it's gonna look like an LSU Bowl showdown. You hear me? Roll Tide."

Sasha turned around to face her with a severe scowl. "I

speak dozens of languages and hundreds of dialects, but be damned if I caught a single word of that. Am I the only one completely baffled?"

Sundown cocked his gun. "He said he loved her. She said, 'I love you, too.' Now shush."

Sasha stood there moving his finger back and forth as if repeating her words silently in his head. After a second, he turned to face Jess. "How the hell did you get *that* out of what she said?"

Urian glared at Sasha. "The man speaks Southern football, now shut up."

"Southern football, my ass," he mumbled before he turned into a wolf and dashed into the woods after whatever was approaching.

Cabeza drew a strange triangle-shaped weapon Kateri had never seen before. "If I accidentally kill Sasha, you think anyone would hold it against me?"

"Yeah, unfortunately." Sundown sighed. "Zarek would tear you apart over it."

"Psycho Zarek?"

"Yep."

Cabeza clapped Ren on the back. "Then I shall blame you, *amigo*, should I slip and yield to my urges."

Ren gave him a wry stare. *"Gracias."*

"De nada."

Suddenly, and just as she remembered that so long as Ren's eyes were blue, he wasn't immortal, the forest around them attacked. Literally. The trees. The foliage. Demons.

Ren lowered his bow and moved to cover her. "Cabeza? *Huitzauhqui, por favor!"*

286

Cabeza manifested the huge paddle weapon with the jagged edging and handed it off to Ren. Sharper than a machete, it cut through everything it touched. Ren backed her up against a rock wall so that nothing could attack her from behind.

Kateri opened fire on every target that was within range. Sundown unloaded his shotgun, while Urian fought with a sword and Cabeza with a different kind of war club.

Ren cursed as more demons crawled out from the ground to attack. He'd lied to Kateri. His powers were still down, so he was as mortal as she was. But at least the others hadn't outed him for it.

The worst part was that he couldn't refill her quiver or blast them.

Or could he?

He looked at Sundown, who had yet to reload. That meant that Jess was able to create the rounds. . . .

Closing his eyes, he summoned another quiver. It appeared instantly in his hands. Thank the gods!

He turned and handed the arrows off to Kateri, then manifested fireballs to throw at their attackers. They shrieked and screamed as fire hit them and drove them back.

It was a thing of beauty.

Kateri hesitated with her next shot as she saw Ren drop his weapon. He leaned his head back and spread his arms out wide. Arching his back, he chanted under his breath in a language she'd never heard before.

In a single blink, heavily stylized armor, unlike anything she'd ever seen, appeared on his body. A deep dark purple that was edged in gold, it covered him from neck to toe.

Steel gloves shaped like talons complete with long claws curving over his fingers, both to protect and to fashion weapons for him, enveloped his hands.

The front of his hair was now pulled back from his face and secured with eagle feathers at the crown of his head.

A heartbeat later, similar armor covered her. She shivered at the feel of it. Instead of being heavy, it was air light. But more than that, it felt like it was breathing.

It's demonic.

Conjured from the powers that he'd inadvertently inherited while breast-feeding from the crow–demon. Amazed by it, she returned to shooting, only to learn that he'd put some kind of force field around her so that her arrows couldn't go more than a few feet before striking it and falling to the ground.

With her safe and secured, he lowered his head into the warrior's countenance that sent chills over her. Then he laid into the demons with a skill that was truly frightening.

This was the creature who had battled her father night and day for a solid year. Three demons attacked him at once. Ren caught one with his claws under its chin. Screaming, it staggered back while another moved to stab him with a short sword.

Ren caught it with his hands, disarmed the demon, then rammed its weapon straight through the demon's stomach. The third turned to run, but Ren wouldn't let it. He sent a blast into its back.

Sundown lowered his gun as Urian moved to stand by his side. "I'm feeling a little unnecessary right now. How about you, Cowboy?"

"About as useful as warts on a pig's bottom."

They turned to look at Kateri.

"Did you know about this?" Urian asked her.

"Kind of, but it's more impressive in live action."

And it was.

Until a bad feeling went through her. *He is the Thunderbird.* . . .

She didn't know where that thought came from, but in her mind, she saw him as the destroyer of legend. While thunderbirds could be protective, they were also known to unleash their wrath against the world and to tear it apart. They destroyed everyone and everything in their path. That was why her father had placed a thunderbird on Ren's necklace that denoted him as a Guardian.

Cabeza fell back to their position. "We're in trouble."

Jess gave him a doubting grin. "How you figure?"

"The *pendajo* fighting Ren is Chamer. He's the husband to Ixtab. The suicide goddess."

Kateri started forward, but couldn't go far before the force field cut her off. "We have to help him."

"Help who?" Urian asked. "From where I'm standing, Ren's winning."

And if he was fighting a regular demon, she might believe it. But this was a god.

He's going to die. . . . She could feel it with every part of her.

Ren staggered back as Chamer kicked him hard in the chest. What the god didn't know was that it didn't hurt. The beauty about this brand of armor was that it drew power from hatred and malice. The more the god sought

289

to hurt him, the stronger the armor made Ren. And the weaker the god would become.

"You will *never* leave here," Chamer snarled. "All of you belong to us now."

Ren laughed. "Do you know what happens to a god when you kill him? You gain his powers."

Chamer attacked him again.

Ren met him stroke for stroke without hesitation.

The god tried to blast him.

Ren arched one brow. "Are you done?"

"You should be in pieces. I don't understand."

Ren grabbed him by the throat. "Then let me explain the rules. We both draw demonic powers. And because yours are demonic in origin, they make me all the stronger. So summon every god here. Let me drink of their powers until I'm drunk from it." He laughed evilly. Then he sank his teeth into the neck of the god and drank his blood.

Kateri went cold at the sight. "Is he supposed to do that?"

"No," the three of them said in unison.

Cabeza slid his gaze to the other two men. "One of us should go and break that up, I think."

Urian clapped him on the back. "By all means. Go for it."

Sundown handed his gun to Kateri.

"What are you doing?" Urian asked.

"I don't want Ren to shoot me with my own weapon. If he goes for my throat, I'm expecting one of you to grow a set and pull him off me." Sundown headed to Ren.

At his approach, Ren raised his head and licked his bloody lips. His eyes glowed a deep, scary red.

"Why don't you go ahead and let the not so nice god go, Ren?"

"I am Makah'Alay. And you should fear me."

"Ain't real big on fear. I tried it once, and well ... didn't like the taste of it. Burped it up for days afterward and have no intention of doing *that* again. Now let the god go before we have to do something we're both liable to regret."

Ren tilted Chamer's head back, exposing the wound in his throat. He sniffed at it as if the scent of the blood was the finest nectar made. "Why don't you leave? I think I'll stay. I like it here."

Chamer summoned Ixtab to him.

With long black hair and skin of the finest caramel, she appeared, then froze at the sight of her bleeding husband.

"Get them out of here, Ixtab. Or they'll destroy us!"

She raised her arm, but Sundown stopped her.

"We're one man down and we're not leaving here without him."

She curled her lip. "The wolf? Take the beast. We don't want him here either."

One second they were in the forest, in the next, they were back at Ren's trashed house.

Even Sasha, who was still in wolf form and bleeding profusely.

"I'll get him to Sanctuary," Cabeza said, rushing to pick him up and teleport him out.

Sundown retrieved his gun from Kateri's hands. "I might be needing this after all."

Urian stopped him. "You know, a gun against a demon is a real bad idea. It won't kill him, but it will piss him off."

"Yeah, but it'll make me feel better." Sundown started past Urian, but Kateri cut him off.

She went to Ren and cupped his face in her hands. "Baby? What's going on?"

Ren heard the words, but he couldn't understand them. Any more than he could comprehend why this strange woman was touching him. His anger surged.

Until he caught a whiff of her scent.

Kateri. Images of her making love to him filled his head. He placed his hand over her heart so that he could feel it beating beneath his palm.

"Ren?"

Help me, Kateri. He wanted to go back to her. But he felt so lost.

She pulled him against her and held him tight. "It's okay, sweetie. We're home now. You're safe."

Safe. He'd never understood that word.

But as she rocked him back and forth, strange emotions and compulsions warred inside him. One was for him to bite her and taste her blood, too.

The other was to protect her. To make sure no one ever preyed on her.

"Look at me, Ren."

He did. He stared into a pair of eyes that were filled with . . .

She kissed him. The moment her lips touched his, he remembered how she'd looked holding her bow and refusing to back down.

"A'ight, baby. But just so you know, you get hurt, I'm opening up a can of 'Bama whup-ass on them so big it's gonna look like an LSU Bowl showdown. You hear me? Roll Tide."

In that one memory, he found himself. *Is this what it feels like to be loved?*

Her hand toyed with the hair at the nape of his neck while her tongue teased his. When she pulled back, he was so light-headed that for a moment, he feared he might fall.

Kateri breathed in relief as she saw his eyes return to blue. There were still little flecks of red in them, but he seemed to be back to the Ren she'd made love to. "Feeling better?"

"If I say no, will you kiss me again?"

She laughed. "I'll kiss you either way." Her laughter died as she glanced down to see the red teardrop around his neck. The only time she'd seen him wear it had been in the visions where he fought her father. "Where did this come from?"

Ren looked down to see what she was referring to. His breath caught the instant he saw the crystal that contained Windseer's blood. The blood they'd used to tie him to the Grizzly Spirit.

In his mind, he heard the evil bitch curse him, and he finally understood. When the Guardian had freed Ren from Grizzly's hold, Windseer had been forced to return to Grizzly's service. She'd only been freed the first time because she'd delivered Ren to him, and her freedom was based on Ren's slavery.

No wonder she hated him so badly.

But he couldn't tell Kateri that, and he was grateful

293

that she couldn't divine its significance that marked him as Grizzly's slave. "It's nothing."

Kateri knew he was lying. She just didn't know why. But she decided to trust him. Perhaps he had a good reason for it. However, he better not make it a habit. She hated a liar worse than anything, but she wasn't naïve enough to think that there was never a time when a lie was needed. Like all the instances when they were kids and she'd tell Sunshine one of her paintings was beautiful while the truth was she thought it stunk.

He's hiding something from you.

And it was bad. She couldn't shake that feeling no matter what. Worse, images of him on a homicidal rampage wouldn't go away no matter how hard she tried.

In them, he destroyed the entire world. And there was nothing she could do to stop him.

Chapter 16

Acheron Parthenopaeus paused as he entered Kateri's bedroom. While her home was modest, the interior was filled with warmth.

Like his own house in New Orleans.

A smile curled his lips as he thought about his wife and son. He couldn't wait to get them back home and have all of this nastiness put aside.

If it didn't kill them all.

His mother would be thrilled to hear his doubt. But he didn't want to think about her right now. He had to find Kateri's time stone and get it to her. Time was running out and the gates were so thin, they were translucent.

"Damn, there's a lot of rocks in here," he muttered as he saw them all around the room. There were even more in boxes in her garage and a huge pile on her covered back porch. He'd never seen anything like it.

The woman was obsessed.

"It's been a long time, Acheron."

He froze at the sound of a voice he hadn't heard in centuries. Turning, he saw the shade of the extremely wise medicine woman he'd met on a previous doomsday avoidance mission. "Ixkib. How have you been?"

"Not as well as I would have liked, but I'm glad to have your help, old friend."

"Glad I'm still here to do it."

She laughed. And by that, he knew it wasn't the real Ixkib. Though she looked like her, she didn't have the same laugh. Dread filled him. "Who are you?"

"You know me."

Acheron searched his mind, but he couldn't tell who it was. "No, I don't."

But as soon as those words left his lips, he realized how wrong he was. He did know her. . . . "Tiva." The goddess of unraveled time. While her twin brother oversaw time itself and kept it in order, Tiva lived to destroy lives.

Zev was the one they called Time.

Tiva was Untime.

She clicked her tongue at him. "Always brilliant. Thank you for leading me here, by the way. I appreciate it. I would never have found this place without you." She moved to go through one of the boxes.

Ash pulled her away. "I can't let you do that."

She sneered. "You can't stop me."

"Oh yes, I can." Ash felt his body start to glow as his god powers surged. "You want to try me?"

Kateri was still worried sick about Ren. Though he said he was fine and they were both back in normal clothes, she had her doubts. Something didn't feel right.

Now that he was resting in his bed, she'd snuck away for a cup of coffee. She sat at the kitchen table with Cabeza, who'd returned a little while ago to let them know that Sasha was being tended to and would make a full recovery.

Kateri hung up the phone to smile at Cabeza. "Sunshine said that they're all fine and that Rain is driving her up the wall. She wants us to hurry so she can go home before she kills him."

Cabeza laughed.

Sobering, Kateri raked her hand through her hair. "I still don't understand why all of this has fallen to me. I get that Sunny isn't completely American Indian because of her mother, but—"

"Your grandmother was a very special woman," Cabeza said, interrupting her train of thought. "Back before records were kept, a fierce battle was fought between our peoples. Ahau Kin was our god of the underworld and time, and we're exceptionally lucky we didn't meet him while we were down in Xibalba. Of course, Ren might have enjoyed his blood more. Why risk it? Anyway, you do know who he is, don't you? He's almost always shown at the center of our calendars."

"The god with the jaguar face. Ren already covered this with me, and said that Ahau Kin was the father of the Anikutani."

He inclined his head to her. "When the other tribes went after Ren's people, their hatred and attack so angered Ahau Kin that he cursed them and divided them for all time. His intent was to send mankind out of this existence and to banish them to the realm of the underworld so that he'd never have to see them again. . . ."

His words made her mind flash to one event in particular. It was in a dark, small village where fires burned all around. Ahau Kin was walking through the center of the village, making sure there were no survivors.

All of a sudden, he saw a young woman holding her neighbor's baby, trying to protect it.

He went to kill them, but rather than cower, she stood her ground.

"What you're doing is wrong!" she shouted fearlessly. "You are supposed to be better than us, but you're not, are you? My father always said that being an asshole to others doesn't make you feel better, and it if does, then I really do feel sorry for you. How awful to hold all the power in the universe and to not have any better means of coping."

Her words stunned him. Here she was, a puny human, and she dared confront him. Not with weapons.

With words.

That courage and wisdom in one so young and pure touched a foreign part of him. It made him admire her, and for that reason, he couldn't bring himself to kill her. Instead, he took her as his human bride and she gave him a hundred sons and thirty daughters. For the first time in the history of the universe, Ahau Kin was truly happy. But due to his actions against the mainlanders, he'd caused a rift in the cosmos.

An imbalance of darkness brought on by his hatred.

That evil swept into this world, devouring everything it touched. Worse, it went for his human family.

To save the children he loved so dearly from being killed, Ahau Kin drove that darkness back, he banished it past the crossroads in the sky where the tree of life forms a bridge between this world and the dark one. Ahau Kin put it there so that it couldn't harm his family.

But the darkness was strong and it wouldn't stay there. He knew it the moment he sealed the gate.

"Every year from that day forward, whenever the winter solstice sun crosses the sky archer, it causes the heart of the sky to open." It was her grandmother's voice Kateri heard now, telling her this story.

"And from that doorway, all that darkness and all the evil it entails is able to climb down the sacred tree and return to earth to wreak havoc and come for the children of Ahau Kin."

To save his children and those they protect, Ahau Kin plucked a piece of the sun from the sky and locked it inside a special stone. Whenever the stars were to align with the solstice and the gate was to weaken and allow them to leave their prison, the Ixkib—the soul jaguar who was a direct daughter from Ahau Kin's wife—was to use the stone to drive that darkness back into the sky and seal it shut, thereby resetting the calendar until the next alignment. But should his children exist no more, then the world of man will cease. . . .

Kateri was the last of that direct line. Her mother had been designated as the Ixkib. And the darkness knew it. It'd come for her and killed her.

Just as it killed her grandmother. Her home invader had never been caught because it had been a demon who took her life.

The only reason Kateri had survived was because her father and stepfather had been sent to keep her safe and had hidden her from the evil that wanted her dead. But for their care, she would have died as a child. . . .

Bullshit. She didn't want to believe it. But she knew the truth now.

It was why she'd never studied Mayan history. Her father had put that dislike into her to keep her away from anything that might alert her enemies to her whereabouts.

And her grandmother, knowing that one day the time stone would be hers, had taught her to love and collect rocks and minerals. Their combined strength kept the time stone shielded and off the grid of those who would have destroyed it.

In her mind, Kateri saw the stone that she needed perfectly clearly. How stupid of her to not have known it immediately.

Her grandmother had always referred to it as the Eye of the Sun, saying that it was the single most powerful stone she had in her collection. The same color orange as the official Cherokee flag that bore seven stars—one for each clan of the Cherokee nation, and the same number as the Pleiades stars—along with the one solitary black star in the upper corner that signified those who'd died tragically on the Trail of Tears ... the same darkness that they were to always guard against.

For that matter, even their peace flag held the Yonegwa constellation—seven red stars against a field of white. . . .

And it was a stone that was only found in Mexico. All Mexican fire opals were rare, but seldom did they show the play of color that was common to the more familiar "black" and "white" opals found in the rest of the world.

As a child, Kateri used to believe that her grandmother's opal winked at her. That it was trying to tell her a secret.

Now she knew what its secret was.

Her grandmother's opal had actually come from the sun. Ironic really, given the fact that it was set into a necklace that had always reminded Kateri of a Mayan-styled sun from one of their glyphs. . . .

Unbelievable.

She frowned at Cabeza. "What do I have to do with it?"

"On a cave wall that only a Guardian can see, there will be a mural of a thunderbird and hummingbird. You'll have to take the Kinichi—the sun's eye—and place it into one of their mouths . . . whichever one has a spot of the thunderbird so that it can carry the eye into the heavens and drive the darkness back. Once done, the stone will be returned for your safekeeping."

"And this mural is located where?"

"The Valley of Fire."

Which was why they'd brought her to Las Vegas. The Valley of Fire was where her father had gone to rest after his battle with Ren. In the heart of the Valley was a cavern that was critical, as it formed an intersection between all the gates of this world and the realms no one wanted opened.

Honestly, she didn't want to believe in any of this.

But every time she had that thought, she heard her grandmother's voice. "You don't have to believe in something for it to be real."

God love her grandmother for that one single truth.

She looked up at Cabeza. "Have you ever felt so overwhelmed by responsibility that all you wanted to do was curl up in your bed and become a vegetable?"

"*Si*, but I was in the midst of battle at the time and

couldn't dwell on that wish." He lifted his coffee mug in a silent salute. "Just like you, *bonita*. No time to dwell."

She nodded. "Can I ask you something?"

"I put the seat down. I swear it."

She laughed at his unexpected comment. "Seriously, why do you speak Spanish when you're actually Mayan?"

"Because when I speak my native language no one, other than Acheron and a small handful of other Dark-Hunters, can converse with me in it. And I learned Spanish long before I learned English. I spent two thousand years in Spain, Basque, and Portugal before I was allowed to come back to my homeland."

"Wow," she breathed. "That's incredible."

"I don't know about incredible. Long, *si*. Definitely . . . It was hard to get used to at first. Things over there were very different from what I was used to here. It was a solid month before I could even secure my pants properly. Led to some rather embarrassing moments, especially when I'd have to explain to others why the Daimons got away and my pants were at my ankles. Unfortunately, we didn't have Google back then to look it up. Hard, hard times."

She laughed again. Once Cabeza lowered the thirty-foot-thick walls around himself, he was quite entertaining. "Since you're so talkative . . . why do they call you Cabeza? I have to know."

He gave her a sardonic grin. "I always tell people it's from the heads I collected in battle."

"But that's not the truth, is it?"

He shook his head. A deep, dark sadness came over him. For several seconds, he didn't speak. "When I was a boy . . . ten, my older brother was killed by Chacu's father.

302

It was a bad time in Tikal back then. The Snake Kingdom was always attacking us. In one such attack, they went after a group of children and wounded several. My older brother stayed behind to draw their fire so that the boys could get away. They made it back, but the price of that safety was my brother's life. Barely fifteen, he didn't last long against an entire band of seasoned warriors. Those bastards took my brother's head and would play ball games with it. When my mother found out, it broke her heart all over again. She say it was like having him murdered every time they did it. She says she would never be able to sleep so long as they dishonored him so. I couldn't stand to see her so miserable so I snuck over to their capital city and found my brother's head, then I brought it home to my mother so that she could sleep again."

Kateri placed her hand over her heart as tears filled her eyes. "How awful for you. I'm so sorry."

Cabeza shrugged. "Bad for me, *si*. For my mother, much worse. I lost my brother. She lost her son ... Much, much worse." He cleared his throat. "My uncle, he was a bit *loco*. So he started calling me Head as a way of celebrating my bravery and loyalty. To remind me and others that the most honorable thing in life is not to live it selfishly, but to take risks for those we love. He used to say being a man is not about killing or taking. It's not about proving your worth or seducing women. It's when you are willing to give up your life rather than watch your family cry or be degraded."

"He was right."

"He was, indeed, and so to this day, in honor of him, I still go by it."

"And you definitely do honor to it and to your family."

He looked away, but not before she saw the shame that darkened his gaze. She started to ask him to explain it. Then thought better of it. Whatever was in the past hurt him deeply. And she was grateful that her powers didn't show it to her. Because if it could make a man who, at age ten, went into an enemy city to bring back his brother's head . . . it had to be bad.

And some memories were too awful to share.

"I think I'll go check on Ren."

He inclined his head to her, but didn't speak.

Kateri hesitated at the door and turned back to watch Cabeza. He pulled the ring from his pinkie and stroked it while lost in thought. As he did so, she had an image of a beautiful woman. Tiny and sweet. Kateri had no idea who the woman was, but she left him to his memories as she headed down the hallway to Ren's room.

He lay sleeping still. Worried about him, she sat down on the bed and felt his brow to see if he had a fever. The moment she touched him, he opened his eyes, which were still blue, then frowned.

"How did I get here?"

"Don't you remember?"

Ren searched his mind for an answer. He saw Windseer and then . . . nothing. "We were under attack. That's the last thing I recall."

"You have no memory of attacking a god and drinking his blood?"

He winced at that. "Tell me I didn't."

She nodded.

Cursing himself, he felt sick. That was the thing about

drinking preternatural blood. The aftertaste was lethal and the indigestion vicious. "Which god?"

"Crap . . . what did Cabeza call him? He's the one married to the suicide goddess."

Oh, this was bad. "Chamer?"

"That was it."

Ren ground his teeth. "Well at least I won't be stuttering for a long while."

She widened her eyes. "Drinking blood affects your stuttering?"

"Yeah, it's totally screwed up, right?"

"It's definitely something."

"So how did we get back here?" he asked again, returning to his primary question.

"You freaked the god out so badly, he banned us from his underworld and threw us out. Good job, there. Who knew that was all you had to do to get free?"

Ren ignored her sarcasm as his thoughts churned. Grizzly must have possessed him and made him do that. His gut tightened with the fear that she'd seen it all. "Was I . . ."

"Possessed? If you have to ask . . ."

He was possessed and she had seen every bit of it. Damn. Then, he froze as he remembered Kateri holding him. Somehow she had reached through the demon to pull him out.

Just like her father.

Well, not *just* like her father. The Guardian had beat the hell out of Ren to do it. Literally. He much preferred Kateri's way. Though to be honest, he was glad her father hadn't attempted *that*. Her father hugging him like a lover grossed him out even more than drinking god blood.

No wonder he felt hungover.

Which he shouldn't feel if he was a Dark-Hunter. "What color are my eyes?"

"Still blue."

Double damn.

"By the way, you are sex on a stick or more apropos sex in a can when you wear demon armor." She sucked her breath in sharply between her teeth. "Ooo baby. Nice."

He vaguely recalled summoning it. "I got the ability to summon it from my nurse. But the armor itself was a gift from my mother."

"Really?"

He nodded. "After I died, Artemis showed up with it and told me that I could access it with the demon powers."

"Nice gift."

"I would have rather had my mother."

"I know, baby." She laid herself down by his side and placed her hand over his heart.

Ren closed his eyes as her scent hit him all over again. Between that and her touch, his body went instantly hard. But worse than that were the feelings inside him. Feelings that wanted to stay with her like this forever.

Feelings that went wild as her breath fell against his nipple while she drew circles over his chest.

"You're killing me, Kateri."

She lifted herself up to look down at him. "I wasn't trying to kill you, sweetie."

But as his gaze fell to the gap in her shirt that clearly showed her breasts, he was sure this was terminal.

Her smile turned seductive as she slowly kissed her way down his body. His senses reeled. Why couldn't he have found her when he'd been human? His life would have been radically different had they met then.

But she hadn't been born. Not until centuries later . . .

Oh, gah, I'm a dirty old man. One who was old enough to be her great-grandfather times a million.

That thought scattered as she took him into her mouth. Groaning from the ecstasy of her tongue caressing him, he cupped her cheek in his hand and stroked her jaw with his thumb. She was so beautiful. So perfect.

And the sight of her on him . . .

How can I let her go?

But he knew he couldn't keep her. Not as a demon. Not as Grizzly's slave. Somehow he was going to have to find the courage to walk away from her and continue to live eternity without her.

Just the thought of it felt like a punch in the gut. For the first time in his life, he could see himself growing old with someone. Having a family . . .

When he'd been mortal, those things had been vague and undefined. But now they were crystal-clear and he could see her face.

Grizzly had found a whole new level of hell to relegate him to.

Kateri hesitated as she felt Ren tense. Afraid she'd hurt him, she pulled back to see the hottest expression on his face. It was feral and hungry. He pulled her up to lie over his body so that he could give her the most incredible kiss of her life. His fangs brushed her lips as he buried his hands in her hair and fisted them without hurting. It was as if he was trying to consume her. That kiss left her breathless and weak.

Rolling her over, he used his powers to strip her naked. His muscles bunched and tightened around her while he teased her ear with his tongue until she saw stars. His hands seemed to be everywhere at once, stroking and delving, heightening her pleasure until she couldn't think straight.

He lifted himself to stare down at her an instant before he filled her.

She cried out at how good he felt deep inside her body. Biting his lip, he thrust himself against her hips, driving himself in even deeper. No one had ever made love to her like this. Like she was the air he needed to survive.

Ren pressed his cheek against hers and held her as tight as he could. He never wanted to let her go. He never wanted to leave her arms.

For the first time in his life, he fully understood what it meant to belong to someone else. Body and soul. There was nothing he wouldn't do for her. He would crawl naked over broken glass in the lowest pit of hell just to make her smile.

And when she came in his arms, crying out his name, he found a level of heaven he'd never known existed. One he knew he'd never have again.

Damn you, Fates.

And damn him for being such a fucking idiot that he'd screwed up his life so badly.

Clenching his eyes shut, he joined her release and

shuddered against her. She ran her hands over his back as she buried her lips against his neck and tormented him with light, sweet kisses.

"Are you all right, Ren?"

No. Once he walked out of her life, he'd never be all right again.

But he couldn't tell her that.

"Fine. You?"

"Worried about you. There's something I can feel, but I don't know what it is."

"It's called nerves."

She snorted. "I know what those feel like. They came out to play with all their friends the entire week before I had to defend my dissertation."

He didn't respond to her attempt to make her laugh as he reluctantly slid out of her and rolled onto his back. She snuggled up against him and sighed contentedly.

So this was what normal felt like. . . .

He'd never experienced it before. How could any man have something this precious and crave anything more?

Kateri watched the emotions play across his face, wishing she could identify them. The only thing she knew for sure was that something bothered him.

A lot.

"So . . ." She stretched that one word out. "If we survive all this, what will happen to us?"

"You'll go back to teaching and—"

"No, I don't mean us as in you and me. I mean *us*."

Ren winced at the wave of pain that gutted him. He'd never been an "us" before. Never had someone who wanted to put him in her future.

It was something he craved so badly ... so desperately, he could taste it.

If I still had my soul, I'd sell it to keep you. . . .

And if wishes were Porsches, they'd all ride free and in style. He swallowed against the pain in his heart. Here in this one moment when he wanted nothing to spoil it, he was going to have to shatter the only heart that had ever loved him.

I am a bastard.

"There is no us, Kateri. There can never be an us."

Kateri held her breath as those words kicked her in the teeth. *What? You had to know this. Why are you so surprised?*

He was an immortal warrior. She was a geologist. Other than hot sex, what did they really have in common?

Not a damn thing.

He tilted her head so that she could look at him. "Are you all right?"

Refusing to let him see the depth to which she'd been hurt, she nodded. "Fine. I'm a big girl, Ren. I'm not one of those doe-eyed romantics who expects a ring just because we slept together. At least I wasn't your one-night stand." She got up and headed for the bathroom.

Ren ground his teeth at the pain he'd seen in her eyes. *You're the only woman I have ever loved.* She was the only woman he would ever love.

But love wasn't for mongrel creatures like him. And it shouldn't be. He'd destroyed too many lives. He didn't deserve happiness after he'd taken it from so many others. He didn't even deserve to have had what little she'd given him.

Draping his arm over his eyes, he tried to banish his

310

emotions and thoughts. Instead, he went back to when he'd been a teenager with Coyote.

"Did you hear? Choo Co La Tah is getting married."

Ren had frowned at his brother. "Already?"

Coyote nodded. "Her parents arranged it with his. I heard she's beautiful. Not as beautiful as my bride will be, I'm sure, but I'm happy for him."

"I would th-th-think there are-are-are-are more important th-th-things than just looks."

Coyote burst out laughing. "Don't th-th-think, Makah'Alay. It's embarrassing. What could be more important than her looks?"

He always hated whenever Coyote did that. It was bad enough when it came from others, but it stung worse when it was his own brother. Unwilling to be mocked further, he shrugged.

Coyote sighed. "Can you imagine having a beautiful woman in your bed every night who belonged to you? One you could screw all night long for as many hours as you wanted, and she couldn't say no because she was your wife? Oh, sorry. I keep forgetting you're still a virgin. We really need to take care of that. You want to try the brothel again?"

Horrified, Ren shook his head. The last time he'd made that mistake, the prostitute had turned him away. *We don't serve retards here. Take him somewhere else.*

For weeks after that, he'd had to endure comments from Coyote about how no one knew whores were picky, and how awful when you were so pathetic you couldn't buy a bargain-priced whore for an hour.

Coyote had slapped him on the back. "Poor Makah'Alay.

But have faith, brother. I'm sure there's a whore out there who'll have you one day."

Ren sighed. In over eleven thousand years he'd only found two women who would sleep with him. One had been an immortal slut who had stolen his humanity.

The other was a lady who had given him her heart.

Wanting to ease whatever pain he'd given her, he got up and went to the bathroom. Her sobs while she showered stopped him dead. They kicked him so hard that for a minute he couldn't breathe.

Unable to stand it, he went to the shower and pulled the curtain aside. She gasped, then cried harder.

Ren took her into his arms and held her tight. "I love you, Kateri," he whispered. "You're the only one in this world that I have ever really loved. I would sell a kidney to shoe your feet and I'd sell my soul, if I still had one, to make you smile."

Kateri trembled as she heard the sincerity in his voice. He meant that. "Then why did you say—"

"Because I can't be with you. Once we reset the calendar, I have to go back to what I was . . . and so do you."

"Why? Sundown was a Dark-Hunter. Talon, too. Now they're married. Why can't that be us?"

Because they were luckier than he was. And they hadn't sold their freedom to buy back their wives' lives.

"Please don't cry, Kateri. I can't stand to see you sad."

"I'm sorry." Stepping back, she pulled him into the shower with her. "I love you, too, you know."

He savored the sound of sincere words he'd never thought to hear. They were even more beautiful when spoken from the heart.

Sniffing back her tears, she soaped her cloth, then used it to bathe him. "Were your eyes always blue?" she asked as she lightly fingered the bow-and-arrow tattoo on his left hip.

He nodded. "They thought for the longest time that I was blind. It took me years to make them understand that I could see perfectly."

"I take it they're from your mother."

"Yeah, and my father hated them. He said it was just like looking at her all over again and that they made his skin crawl with revulsion. Sometimes he'd just walk by and slap me for having them."

"How awful!"

He shrugged. "Believe it or not, you get used to it. You know you're going to get slapped for something so you don't even react when it comes. Besides, the slaps didn't hurt all that much. I preferred those to being lashed by his tongue."

She couldn't imagine being hit over something she'd been born with. Something she couldn't help.

Something so beautiful and unusual.

"You know, Ren, I think you're the most fascinating person alive."

She could plant corn in the furrows his frown created on his forehead, they were so deep.

"Why?"

If there hadn't been so much doubt and confusion in that one single word, she'd have laughed. But he really, truly didn't see it.

"You're born of two entirely different ancient cultures. Your mother was a goddess, Ren. An actual Greek goddess who loved you so much, she sent another goddess to watch over you. You said you understood Apollymi. While your mother didn't try to destroy the world over you, you were her world. She loved you so much that the worst punishment Zeus could give her was to cast her into the sky as a comet so that she would never see the baby she loved *so* much. And yes, your father was definitely a dick, but he was also the chief of a tribe of legendary fighters. *You* were one of those warriors that our people still talk about in hushed and reverent tones. You led an army ... okay, it was an evil army, but you led an army of demons—*you* have demon blood and powers. And you fought my father for a year and a day. Gracious, Ren, you're the most fascinating man I've ever met. You draw power from three different cultures. How many people can do that? Seriously? That's impressive. *You're* impressive."

Those words made his heart race.

No, not the words. The passion behind them. She meant every one of them. They weren't spoken out of flattery because she wanted something from him. She meant every word she spoke.

"I love how you see the world, Kateri." Most of all, he loved how she saw him.

As she soaped his chest, she paused at the necklace. "Where did this come from? You didn't have it earlier."

Ren hesitated. He didn't want to lie to her, but he damn sure couldn't tell her the truth. "It came with the armor."

"Oh. It's very cute."

"Thanks," he said drily. "That was so the look I was going for."

314

She laughed at his sarcasm. "Sorry. It looks all hot and manly on you."

If she only knew . . .

He could never remove it, and with it, Grizzly could summon him anywhere. Anytime.

So long as you wear it, Kateri's safe. That thought was the only thing that made his slavery bearable.

"Hey, Ren?" Sundown called from the hallway. "You in there?"

"Yeah."

"Have you seen Kateri lately?"

He gave her a lopsided grin. "Um . . . yeah."

"Where is she?"

He opened his mouth to answer, but wasn't sure what to say. He didn't want to embarrass her. Most likely, she didn't want them to know she was sleeping with him.

But before he could think up an answer, she called out to Jess. "I'm in the shower with Ren."

"Oh dear lord, I am so sorry. I most certainly did not mean to disturb either one of you. As you were. This can definitely wait for later. Y'all take your time. Whatever you need. We'll . . . uh . . . hold down the fort. And I am so out of the hallway."

Ren felt terrible as he heard Sundown's footsteps retreating. "I'm sorry, Kateri. I didn't mean to embarrass you."

She arched a brow at his statement as she sank her hand down to cup him. "You didn't embarrass me, sweetie. I don't care if he knows. We can shout it from the rooftop if you want."

That was something he'd never get used to.

She took her time bathing him and was very thorough

as she did so. By the time they were finished, there was no hot water left and it was pitch dark outside. He hated to get dressed and leave her, but the end of the world respected no one.

Toweling his hair dry, he went into the living room to find that Urian, Sundown, and Cabeza had been joined by Acheron. But it took him a second to recognize their fearless leader with his short hair.

Now there was something terrifying. "What happened to you? You get into a losing argument with a pair of scissors?"

Acheron rolled his eyes. "Damn, all of you are going to make this hard on me until it grows back. I swear. What's more important? Armageddon or my haircut?"

Kateri paused in the hallway as she heard that deep, rumbling voice that spoke in an accent the likes of which she'd never heard before. So this was the mysterious Acheron who led the Dark-Hunters.

The son of a goddess who'd almost ended the world over what had been done to him.

Curious, she stepped into the living room and froze. She wasn't sure what she'd expected to find, but it certainly wasn't . . . *this*.

Yeah, okay, Lord King Badass had just entered the building. Her jaw went slack as she skimmed the ridiculous height of the latest man to join their party. Just shy of seven feet, he had short black hair framing a face that appeared to have been flawlessly chiseled from granite. He held an aura so dark and powerful that it made the hair on the back of her neck and arms rise.

316

Out of all the scary things in the room, he definitely put the others to shame, and that was not an easy thing to do.

Pinning her with a gaze that left her completely immobile, Acheron strode forward with the most predacious walk she'd ever seen. Something not easy to carry off when you considered the fact that he was physically very pretty and surprisingly young.

Probably no more than twenty or twenty-one, he was absolutely beautiful ... almost angelic. Except for that aura of lethal authority that bled out of every molecule he possessed. Yeah, this was a man used to riding herd and having to cow warriors like Cabeza, Sundown, and Ren.

And she couldn't take her gaze away from his spooky eyes. They literally swirled with a hazy silver color ... and they were filled with the promise of death.

Swathed completely in black, he had his hands tucked into the pockets of a long leather coat. He pulled one hand out and reached for her.

She instinctively took a step back.

Luckily, he had a sense of humor about that. "I'm not going to hurt you, Dr. Avani. I promise. I only bite when given an invitation to do so."

And he had manners too. . . .

Freaky.

He opened his huge hand to show her her grandmother's necklace.

Stunned, she gaped at him. . . . Granted, she had to crane her neck to do so. "How did you know where to find it?"

"I have my evil ways."

Yeah, I bet you do. She took it out of his hand and for the first time really saw it for what it was. The thick gold chain was forged in such a way that it was much lighter than it appeared. But it was the fire inside the stone that was truly exceptional. As a kid, she'd had no idea whatsoever how rare a stone this was.

As a geologist she knew there were probably only a handful of stones ever created that came close to this perfection. Most fire opals were opaque like a regular gemstone. In spite of the name they bore because of their typical orange or red color, fire opals seldom showed the play of color other opals were known for. And in all her studies, she'd never seen one with the color play this one had. It really did look like it was a piece of the sun.

"Thank you," she breathed.

He inclined his head to her. "By the way, my wife had no idea what the writing on the seal was, she—"

"Your wife?" Kateri hated interrupting him, but he didn't look old enough . . .

Yeah, duh, what was she thinking with this group? He was an Atlantean . . . older than dirt and dirt's great-grandfather.

Acheron took her interruption in stride. "Dr. Soteria Kafieri Parthenopaeus."

The way he said that, it melted like chocolate on your tongue. It rolled so fluidly and with his accent . . .

Wow. His wife probably made him read everything out loud, including cans and cereal boxes, just to hear the cadence of it.

The downside was that his accent was so thick that at first she had no idea what he'd said, until it suddenly clicked. "Dr. Par . . . Par . . . Parthen . . . Par . . . yeah. Ancient Greek scholar. Fluent in many dead languages. Fernando e-mailed her a photo of the stone."

Acheron laughed, then nodded. "The real reason I fell in love with my wife. She can not only pronounce my last name without stumbling over it, she can actually spell it."

The men all laughed but Kateri felt awful.

"It's okay, Dr. Avani," he said good naturedly. "My first name isn't much easier, it's why I usually go by Ash. It's harder to trip over and it doesn't take me an hour to write it out."

Thank goodness the man had a sense of humor about it.

"Did she recognize the language?" she asked, trying to divert the conversation to something less embarrassing.

"Lemurian."

That was the last thing she'd expected to hear. "Shut the front door! Really?" she breathed, then shook her head. "No. It can't be. Biogeographists debunked that myth a long time ago."

He grinned at her, showing off a little bit of fang. "Yeah, well, they don't know everything, do they?"

Very true. Case in point, she stood in front of a giant from Atlantis who was flanked by a cowboy, Mayan prince who had carried off a lycanthrope, ancient Greek vampire, and a real Keetoowah whose mother was a Greek goddess. Yeah. . . .

"Guess not," she said, returning his smile.

"Did you have any trouble getting the stone?" Ren asked.

Ash hesitated. "Define 'trouble.'"

Ren cursed. "What happened?"

"Tiva. Our little time bitch broke out early and she was hellbent on using the stone to lock down her brother. Luckily, I was more hellbent on keeping her away from it. I'm thinking when the first gate was breached."

Ren and Cabeza paled. "When did the first gate go down?"

"While you were in Mayan hell. We've had our hands full on this side. May the gods have mercy if another gate opens. And since you're most likely not aware of how much faster time travels on this side . . . tonight at midnight. Reset the 'damn' calendar 'cause I don't want to spend eternity cleaning up your mess." He looked over at Urian. "And you'll have to sit it out."

"Why?"

"You're related to a Greek god. You hit the Valley and you'll be real sorry for the last few minutes you're alive."

Urian pointed to Ren. "He's a cousin."

"Who is also Keetoowah. They'll let him in. He's an exception."

"Well, that sucks. What if I wanted to go sightseeing?"

"I'd suggest an online tour." Ash met Ren's gaze. "As a heads-up, I waited to bring the kinichi, as it is a beacon to all kinds of paranormal creatures who want to control time." He turned to face Kateri. "Your grandmother was one powerful woman to keep that under wraps. I am very impressed."

"Thank you. She *was* exceptional."

Ash stepped back. "And on that note, I'm off to help hold the gates."

Just as he started to leave, another light flashed in the room.

Cursing, Ren grabbed Kateri and pulled her behind him. His eyes turned vivid red as his armor reappeared. His hands exploding into fireballs, as he faced what must be another demon.

Ash, Urian, and Cabeza, however, didn't react to this new presence at all. Except for Ash who reached out to lower Ren's arm. "Stand down."

"He's a demon. High level."

Ash gave him a bland stare. "Yeah, well, his highest level is functioning as a perpetual pain in my ass." He turned his attention to the newcomer. "What do you want, Nick?"

Kateri wasn't sure what to make of this man. At least six foot four, he had a bow-and-arrow mark on his left cheek that was identical to the one Ren had on his hip. But even with that mark, he was incredibly handsome.

"I was asked to come here."

"By whom?"

"Artemis."

Ren exchanged a bemused frown with Kateri. "Why would she ask that of you?"

A wry, evil smile curled his lips. "I am a messenger, after all. It's what I was created to do."

The way he said that shivers over her. And in that moment, she flashed to Nick's real form. His skin should be black and red, with glowing eyes and gold armor. In his true body, he was a winged demon. One of the highest level. He was evil in its purest, rawest form.

And she didn't trust him even the slightest bit.

Ash shifted his weight to one foot and assumed a total power stance that said, *boy, don't make me kick your ass all the way to the state line. 'Cause I will. And no, you won't enjoy it.* "You still haven't answered my question. What are you doing here? And to stop the semantics game . . . what missions or message did Artie put you on?"

"I'm to protect Artemis's blood and make sure the gates stay sealed tonight."

Acheron appeared stunned by those words. "Really?" His tone dripped with sarcasm. "I would think you'd have a vested interest in seeing them opened."

Nick snorted. "You don't know me as well as you think you do."

Acheron swept his gaze over them. "Guys? Will you give us the room, please?"

One by one, they filed out.

Ash didn't speak until he was alone with Nick and he was sure none of the others could hear their discussion. "Cut the shit, boy. I know what you want, and why you want it, and you can't have it."

Nick rolled his eyes. "I'm tired of fighting with you, Ash. I know what you think of me and I *really* don't care. But let me tell you a few things you don't know about me, Lord Omniscient to most. You've asked why I'm with Artemis. It's the one place I can go where Stryker can't see through my eyes. Well . . . he *could* see, if he wanted, but since the sight of his aunt sickens him, he withdraws from me the minute I enter her temple. And I finally have a modicum of peace."

Damn. Nick did have it bad if dealing with Artemis's tantrums and moods was his idea of serenity. Ash almost felt bad for the Cajun. "There are ways of blocking him."

"No, there's not. Not the way your mother has him

322

trained. Thanks for that, by the way. You could have slaughtered Stryker and you passed."

Ash shrugged. "I could have slaughtered you, too."

"Can't tell you how much I appreciate *that* kindness."

Ash took a step toward him. "Nick—"

"Don't Nick me. You have no right. You brought back Amanda and Kyrian. You left my mother dead."

Ash winced at a truth that burned him as much as it burned Nick. "I know. But I couldn't bring her back, Nick. Not really."

"Because she didn't want to be here anymore. I know. She was sick of her God-awful life and happy to be dead. You felt sorry for her and so you left her dead to keep her from suffering. Thanks for the consideration. I deeply appreciate it, *cher.*"

Ash heard the anguish underneath those words and it scorched him. At one time, he and Nick had been best friends.

No, they'd been closer than that. He considered Nick his brother, and he hated to see Nick in this much pain. "Your mother loved you. You were her life."

"Apparently not. But I've accepted that."

"Then why do you want the time stone?"

Faster than Ash could react, which said a lot about Nick's skills, Nick grabbed him into a headlock.

Ash started to fight until he realized what Nick was doing. While Ash could see into the future, he could never see the lives of anyone who'd become close to him.

But Nick was able to use his powers to show him what Nick was going to become.

And it was terrifying. Through Nick's eyes, Ash saw

323

Nick's true demon form and the army he led against the world. Gone was the fun-loving boy who used to tease Ash. The one who had wormed his stupid way into Ash's heart, and taught him a lot about human life and normality. Damn, how he missed their friendship.

"My mother is the only thing that kept me human, Acheron," Nick growled into his ear while he continued to share his bloody and brutal destiny with him. "Every single day I live without her, I lose more of my humanity. There's nothing that anchors me now. Do you understand?" He released him.

Ash struggled to breathe as the images began fading. "I thought you hated me."

"I hate every fucking body. Don't you understand? I can't help it. Welcome to the club. Now let's light the sign that we're open for business." He raked a sneer over Ash's body. "Newsflash, Atlantean—you're really nothing special to me. Hatred is who and what I am now. It rules me entirely. Menyara has tried everything, as has Artemis. Nothing works. Without an anchor, I can't stop the metamorphosis." He gestured toward the door the others had left by. "You're afraid of the gates? I pick my teeth with the bones of better evil than anything those gates guard. When I become the Malachai, there is nothing that can stop me."

"The Sephiroth."

Nick shook his head. "I've seen me kill him. Jared is weakened by his past and guilt, and by the weight of a conscience I am losing day by day. When I no longer have mine and he still has his?" He shrugged. "You don't want to know how easily he dies. Remember, he's like my mother.

He wants to die. He's long done with this world and everything on it. He even tried to kill me so that he'd be released."

Ash swallowed as he remembered the past. Nick was right. Jared wouldn't put up a fight, and without that . . .

Nick would destroy everything.

While Ash was considered a final fate god, he wasn't the only one. Almost all pantheons had at least one god of fate. They all basically balanced each other out. But Nick wasn't a god. While Nick's predecessors had been created from the same primal source of power that fueled the gods, Nick's species had been created as a servant for Ash's mother.

To end the world.

Ash was the only person who walked among humanity who knew the real origins and role of Nick's demonic race. Back before time itself, there had been six gods who sprang from the primal source. Three who clung to good and three who craved evil. Three gods of creation and three of utter destruction.

After they'd fought the *Primus Bellum* that almost destroyed the earth and all humanity, those gods had slept for a long time. Until Nick's premature ascension to his Malachai powers. Then two of the dark ones had awakened. Noir and Azura.

They were scouring the earth in search of their missing half-sister, Braith, while never knowing that Braith sat imprisoned in the Atlantean hell realm. That she had given birth to a son . . .

"I can help you, Nick."

"Yeah . . . then bring my mother back."

325

To those who didn't know better, that sounded like a whiny child. But that wasn't what Nick was saying and Ash knew it. Nick was a creature of destruction. While his powers were virtually infinite, they were not without some limitation.

The Malachai—the nuclear bomb for evil—was a tool of annihilation. He couldn't create or restore life. He could only take it.

Nick couldn't walk through time, not without a tool such as the time stone. Nor could he identify a god until he was either sent to kill it or it revealed itself to him. Nick could tell it was paranormal, but not what degree. However, once identified as a god, Nick had all the power he needed to kill it and take its powers.

And Artemis had sent Nick in to guard the Ixkib. . . .

He would laugh if it wasn't so typical of her. How could the twin sister of Apollo—a god of prophecy—suck so badly at seeing the future?

"I can't get your mother back now, but if you can trust me again . . ."

Nick let out a sinister, bone-chilling laugh. "Trust? My father trusted and what did it get him?"

Ash shook his head. "Trust had nothing to do with it. Your father died because he sired another Malachai. Had you not been born, he would still live."

"I still won't trust you."

"Fine, just stop trying to kill me."

Nick sighed, and for a second, he was again the smart-mouthed Cajun kid Ash had welcomed as a friend. "I can't promise that either, boy . . . have you not been listening to me? I'm speaking English here. I can't stop my true nature. It's like asking the moon not to rise or the ocean to quit making waves." He spat each word out separately. "My nature is death. You're alive. That sheer fact, regardless of any other, makes me want to kick your ass and kill you. This is why I need help, and I can't go to a therapist. I just might eat them and I don't like the taste of human...." Ash didn't even want to know how Nick knew he didn't like the taste of human. "At least Artemis has a fighting chance if I go bad on her."

"We will get through this."

"You better be right, Ash. 'Cause if you're not . . ."

Ash's mother would finally win and the world of man would lose everything.

Chapter 17

Ren took a moment to study Kateri while she napped on his bed. A bed he'd never shared with anyone before. One he'd never even dreamed of sharing with another.

Yet there she lay, naked and entwined in his dark brown sheets. Her long dark brown hair spilled over his pillows. She had one hand curled beneath her chin and one leg bent and jutting out from beneath the sheet.

Her right arm dangled over the side of the bed. Kneeling down, he touched her wrist and leaned down to inhale the precious valerian scent that she wore. A scent that would haunt him forever, along with the gentleness of her touch.

"I love you," he whispered as he pressed his lips to her wrist, then nuzzled his cheek against her palm. They had spent the last few hours together, exploring every inch of each other's bodies.

And he was definitely ticklish.

She thought this was the beginning of their future together.

He knew it was the end. It had to be. There was no choice. Grizzly would devour her and laugh while he did it. Worse, he'd make Ren watch.

I will miss you. Always.

His only hope was that one day she'd find a man worthy of her love, and that he'd make her as happy as Ren would have tried to had he been lucky enough to keep her with him.

But it wasn't meant to be.

You know, Ren. My grandmother always said that life isn't about knowing who you are so much as it is about knowing who you're not. Who you are can always change. We strive to be better, and we should greet every day we live with a desire to make it better. But who you're not never changes. And you, my precious, are a hero. Even when you were hurt and angry, you only went after the ones who hurt you. Never the ones who didn't. Because you're not that man who kills for no reason. You are not the person who lashes out against the innocent and hurts them. You will never be that man. And that is why you are a hero in my eyes, and why you will always be one.

He would carry those words for the rest of eternity and let them offer him comfort while Grizzly rained down misery on him.

Rising, he leaned over her and kissed her head. With one last look, he changed into his crow form and left her to the protection of his friend and allies.

Due to the coming storms, the night winds were against his wings. It felt as if they, too, were trying to destroy him, and drive him into the ground far below. In just over twelve hours the equinox would arrive and the path would open and unleash its hell.

Unless Kateri reached the Valley by 3 A.M.

She'd make it. The others would make sure. His job was to make that trip as easy as possible for them.

Dreading what he'd find on his arrival, Ren flew to the one place where his brother would feel safe. The cave where Coyote always retreated to whenever he wanted to draw strength.

Ren came in low to survey the landscape before making his presence known to his enemies. The shaft was empty. He took a second to transform into a man and cover himself with his armor. The Coyote was ever a trickster. He should never be underestimated.

With the same stealth he'd once used to track elusive game, Ren crept down the shaft until it widened into an earthen room. The red walls were decorated with ancient glyphs. Some appeared to be space aliens, but he knew they were ceremonial masks taken from the collective memory of the demons that had long ago been banished from this realm.

Before man taught himself science and reason, he had sought to blend in with demonkyn, hoping that the demons would be fooled into thinking he was one of them and would leave him alone.

It'd never worked, but it had been a nice effort and it had given the demons countless hours of entertainment as they laughed at the stupid humans who tried to mimic them.

Ren drew up short as he saw Choo Co La Tah tied

against the wall. Thank the gods, his friend was still alive. Though, judging by the horrendous condition Choo was in, Ren was pretty sure his friend wasn't thanking anyone for the fact.

Least of all him.

As silent as a wraith, Ren crossed the room and touched Choo's hand.

Choo Co La Tah flinched, then let out a relieved breath as he saw Ren standing in front of him. "It is you, is it not?"

As ludicrous as that proper English accent had always sounded coming out of Choo's mouth, it was doubly so while his friend looked like he'd gone a few rounds posing as Mike Tyson's weight bag.

"It's me, Choo."

"Strange how life goes, isn't it? One day you're king. The next, you're a discarded pawn. Who would have dreamed all those times I laughed at you, and allowed Coyote and others to torment and humiliate you when we were children that I'd one day be reliant on your good grace and decency to save my life."

Ren cut the ropes around his wrists. "Damn, Choo. Only you could be this chatty after being beaten to the brink of death."

Choo Co La Tah managed a bloody smile at that. "Thank you, Makah'Alay."

"For what?"

"Being the better man. It takes a great deal of courage to save the life of someone who wronged you. Badly, at times. Thank you for not holding on to grudges."

Ren scoffed as he draped Choo's arm around his

shoulders. "I do hold on to them, Choo. I kill you every night in my thoughts, and wish festering, puss-filled boils on your crotch."

Choo laughed, then winced in pain.

Applause erupted.

Ren froze as Coyote entered the room from a different shaft.

"Look who's p-p-p-playing hero."

Ren rolled his eyes. "How many weeks did you spend thinking up that one?"

"Funny, I don't remember you having the mental ability to conjure such witty retorts. Was that one of the powers you sucked from the tit of your demon bitch?"

Ren smiled evilly. "Oh, I sucked a lot of things from a lot of people." He gently lowered Choo Co La Tah to the floor.

Choo hissed in pain. "He intends to kill you."

"I know, Choo. It's okay. I intend to kill him first."

Coyote arched a brow at that. "Do you?"

Ren nodded as he looked around the small room. "You're screwed now."

"How so?" Coyote asked in that overly familiar mocking tone.

Ren manifested a short throwing spear similar to the one the Avenging Spirit had used to kill him. "You have no one here to change places with." While Ren could teleport, Coyote could only transpose. "I can't really kill myself, and poor Snake . . . what was it Father used to say? Beware the cups you drink from as you are likely to fall victim to whatever disease infects those who drink with you."

"Is that what he screamed out when you cut his throat?"

Ren shook his head. "He actually died laughing."

"I can see why. The pathetic can't attack outright. They have to resort to trickery to win."

Now *that* was hysterical. "I'm not you, little brother. There was no trickery involved. I told him I was going to kill him. Just as I'm telling you. He made the decision to laugh at me, instead of running. I guess stupidity does run in our blood after all."

Shrieking in outrage, Coyote ran at him with a raised club. Instead of manifesting his own, Ren jerked back, out of the way.

"Why aren't you attacking?"

"You lived with me all those years, Anukuwaya, and yet you never once saw me, did you, brother? I guess that's only fair, as I never saw you either. Not really."

Coyote pulled back. "What do you mean?"

"He doesn't fight," Choo said from his place on the floor. "Ren lies low and watches his opponent exhaust himself with petty posturing. Then, once his enemy has exposed his weakness, your brother strikes once with lethal accuracy."

Coyote lunged at him. "You fought the Guardian."

"I did do that. But that's because, unlike you, he knew me and he knew how to attack my weaknesses to goad me against my better judgment."

"I know your w-w-w-weaknesses, too!"

"No. You know my faults. They are not the same thing. In fact, the Guardian and his daughter have taught me much about myself and others." He twirled so that Coyote's next blow missed him.

"Something other than how to speak without stuttering?"

"No. That is something I owe Grizzly. What the Guardian taught me was that we grow stronger and more intelligent as we learn to compensate for our faults. Unlike others, we have to teach ourselves to adapt quickly so that we can finally master what others take for granted. When something comes too easy for you, you never learn the skill of improvement or flexibility. Of thinking up a better, more concise way to do it. Most of all, you don't learn determination and how to roll with a punch. That was what allowed me to fight him for a year. Because I couldn't speak without your mockery, I learned other ways to communicate. Because you spoon-fed me a daily dose of pain, I didn't feel his punches."

Ren ducked another blow. "And because you taught me to hate myself, I learned to value others more. I kept fighting the Guardian, not for my own well-being, but for Buffalo's. Had it been my death solely that concerned me, I would have allowed him to take my head and end my pain. But I feared that should he defeat me, he would kill my one and only friend, and leave me alone in the world again. *That* is why I fought him so relentlessly. My flaws became my strength. Your mockery and cruelty were the fuel my determination needed to see me through the darkest hours of my life. For that, my brother, I am forever in your debt."

Coyote stabbed at him.

Ren sidestepped the blow and caught his arm. "But weaknesses . . . those are the most dangerous weapons in the universe. Weakness is not a physical trait. It's not a stutter or a bad hand or missing leg. Weaknesses are the

335

ones who live in our hearts. They can motivate us to the highest level and they alone can utterly destroy us. There was a time, brother, when you were my weakness. When I charged headlong into a boar, knowing I lacked the equipment to fight it—*that* was a weakness. I cared more for your life than mine."

Coyote sneered in his face. "You never loved me. You did that for attention. 'Look at me! I'm the hero. I'm the better warrior.' Everything you did, you did to show me up, and you know it. But I wouldn't let you steal my thunder. I showed you who the better man was."

Ren shook his head. "What you showed me was a pathetic little boy, crying for every drop of attention you could grab even though it was always lavished on you. It still wasn't enough. All these years, I have carried guilt in my heart and tortured myself over what I did to you. Did you ever once consider what you did to me?"

"I never did anything to you to warrant your torture. I was your brother and I loved you. Yeah, I played a prank or two. That's what children do. It was all harmless."

Ren shook his head at his brother. There had never been anything harmless about Coyote's actions. "You lied and you stole everything you could from me. When that wasn't enough, you insulted and mocked things I couldn't help."

"You tortured me, you bastard!"

Ren grabbed Coyote's hair and jerked his head back. "See the past. Not through your lies, but through the truth."

He pulled Coyote back to the small home Ren had seized as his headquarters. Unlike his brother, who had taken over their palace after their father's death, Ren had wanted nothing more than a modest place to call his own.

As soon as Coyote entered his domain, Ren had been suspicious of his intent.

"What do you want?"

"I am going forward with my marriage to Butterfly and wanted to bring you my offering for your attendance." Coyote had smiled winsomely. "I miss my brother. We used to sit and talk every night."

No. Ren would clean Coyote's weapons and test them, then prepare his brother's bed while Coyote chattered on about the woman he'd most recently been with and all the changes he would make once he was chief. *Makah' Alay, fetch me wine. Food. A chamber pot.* Coyote had treated him as a slave while mocking him constantly.

But Ren hadn't remembered any of that as he saw his brother again. "I thought you'd be mad at me over what I did to Father."

"You made me chief. How could I be angry over that? Had Father been worthy, he would have killed you, instead." Coyote had held a jug of wine out to Ren. "Let us drink to your victory and my position." He tipped it at Ren. "You first."

Without thinking, Ren had trusted him. But the poison had hit his system hard and sent him to the floor within a few seconds after drinking Coyote's "offering." Sick and disoriented, Ren had groaned from the cramps in his stomach. "W-w-w-w-what—"

"D-d-d-d-did I do? I poisoned you, you moron. Did you really think I'd let you live to take my place? No." Coyote had kicked him over, onto his back. Then, after pinning him to the floor with one knee, he moved to stab Ren's heart.

But the Grizzly wasn't willing to lose his host. The red pendant had flashed and the knife had been unable to pierce Ren's flesh. Better still, the demon stone had absorbed the poison in his body, and within a few heart-beats, he was back on his feet.

He seized Coyote by his throat. "How dare you!"

"Release me."

"So you can poison me again?"

"No. I intend to turn everyone against you. It won't do you any good to be a leader when everyone's dead."

Ren frowned at his brother's psychotic reasoning. "Why would you do that?"

"Because if I can't rule them, be damned if my retarded brother will."

"I'm not retarded!"

Coyote had curled his lip at him. "That's because you're too retarded to know just how stupid you really are."

Ren had slung him against the wall.

Even though he was limping, Coyote dared to laugh at him. "Do you really think your men follow you? They follow the Grizzly Spirit. Makah'Alay is a joke. They mock you behind your back."

Ren had grabbed him again.

"Go ahead and hit me. I dare you. You're not man enough. We both know it."

"Shut up!"

Coyote laughed even harder. "You don't order me around. I refuse to follow someone so revolting and stupid that not even a whore will let you touch her tits.

338

Remember? We offered her four times the going rate and still she wouldn't even show you one. But I fucked her until she howled like a bitch desperate for my cock."

His anger burning so fiercely now that it was almost tangible, Ren pulled Coyote back to the present where they were once again facing off. "You goaded me. Every time I started to free you during that year, you ran your mouth and threatened, then insulted me."

"You were a coward."

"Yes, I *was* a coward and a pathetic fool who thought if I obeyed well enough and licked your ass enough ... if I swallowed all your shit with no complaint, that maybe, just maybe you would love me back. But what I learned from the Guardian's daughter is that love doesn't happen like that. Love isn't an obligation. You don't owe someone your loyalty and you damn well don't owe them your heart. It's an emotion, and it's born from mutual respect and generosity. It is not cruel and it is not judging. It comes from a willingness to live in complete and utter misery for the benefit of another. But when it's real, you don't feel that misery at all. The thought of their face, the scent of their skin brings a light to that darkness so bright that it drives out everything else."

Coyote sneered at him. "Congratulations, Makah'Alay. You finally allowed a whore to turn you into a woman."

Ren shoved Coyote away from him. Then as he moved to take Coyote's life, he heard the sound of men running toward them.

Coyote laughed. "Thank you for that award-winning chick speech, brother. Now ... let me show you how a man deals with things. I believe you haven't met my new friend Chacu . . . but you might remember his men that you sealed in hell. If not, I can assure you, they remember you."

Shit . . .

Sorry, Grizzly. His brother had just unleashed the one army that could kill him.

Demonstone or no demonstone.

Chapter 18

Nick tossed Kateri over his shoulder as they hiked through the hinterlands of hell to find the right cavern that no one other than Ren or Choo Co La Tah knew the exact location of.

"He's in trouble. I can feel it."

Nick swept his gaze around the others—Sundown, Cabeza, and Sasha who was limping, but who refused to, as he so eloquently put it, 'lie down and lick his crotch while they either saved or condemned the world.'

"Why am I the one holding hellcat when out of this group, I'm the only one who doesn't really have to fear the gates opening?"

Sundown clapped him on the shoulder. "'Cause you're just that kind of man, Nick. And we appreciate it."

Nick snorted in derision. "You're so full of caca, Cowboy—no wonder you only wear shit-kickers."

Sundown flashed him a wicked grin. "I happen to like my cowboy boots. My woman says they make me look sexy."

Nick let out a "heh" sound. "I should have had Andy buy you scratchy wool long johns when I was a Squire."

Kateri stopped squirming at the word she wasn't familiar with ... at least not in the way he used it. "What's a Squire?"

"Humans who help Dark-Hunters," Sundown said. "Obviously, mine was named Andy."

That made her heart lurch. "Was? Did something happen to him?"

"Yeah, little booger up and married on me a few months ago, and ... well, I was going to say moved out. But that's just a pipe-dream I had once. I can't get him out no matter what I do, but I keep trying. Luckily the house is so big I don't ever really see him unless he runs out of eats or coffee, and has to mosey over to my side in the middle of the night to raid my cupboard or fridge."

"How big is this house?" she asked.

"Don't ask," the three-men-not-Jess said simultaneously.

Okay, now she had to know. "How big?"

Sundown chuckled. "Sixty thousand, give or take a few."

"You mean six thousand."

"No," Sasha said. "Sixty. You can land a 747 jet in his backyard."

She gaped. "Where do you live?"

"Vegas."

Wow ... she didn't even want to contemplate how much something like that would cost in Vegas. "Now I have to be nosy. How much does a Dark-Hunter make?"

Nick laughed. "Let me put it to you this way. Those boots Jess is so proud of? Five grand."

That confused her more. "Then why is Ren's house so small?" While it was comfortably furnished, it wasn't elaborate. His sparse furnishings kind of reminded her a lot of IKEA.

"He don't got horses to accommodate." Jess made it sound so simple.

But it was Nick who really told her what she wanted to know. "Ren doesn't need much. He wants even less. Most of his pay gets donated to charity. Hell, he doesn't even have a Squire. And he never has had one."

"Why not?"

"It's up to the Dark-Hunter. Some," Nick cut his gaze to Jess, "like them, and others,"—he looked over to Cabeza—"can't stand humans of any sort. I have a feeling Ren falls into that latter category."

No. No one who donated the bulk of their money to charity hated people. But given his past, it made sense that Ren wouldn't want someone in close quarters with him.

Nick twisted to look at Jess. "For the record, Sundown is no longer a Dark-Hunter."

That surprised her more than anything else. "I didn't know they could stop."

Jess clicked his tongue. "It ain't easy on a Hunter. Not by a long shot. But somehow, some of us have muddled through."

Nick stopped dead in his tracks. This time when he spoke, his Cajun accent was as thick as Jess's Southern drawl. "Not easy? Cowboy, I know you did not just say that to moi. I'm the one who had to go up to Artemis and get your soul back *pour tu*. Having Abby stake your ass to put your soul back in is a Mardi Gras-style cakewalk. Trust me, *cher*."

Sundown scratched at the back of his neck. "Well, there you go. That's basically how we get out. Personally, I was going to stay in, but we decided we wanted kids, and since Dark-Hunters can't have young'uns . . ."

"They can't?" she asked.

"Nope," they all said in unison. Did they practice that? But at least it took one concern off her table. Ren hadn't left her pregnant.

She tugged gently on Nick's jacket. "You can set me down now. I'm calm."

His expression skeptical, he obeyed and put her on her feet in front of him. "Remember now, *cher*. I can catch you and not break a sweat. So no more running after Ren and risking your neck. At least not until the calendar's reset. Then, you can be as stupid as you want, and I'll let you."

She let his comment go as she focused on what really mattered to her. "Could you get Ren's soul back?"

Nick groaned as if she'd just asked him for a kidney. "I damn sure can't say no to that face. Poor Ren. You must have him beside himself when you do that."

Not really . . . at least not that she knew of. And since she didn't know Nick all that well, she wanted to make sure he didn't find a loophole on her.

"*Would* you get his soul back for us?"

This time, he growled. "He has to request it, but yeah. In spite of the rumors, I haven't completely gone to the dark side yet. But damn, those cookies are good." Come to the dark side. We have cookies.

Someone spent way too much time on the Internet. Smiling, she stood up on her tiptoes and placed a chaste kiss on his scarred cheek. "Thank you."

"Ah, *cher*, that ain't right. Laying lips on me to help another man out? Cold, *cher*, cold."

She frowned as she glimpsed a different Nick. One who was a lot younger and much happier. It was something he was remembering, too. "You're not as far gone as you fear."

Nick scoffed. "It's hard to know how far down you are when there's not a speck of light to judge the darkness by."

"But the scariest part of the dark isn't what's really there, but rather what we imagine from our own fears."

"Then, *cher*, you don't wanna ever come to my closet. I promise you, there's a lot more than just skeletons hanging in it."

She could believe that. And that brought her right back to what had started all of this. . . . "Ren is in trouble. I know it." She could feel it with every part of her.

"You read the note," Sasha said from between clenched teeth. "He said he would meet us at the cave. Bastard could have left a map, or an address, or latitude, or longitude, or something, but nooooo. . . . he leaves *you* a note. Screw the rest of the world. Y'all can all die if you want. Just don't make my woman worry about me."

Nick snorted. "You obviously have never had a mother or a girlfriend. You do not go to the bathroom without letting them know, 'cause this hell's fury coming at us? Ring Around the Rosies, baby. I'd much rather face an armed demon horde drunk on the scent of my blood, than one riled woman who's been worrying herself sick about where I've been. Ain't a diamond cut big enough in the entire universe to make *that beast* smile and save your really important jewels from being drop-locked out your nostrils."

Cabeza froze.

"Something wrong?" Jess asked.

"Not sure. It's a ... feeling." He cocked his head as if listening for something. After a second, he indicated Kateri with a jerk of his chin. "Go on. I'll catch up."

Her heart pounded with trepidation. *Please, Cabeza, be the angel I think you are. . . .* "Are you going after Ren?"

"Si."

For that, she could kiss him. "Thank you."

He winked at her. "Hey, I'm Mayan. We live to fight. Don't worry, *chica*. I'll have him back to you before you miss me." Then, he was gone.

Kateri bit her lip as another wave of worry crashed over her. And with it came anger of tidal proportions. Where were those powers her grandmother and father had promised her? They'd said they would kick in when she needed them.

Well, I need them now.

Unfortunately, neither her powers, nor her parents were listening, and all of them appeared to be on their own schedule. One she wanted to rush. How could she save the world without them?

But that wasn't her biggest concern.

Please be all right, Ren. Honestly, she wasn't sure she'd want to save the world if he was no longer in it.

Ren spat the blood out of his mouth an instant before Cha-cu seized him again, and slammed him back into the wall, face-first. The good news? He ached so much, it no longer hurt. The bad news? He ached so much, it no longer hurt to be slammed, face-first, into a wall.

Just kill me already and be done with it.

But they were having way too much fun beating on him. And while he'd stood strong against the Guardian month after month, the Guardian had only been one being. Against nine huge, immortal warriors, four of whom dwarfed him, with thousands of years of combat training each?

Sucked to be him tonight, and he was getting the ever-loving shit knocked out of him. And if, by some miracle, he got out of here in one piece, he was definitely going to feel it later.

"Hold him," Coyote snarled at his attackers.

Two seized Ren's arms and two his legs, while another planted one herculean boot right on his crotch to keep him from resisting. The bald bastard pressed down enough to let Ren know he meant it, but not enough to really damage him.

Yet.

May the gods help his jewels if the bastard sneezed.

His breathing labored, Ren looked up to see Coyote with war club in his hands.

Ah, shit . . .

The bastard was going to cut his head off. *Yeah, that'll kill me.*

At least it'll be quick.

Coyote twisted his face into a snide smile. "Where's your soliloquy now?"

Ren laughed at him, then licked at his bloodied and bruised lips. "It's 'monologue,' moron. And you dared to call me the stupid one? Now I *am* insulted."

Coyote narrowed his gaze in warning, "Fine, then. Your requiem."

Laughing even harder, Ren coughed up blood, then cursed as it rammed his cock against the bastard's boot. His breathing ragged, he glared at his brother. "I can barely speak, never mind break into song. And the last time I checked, we weren't Roman Catholics, so there's no chance of a requiem from me. Damn, boy. Buy a dictionary. Or better yet, kill me already. I can't take another minute of your uneducated abuse of the English language."

The biggest of his attackers grabbed Ren's chin and lifted it as far back as he could so that Coyote would have a clean shot at Ren's throat. Tensing from the pain that racked him, Ren glared at the asshole whose grip bit hard into his jaw. "I knew I should have killed you motherfuckers instead of imprisoning you. That'll teach me to be compassionate, eh?"

Even though he knew it was completely useless, Ren tried to throw them off him.

Squeezing his eyes shut, he mentally took himself away from the pain they caused, back to the first time Kateri had smiled at him. The first time her lips had brushed against his skin, and she'd called him baby . . .

Coyote dragged the jagged edge of the obsidian glass on

the club across his throat, slicing his flesh only enough to sting. *"À bientôt, mon frère."*

His brother lifted the club for the killing blow.

I love you, Kateri. May the gods watch over you always, and thank you for being the best thing I ever knew. If only he could see her one last time ...

In the next heartbeat, Coyote went flying into the wall beside them, and the one holding his jaw was unconscious on the floor. Coughing to clear his throat, Ren rolled over to see Cabeza doing a death match circle with Chacu.

Chacu raked Cabeza with a sneer. "How's your wife, Kukulkan?"

By the amount of rage and severity of attack that question evoked from Cabeza, Ren was going to lay money that Chacu had had something to do with her death.

And hopefully that was the worst thing the bastard had done to her.

Ren splayed his hands against the earthen floor and pushed himself upright. One of the others grabbed his right arm and snapped the bone.

Okay, *that* he felt. . . .

Before he could recover, four of them were on him.

"We don't need Chacu or Coyote to finish you." As Ren's attacker reached for the Coyote's club, a sonic boom went through the room so fiercely, it knocked everyone off their feet.

Damn, I'm on the floor again. He was getting really sick of this vantage point.

At first, he wasn't sure what had happened to knock them down. Not until he saw Ash grab one of the Gate Guardians and head-slam his ass into the wall. *Yeah, that hurt, didn't it, puta? Slam him again, Ash.* He'd say it out loud, but the last one who'd grabbed him had broken his jaw.

Ash rounded the seven of them up, and left Chacu for Cabeza to finish off. His silver eyes swirling with fury, Ash snarled at the Gate Guardians, exposing his fangs. "You swore to protect the innocent."

The tallest one tried to peacock posture Ash. It might have worked had Ash been a couple of feet shorter. But with those combat boots on, Ash topped seven feet easy. It'd be damn hard to intimidate someone that size if they were human. Toss in the god powers, and mad warrior skills . . .

You go on, bitch, and posture. Ash can probably use the comic relief.

Bald Ugly jerked his chin toward Coyote as he spoke to Acheron. "We owed a favor to the one who freed us. We were merely paying the obligation."

Ash shook his head. "Ah, see now, that was your mistake. Your obligation tripped all over a man I consider a brother. One I don't like seeing ganged up on and beaten to a pulp when I know one-on-one, you'd be picking up busted teeth . . . so I tell you what . . . How about I level this playing field a little?"

Still, the imbecile blustered. Maybe because his muscles were five times larger than Ash's, he thought that gave him the advantage. But one of the first things Ren had learned when he'd shot up to tower over his shorter, bulkier opponents . . . Lean muscle didn't interfere with fighting technique. It made you lethal. And you were a hell of a lot stronger than you appeared to be, so people

350

underestimated the power of your blows. While a single blow from the mountain could lay you out cold, you could get twenty in to his one and have him down first. The mountain had to be accurate.

You? Not so much.

The mountain sneered up at Acheron. "We're not afraid of you."

Ash shrugged nonchalantly. "That would be exponentially foolish on your part. But I'm not the one you need to fear." Ash turned and approached Ren. "You look like hell, buddy."

"Ah, damn," Ren said, trying not to move his busted jaw any more than necessary. "All those hours in the salon wasted. I'd just got my nails done, too."

"You're so not right." Ash held his hand out to him so that he could pull Ren away from the wall, where Ren had himself braced to keep from falling again.

He took Ash's hand with the arm that hadn't been broken, and the moment he did, the pain vanished. Warmth spread through his veins as whatever Ash was doing to him healed his body completely.

Within a few seconds, Ren felt stronger than he ever had before. More than that, everyone else in the room was frozen solid—like someone had hit the pause button on a player.

Ash didn't seem to notice. "You know, Ren, it occurs to me that you never took your Act of Vengeance when Artemis signed you into her service."

"I didn't want it, then."

"And now?"

Ren glanced over to Coyote, who was frozen in the

middle of a furious shriek that made the tendons on his neck protrude, and left his face a mask of ugliness.

As Dark-Hunters, they weren't allowed to arbitrarily kill anyone. There were very strict codes they had to follow. Murdering someone was a big no-no. "You'd allow it?"

Ash arched a wry brow. "You're part demon. Do you really give a shit what I think?"

"The demon in me that knows there's a demon in you who can mop the floor with my raunchy butt tells me to say yes. I care. Deeply."

"You're such a liar," Ash said with a laugh. "And a genius." He jerked his chin toward the group. "So, how about that vengeance?"

There was only one person in the room he truly wanted to lay low. "I'm going to kill Coyote."

"Take them all out if you want. You've earned it."

Ren frowned at the offer. Ash wasn't normally quite this bloodthirsty. Up until he'd married, Acheron had been all Hare Krishna—can't we all get along? Peace and love, brother. Peace and love. Kill the Daimons to free the human souls, but play nice with everyone else.

Yet from the moment Ash's wife Tory had placed that black titanium wedding ring on his finger, Ash had learned the benefits of "You knock on *my* door looking to fight? Then come on in, brother, and I'll put your rabid ass down tonight."

However, given Ash's lengthy past condemnations of wanton bloodshed, Ren wanted to make double sure that they were on the same page. "What exactly do you mean by that? Send them home intact, a little broken up, or in bloody body bags?"

No sooner had Ren asked the question, than seven more Rens appeared in the room around them. They stood before the Gate Guardians and were also frozen in place, yet posed as if they were about to clobber the one in front of them.

What the hell?

Ash folded his arms over his chest. "Relax. They'll vanish once they dispense of their assigned target . . . in whatever way you want them to. And you'll be none the weaker for it. Their powers don't draw from you."

Ren gaped at Ash's abilities. While he'd known the man had mad gpd powers, he'd had no idea that insta-clone-a-warrior was one of them.

"How did you do that?" Ren breathed. "For that matter, how can you even be here? I thought you couldn't help us tonight."

Ash shrugged. "Hope you don't take this the wrong way, but your gene pool is a little shallow when it comes to intelligence. The hallowed part of the Valley doesn't begin for another five miles in." He flashed a fanged grin at Ren. "Great place to set up camp, huh? I'd laugh at your brother's arrogant idiocy if it wasn't so pathetic. Anyway, I thought you were going in with the others, not detouring here. Had I known this was your plan, I'd have had your back all along. Sometimes, Ren, you have to remember that you do have friends now. And some of us have been around for a very long time. Like a permanent boil on your ass, I'm kind of attached to all of you."

Ren laughed. "I will remember that. Thank you."

Ash inclined his head respectfully. "I shall leave you and Beza to your fun. I'll take care of Choo Co La Tah for you, and continue holding the line against the vermin breaking though the barriers." He headed over to where Choo lay in an unconscious lump.

"Acheron?" Ren took care to use the true Atlantean pronunciation of his name with a hard C and audible H. "*Herista.*" *Thank you.*

Ash tapped his heart twice with his fist, which was an Atlantean gesture for blood family. *"Atee, mer, atee."* *Anytime, brother, anytime.* Then, turning, he picked Choo up and vanished with him. As soon as Ash was gone, everyone returned to normal.

One day, Ash really needed to come clean about the full extent of his powers.

But that wouldn't be tonight.

Tonight, Ren had a gate to seal, and a rat to catch. One whose eyes were now widened by fear as Coyote realized he had eight Rens to fight now.

One of whom was severely pissed off and wanted his blood over the beating Coyote had ordered.

Ren left his duplicate army to fight the others while he headed straight for Coyote. As soon as his brother saw him coming for him, Coyote did what he did best.

He ran.

Ren picked up the pace as he ran down the shaft, after Coyote. Tired of chasing the jackrabbit, Ren teleported himself in front of Coyote.

Still looking behind him, he slammed into Ren's chest, then staggered back.

Ren gave him a pitiless glare as Coyote scurried backward on the ground, like a creepy contorted possessed human in a horror movie. *Stand up and face me like the*

354

man you claim to be. . . . "I will never understand how our father was so blind to your true nature."

Finally discovering some semblance of a backbone, Coyote stood up and lifted his chin defiantly. "What are you going to do? Kill me?"

Ren pulled the hand forged knife from his boot, and glanced down at it. It was one of the very few items he'd managed to hang on to from his human life—one of the very few things he'd owned as a human. Simple and elegant, it had a crow etched down one side of the blade and a hummingbird on the other. A bit of whimsy he'd put there one night when he'd been unable to sleep. Too many bitter memories had often robbed him of his rest.

But he'd always had a strong affection for weaponry.

One of the things he'd learned as a boy was metal-lurgy. He'd watch the smiths smelt different compounds, taking mental notes on what they did so that he could duplicate it in private.

By the time he was twenty, he made all of his own weapons. His bow, arrows, war club, and knives. And he'd learned, courtesy of Coyote's "pranks," to sleep with his weapons so that if they were touched or tampered with, he'd know instantly.

There was no worse feeling than to entrust your life to a tool that malfunctioned or broke while you were under attack.

And he had the scars to prove it. As a human, his weapons had been the only thing he'd ever taken pride in. Unlike people, they didn't mock him. They didn't leave him, and they protected him when no one else would.

He still felt that way about them.

In fact, the garage at his house was a forge. Since he could fly and teleport, he had no use for a car. There was no need in wasting prime space when he could use it for the only thing that gave him real comfort.

"Say something," Coyote snarled.

"Sorry. I was lost in thought for a moment."

"Are you insane?"

Ren laughed. "Given our genes? It's a safe bet." He sobered and narrowed his gaze on Coyote. "Tell me something . . . do you remember that time when I was nineteen and for my birthday, I made a matching set of knives as a gift for you and Father?"

"Yeah? So?"

"Do you remember what you did?"

"No. I don't even know what happened to them."

Of course he didn't. Why should he? "I remember it." With a clarity he would give anything to purge out of his memory. "I gave you yours first, and you convinced me that Father wouldn't take his from me. That he would criticize it as being inferior. So I allowed you to give it to him while I watched. He assumed you'd made it, and he embraced you for the gift."

"Father was bad that way."

"No, Anukuwaya, *you* were always bad that way. You're a shadow walker. A treacherous creature from the dark that pretends it's from the light. It's shimmery and beautiful, but it has no substance. No loyalty. When we were human, I never saw it in you, because I cherished you as my brother. I didn't want to see it. And Father, even after Buffalo told him I was the knife's creator, said it was the best one he'd ever seen. It was the only time in my life he looked at me with anything other than contempt. But you couldn't stand it. The jealousy ate at you. And you couldn't let me have those two minutes of his affection. Instead, you thermal-shocked the blade so that it would snap, and then showed it to Father, who thanked you for saving his life from my incompetence. Angry at me for having given him a defective knife, he threw it at me while I ate dinner alone in the kitchen."

Ren opened the front of his shirt so that Coyote could see the scar on his shoulder where the knife had hit him while he sat unaware of his father's rage. Their father had thrown the knife so forcefully, that it'd knocked him off his seat, and laid him out on the floor. Stunned, Ren had stared in horror as his father curled his lip and cursed him. "It was a fine weapon. It tore through my flesh and sinew and muscle like they were butter, and the tip embedded in my bone. If nothing else, you should remember that. It was over a year before I had full range of motion in my arm again." Though to be honest, there were still some things he couldn't do with that arm.

He held the knife up for Coyote to see it. "It's been one of the best weapons I've ever owned. Eleven thousand years and the blade is still as strong as ever."

"Why would you keep it, you sick bastard?"

His anger rose up in his throat to choke him, but Ren shoved it away. This wasn't about fury. It was about retribution for a lifetime of misery Coyote had served him. "Because I wanted to make our father proud, and you happy, I melted down my mother's necklace as part of the blades. The cost of a gift is never important. The important part is that it comes from the heart, and that it holds emotional value to the giver. There was nothing I treasured more than her necklace ... except you and Father. So I keep this knife that I used to remind myself to be humble and to never, *ever* trust another with my life. To make sure I always knew where other people stood in relation to my position at any given moment, so that no one would ever stab me again while I was being inattentive to my surroundings."

Moving closer to him, Coyote rolled his eyes. "I miss the days when you stuttered. You never rambled on back then about bullshit."

"After tonight, you'll never have to suffer my presence again. And never again will you take, harm, or threaten those I love."

Coyote scoffed as he came to rest right in front of Ren. "You can't kill me. I'm your brother."

Ren pulled Coyote against him into a brotherly hug, then the instant he felt Coyote relax, he stabbed him through the heart. "From another mother," he whispered in Coyote's ear as he held him in his arms. "And the Keetoowah only count relations through their mother's bloodline. . . . *He* is no brother of mine. And I owe him nothing." Those had been the exact words Coyote had said to the priest when he'd asked his brother how Coyote wanted Ren buried.

More than that, Coyote had added, "He is not a true Keetoowah and he died with no honor. I don't care what you do with his body, but do not insult or desecrate our beloved dead with a foreigner's remains."

Instead of having a funeral fit for a chief's son, Ren's body had been dumped in the pit they used for garbage.

358

And Coyote would never have thought of him again had Artemis not restored Ren's life.

Gasping for air, Coyote reached up with his hands, trying to choke Ren as he died.

Ren shoved his brother away, and let Coyote fall to the floor where he writhed for a few more seconds. Once Coyote was dead, Ren did what Coyote had done to him all those centuries ago. He stepped over his body and went about his business.

At least he tried to. But he'd only taken three steps when his necklace heated up, and burned his skin.

Shit . . .

While Coyote had tried to choke him, their mingled blood had touched the demonstone.

The Grizzly would now be freed.

And I am owned. Forever.

Sick to his stomach, Ren rushed back to where he'd left Cabeza battling Chacu, to find his friend standing alone in the center of the room.

Ren slowed. "Where's Chacu?"

"Little *puta* ran home for his mother. I swear . . . one day I will drink the blood from his heart and eat it. . . ." He jerked his chin toward the blood on Ren's shirt. "*Et tu?*"

"The Coyote howls no more. The bastard is forever silenced."

He nodded in understanding. "I am sorry, and I am happy for you."

Ren let out a short laugh. "Yeah, that sums it up, doesn't it?"

"It does, indeed, my brother."

Ren took a moment to savor that last part. The only

time Coyote had claimed him as a brother was to manipulate him. But the ones who meant it when they said it to Ren had no blood relation to him whatsoever.

He would miss them while he served Grizzly.

Not wanting to think about it, he chucked Cabeza on the arm. "Shall we save the rest of the world now?"

"Sure. Why not? If everyone dies, I'd have to cook my own food, and I cook like shit. How about you?"

Ren laughed. "Only fry bread and okra, and I make no claims to the edible state of either."

"Then we'd best be saving the rest of the world."

Kateri cursed as she realized she was out of ammunition. Again. What she wouldn't give for a Hollywood weapon that never ran dry while you were taking fire.

Sasha was off in the darkness alone, fighting in wolf form, trying to keep as many away from them as he could, while they were pinned down, unable to go anywhere near the cave they had to reach really soon, or all of this was for nothing.

Provided that was actually the cave they needed. There was still some debate about the exact location of where the mural was. Without Ren . . . Yeah, this night might not have the best ending.

She shot her last arrow at a demon that was flying straight for Sundown. "Nick! More ammo!"

They appeared instantly in her quiver. Okay, Nick was better than Hollywood. Except he couldn't conjure C-4. Well, he could, in theory, conjure it. The problem was, none of them knew how to use it.

"Thanks."

Nick went back to fire-balling their attackers. He shot so many so fast, it looked like a Fourth of July celebration.

Jess continued to shoot at the raven mockers and demons as fast as his shotgun would load, cock, and aim— which was surprisingly fast in his hands. The barrel of that thing had to be hot enough to raise a blister.

But for every demon they destroyed, it seemed like ten more came in to replace it.

Sundown cast an irritated glare at Nick. "Can't you command these things to die, or something?"

"Yeah. Sure can, but, here's the big green pickle . . . if I use those powers, they'll pierce through the weakened gates, and open them instantly. I'm the top tier, Jess. That power tends to draw out other demons like Mardi Gras beads to naked beasts, and depending on the demon's level, can even strengthen them. Think of me like a homing beacon of the damned."

Jess reloaded. "That don't seem like a whole lot of fun."

"It's a jolly fucking Barrel of Monkeys." Nick sent more fireballs to the demons.

Amused by Nick's acerbic nature that could make light of a very dangerous situation, Kateri blew air across her wrist that was stinging even with a guard on it. Her fingers were numb and she was sure if she survived to sleep again she was going to have nightmares about ghostly fanged things screaming at her as they died.

This is hopeless. She didn't say it out loud, but she felt it. She was sure they did, too.

None of them could move forward toward the caves. She was so exhausted from fighting that all she wanted

361

to do was lie down, and let them have her. In fifteen minutes, it wouldn't matter anyway.

It'd be too late.

Fifteen minutes.

Strange how, as a student, especially in a boring class she hated, fifteen minutes had seemed an eternity.

Now . . .

It wasn't even enough time for her brief life to flash before her eyes.

She ducked as something that reminded her of a flying monkey went over her head, spitting at them. It was acidic saliva she realized as it hit the rock a few millimeters from her hand and dissolved it like sugar in hot water.

Jess stood and shot it three times. It recoiled as it was hit, but it didn't kill the beast. "Didn't your mama never teach you no manners? You don't spit at no lady." He knelt to reload. "Flipping animals."

"Demons, Jess," Nick reminded him.

"Damn flipping demons." He narrowed his gaze at Nick. "Holy water work on them?"

"Only some. Remember, I still take Communion on Sundays and was an altar boy as a kid."

"Yeah, that ain't right."

"Couldn't agree more." Nick shielded her just as she would have been hit by another wave of flying uglies. Then he stood to open fire, literally, on the ones who'd almost killed her.

Nick would have teleported them into the caves, but since he knew so little about them, and absolutely nothing about their interior, he could slam them into a wall, and kill them by attempting it. Not to mention, they would be trapped inside, which made it easier for the demons to kill them.

She nocked another arrow. But what she really wanted to do was crawl into a hole and wait for all of this to end.

C'mon, Kateri. This isn't just about you. She glanced around at the men who risked their lives to protect her. Jess with his new baby. He didn't want to be here. But here he was without a single complaint. Nick who, well according to him, was only living to piss certain entities off. Sasha who had a crush on someone he wouldn't name, but who'd sworn that if he lived through this, he was going to ask her out. Fear be damned. Cabeza who would say nothing about his life.

Most of all, Ren. He'd given her his heart . . . the only part of himself that still belonged to him.

The one part he'd never given to anyone else.

In that heartbeat, she saw herself as a young teen in the cemetery with her grandmother on Memorial Day. They always went there to put a red, white, and blue rose on the grave of Kateri's grandfather. And her grandmother, who was tougher than nails, who never shed a tear for anything, would stand there and cry for the husband she'd loved so dearly.

"How will I know when I love someone like you did Grandpa, Grammy?"

"Oh baby," she'd said, brushing Kateri's hair back from her face, "that's an easy answer. When you know you'd be willing to lay your life down to save theirs without thought or hesitation. When five o'clock comes, and they're not home like they said they'd be, and you panic and can't breathe for fear they're not coming through that door ever again. When the thought of laying them in ground hits you so hard, you can't breathe for it. Most of all, when something good or bad happens to you, and they're the first one you want to share that news with. That's how you'll know it's love, baby. There won't be any doubt whatsoever."

Kateri had never fully understood her grandmother's explanation. Not until she looked into a pair of shockingly blue eyes that carved one man's name into her heart and soul, and made her realize that her life that had seemed so perfect and happy, had one thing missing from it.

Ren.

And if she didn't seal those gates, the things it held back would come for him.

Hoping she lived to regret this blatant act of stupidity, she headed for the caves. She thought she was running alone, until Nick grabbed her an instant before a ball of fire exploded next to her.

More demons came at them, cutting them off.

Crap. It was no use. All she'd done was move them from cover and left them exposed to die.

I'm so sorry.

"Need a hand?"

Her heart pounded at that deep, familiar voice as Ren appeared next to her. "You're here!"

"Where else would I be?" Ren frowned as he surveyed the madness they were knee-deep in. "Why are you under such heavy fire?"

Nick gave him a droll stare. "Oh, I don't know. But we're really enjoying it. Fear has such a wonderfully romantic scent to it that they ought to turn it into cologne and deodorant. Eau de Ew. Let's all just take a minute, and bask in it."

While he could be annoying, Nick had moments of profound sarcastic humor.

Cabeza cleared his throat as he appeared beside Jess. "We have five minutes, people. Then, it's going to get a whole lot worse."

Ren held his hand out to her. "You ready?"

"Absolutely."

She placed her cold hand inside his that was so warm, it sent chills over her. The strength of him was electrifying. And if she had to die tonight, she was glad his would be the last face she saw.

Ren flashed her into the cave effortlessly. Having spent centuries here, he knew every inch of this valley like the back of his hand, and he knew exactly which cave held the mural they needed for the Reset.

But it was so dark inside, she couldn't see anything at all. Not even her own hands.

Until Ren used his fireballs to light the torches, which were spaced out every few feet on the earthen walls decorated with thousands of prehistoric glyphs. They were beautiful. Fernando would be in his glory to explore something this pristine.

"The thunderbird is over here." Ren led her to the other side of the cave, to the flattest wall there.

The whole expanse of it had been painted with a colorful mural, which told the entire story of how the world had been saved by the first Ixkib when she'd faced down an angry god.

It showed Ahau kin gifting the Kinichi to her.

But Kateri didn't see what she was looking for. And time was ticking way too fast. They had a mere handful of seconds before the gates unlocked. "Where does the Kinichi go?"

Ren pointed up toward the ceiling where a giant thunderbird rose above the scenes below. Over the thunderbird's head was a tiny hummingbird. You couldn't tell if the thunderbird was following or pursuing the hummingbird. Were they friend or foe? It was impossible to tell. But it was positioned right between the thunderbird's open beak.

Kateri wanted to weep in frustration. "Well ain't this a bitch? How long did they think my arms would be for me to reach into the mouth of *that* hummingbird? I don't suppose you have a vat of radioactive isotopes I can throw myself into and quickly mutate, do you?" It always worked in the movies.

And of course, there was one other obvious problem. "Where exactly am I supposed to put the stone?" The wall was completely flat without a single crevice in it.

"We'll find it, don't worry."

Now look who had found his optimism. *Great timing, bud.*

As Ren moved toward her, out of nowhere, a blast struck him hard enough to send him straight to the ground.

Reacting on instinct, she nocked an arrow, and turned to fire. But the moment she sighted her target, she froze.

No . . . It was impossible.

WTF?

Kateri couldn't believe her eyes. It had to be a dream. Major hallucination.

Something.

She lowered the bow. "Enrique?"

"*Si*, Dr. Avani."

Gaping, she tried to make sense of this as he moved closer to her. "What are you doing here?"

He smiled coldly. "I'm here to see *you,* of course."

Of course?

"I don't understand. How did you know I was here?"

"Veneno," he said simply. "I captured him when he attacked Chacu in your lab . . . I wasn't as frozen as you and Cabeza thought. And I spit down the necks of all those so-called experts who tell people torture doesn't work. To that, I say they don't know how to do it right. I, personally, have never had it fail me."

It took her a second to register the name of his victim.

Ren started for her, but Enrique blasted him into the opposite direction. "If you want her to keep breathing, stay back."

Kateri's watch started beeping to let her know they were in the final countdown. She had to get past Enrique. Now!

"What do you want?" she asked him.

"Hand me your time stone, or I will hand you your boytoy's stones."

She looked at Ren, still unsure whether or not this was a dream.

"Don't do it, Kateri," Ren said adamantly. "He's not human. Whatever you do, don't let him have the stone."

She shook her head. "He's my grad assistant."

Enrique laughed. "Yes and no. Enrique was your grad assistant. But I was actually your prisoner, Dr. Avani. Until Chacu unknowingly freed me."

None of that made sense to her. She scowled at Ren. "What do you mean he's not human?"

Enrique hissed. "Stupid *puta*. I told you ... I'm *el peuchen*. You brought back my *cárcel* from your first excavation with Fernando so that you could test it. Because of those tests you ran, I was able to break free of my *cárcel*. But I couldn't escape that damn campus. Not even after I took over your assistant's body. His great-grandmother was indeed powerful. And I've enjoyed devouring his soul. But now, I'm done. I want what I came for."

He reached for her.

Ren blasted him back. "Don't you dare touch her!"

Enrique turned on Ren, and shot something that went straight into his chest and splintered into fragments.

Ren cried out in pain as Kateri shrieked in anger. By the sound of Ren's voice alone, she knew how bad it was.

He would never, ever cry out like that.

She tried to get to him, but Enrique wouldn't let her.

"Give me *el piedra*! Now!

For Ren's life, she was willing to give him anything. But she wasn't dumb enough to think for one minute this demon would allow them to leave here alive.

Think, Kateri, think . . .

He started for Ren to finish him off.

In that one instant when she was convinced she'd lose Ren forever, she felt it. A peculiar inner snap. Like the tiny pinprick in a dam that came right before the force of the water exploded it into a violent flood. And

368

when that inner flood came, it saturated the room with bright light that shot out from her entire body. A light that pierced Enrique. Screaming in pain, he recoiled, and tried again to reach Ren.

The moment he moved toward Ren, her light stabbed him, over and over.

His face changing into an ugly demonic beast, Enrique attempted to reach her. The light intensified and, finally, exploded him into a thousand pieces.

Horrified, relieved, and terrified all at once, she ran to where Ren lay on the floor in a pool of blood. As gently as she could, she turned him over and held him in her lap.

His face pale and clammy, he could hardly breathe. His lips were turning blue. God, there was so much blood. . . .

Ren covered her hand with his. "You have to reset the calendar."

Screw the damn calendar.

"You're hurt." Worse, it looked like he might be dying.

Ren licked his lips. Each breath he took made a hollow, rattling sound in his chest. "It doesn't matter, Kateri. The calendar is more important. Go, and I'll wait for you."

"Don't you dare die on me," she warned him. "I mean it."

"Go."

Nodding, she ran for the glyphs again.

This time, when she looked up, she saw something different. New details she'd missed before. Details that were only evident now that she had her father's and grandmother's powers.

Perspicacity. The ability to see anything hidden or masked.

Now, total clarity was hers. The thunderbird was a symbol for Ren and his metamorphosis from destroyer to protector of the world. That thunderbird was being sacrificed for the hummingbird so that it could send its eye into the sun. The open beak that surrounded the hummingbird did so to protect the hummingbird with its dying breath.

But she still didn't know how to reach the damn thing from the ground.

Believe. Ren's voice in her head was so strong.

She glanced over to him to make sure he was still with her.

I will always be with you, Waleli. It took me eleven thousand years to find you. Do you really think I'd leave you now?

Tears gathered in her eyes. "I do believe." And for the first time in her life, she meant that. Even though it was total and utter insanity, she believed in the ludicrous.

She believed in the paranormal.

All of it. And most of all, she believed in Ren. His love wrapped around her, giving her strength and resolve. With him by her side, she finally believed in the impossible. *I am the Hummingbird—the bridge between night and day. The messenger of the sun who carries the hope of mankind.*

As thoughts filled her head, it felt as if a weight left her body, and she began to float.

No, not float . . .

She flew.

One moment, she was on the ground, and in the next, she was high above the floor. Oh this . . . this was scary.

And it was a whole lot of fun.

Suddenly, Enrique reappeared.

Didn't I kill that bastard?

"Give me the stone or I'll kill him!" Enrique held a knife to Ren's throat.

Without hesitation, she started to return, but Ren threw his arm out, and gently blasted her with wind, lifting her up higher.

Save the world Kateri.

Tears filled her eyes. "You *are* my world."

And you are mine. Now please, Kateri, if you love me, finish the task we were given. Reset the calendar, and then we'll kill this asshole.

Only Ren could make her smile when she was this scared and upset.

Nodding, she reached up and realized that from the ground the painting was a *trompe l'oeil* that made it appear flat. From up here, she saw the small space in the heart of the hummingbird that had been cut like a puzzle piece specifically to hold her necklace.

As soon as she touched the painting, she had total clarity of thought.

Eye. Heart. Soul. I am the power that drives out the evil. I, alone, can fight it and keep it from the most vital parts of my being.

The sun wasn't just the light that banished the darkness. It was the warmth that kept away the icy chill of hurt and harm. *Focus on the things that make you happy, that fill your heart with joy. They are all that matter, and they are what will keep you safe. They are what will keep you strong even in the worst storm.*

And that joy was what gave her a heart. Her hand shaking, she placed her necklace inside the hummingbird.

Lightning ricocheted through the room. The hummingbird

fell back into the mouth of the thunderbird as it shot an orange light straight up through a small hole in the top of the cave.

She turned her face away to protect her eyesight from the searing beam that shone brighter than high noon on a summer's day.

"No!" Enrique screamed in horror. He turned to throw his knife at her.

The moment he did, Ren rose up from the floor, and snatched the red stone necklace from his neck. He looped it around Enrique's throat at the same time Enrique let fly his knife.

She ducked the knife, and for a moment thought Ren was using his necklace as a garrote. Until he fastened it around Enrique's neck and stepped back. "Enjoy *Cárcel Infierno, amigo.*" Give Grizzly and Windseer my best.

Enrique screamed as the floor opened and sucked him into it. He tried to fight, to hold on to the surface. But it was useless. The ground swallowed him whole.

As soon as Enrique was gone, Ren hit the deck. Hard.

Forgetting her own necklace, Kateri flashed herself to his side. Cold dread and all-out terror filled her. He was so pale. His breathing so shallow.

She carefully placed his head in her lap and brushed the hair back from his handsome face. "Baby? You're not going to die, right? You're immortal."

He shook his head. "The blast pierced my heart. I'm dying, Kateri."

"No!" Tears blinded her as agony tightened her chest. She couldn't lose him. She couldn't. "Don't leave me, Ren. Please. I need you."

Ren savored the words that he'd never expected to hear out of another person's mouth. And to have them come from someone as remarkable as his Kateri ... It was more than he could ask for. More than he deserved. *Thank you for saying them.* How he wished he could stay with her, but fate had made other plans for the two of them. "You don't need me, my precious. You were fine without me."

"I might have been fine. But I wasn't excellent. Not until you barged into my world, and stood by me while I was under fire. I don't want to be alone anymore, Ren. Just because I can stand alone doesn't mean I want to."

He kissed her cheek. "Don't cry, Waleli. . . . It's better this way."

Was he insane? How could *this* be better? "How?"

Before Ren could respond, a huge bear of a man appeared before them. Dressed in tanned buckskin, he was fierce and well-muscled. With his lip curled, he raked them both with a hate-filled sneer. "He sold his life to me, and this is his attempt to get out of his slavery."

"Leave her alone!" Ren growled.

"Oh please, Makah'Alay, don't bother. You have nothing with which to bargain anymore. In a few minutes you won't even have your life."

Kateri went cold as some foreign part of her recognized this man even though she'd never seen him before.

Grizzly.

"Now I've come to claim what little life he has left. He owes me that much."

Kateri refused to let go. "I don't understand. Why would you do that?" she asked him.

Grizzly answered through gritted teeth. "For *you*." He spat that out like it disgusted him. "He was always stupid."

"No," she said, fiercely. "Ren was never stupid. But you . . . You should have taken his offering when he sent Enrique in his place."

Grizzly snorted. "A pitiful replacement." He reached for Ren.

"You're not taking him," she growled, ready to fight to the death for Ren. Summoning every ounce of her father's and grandmother's powers that she could, she blasted Grizzly.

The weight and strength of her attack shocked him. But it was too late. Her powers were too strong now. And by coming for Ren, he'd brought out the grizzly bear spirit in her.

No one touched her family.

No one!

Rising to her feet, she went after him with everything she had. Over and over, she blasted Grizzly as her fury unfurled and unloaded. Not just because he dared to come here now. For everything he'd done to Ren, and for going after and killing her father. He had taken or attempted to take everything from her.

And he'd taken enough.

"You've done all the harm you're going to. The Grizzly stops here."

He laughed at her. "What could you ever do to me? You can't kill me. I'm immortal."

"No, but I can banish you back to the source that birthed you. I'm sure you remember the boiling pain and agony. May you enjoy burning there for all eternity."

He tried to run, but she wouldn't let him. He'd given Ren and her father no quarter, and so she gave him none in return.

She blasted him harder. Faster. Deadlier.

Grizzly screamed as she sent him to the worst imaginable fate for any immortal being.

"What the hell happened here?"

She turned at Sundown's thick drawl.

"And what the hell happened to you, buddy?" Setting his shotgun aside, he sank down beside Ren whose skin now had a scary bluish tint to it. Tears filled her eyes as Sundown reached to check Ren's breathing.

Ren didn't respond.

Afraid he was already gone, that he had died alone while she fought Grizzly, she rushed back to him. "Ren?"

He opened his eyes, but couldn't focus them on her. They danced around as if he couldn't control them at all. "Thank you, Kateri."

"For what?"

"Coming back for me."

That opened the floodgate for her tears. "I would always come for you, Ren," she sobbed. "Through hell, storms, and demons. Nothing would ever keep me from your side. And I can't lose you. Not like this. Dammit, fight for me!"

He licked his lips. "I'm trying. It's why I'm still here. But I don't think they're going to let me win this one."

Desperate to save him, she started going through his pockets.

Sundown scowled. "What are you doing?"

"I'm looking for his *degalodi nvwoti*. His medicine bag."

Ren caught her hand. "*Osda.*"

"It's not all right," she breathed in contradiction. Locating his bag in his front pocket, she pulled it out, then opened the red deerskin pouch, and started going through it, looking for something that could heal him. She wiped angrily at her damn useless tears. *I have to save him.*

She'd lost everyone she'd ever loved, and if he died, she'd never forgive herself. *I'm cursed.* She knew that for certain now. Every time she dared to let someone into her heart, they paid the ultimate price for it. *I will not lose another! I won't.* Because she knew, that if she lost Ren, she would die, too.

Determined to save him no matter what, she sorted through his stones and feathers . . . spiritual items he'd spent his life gathering together. Just like her grandmother.

Just like her.

Items that gave him strength and courage. Items that reminded him of who he was, and who he wanted to be. Going through someone's *degalodi nvwoti* was more personal than reading their diary.

And when she pulled out a hummingbird fetish that had been secured to a pink heart-shaped rose quartz by the small red Bama hairband she'd been wearing when they met, she started sobbing so hard, she couldn't breathe.

Ren reached for her. "Please don't cry, Kateri. It breaks my heart to hear your tears."

But she couldn't help it. With this one item, she fully understood the depth of his love for her. He had created a personal symbol for her, and placed it in his medicine bag—the one thing she knew he would never be without.

Suddenly, another bolt of lightning shook the room, and sprayed debris over them.

Shit! Furious and needing to draw a blood-heart sacrifice from someone over this, she shot to her feet, ready to battle.

And this time, she was going to enjoy the killing.

But as she dropped into her fighting stance, she hesitated.

Nick stood in front of her in his human form, but he had his black demon wings spread wide. His dark hair was tousled and the bow and arrow mark was so faint, she could barely see it now.

He came forward with a jet crystal.

With a ragged breath, she frowned at it. "What is that? A healing stone?" She reached to touch it.

Nick caught her hand. His eyes burned into her. "It's Ren's soul. When I saw he was dying, I went to get it from Artemis. If you restore his soul to his body on his last breath, it'll bring him back and release him from Artemis's service."

Hope tore through her. "Really?"

Nick nodded.

"No!" Ren growled.

Was he insane? Kateri gaped at him. "Why not?"

"Because it'll burn and scar you. Badly. Tell her, Sundown."

Jess nodded. "He's right. It's an awful scar, too. When Abigail released mine, it fused two of her fingers together. Every time I see them, it kills me, and I hate that I caused her that much pain."

"I don't care." She reached for the crystal again, but Nick caught her hand.

"If the pain makes you drop this before his soul returns to his body, you will destroy it, and condemn him to an existence of unbelievable agony. So before you take it, understand that you can't let go, no matter how much it burns you."

"I would never, and will never let go of him," she said with the full weight of her conviction. She knelt beside Ren. "And if I don't do this, I will damn myself to a far worse hell."

Ren's gaze finally stopped shaking and held hers.

"If you could save my life, would you mind being scarred from it?" she asked him.

"No," he whispered emphatically.

She smiled, then looked at Jess. "I don't know Abigail, but I'm pretty sure every time she sees that scar, all she thinks about is how lucky she is to share her life with you. And I'm certain that on those days when she wants to beat you over something you've said or done to tick her off, it saves your butt, because it reminds her of just how far she was willing to go to have you."

Jess swallowed. "Damn Ren, she's a keeper."

Ren coughed up more blood.

"Hang on, sweetie." She reached for the crystal, but Nick pulled it out of her reach.

"I'll give it to you right when it's time. No need in you being hurt any longer than necessary."

"Okay." Kateri moved to put Ren's head in her lap so that she could hold him.

Ren reached up to take her hand. "If you drop it, I won't mind. I'll know that at least you tried."

She laughed through her tears. "I'm not going to drop

it. But when you're back to normal, I might drop *you* on your head for thinking I would do such a thing."

He smiled, then tensed.

"Ren?"

His hand fell away from hers.

"Ren?"

Don't panic. You'll bring him back.

But it was hard not to.

Nick tucked his wings down around his body. "You'll have to place the crystal on the bow-and-arrow mark. That was where Artemis took his soul from. It's where it will want to return." She tried not to stare at the mark on Nick's face. Artemis must have been cupping his cheek when she took his.

"It's on his hip." She looked at Jess.

"Why y'all cutting them eyes at me? I ain't undoing his pants. I love the man. But I don't *love* the man. . . . That right there's your job, woman, and I don't mean that in a sexist or homophobic way. I just don't want to touch another man's junk if I can help it. And that's a personal choice guaranteed by the Constitution."

Shaking her head at Sundown, she carefully placed Ren's head on the ground, then scooted down so that she could undo Ren's fly and open his pants enough to expose the mark on his hip without embarrassing him. Of course, that would be easier if he wore underwear, but . . . Her mission accomplished, she slid a teasing smirk at Jess. "I'm pretty sure Ren doesn't want you touching his junk either."

With a short laugh, Sundown moved to make more room for her. "Damn straight. Literally."

Nick came closer. She reached for it, but again Nick stopped her. "Wait for his last breath."

It came thirty seconds later. And that was the worst moment of her life.

Ren expelled it, and the light faded from those remarkably blue eyes.

Please don't screw up. Please don't screw up. . . .

Nick gave her the crystal. "Now."

To her amazement, she felt no pain whatsoever. None.

Grateful to her adrenaline or whatever spared her from hurting, she placed the crystal over Ren's mark.

Nothing happened.

Panic tore through her. Was it the wrong stone? Had she messed something up? "It's not working. What did I do wrong?"

Nick placed a comforting hand on her shoulder. "Give it a second."

It still wasn't working. She wanted to scream.

But then, just as she was about to attack Nick for killing him when they should have been trying to save his life, it happened.

Ren sucked his breath in hard and arched his back. Panic contorted his features as he met her gaze, and held it with those blue eyes that again sparkled with life.

And this time, his soul.

Cupping his face in her palm, she smiled at him. "Hey, baby. Welcome back."

Nick took her hand that held the crystal and pulled it away. "You can let go now."

"Sorry. I didn't want to take any chances."

Nick frowned as he saw her unscarred palm. "You weren't hurt?"

She shook her head.

"Well, good." Nick flashed a grin at her. "*Mazel tov.* He's all yours now. Take good care of him." And with that, Nick vanished.

Kateri laced her fingers with Ren's as he came to terms with being human again.

He glanced up at the mural in the ceiling. "Did we make it in time?"

"I'm not sure. I think we did." Biting her lip, she met Jess's gaze. "Did we?"

He pushed his cowboy hat back on his head and shrugged. "We won't know for sure until 11:11 a.m., but yeah, I think we did. By the skin of our teeth."

Cabeza yawned from across the room, and Kateri felt bad that she'd been so fixated on Ren that she'd forgotten about them.

"I don't know about the rest of you, but I need some sleep," Cabeza said. He clapped Sasha on the back. "Either wake me for the Apocalypse or, if the world's still here and not overrun with demons, I'll see you at sunset." He saluted them, then vanished.

Sasha duplicated his yawn. "Yeah, I could use some beauty sleep and a masseuse myself. See you guys later. Hopefully under much better circumstances."

"Take care." Kateri surveyed the damage around them that the lightning and fight had caused. While it was an impressive mess, it didn't look like it'd stopped the end of the world.

Ren tugged her hand to get her attention back on him.

"What, sweetie?"

He rose up to give her the hottest, sexiest kiss in the history of humanity.

And when he pulled back to rub his nose against hers, he offered her the sweetest smile she'd ever seen. "So tell me, Kateri. What does the future hold for *us*?"

Us . . .

That one word and his question filled her with the warmth of a million suns.

Before she could answer, Jess stood and swung his shotgun up to rest on top of his shoulder. "Ah hell, boy, I can answer that one. A whole passel of kids, and a life that's damn worth living."

EPILOGUE

July 28, 2061

"Is everything ready?" Kateri asked as she joined Ren beside the largest of the bonfires they'd made.

"I think so." Ren glanced around at what amounted to a year's worth of preparation for this night.

Actually, that wasn't true. He'd been waiting for this his entire life.

In more ways than one.

"Waleli!" Ren shouted sharply. "Put your coat on, the desert air is chilly. You could catch a cold."

His youngest daughter rolled her eyes at him. "Dad, really?" She gestured to her four sons, who towered over her slight frame. "I have grown children of my own. I think I know when I need a coat. Besides, it'd be the first time in my life I ever took sick."

Laughing, Kateri draped a sweater over Waleli's shoulders, then kissed her cheek. "He only fusses because he worries about you."

"I know, Mom." She walked over and placed a kiss on Ren's cheek. "I love you, too, Daddy."

Those words never failed to make his knees weak or his heart soar.

As Waleli started away, Ren took her hand and stopped her. Without a word, he kissed her knuckles, and took a moment to offer a silent prayer of gratitude for his family. His daughter squeezed his hand before going to see after her husband.

"P-p-p-papa! It's t-t!" Parker, their six-year-old grandson, broke off into an angry growl as the word refused to leave his mouth.

Ren picked him up and held him tight. "It's time?"

He nodded.

"All right then, would you like to do the honors, little bit?"

Parker nodded more vigorously.

Ren sank down on one knee and stood Parker before him. "You can talk to me, Parker. Any time. I'm in no hurry and there's no sound more precious to me than your voice. So you don't worry about how you sound, okay?"

"I love you, Papa."

Ren kissed him on the cheek, then took the torch from Kateri's hand. He held it out for Parker. "Be careful. Don't get hurt."

Parker ran to the lines they had drawn in the desert and lit them. The flames roared across their massive drawing that made the Nasca lines in Peru look paltry. Burning even higher and brighter as they spread, the fire lit up the entire desert region. And those flames danced and played with colors in Kateri's fire opal necklace. Since they'd retrieved it that night in the cave, she had never taken it off again.

Ren draped his arm around her shoulders. With his entire family gathered around him, he looked up at the sky and waited.

Within a few minutes, they saw the comet as it flew over their heads.

"Wave, everyone!" Kateri shouted. "Let your grandmother know how much we love her, and how grateful we are for her son."

Teri, their eight-year-old granddaughter, looked at her with wide eyes. "Do you think she sees us, *Elisi*?"

Ren swung her up on his shoulder. "Yes, I do, *sogainisi*. I think we built a monument in her honor so large, even the Martians see it."

It was an eight-mile-long thunderbird with a hummingbird under its wing—not because it was being protected by the thunderbird. It was there because it was the wind that carried the thunderbird to the heavens.

And in the center of the thunderbird, with the help of Acheron and Tory, they had written in ancient Greek— *S'agapo. I love you.*

He hoped his mother saw it as she passed over, and knew that he was still here, and that though they had never met, he was grateful to her for the life she had given him.

Teri sighed as he set her back on her feet. "There are no Martians, Papa. Scientists debunked that theory a very long time ago."

Exchanging a laugh with Kateri, he grinned. "I swear

there are some traits that have to be genetic, no matter what they say."

Kateri gave him the sweetest kiss, and hugged him tight. "So tell me, baby. Was Sundown right about us?"

He glanced around at their four sons and three daughters, their spouses, and the twenty grandchildren they already had, and the one that would be born this fall who was being carried by their youngest son's wife. "Yes, he was. But it's you I have to thank."

"For what?"

"Sharing a life with me, and making it so that even the worst days I have now are still the best days I've ever known."

Do you love fiction with a supernatural twist?

Want the chance to hear news about your favourite authors (and the chance to win free books)?

Keri Arthur
S. G. Browne
P.C. Cast
Christine Feehan
Jacquelyn Frank
Larissa Ione
Sherrilyn Kenyon
Jackie Kessler
Jayne Ann Krentz and Jayne Castle
Martin Millar
Kat Richardson
J.R. Ward
David Wellington

Then visit the Piatkus website and blog
www.piatkus.co.uk | www.piatkusbooks.net

And follow us on Facebook and Twitter
www.facebook.com/piatkusfiction | www.twitter.com/piatkusbooks

piatkus